TWO UNFORGETT...
NOVELS BY HEA...
IN ONE V...
A $7.98 VALUE FOR ONLY $4.99!

TENDER TAMING

Whitney discarded her boots and curled onto the floor bed, her eyes tightly closed. A moment later White Eagle joined her, his length inches from her own. He was silent for so long she was sure he slept; then he spoke harshly in the darkness. "You're being ridiculous."

"About what?"

"Do you really think one or a hundred garments would stop me if I decided to attack your precious body? Don't flatter yourself that you're such a prize, and don't deceive yourself into thinking you don't want me. You were mine from the moment we met."

WHEN NEXT WE LOVE

"I don't like you, Derek. Is that so difficult to comprehend? I don't want to be near you. I don't want to be in this house and I particularly don't want to be in your room and I especially don't want to be in your bed—"

Leigh was rudely interrupted as Derek's hand clamped over her mouth. Then, with one swift movement, he was on top of her, and when he spoke, his eyes blazed.

"You, Mrs. Tremayne, are a liar! When I kissed you earlier you certainly responded. With amazing eagerness and expertise, I might add. Of course, you have had your share of practice!"

HEATHER GRAHAM

TENDER TAMING AND WHEN NEXT WE LOVE

LOVE SPELL NEW YORK CITY

LOVE SPELL®

March 1994

Published by

Dorchester Publishing Co., Inc.
276 Fifth Avenue
New York, NY 10001

TENDER TAMING

For the Florida Everglades,
the Miccosukee, and Debbie Craig

CHAPTER ONE

The windshield wipers squeaked in a monotonous rhythm as Whitney Latham sat tensely hunched over the wheel, her knuckles white from the tightness of her grip, her bright green eyes wide and glued to what she could see of the road. The storm, which had been only a light patter of rain when she had left the civilization of Ft. Lauderdale behind, now thundered upon her with a ferocity as savage as the primitive swamp that flanked each side of the two-lane highway known as Alligator Alley.

A jagged streak of lightning blazed with sudden brilliance across the black sky, followed immediately by an ominous roar of thunder. Whitney emitted a startled cry and the wheel twisted violently in her hands, causing the car to jackknife on the slick pavement. "Damn!" she muttered, fighting to bring the auto back into control. She should pull off the road, but she was afraid to try. She might pull right into a canal!

"Some 'two-hour' drive!" she moaned aloud, remembering the words of the friendly waitress who had suggested the short cut rather than an extra drive of thirty miles down to Miami and the Trail. But in daytime, with a sunny sky overhead, it probably was a pleasant and short enough excursion. She had only herself to blame for rushing onto the highway with darkness—and the rain—descending. Her eagerness to manage her new job efficiently had prompted her to reach her final destination, Naples, with all possible speed, and consequently she had shunned

9

the idea of staying in Ft. Lauderdale for the night. It had not occurred to her that the road, which cut in what the map showed as a straight line across the Everglades, could possibly offer mile after mile of absolutely *nothing.* It seemed like endless hours ago that she had passed the last signs of humanity—an Indian restaurant and a billboard that announced WILLIE'S AIRBOAT RIDES. That had been before the total blackness of the stormy night had fallen. It had been a good thirty minutes now since she'd even seen another car! But then the natives of the area were probably bright enough to stay off the road in this type of weather.

"I'm going to make a marvelous public relations director!" she mocked herself lightly, aloud again to bolster her morale. "I don't seem to know a thing about the land that's going to be in question!"

She really didn't know if she was even near the land that interested her. When she had been offered the new position, she had said yes without hesitation. The job would take her away from the slush and snow of a Richmond winter—and away from Gerry. As an ex-husband, he had become as paternal and protective as a second father. She didn't need a second father. One—who had failed to realize that she was twenty-five, a college graduate and a mature, competent woman—was enough!

A smile twisted her lips despite her predicament at the thought of her father and Gerry. She would never—never, never!—tell them that she had "maturely" and "competently" driven herself into what was appearing to be the Twilight Zone. They would surely shake their heads and attempt to shackle her back to the kitchen!

Her grin faded as her gaze focused briefly on the gas gauge. The needle was bouncing below the reserve line. "Oh, God!" she groaned reproachfully, directing her comment to the divinity as if He were seated beside her in person. "Why are you doing this to me?" She could hardly

10

see ahead of her; how would she ever find a service station if there was one to be found?

Again she berated herself for not doing a more thorough study of the area and the problems she would be called upon to solve. In theory her idea of reaching her destination and learning the particulars of the job in the city where she would be headquartered had seemed sound. She would have a whole week to study the situation up close before her first meeting was scheduled. She knew the basics. Her firm, T and C Development, had purchased land from the federal government. The company was planning a wonderful family community, but now the land was in dispute. The Seminole Indians were claiming that prime portions of the land belonged to them. Rather than anticipate long years of court battles, T and C had decided first to attempt to deal with the Indians on their own. Hence the PR.

Whitney didn't doubt her capabilities for a minute. She loved dealing with people, and with T and C behind her, she was sure she could work out a deal beneficial to both parties. In her two years with the company she had worn down the top brass of some of the nation's most influential corporations; surely she could handle a small tribe of Indians!

Although Whitney wasn't aware of what it was that made her so perfect for her work, an outside observer could have easily told her. Of medium height and slight build, she was a willowy beauty. Her face was a classic oval, her nose pert, her chin determined, her large green eyes vivacious and sincere. The dark brunet hair that framed the alabaster skin of her features was styled in a long, feminine, feather cut that thoroughly proclaimed her a woman, while the dignity of her stature, movements and cool, quiet voice announced that she was not one to be dealt with lightly. She tackled each new problem with vital energy, intuitively looking beyond the obvious, objectively open to thoughts and ideas other than her own.

Whitney was inching along now, the rain having become a solid sheet of gray which her bright lights illuminated but failed to penetrate. The car practically came to a stop as she chewed her lip nervously and decided she would have to pull off the road and onto the embankment. Carefully she braked and hedged the wheel to the right. She breathed a sigh of relief as the auto halted without sinking into the muck. The ground of the embankment was sturdy.

Leaving the emergency blinkers on, she switched off the ignition and fumbled in her purse for a cigarette. She had been craving one for an hour but had been afraid to lift her hand from the steering wheel long enough to light it. Now she inhaled deeply, flexing her long, taut fingers. Once the rain cleared, she would be fine. She had to be close to Naples. And somewhere along the road there *had* to be a service station.

Allowing her mind to wander as she watched the pelting rain pummel the windshield, Whitney idly began to wonder about the man who would be her main opponent in the land deals. All she really had to go on was a name: Jonathan E. Stewart. He sounded like a crusty old crusader, some ranting do-gooder determined to hold sacred the cause of the Indian. Oh, well! she thought philosophically, it was her job to deal with difficult people. She hoped she would be able to convince old Jonathan E. that the proposed community would valuably aid the Seminoles both economically and socially. Jobs, schooling, and better housing would be available to all.

Crushing her cigarette into the BMW's compact ashtray, Whitney smiled gratefully as she realized that the rain was finally slowing to a drizzle. Flicking the key in the ignition and switching the brights back on, she noticed a broken sign lying haphazardly on the ground not twenty feet away. The heavy rain must have torn it from a post. Straining her eyes, she could just make out the blessedly wonderful word GAS and an arrow that pointed into the swamp.

Frowning, Whitney scanned the dark, cropped embankment and the fields of high sawgrass that loomed beyond in the night. She switched to her low beams and then back to her high beams. Yes, just past the sign there was a road. Creeping slowly to it, she discerned that it was solid—just dirt and gravel, but mercifully unflooded. And in the distance, peeking dimly but surely, glowed a sure sign of life—light! Almost giddy with relief, Whitney eagerly began her drive through the swamp.

With the rain receding, she rolled down her window and welcomed the fresh night air that washed through the small car. Along with the air came the eerie sounds of the primitive environment—the low, musical chirping of a thousand insects, the guttural croak of a bullfrog, the high-pitched and mournful scream of a startled bird.

The darkness, compounded by the sawgrass that bordered her, rising several feet higher than the car in spots, suddenly caused chills of fear to creep along her spine. She was facing danger, she realized for the first time. The longer she drove, the farther away the light seemed. She was truly in no-man's-land. Legends she had heard of the Glades came to her mind—legends of alligators, snakes and quicksand. In the sterility of a Richmond high rise, the stories had seemed things of the past—fairy tales as extinct as dinosaurs.

But she was driving into reality—a very present reality. She could well imagine being lost in this desolation, dying a slow, agonizing death of snakebite and wandering mile after dismal mile in the sweltering bog. . . .

Stop it, girl! she warned herself with a firm shake. She was in a car on a high road. Alligators did not attack BMWs. Nor did snakes climb through moving windows. Now as to quicksand. . . .

The light was standing still, increasing in brilliance.

Within minutes she would reach it. Not even a half-mile farther—

But the BMW sputtered, choked and died, rolling to a standstill. Damn! Whitney's hands fruitlessly crashed onto the steering wheel, accomplishing nothing but causing tender spots that would turn to bruises. Knowing that it was her own stupidity that so thoroughly infuriated her, she still swore a spate of oaths to the betraying machinery. She had to yell at something!

Sitting perplexed, in disgusted disbelief she watched the slow tick of the second-hand dial on the dashboard clock. It was nine o'clock. The first pink streaks of dawn were still a good ten hours away.

"You deserve the mess you're in!" she told herself crossly, not relishing spending a night in the car with the frightening noises cascading around her. She didn't relish the thought of sleeping in the car, period! Having been raised in a distinguished old Virginia home by moderately wealthy parents, Whitney was admittedly accustomed to all the creature comforts.

"Competent and on my own!" she chided herself in exasperation. "Oh, for a shower and a Holiday Inn!" She extinguished the lights and curled her leather shoulder bag into her arms to form a pillow as she stretched as comfortably as possible across the front seat. "One day I'll be able to laugh about all this!" she assured herself glumly. "Now sleep! You have no choice. . . ."

But as soon as she closed her eyes, visions appeared before them—visions of her running through the Everglades, lost in the woods, shrouded in darkness, deadly menace lurking everywhere. . . .

Snapping back to a sitting position, she blinked in the darkness. The noises coming through the window were a cacophony that rose shrilly in her ears. Were birds supposed to shriek like that in the night? Chills flooded down her spine again in a mad race, numbing her. Something stung her nyloned leg and she feverishly slapped at it. A mosquito, she told herself, only a mosquito . . . but she couldn't see anything. Rolling up the window and turning on the lights simultaneously, she stared at the palm of her hand. Definitely a mosquito. A very squashed one. Breathing deeply in the small confines of the car, she tried to calm her growing unease and convince herself to turn the lights off again. If she didn't she would have a stone-dead battery by morning.

Turning the lights off, she lay back on the plush interior. The car had been a present from her father, and for normal driving it was the utmost in luxury. Unfortunately, for sleeping it was too small and cramped!

Whitney couldn't keep her eyes closed. The scary, rustling sounds of beasts and foliage bore down upon her loudly despite the closed window. And now the closed window was adding another element of discomfort; it was confining her to a prison of humid heat.

Emitting a resigned whistle, Whitney sat back up. Try as she would, she couldn't sleep. Part of the problem, she was sure, was the hour. She hadn't been to bed at nine o'clock in years.

"So what do I do?" she asked herself, raising helpless hands to the faint illumination of the green-glowing dials. "Play twenty questions with myself? Why didn't I have the sense to find out what kind of road Alligator Alley was? Why didn't I study up first on the swamp and the habits of venomous reptiles . . . ?"

"Ugh!" With a shudder she groped and reached for another cigarette. Her initialed silver lighter flared high with fire, stressing the completeness of her solitude. With the smoke issuing around her, she rolled the window back down a crack. The night noises increased—the nerve-racking chirping loudest of all. Glancing at the dash clock, she was dismayed to discover it was only nine fifteen. Just a quarter of an hour had elapsed!

"Stupid! Stupid! Stupid!" she hissed. If only she had thought to fill the damn tank back in Ft. Lauderdale! But she hadn't known she wouldn't come across a station. She should have known! She should have been prepared; efficient people were always prepared.

"I am not a nitwit!" she assured herself. "Everyone makes a mistake in judgment at some time or another." And wasn't that what she had always fought for? The right to make her own mistakes?

"This was one hell of a mistake!" she snapped with self-reproach. Tiny beads of perspiration were forming across her nose. I'm going to melt! she silently wailed. She sat still for another moment, then rolled the window all the way down with a vicious movement. She simply couldn't endure the stifling heat.

A bump sounded on the rear of the car, and she twisted around in panic. Holding her breath, she waited. But there were no further thumps or jiggles. The blood stopped its crazy thudding through her veins slowly, and she gulped air back into her lungs. The clock read nine twenty.

"I can't do this . . . I can't do this . . . I just can't!" she whispered, her voice verging on a sob. "I just can't sit here doing nothing anymore! I'll go crazy," she muttered, the terrible feeling of claustrophobia closing in on her.

But her alternatives weren't good; they involved leaving the safety of the car. Keeping her eyes narrowed speculatively on the light in the distance, she began to rationalize.

She could walk half a mile in ten minutes. Ten tense minutes and then she would be . . . where? Somewhere, at least!

The road was high. It wasn't flooded. She had a flashlight in the glove compartment and she could keep it trained on the path. Animals were afraid of humans, weren't they? As long as she didn't bother them, she was safe.

The decision for action was making her feel better already. Stupid it might be, but it was her choice. And anyway, if she could make it to the service station, the proprietor could fill her tank tonight. Then she could be

16

out of the dismal swamp and into a shower at a Holiday Inn.

The anticipation of a cooling shower was the deciding factor. Reaching into the glove compartment, Whitney extracted her flashlight. Her hand hesitated over a small spray can. Shrugging, she grabbed the can. Wryly admitting she had no earthly idea of what the effects of Mace might be on an alligator, she decided she might as well have the slight protection along with her anyway.

Whistling for bravado softly through her teeth, Whitney rolled the window up—in case of more rain—and climbed from the car. Training her eyes on the small pool of light from her flashlight, she started walking. Her slick heels, attractive and smart in the city, were a painful hindrance on the path. Nor was her soft beige jersey dress conducive to a stroll through the Glades. The sawgrass and brush grew closer and closer to the path as she walked, ripping against her clothing and flesh like mystical, haunted fingers that would hold her with evil intent. Her steps became hurried; she broke into a jog.

The sturdy gravel broke off abruptly and her feet sank into mud clear to her ankles. A nervous, frantic sob escaped her as she tried to flounder from the mud, losing her shoes in the process. Pull yourself together! she silently warned, fearing that panic would soon send her racing crazily into the sawgrass.

Each sucking step she took was an exercise in agony, but the lights ahead were so close that she could almost reach out and touch them. Allowing anticipation to outweigh caution, she once again tried to hurry. A root deep within the bog caught around a slender ankle and sent her sprawling into the swamp face first. Gritting her teeth against pain and hysteria, Whitney muttered a few well chosen oaths and stumbled her way back up. Wiping the mud from her face, she was dismayed and horrified to realize she had lost both the flashlight and the Mace, but the very real fear of a venomous snake kept her from

17

sloshing too thoroughly through the unfathomable depth of the pitch-black, oozing earth to find them. Catching sight of a foot-long piece of broken root, she held it firmly in her right hand as she doggedly crept forward again, carefully, her form almost as dark as the night, with her beige dress doused in the mud and her hair sodden and clinging to her head. "I will not panic . . . I will not panic . . . I will not panic. . . ." She repeated the words softly in a chant to quell the tremors that raged through her.

But she was panicking. Over the ceaseless noises around her, she could faintly detect a new sound.

Something was following her. Its pace increased with hers, then decreased with hers; a constant entity. Halting totally for a minute, listening with abject fear, Whitney realized that whatever it was patiently waited for her to make a move. The light ahead was close. No longer concerned with caution but giving way to the terror that gripped her, Whitney thrashed ahead recklessly, making for the ignominious security of the light.

Another root caught her foot and she slammed back down to the ground, thoroughly stunned. This time the noise behind her did not stop. A form rose above her in the darkness and she instinctively struck out with the club of broken wood, flailing feverishly.

A very human grunt of pain reached her ears and the wooden club was wrenched powerfully from her fingers. "Don't hurt me!" she pleaded in a garbled sob. "Oh, God, please don't hurt me!" It was too late to be thinking about it, but maybe her father and Gerry had been right. Maybe a woman's proper place was home, her life in the kitchen . . . at least then she would have a life! At the moment her fear was so intense that she would have bargained with the devil himself just to know that she would live. . . .

The beam of a powerful flashlight suddenly flared in her face. Blinking in the unaccustomed brilliance, Whitney choked, "Pleeease. . . ."

A grunt was her only verbal reply, but she was gently

hoisted from the mud by a pair of strong, masculine arms. She was not being attacked. The arms carried her toward the light that had been her own destination.

The man holding her seemed to have no difficulty maneuvering a silent and graceful trail through the muck, nor did it seem that her weight was any more troublesome than a feather to him. In a matter of minutes she could see that the light was coming from a small wooden cabin that appeared more inviting than the Washington Hilton. Another moment and they were mounting three planked steps and the door was being firmly kicked open by a high-booted foot. Inside, the cabin was surprisingly cool and comfortable, furnished sparsely but adequately with large leather and wood couches that sat upon deerskin rugs.

Whitney was deposited upon one of the couches, and she finally had a chance to take a good look at her unknown-assailant-turned-rescuer. Her eyes traveled from the high black boots to form-fitting, worn jeans that hugged tightly muscled thighs and trim hips, then on to the powerful chest she had leaned against. It was clad in a simple, now muddied, white cotton shirt. Above the broad shoulders were a strong, corded neck and a face that left Whitney speechless with amazement.

The man was an Indian. Or was he? The best of two races seemed to be combined in a profile as proud as a hawk's—sharp, rugged and severe. The cheekbones were high, the nose long, straight and imperious with an ancient dignity. The lips were sensuously full, grim and tight.

His hair was raven black, almost blue black in the gaslight, and long—reaching to his neck. But the most startling aspect was his eyes. Brilliant as diamond studs against the handsome bronze of his face, they were a blue as bright as a summer sky and as intense as a blazing sun. They were bordered by high, well-defined brows and framed by lashes as musky and dark as the sinister night.

Totally unnerved, Whitney uttered a tactless exclamation. "You're—you're an Indian!" she stuttered. Remorse at her lack of diplomacy filled her immediately. He had dragged her from the mud and she was spilling muck all over his neat cabin. "I'm sorry," she mumbled, tripping over her words as he continued to survey her silently. "Not that you are an Indian—" Oh, God! What a thing to say! What was the matter with her? But he wasn't helping any, not saying a thing—just staring at her with what might be a quirk of sardonic amusement twitching the tight line of his lips.

"You do speak English?" Whitney snapped, irritated by his silence and the annoying feeling of inadequacy he was instilling within her. He was making her appear to be a blithering fool!

"Yes." His voice was velvety; a deep, rich baritone.

Attempting to draw on some dignity—which was difficult when she was sitting in a huddle with bare feet, torn stockings and her hair and clothing plastered to her smudged body—Whitney spoke again, haughtily, slowly, thinking out her words before she uttered them. "Forgive me if I sounded terribly rude. I thought I was following a road to a service station. I can see now that this is your private property. If I could just use a phone—"

"A phone!" The black brows rose in ridicule. "Sorry. Southern Bell hasn't installed lines yet in this block of the Glades."

Whitney's emerald gaze flared like firelight as she flushed uneasily. Without a flicker of facial movement or the slightest change in intonation, her towering host had aptly proved his complete knowledge of the English language. "Forgive me," she repeated, unable to keep the acid from her own tone. "I'm afraid I'm unfamiliar with my surroundings."

His arms were crossed negligently over his chest as he stared down at her with an austere, emotionless expression that still managed to convey to her his belief that she had just mumbled the understatement of the year. Whitney's flush heightened as his electrifying blue stare wandered briefly over her entire person from muddied head to muddied toe with ill-concealed contempt. Yet despite the anger his gaze elicited, she experienced a new type of chill—one that hinted of fire rather than ice. It was as if his eyes could really send out jolting currents of heat. Unwittingly she found herself studying his form again, remembering the comfortable security of being carried in the strong arms . . . resting her head against the rock-hard chest.

"Umm—I—" she was babbling again, bewildered by the intensity of the physical reactions he was evoking from her while merely standing above her. Why was she behaving like a schoolgirl? He was ruggedly handsome and undoubtedly attractive; that she grudgingly acknowledged. But she had met many men with blatant sex appeal. Maybe that was the difference. This man's inherent sexuality was in no way blatant or contrived. It was part of his essence, natural and almost untamed, like the elements around them.

"My name is Whitney Latham," she offered, squaring her shoulders. "I know you think me a complete fool and I do apologize. But I really could use your help—" Something flickered through his ice blue gaze as she mentioned her name and then was gone. Something that appeared for that minuscule portion of time to be recognition and—and dislike! Why? Whitney wondered. Maybe she was imagining things. She had to be! His face gave away about as much as a statue of chiseled granite.

"There is little I can do to help you except offer you the hospitality of the cabin—such as it is," he interrupted curtly as her voice trailed away. "I don't know how you managed to get an automobile anywhere near here. I can't even get a dirt bike or jeep back to the highway now."

"Oh!" Whitney's lips formed a circle of dismay.

"My brother will be by in the morning with the airboat," he supplied more kindly, her forlorn expression

21

having touched whatever semblance of a heart he had. The hint of a grin twitching around his eyes, he left his towering stance to move with swift grace to the left side of the cabin, which served as a makeshift kitchen with a butane stove, sink, cabinets and some sort of small icebox. Setting a battered gray coffee pot upon the stove, he added, "In the meantime I can offer you a warm drink and a shower —cold, I'm sorry to say. And a dry place to sleep for the night."

"Thank you," Whitney murmured.

The coffee began to perk immediately, as if it had been hot and ready before she interrupted him with her unexpected arrival. In a daze Whitney watched the brown liquid bubble. The night had not gone at all as planned! She should be in a comfortable hotel room right now, sipping a cool, delicious glass of wine. She should be showered and clean, pampered with her favorite soaps and fragrances, *reading* about the Everglades. Instead she was a tired, dispirited, mess! The uninvited guest of an intimidating dark stranger in the middle of the forlorn and desolate swamp. . . .

"Tell me," he said, his blue gaze unfathomably upon her as he brought her a cup of the steaming black coffee, "how did you come to be prowling around my cabin?"

"Prowling!" Whitney repeated indignantly, bristling at his insinuation. "I wasn't prowling! I was trying to get help. There is a sign out there that says gas—"

"The storm must have blown it down from somewhere."

"Nevertheless, there is a sign by your road," Whitney informed him stubbornly. "I needed gas so I followed the arrow off Alligator Alley. Then I ran out completely about half a mile back—"

"So you walked through the swamp in your bare feet?" He shook his head slightly as if acknowledging that there was indeed a Great Spirit who must look after fools and ignorant women.

22

"Yes. No," Whitney retorted. "I lost my shoes in the mud—"

"Don't you know a damned thing about the Glades? Only a complete idiot would come walking out in this terrain in the middle of a stormy night!" His tone was a growl, his stare a dagger that pierced her. "You must have wanted something very badly."

Whitney gasped, stunned more by his hostility than his blatant insult. Not in a position to tell him where to shove his opinions, she carefully lowered her own tone to one of controlled anger and coldly replied, "I think we have established the fact that I acted foolishly. And I do not know much about the terrain." Gaining momentum as her irritation increased, she grated, "And yes! I did want something very badly—help! I was frightened to begin with, and you nearly scared me to death! Why were you skulking after me?" Come to think of it, she thought as she awaited his reply, he was still scaring her to death! What did she know about him? He was charismatic and compelling; he was rude and dominating. She was literally his prisoner in the frightening Glades.

"Madam," he answered slowly, sipping his own coffee, "even I do not have perfect vision in the darkness. I seldom receive social calls at my cabin on flooded nights like this. I heard you; I followed you to find out who you were and what you were up to. Then I did try to help you and all I got for my efforts was a lump on the forehead."

Whitney gnawed her lower lip pensively. There was an ugly black bruise sprouting along his temple where the blow from her makeshift club had struck. "I—I'm sorry—I didn't know what you were—you might have been an alligator or—"

The deep, mellow sound of his laughter interrupted her; his amusement was now open and more infuriating than ever. "This is incredible!" he said as he chuckled throatily. "You were going to ward off a hungry alligator with twelve inches of mangrove root?"

"Well, I started off with a can of Mace—"

"Oh, Lord!" he scoffed. "That's even better. Macing an alligator!"

Fighting her rage and discomfiture, Whitney tried to lodge a protest. "I—"

"Never mind." He sat across the room from her and turned his quizzing to another vein, still keeping his steadfast eyes locked upon her. "Where were you headed?"

"Naples—of course!" Even she knew the highway led in only one direction. "Why?"

"Just curious. It's so pathetically obvious you've never been in these parts, I thought I'd make sure you were in the right state."

That was the final straw. She had admitted her stupidity, her foolishness. She had apologized profusely for it. There was no way she was going to sit and quietly accept insults from this arrogant know-it-all! Storming to her feet with a spray of mud, she declared imperiously, "That's enough! I don't have to endure this from some alligator-wrestling Seminole—"

"Miccosukee," he interrupted with droll complacency, her outburst having amused him further rather than angered him.

"Pardon?" Startled, Whitney dropped her raving from inborn and inbred politeness.

"Miccosukee," he repeated, a handsome smile spreading across his face. "Same nation, different tribe. The US government recognized us years ago." As she stared at him, lost and still confused by his words, he added, "But I do wrestle alligators now and then. Don't all of us Glades Indians?" he asked, his bronze face guileless with pretend naiveté.

Releasing a pent-up breath, Whitney found herself laughing. He was teasing her, but then she deserved his words. She did have preconceived notions about a people of whom she was totally ignorant. "I don't know," she answered with a return smile prettily highlighting her face

24

despite its grimy condition. "*Do* you all wrestle alligators?"

He sipped his coffee and grinned enigmatically. "Are you here on business?"

"Yes, I am."

"And what might your business be?"

Whitney decided that answering his questions could cause no harm. His frank, unwavering stare was still upon her and his queries were domineering and autocratic, but he did seem to have a sense of humor. Besides, she was in his cabin and at his mercy.

"I work for T and C Development," she said. Suddenly realizing that he was one of the Indians she would be trying to cajole to her point of view, she warmed to her subject and became professionally charming. "We have a land dispute going with the Seminole Nation," she told him truthfully. "I'm supposed to work with a Jonathan E. Stewart and come to an equitable conclusion." Almost to herself she frowned and added, "I wonder why the Seminoles didn't choose one of their own to enter the negotiations?"

Amusement was back in his glacial eyes. In fact, they were twinkling away merrily. "The council believes Stewart will represent them with their best interests at heart," he answered.

"You know about this!" Whitney exclaimed, very eager now to hear anything her host might have to say. "Do you know Stewart?"

He rose with sudden agility and took her empty mug from her hand. Walking back to the kitchen area with his silent tread, he disposed of the mugs on a butcher block and replied, "As a matter of fact, I do." Spinning on a heel, he turned to a bureau and bent with the lithe grace of a beautifully powerful cat to comb through a drawer. Watching him, Whitney couldn't help but indulge in wistful admiration. He was as tightly muscled and sleek as a magnificent animal. Probably, she mused, the long years

25

of exercise, manual labor and life in the Glades had given him the superb tone more urban men worked for diligently in sports rooms across the country yet never achieved. What did he do for a living, she wondered. Fish? Hunt? Wrestle alligators . . . ? With his proud and noble profile, she couldn't imagine him in some innocuous occupation.

Whitney blushed a bright crimson as he turned back to her, the light of crystal in his eyes telling her clearly that he had read her thoughts and again found them amusing. "What is—uh—Jonathan E. Stewart like?" she asked, feigning indifference to his look.

He answered with a chuckle and a friendly question. "What do you imagine him to be like?" He had pulled a flannel shirt from the drawer and held it as he walked nearer to her.

"Crusty, old and hard to deal with!" Whitney returned honestly, too unnerved to lie or hedge diplomatically. "Am I close?"

"You will find him hard to deal with!" was the reply. "Here." He tossed the flannel shirt to her and Whitney quickly threw up her hands to catch it. Pointing to a curtain at the rear of the cabin, he said, "Shower is that way. You'll find everything else you might need—except hot water. I'd like to meet you devoid of mud, and then I'll try to help you a little by giving you a brief education on the Seminole Nation." Grinning contagiously, he moved to her side and offered her his hand.

Glancing nervously at it, she noted that it was firm and tanned although lighter than she would have expected, and the long, wiry fingers were oddly well manicured and neat. His touch sent another strange heat-chill through her, and she glanced at him tentatively as she came to her feet and brushed past him, her head tilted up as he ranged a good foot taller than she. His masculine scent assailed her at this close range, a pleasing scent that was low-keyed and woodsy, pleasing and titillating, a scent that fit his aura of virility to a *t*. "Thank you," she murmured uneasily, clutching the shirt to her breast and rushing past him to the curtain, completely bewildered by his effect on her and therefore nervous as a stray kitten. What was the matter with her?

The bathroom was surprisingly modern. New tiles sparkled in the shower stall, contemporary porcelain and brass formed a sink and its fixtures and an intricately carved wooden cupboard hung above the sink. Double shiny fixtures adorned the wall; apparently her host was planning on providing hot water at some future date. At least, she decided, a modicum of civilization had come to the Glades! The room offered a great deal in the way of efficiency except—except there was nothing between her and her host but the curtain. . . . Crunching her lower lip, she curiously pondered the uniquely compelling stranger as she tentatively began to doff her mucky clothing.

She was sure he wasn't going to come barging through the curtain. However rude his comments might have been, not one was in the least insinuating or suggestive. He had seemed totally unaware that she was even of the feminine gender—except to sniff disdainfully at her sex's foolishness. Any indecent thoughts had been generated in her own mind. No! Whitney protested her silent admission with horror. But yes. She—who had decided after her short-lived and stoic marriage that great and erotic passion was something only read about in books—was wondering yearningly what it would be like to have those strong arms wrapped around her with desire . . . the tight lips with their sensual play of amusement softening to caress her flesh . . . the whole of his sinewed body exposed to her appreciative view. . . .

A cold shower is just what you need! she scolded her muddy reflection in the mirror above the porcelain sink. How ridiculous! She did not—repeat, did not—like domineering men, and *he* would certainly fit such a description. Tomorrow she would get out of here and never see him again. She would forget these strange feelings that were so

27

foreign to her . . . forget the dizzying sensations he had awakened that she, for all her sophistication and assurance, hadn't known or even believed existed. . . .

His voice, just outside the curtain, caused her to jump. She had forgotten that he could move without a sound. A soft, husky chuckle sounded. Through the curtain he knew he had startled her—he knew he had sent her blood racing.

"I wanted to let you know there's a clean towel over the rack and soap and shampoo in the cabinet behind the mirror."

"I found them; thanks," Whitney answered shakily in return.

Nothing more followed. Had he moved away again? Her wide green gaze lighted upon her own reflection. Did he know that he frightened and yet magnetized her, this half-breed with his brilliant, knowing blue eyes. That he shook her cool confidence to the core?

Appalled by her own thoughts, she scoffed but couldn't deny them. A strange longing swept through her as she peeled away her torn stockings and slip. Did he find anything appealing about her? Her skin, beneath the crust of mud, was good, soft, silky and pampered. Her figure tended to the slim side, but it was adequately curvy and her breasts were high and firm and . . . and what? Not voluptuous, she thought with a sigh.

Although confident that she was attractive and cut a pleasant appearance, she just didn't know if anyone would ever refer to her as enticing. She had entered marriage with shy eagerness, sure that she would discover the sensual pleasures of life and love. She had been sadly disappointed. To staid Gerry, the act of love was performed without fanfare, never spoken of and indulged in only in darkened rooms. Like an anachronism from the past, Gerry believed that sexual release was something needed strictly by males and that passion in a woman hinted of sheer wantonness.

Embarrassed and humiliated, ignorant and young, Whitney had buried her own feelings, the hint of desire she had learned and the fantasy yearnings she was convinced were abnormal. After their friendly divorce, she had remained cool and untouched, convinced that there was nothing to be found in the many overtures she had received and rebuffed.

But now her mind turned to her host. If she was ever to have such a man, she wouldn't know what to do with him! She would be too frightened of her own inadequacy ever to come to the point of . . . *Stop!* she silently wailed. What on earth was possessing her? She was a career woman, authoritative in her own world. The man outside was a stranger—educated and cultured, maybe, but still a stranger! Hostility had flared between them more than any other recognizable emotion. She didn't even know his name!

That thought stopped her, her hand pausing on the water fixture. Glancing at the curtain, she straightened and tentatively called, "Excuse me!"

"Yes?" the velvety baritone inquired politely.

"I just realized I'm standing in your shower and I don't even know your name," Whitney warbled apologetically.

There was silence for so long that she began to wonder if he had heard her. Just as she opened her mouth to speak again, she heard a soft rustling at the curtain and another throaty chuckle.

"My name is Eagle," he said quietly. "In the Seminole Nation I am known as White Eagle."

There was silence beyond the curtain. Whitney turned the spigot, and the refreshingly icy water cascaded over her.

CHAPTER TWO

Emerging from the shower fifteen minutes later, remarkably refreshed and respectably if awkwardly clad in the red flannel shirt, which reached her knees, Whitney discovered that White Eagle seriously intended to give her lessons. He had shed his own muddy shirt, and his broad chest gleamed a golden bronze as he sat crossed-legged at the hand-carved coffee table, his attention focused on an assortment of books and maps. Hearing her approach, he patted a spot beside him on the deerskin rug and smiled. "If you're going to meet with old Jonathan Stewart and tell him how to run a swamp and improve the lot of the Indians, you'd better go in with a little background information," he told her, his eyes sparkling with mischief. "And since you seem to like muck walks in the rain, we'd better start with the environment!"

Hiding another flush by furiously toweling her wet hair, Whitney sank down beside him, annoyed at the erratic thumping of her heart caused by the proximity of his bare flesh. Her lashes fluttering over the soft skin of her cheeks, she nonchalantly agreed. "All right, White Eagle, I may seem a fool to you, but I am eager to learn. And I really do intend to do all that I can to help the Seminoles and the Micco—Micco—"

"Miccosukees," Eagle supplied, his grin broadening. Handing her an expensive new hardcover book, he added, "This will explain the different tribes that make up the Seminole Nation. You can take that and read it at your

30

leisure. The information is important, but it won't save your life if you do any more swamp walking."

"I can't take your book!" Whitney protested, ignoring his taunt. To an Indian living in the Glades in a one-room cabin, the cost must have been prohibitive!

White Eagle shrugged. "Return it to Stewart, then. Now—on to venomous snakes." He opened another book and pointed to the four large pictures of the creatures that spanned the pages. "These are the four fellows you have to worry about in this part of the country—the coral snake, the eastern diamondback, the pygmy rattler and the water moccasin. These guys"—he pointed to the black moccasin—"are the ones that might have gotten you tonight. They are swamp dwellers and highly aggressive. The coral snake has the most toxic venom, but its bite is tight and it can only sink its fangs into areas of flesh such as that between the fingers and toes. You won't see many of the diamondbacks if any; drainage has sent them north. The pygmy is numerous, but he's a hammock boy; he prefers the high pine lands."

A shudder rippled through Whitney as she listened to his cool dissertation. She had been a far greater fool than she had imagined! The thought of one of the vipers finding her bare feet in the muck was numbing. Swallowing, she glanced sheepishly at White Eagle, who had grown silent. His unnerving crystal gaze was speculatively upon her, and she hurriedly looked back at the book. "I can see them in the pictures," she said quickly, "but what do I do if I run into a snake outside? Ask him to hold still so that I can study his markings and compare them to the book?"

"No," Eagle said quietly, refusing to respond to her nervous sarcasm. "You watch out for any snake. Most of them will give a nasty bite if aggravated." Flopping open another book, he resumed his brisk, educational tone. "Alligator here, crocodile there. Notice the difference in the snouts. Both can be found in the Glades, alligators in the freshwater, inland regions; crocodiles in the outlying, mangrove island regions—that's coastal. Both can be nasty and aggressive, but if left alone, they tend to go their own way." Turning pages slowly, he went on to point out the Florida bear, panther and deer, mentioning a few traits of each. By the time the book snapped closed, Whitney had become deeply immersed in the pleasant drone of his voice and was sorry that her lesson had come to an end.

"More coffee?" he inquired suddenly. "Or if you like, I can make tea."

"Coffee would be fine," Whitney replied quickly, once more terribly conscious of his broad, bare chest so close beside her. The rippling gold skin was smooth and tight, completely devoid of hair. Not an inch of skin could be pinched from his form, and Whitney longed to reach out and touch it and feel the sleekness. Whoa, she told herself, suddenly dizzy and keenly aware of his clean, masculine scent. Time to move!

Stumbling in her haste, Whitney tripped over her own feet as she tried to rise from her crossed-leg position. A strong hand immediately snaked out to steady her.

"Thanks," she murmured, lowering her lashes and walking gingerly to the window. White Eagle silently rose after her and calmly began to prepare a new pot of coffee.

Leaning her forehead against the cool pane of glass, Whitney stared out into the black night. What an unusual trick of fate the evening had played upon her! Little more than an hour ago the Glades and its inhabitants had been but words and pictures in her mind. She had inadvertently stumbled into a situation that was proving more educational than any book had ever been. *That* she had to appreciate. The strange things that the remarkable Indian was doing to her unraveling composure were another matter entirely. . . .

White Eagle was watching his surprise guest, assessing her with a curiosity that would have stunned Whitney were she to know its cause. His crystal gaze softened momentarily; she looked like a beautiful, woebegone child as she stared out the window, her hair drying and fluffing around the delicate contours of her creamy face; her arms clasped tightly around a slender form that seemed incredibly petite beneath the drooping tails of his huge shirt. Then White Eagle stiffened imperceptibly; his gaze hardened again to that of a glittering gem. She was accepting his hospitality and responding with intelligence to the lessons he had attempted to give her. But she had a job to do, and that was where her interest lay. Every aspect of her—her poise, her dainty appearance, her chic though destroyed clothing—all spoke of spoiled affluence. Her attitude was condescendingly kind. A spark of anger ignited within him as he thought of her as yet another outsider determined to cause "beneficial change" while understanding nothing of the true problems.

She turned to him suddenly with a wistful smile, and a tightness gripped his throat. God, but she was lovely!

"Tell me," she said with a slight shudder, "why would anyone choose to live out here in this bleakness?"

Eagle smiled with thin lips, a motion that did not reach his eyes. He turned his back on her to pour the coffee. "The Seminoles didn't choose to live out here originally. The name itself has two meanings: 'runaway' and 'wild.' " Having poured the coffee, he sauntered over to her and continued in a biting tone. "A brief history: The Seminole and Miccosukee tribes are the descendants of the Creek Confederation—Georgia Indians. They began to migrate south in the eighteenth century, absorbing the remnants of the earlier tribes who had been mostly massacred. When Jackson became president, he determined to transplant or annihilate the Indians in Florida. The Seminole Wars began. Some of the clans signed treaties and allowed themselves to be shipped west. Others refused to be conquered. They fled further and further south, forced to the sanctuary of the swamp. They learned to live with it, adapt to it and appreciate the beauty of it. It became their land; they *never* surrendered to the United States government.

33

And that, young lady, is why land simply cannot be stolen any longer. Warriors can no longer take the battle to the field, but the people *can* wage war in the courts with the rights of the citizens they have become!"

Whitney found that she had backed herself into the wall as his speech had grown more intense and vehement. He had actually advanced upon her with barely controlled anger, his hands tight fists around his cup. If his blue eyes and cultured voice had lulled her into believing him to be harmless, his proud, towering fury now dictated otherwise. She could well imagine his eyes flashing within the noble countenance of his carved features if he was challenged or angered.

He stepped back abruptly, aware that his menace had caused her eyes to open with fearful alarm. "Sorry," he murmured, his voice returning to its cool, controlled baritone.

Whitney drew a deep breath. "I think I understand—"

"Do you?" The interjection was contemptuously cold.

"Well, yes, damnit!" Whitney countered. "And *I* don't want to steal anyone's land! I want to see that the Indians lead better lives—"

"Better than what?"

"Than what they lead now! I want to improve their living conditions—"

"Oh? And what are those conditions?"

"Well. . . ."

"You don't know a thing about it!" White Eagle muttered disgustedly, pacing across the room and dropping to the sofa, one barefooted, jeaned leg crossed in an L over the other. "Here we have her, folks, Miss Southern Homecoming Queen, ready to change the lot of the Indian without mussing her hair or dirtying a single polished nail!"

"How dare you judge me!" Whitney gasped, her temper frayed to a reckless breaking point. Stalking him in return, she followed him to the couch and glared down at him furiously, her eyes snapping with bright emerald lights.

"*You* don't know a thing about *me*. I'm from the city, yes, and I have a great deal to learn. But who the hell are you to decide that I don't plan to investigate what I'm doing? You're sitting here in a log cabin, content and comfortable! You're not living in one of those thatched-roof things —"

"Chickee," Eagle interrupted, and Whitney saw that his anger had dissipated and that he was hiding the twitch of a smile again. "The thatched homes are called chickees."

"Whatever!" Whitney sighed with exasperation. "I don't see you living in one."

"Ah, but I have, and that's the difference," he told her gravely. "Would you mind not ranting right above me?" He pointed to her hand, which held the cup and had been gesturing with emotion. "I'd just as soon not have the contents of that thing spilled all over me."

Deflated, Whitney glanced at her cup and spun away from him, still ready to do battle despite his sudden change from anger to amusement. "I repeat—you are no one to judge me. You are obviously half white, well educated and not too immediately concerned with the hardships—"

"Stop!" he ordered, a grim smile curved into the thin line of his lips. "Let's start over. Make a peace treaty." Setting his cup on the coffee table, he indicated that she should sit beside him, and when she warily complied, he twisted so that his long legs were folded beneath him and one arm stretched along the rear of the couch. Crooking it, he rested his head lightly upon the knuckles of his hand in order to give her his complete, undivided and interested attention. "Okay, now," he teased mockingly, "tell me what you would do."

Whitney returned his crystal stare unwaveringly. "I would give these people homes. I would build schools. I would—"

"You would civilize them," Eagle interjected softly.

It wasn't an angry or a mocking comment. Whitney

puckered her brows with confusion. "I don't know what you mean."

Eagle raised one dark brow and shook his head slightly. "Never mind. I believe that your intentions are good, but you are lacking one basic understanding."

"And what is that?" Whitney demanded.

"It is not something that can be told," Eagle told her. "It must be learned and absorbed. It has to be lived."

"Great!" Whitney sneered. "You're telling me that I need to learn something, then you're telling me that I will never learn it!"

"I did not say that."

"Well, what do you want me to do?" she exploded, unconsciously tilting her chin to an arrogant angle. "Die and come back to life as an Indian?"

"Hardly." Eagle's bright eyes were dancing devilishly. "I want you to get to know the Seminoles and Miccosukees. So far all you've told me you know is that the Indians live in grass hovels and wrestle alligators, and that to improve their deplorable lot, you would put them into rows of whitewashed houses away from this 'bleak' swamp."

"Well?" Whitney snapped curtly. "Is it bad that I want to offer them nice homes on dry land?"

"It is bad that you patronize!" Eagle growled, his features rigid. "If you see J. E. Stewart with an attitude like that, you'll be spending the next decade in court."

"I'll handle J. E. Stewart, thank you," Whitney said acidly. "But I will find out more about the life-styles—"

"And how are you going to do that?"

"I'll visit the damn villages, of course, you idiot!" Pure exasperation had driven Whitney to the crude name-calling; that and a profound desire to wipe the arrogant cynicism from his eyes.

"Idiot?" Both brows raised in a high, black arch. Muscles flexed involuntarily across the expanse of his chest and down the length of his arms. Whitney shrank into the

36

couch, regretting her snide comment and fearing that she might have incited him to violence. He stretched a hand to touch her cheek and she unwittingly emitted a small cry of fear. The tension left White Eagle's eyes and he chuckled. "I'm not going to hurt you." His thumb, rough and calloused, traced a pattern along her jawline, and Whitney quivered, not from fear but from the simple yet delicious sensation of the tender gesture.

"Idiot, huh?" he repeated with a laugh. Such a fine thing she was! Like a delicate, porcelain doll. Yet as he watched her liquid gaze upon him, tremulous but full of defiance, self-righteousness and determination, he was overcome by a sense of possessive curiosity. A strange longing really to know the woman beneath the elegant trappings gripped him painfully. At the same time he wanted to break her of the proud superiority she insinuated in so many ways.

Of course, he could easily do that with a few words. But then he would never know. . . .

A full, satanic smile broke across his face, highlighting his eyes with a handsome, rakish glow. Whitney stared at him incredulously, certain she was dealing with a madman.

"What is the matter with you?" she queried crossly. "One minute you look as if you're going to snap my head off, and the next thing I know you're finding me vastly amusing!"

"Nothing, nothing!" White Eagle assured her quickly. "I just had a tremendous idea." Gripping both her small hands within his large ones, he began to quiz her. "You don't have to see Stewart until next week, right?"

"Right, but how did you know?"

"You mentioned it earlier," Eagle said quickly. "I'm assuming you're over twenty-one and on your own, right?"

"Right—"

"No husband?"

"No, I'm divorced—"

"Good! And you seriously want to do what is best for the Indians?"

"Of course!"

"You want to understand them and their way of life?"

"Yes, I told you that—"

"Well, then, Miss Latham," he said smugly, "I am going to help you. I will take you to meet the Miccosukees as you never would purchasing souvenirs from a roadside stand. By the time you meet with Stewart, you will have a very clear and concise picture of just what the Indians do and do not need."

He was quite serious, Whitney realized, but she was more confused by him than ever. "Do you mean you're going to take me to meet your family? That—"

"Not meet them," Eagle interrupted. "Live with them, as one of them."

"*What?*" Whitney shrieked. "You want me to go live in a grass . . . a grass . . ."

"Hovel?" Eagle suggested with amusement.

"A grass *house!*" Whitney shot him a nasty glance and clicked her teeth together. "You spent half an hour telling me how foolish I was to wander into the swamp and now you want me to stay in it with the snakes and alligators and—oh, Lord!—the mosquitoes and spiders and—"

"Yes, I see that you're right," Eagle interrupted coldly. "You'd never make it. Miss Virginia might crack a nail."

"That isn't fair!" Whitney protested.

"Isn't it? I said you didn't want to dirty your pretty little hands and it seems that I'm correct."

Whitney was floundering. While indignantly feeling that she owed no explanations to this overbearing man, another part of her hated the easily read disappointment that he made no attempt to hide. Why did she feel she needed his approval; why did she so long for his respect? She had only met the man tonight!

"You're the one being pigheaded and refusing to under-

38

stand now," she told him quietly, raising her chin. "I wouldn't know what I was doing—"

"I said you were right," Eagle interrupted curtly. "You are too soft. You wouldn't last a day. You'd pass out after an hour's work."

"I would not!" Whitney flared. "I do work for a living and I have for several years."

"Wow, am I impressed!" Eagle jeered lightly.

"Damnit! You think you're the only one capable—"

"I didn't say that. But I'm talking about manual labor, and I'm not sure you're even aware of the definition of the words."

"Of all the conceited audacity!" Whitney flew from the couch in a rage, her hands tight fists clenched to her sides. "I can live your Micco-whatever life-style and never pass out! I am well versed in the meaning of manual labor and most of all—Mr. Eagle—I am sure that I can handle anything that you might dish out!"

"Bravo!" His eyes were sparkling; he was laughing again.

Stunned by his mirthful acceptance of her speech, Whitney realized belatedly that she had been goaded into agreement with his ridiculous proposal. Regret over her hasty words washed quickly through her, but how could she back out now?

Holding her head high, she crossed her arms tightly over her chest. "This is a deal between us, right?" she asked in her best business voice. "We need terms. What are they?"

"Hmmmm. . . ." he said pensively, his eyes guarded as he perused her rigid stance from head to toe, a grin flickering. "I'll have to think about that. The time period will be exactly one week. If you make it, you will understand why the land problem came up. And I will help you all I can; I'll talk to Stewart for you, and I'll make sure you both come to an amicable agreement."

39

"That's fair," Whitney said stiffly. "Do you have that type of influence with Stewart?"

"Yes, I do."

"How do I know that?"

"Neither the Cow Creek Seminoles nor the Miccosukees are liars," he informed her coolly.

"Sorry; no insult intended," Whitney declared, her voice as cool as his. "I'm used to dealing with contracts."

"Indians are known for keeping their word."

"So I've heard."

They stared at one another, two sparring partners, both determined to bring the other down. It was an ancient battle. Their eyes were locked in the simple war of the sexes: the keen, penetrating stare of the powerful man; the rebellious, determined glare of the beautiful woman.

It was Whitney who gave way first, but unwilling to admit any type of defeat, she nonchalantly picked up her cup and sauntered to the battered coffee pot. "We forgot one thing," she said casually. "What happens in the highly unlikely event that I lose? What will be—uh—your winning bet?"

"I don't know yet." Eagle chuckled evasively. "That's what I'll have to think about. I'll let you know by morning."

Whitney's hand was shaking as she attempted to pour more coffee. She had to be crazy! Committing herself to a week in a primitive wilderness. Would she survive on her own? She began praying fervently that White Eagle's family was kind and that they would accept her presence with charity.

A hand suddenly came over hers, steadying the pot. Whitney's skin prickled with anticipation. Eagle was standing behind her, his flesh touching the material of her shirt. "What are you afraid of?" he asked kindly.

Lowering her lashes, Whitney whispered honestly, "Snakes and things in the dark."

Pivoting her by the shoulders so that she faced him,

Eagle gave her a warm, sincere smile. "I'm not sending you into the jungle to be consumed, you know. Don't you trust my ability to protect you?"

Whitney's eyes flew widely open. "You plan to be with me?"

"Certainly. Every day and night. I don't want to miss this for the world," Eagle assured her, his eyes leaving hers to follow his hand as he gently smoothed back a strand of her straying hair. "What did you think? That I was going to dump you in the Glades and leave you?"

"Well, you didn't say," Whitney hedged nervously, stuttering in an attempt to hide the rush of heat that flooded through her at his touch. Day and night! She would sleep in the woods with this man—with this compelling stranger who affected her as no one had before—for an entire week. Her throat went dry and her breathing became short and gaspy. Her heart was pounding mercilessly. Couldn't he hear it? Oh Lord! She was thrilled; she was terrified. Where was her rational thought? If she had any sense in her at all, with the first light of morning she would run away . . . as far away as she could possibly get from the uncanny power of White Eagle.

"I don't happen to have to be anywhere myself for a week," Eagle was saying amiably. With a shrug and a blink she might have missed, he added, "It's a slow season for alligator wrestling."

Smiling weakly, Whitney pulled gently from his hands and strolled back to the couch. "Will your family accept me?" she asked.

"The 'family' I'm taking you to is my grandmother. As you've so observantly noticed, I'm half white. Three quarters, if you want to get technical. But Morning Dew is full-blooded Miccosukee. She is a direct descendant of the great chief Osceola. If anyone can teach you the ways of our people, it is she."

"Oh!" Whitney said, puzzled. If White Eagle was only a quarter Indian, why was he wasting his life in the swamp? Questions about his white heritage rose in her throat, but she didn't get a chance to voice them.

White Eagle followed her and playfully pulled her from the couch. As she stared at him indignantly, he pointed to a pile of sheets and pillows neatly arranged in the corner of the cabin. "Grab yourself a blanket and I'll make up your bed. This is an ingenious non-Indian invention known as a Castro convertible."

Laughing as she sprang from the couch, Whitney obediently retrieved the bedding from the corner of the room. White Eagle lifted the bottom rung easily and the couch unfolded into a large bed. He motioned for Whitney to toss him a sheet, and between them they silently made the bed. Plumping a single pillow on the crisply clean undersheet, Eagle bowed gallantly. "Enjoy, Miss Latham. Tomorrow night you will be sleeping with the stars."

Granting him a dry smile, Whitney crawled hesitantly onto the converta-bed and pulled the top sheet primly to her chin. "Where are you going to sleep?" she asked him nervously. "I—I don't mean to kick you out of your own bed!"

"I'll be on the other couch and I'll be fine," he assured her, smiling down from what seemed an incredible height. Her dark hair was spread in a beautiful, fluffy fan across the white pillow, and the eyes that gazed tentatively at him in return were like seas of jade. An ache shot through White Eagle with a force that almost doubled him over. It was more than simple desire for a lovely woman that pained him, but he refused to question his feelings. Stiffening to a posture as regal as that of any of his warrior ancestors, he growled a quick "Good night" and spun away in a smart turnabout. Moving deftly around the cabin to extinguish all but one of the gas lanterns, he added briskly, "I'll leave this light going so that you won't be in total blackness. Just don't panic in the night and go thrashing about and knock it over."

"I won't," Whitney promised, closing her eyes.

A few moments later she heard a faint creak as he lowered his weight onto the couch opposite her. Opening her eyes narrowly, she could see his form dimly in the pale, remaining light. The muscles of his golden back rippled even in relaxation; the trim length of his legs, still encased in the worn jeans, hung precariously off the couch. He was turned away from her, his black crop of hair resting on a pillow he had bunched beneath his head. Whitney watched him for several moments, then sighed complacently and closed her eyes. Even in the swampland of the Glades, she felt an innate security knowing that he slept just a few feet away, his easy breathing audible if she listened closely.

In her exhausted state Whitney began to dream. She was back in the muck, following a path to the light. She ran and fell, floundered to her feet, ran and fell again. The earth sucked at her, refusing to release its grip. She could see the light clearly, shining so near! But no matter how desperately she clawed for freedom, the muck dragged her down.

A noise came from behind her, and in the confused state of her dream she knew that it had to be White Eagle. But it wasn't. White Eagle stood ahead of her, framed in the glow of the light as a dark form, his arms crossed over his chest, his feet a foot apart and planted firmly to the ground.

Whitney's head turned irrevocably in an out-of-sinc slow motion. She didn't know what she would see behind her and dreaded the confrontation with paralyzing panic, yet still she turned her head, slowly, slowly, slowly.
. . .

Outside in the night, a bird shrieked a high call. It coincided with the earsplitting scream that Whitney rendered as she reared up in the bed, trembling uncontrollably with terror.

"Whitney! Whitney!" Strong arms cradled her as she fought her way from the murky depths of the dream to

43

reality. The blurry world came into focus and she saw that White Eagle was beside her, his face unmasked for once, his eyes naked pools of tense concern.

"I—I was dreaming," she babbled, "about something hounding me. It was coming for me. Oh God! How horrible!"

"Hush, Whitney, it was only a dream." He sat holding her, swaying in a slight rocking motion until her trembling subsided to small shudders.

As her sense of fear lessened with each waking moment, Whitney began to feel faint twinges of embarrassment. Here she was, self-proclaimed rugged woman of the world, wailing like a banshee over a dream!

"I'm sorry," she mumbled, suddenly very aware of the arms that held her with soothing comfort. "I didn't mean to disturb your sleep. I don't usually do things like this—"

He was smiling gently. "It's all right. You really did have a rather hairy first introduction to the Glades. Probably a delayed reaction."

"I guess," Whitney said sheepishly.

Pushing her to arm's length, White Eagle probed her eyes intensely. "You don't have to go through with this deal of ours," he said, his expression carefully guarded again.

Whitney bristled. He was thinking her a cowardly quitter. "I most certainly do intend to go through with our deal, and more important, I intend to win."

Eagle shrugged, and Whitney could see the gleam of perfect white against the bronze of his face in the darkness as he nonchalantly grinned. "That is something only the future will tell!" He released her shoulders. "Are you okay now?"

"I—uh—yes," Whitney answered. He was rising, and a thickness was catching in her throat. She didn't want him to leave her. His touch stilled all thoughts of fear and terror. "Wait!" she said impetuously, clutching his hand. He paused and stared down at her with expectant, raised brows. "Don't go. I mean—" She knew she was blushing furiously and she tossed her head to form a fluffy veil of hair over her telltale features. "I am kicking you out of your bed. You must be horribly uncomfortable on that couch—your feet hang off it! We're going to be sharing a chickee for a week so we might as well share the comfort of a mattress for the night." Not daring to look into his eyes for fear of rejection, Whitney gazed with what she hoped was casual nonchalance at his jaw. There was an erratic tic beating in the hollow of his cheek.

"Are you still frightened?" he demanded tightly.

Miserably Whitney whispered, "Yes."

He gave a funny sigh that sounded like a groan. "Move over," he muttered irritably, "and I'll ward off the nocturnal demons. From this side of the bed, at least."

Whitney scrambled across the bed, scarcely daring to breathe. She had just asked a stranger to sleep with her. God, what was happening to her? But he didn't seem like a stranger; in the short time since they had met, she had come to feel that everything in her life before this evening had been inconsequential. She couldn't imagine anymore *not* having known him.

Hearing the rise and fall of his breathing, she wondered if he slept. He had been so kind when she screamed, tender even. But when she asked him to stay, he had been irritated, brusque. Unbidden tears suddenly formed in her eyes. Oh well, what had she expected? She had burst upon his evening and showered him with mud, then disturbed his sleep. And, however grudgingly, he had complied with her request and now lay beside her so that she might get some rest. She would lie very quietly, not even move. She would not waken him again.

But White Eagle wasn't sleeping. He lay awake tensely, his body groaning in protest. Damn! Didn't she know what she was asking of him? His fingers ached to reach out and touch her; his nostrils were filled with her clean, fragrant scent. Every nerve in his body cried out.

45

Long after she had fallen back to sleep, Eagle still lay awake. He turned on his side to watch her. The rich splay of her hair was spread in wild disarray over the bedding. Her lips were curled in a small, sweet smile. Who was this lovely enchantress, he wondered whimsically, not trusting her gentle countenance. Only time would tell.

She stirred in her sleep and inched closer to him, her small frame curving perfectly against his large one as she unconsciously sought his warmth. Eagle groaned aloud softly. Sighing, he slipped an arm around her and his hand fit over her midriff, just below the soft swelling of her breasts. She nuzzled comfortably in his hold, naturally, as if they had lain together hundreds of times before.

With the warmth of her body radiating through him, White Eagle finally slept. His dreams, too, were of a turbulent nature. The times were long ago, and he was able to follow his natural instincts. And when he found his beautiful witch, he simply made her his and rode away with her into the sunset.

The thought was still with him when he woke to the dawn, and he grinned at himself with wry humor. Wasn't that really what he was trying to do?

CHAPTER THREE

The bright heat of the sun streaming in through the open window brought Whitney slowly out of a deep and pleasant sleep. For several minutes she lay in the groggy, relaxed state that was between unconsciousness and full awareness; then as she recalled where she was and the events of the previous night, she opened her eyes with alarm and quickly scanned the room for White Eagle.

He was nowhere to be seen, but her overnight bag and suitcase were sitting at the foot of the bed. Sometime that morning he had made a trek to her car and procured her things.

Smiling with gratitude, Whitney leaped from the bed to burrow through her clothing. She was thankful that she was well supplied with jeans. Grabbing a pair, she delved through her more feminine blouses and chose a plain, tailored western-style shirt in a light blue denim. Serviceable certainly! She only had one pair of boots with her, and they were fashionable, soft kid leather. They would be better than nothing, she decided. They would be ruined, but they were replaceable and her feet were not!

By the time she had finished dressing and had returned the bed to its original couch state, the pleasant aroma of something cooking began to drift through the window. Giving the room a once-over glance and satisfying herself that she had left it impeccably neat, Whitney brushed her hair into a tie at the back of her neck and hurried out the cabin door.

On the top step Whitney paused and allowed her eyes to roam over the landscape. Things had changed overnight. The cabin, she realized, was built on a spit of high ground, and it was surrounded by a semblance of lawn. In the distance the sawgrass rippled in the breeze, shimmering like foam-flecked waves on an ocean. To the far left she could see an oasis of cypress trees, dripping prettily with moss. The scene, she had to admit, was beautiful.

"Whitney! Come on down."

Her attention drawn back to the present, Whitney snapped her gaze to the right edge of the "lawn." White Eagle, similarly appareled as herself in a dark blue work shirt and black jeans, was leaning over one knee as he poked at a small cooking fire. Whitney caught his brilliant blue gaze, and little butterflies began to flutter in her stomach. How could anyone be so damned, rawly attractive?

And he wasn't alone. A sandy-haired young man in a Coors beer T-shirt and sneakers sat on the other side of the fire with a woman as stunningly attractive as White Eagle. Her eyes were the same brilliant blue, her hair the same slick raven black. It hung down to her waist in shining waves, framing a good-natured, beautifully sculpted face. For a moment Whitney felt her heart pull with the strings of jealousy. Then a silly smile of relief twitched her lips. With the remarkable resemblance, the woman could only be White Eagle's sister.

Her hands stuffed shyly into her pockets, Whitney started across the grass toward them, realizing happily that Eagle had used her first name. In fact, after having addressed her as Miss Latham during their early conversations, he had also called her Whitney when he had come to comfort her after her nightmare. . . .

"Miss Whitney Latham," he was saying now as he stood with the sandy-haired man and the woman, "I'd like ɔu to meet my sister, Katie Eagle, and her husband, Randy Harris."

48

As Whitney accepted their friendly handshakes and returned their welcoming smiles, she wondered uneasily why it seemed that her host had stressed the surname Eagle and glanced warningly at his sister. It must have been her imagination, she decided; no one else had appeared to notice.

"Randy is with the Bureau of Indian Affairs," White Eagle added as they all sat back down around the fire. "He's in charge of some of the cattle projects at the Big Cypress Reservation. He and Katie have volunteered to show you around up there next week."

"Thank you," Whitney acknowledged, studying the woman again as she accepted a cup of coffee from Eagle. Katie wore jeans as did her brother, but her blouse was of colorful Indian design. The handiwork was intrinsic, with row after row of bright trim.

"We're thrilled that you're really interested," Katie told her with an endearing eagerness. "When we first heard that T and C Development was willing to negotiate, we didn't believe it, in all honesty," she said apologetically. "My brother tells me that you're even willing to try life in the Glades for a week." Was Whitney imagining it, or did Katie really cast Eagle a reproachful glance?

"Thanks to your brother," Whitney said wryly, "I've learned how ignorant I am." The flutterings in her stomach were becoming gnawing pains. They had nothing to do with White Eagle; she was ravenously hungry! "What's in the pan?" she inquired, sniffing.

"Good old Indian bacon and eggs," Eagle said with his sardonic grin. "This is going to be your last 'civilized' meal for a while. And the last one *I* will be cooking. In Miccosukee society, the women still do the cooking."

"I'm a good cook," Whitney retorted, accepting the plate he handed her. His reply was a raised brow of amusement.

"Don't let this man get to you," Randy Harris said with a laugh at their interchange. "The Seminoles were counted

49

in with the Five Civilized Tribes back in pioneer days. They were never given to caveman tactics and barbarism!"

Katie Eagle started to say something, but her brother quickly cut her off in their native tongue. Whitney glanced at them both with confusion, then at Randy. "That's Miccosukee or 'Hitchiti,' " he told her with a chuckle, "and I guarantee you, it's not easy to learn! Then if you do learn it and meet up with the Cow Creek Seminoles, you have to start all over again. They speak Muskogee, like the Creeks from Oklahoma."

Whitney smiled wanly. She had never even heard the word "Muskogee" before, nor did she know that Creeks lived in Oklahoma. "What are they talking about?" she asked him loudly, purposely interrupting the conversation that had grown animated between brother and sister. Not only did it seem rude, but she was sure they were discussing her.

"Can't tell you," Randy said with a shake of his head. "They're speeding along too fast for me."

"We disagree on the best way to introduce you to Indian life," Eagle said smoothly. "Right, Katie?"

"Right," his sister agreed with a sigh. "You will enjoy my grandmother, Whitney. She is hard-core Miccosukee."

"That's what Eagle says," Whitney mused, wondering if there was a warning in the words. Still, she felt an element of safety in spite of her niggling suspicions. At least the sandy-haired man and Eagle's friendly sister knew where she would be!

"Look!" Randy said suddenly, his voice a hush as he pointed across the lawn. "One of our peculiar beauties . . . a great white heron."

Whitney followed his pointing finger and watched as the graceful bird closed its mighty wingspan and cocked its head to the breeze. The bird delicately balanced on a single foot for a second, a proud, immobile statue against the blue gold sky, then bunched its muscles and few into the horizon. It was a beautiful sight, Whitney silently agreed.

"Randy's thing is birds," Katie said.

"Wildlife," Randy corrected, offering Whitney a wryly apologetic grin. "I can go off on tangents, so don't let me." He pulled a pack of cigarettes from his breast pocket and offered them around. Thinking with surprise that she hadn't missed smoking all night, Whitney gratefully accepted one and inhaled deeply. "Have to be real careful with these things in these parts," Randy warned, indicating his cigarette and matches.

"You arrived at the tail end of the rainy season," Eagle said as Whitney glanced with a frown at the wetness that surrounded their immediate dry circle. "For six months of the year we're lucky if get a few inches of rain. A fire in the Glades can be a terrible thing. The earth itself burns."

"I'll be careful," Whitney promised, pouring herself more coffee to accompany her cigarette.

"Maybe I'll cure you of the habit before the week is out, anyway," Eagle said, watching her expression as he leaned back on an elbow and musingly chewed on a blade of grass.

"Pardon?" Whitney looked at him suspiciously.

"You won't be smoking."

"Now wait a minute!" Whitney protested. "You keep making up new rules all the time! I didn't make any promises regarding my personal habits!"

Eagle shrugged, imperially allowing her the slight concession. "You can bring whatever supply you have with you. I don't want you running wild into the woods in the midst of a nicotine fit. You won't find much time though, I think, to laze around with a cigarette." He jumped suddenly to his feet and began collecting the dishes. "We have to get a move on. Your 'swamp week' is going to be exact. It starts at noon today and ends at noon in seven days. That is, if you make the first hour."

"Oh, I will make it," Whitney said sweetly, her eyes

51

telling him what she thought he could do with his taunting cynicism. "I've told you that before."

"She's got the look of an eagle about her, too, my friend," Randy said with a chuckle as he scrambled up to help White Eagle thoroughly douse the fire. "Watch it; she'll beat you at your own game."

"Maybe," Eagle agreed good-naturedly, extending a hand to pull Whitney to her feet. "I put a gallon of gas into your car this morning and pulled it around back," he told her. "Go on and get anything else you're going to need for your 'personal habits.' The keys are still in the ignition where you left them. We don't have many thieves running around the neighborhood, but you might want to lock it up anyway."

"Thanks," Whitney said, dusting off the seat of her pants. "How are we going to get where we're going?"

"Jeep and airboat," Eagle said briefly, smiling. "Randy is the 'brother' I said was coming by. He and I will go hook up now. Go on—get ready."

"I'll come with you," Katie offered.

"No!" Eagle snapped at his sister, softening his command with a pleasant request. "I'll need you out here, if you don't mind."

Apparently Eagle was undisputed boss. Katie shrugged and lifted helpless hands to Whitney. "I guess I won't get a chance to know you until next week. I stay with Morning Dew a lot myself, but I have to go back to Big Cypress with Randy now."

If Katie didn't have to go back to Big Cypress, Whitney decided dryly, she was certain White Eagle would find some other place to send her. It was obvious he didn't want his sister involved in any deep discussions with her. Was he ashamed of anything, she wondered. That seemed doubtful. White Eagle was proud. He would declare what he was to the world and the devil himself could go hang.

"I'll be looking forward to next week," Whitney promised the Indian woman. Glancing across the lawn to where

Eagle and Randy were about to round the corner of the cabin, Whitney saw that her host was staring crossly at his sister. "It looks like the big chief is summoning you," she told Katie in a wry drawl. "I guess we will have to talk later."

Katie chuckled, amused by the reference to her brother. "This isn't good-bye yet. We'll be dropping you off at the village. It really is remote." Waving, she scampered off to join the men.

Whitney thoughtfully climbed the steps back to the cabin, realizing she had made grave mistakes in judgment where White Eagle was concerned. Obviously he and his soft-spoken sister had been well educated, and it was equally obvious he had some type of decent income. His books were expensive, his clothing quality. Airboats and jeeps were not cheap. Closing the door quietly behind her, Whitney glanced around the single room of the cabin and determined that a little snooping was in order. Rushing to his bureau, she hastily began to rifle through it.

She was doomed to disappointment. There wasn't a single document, note or paper to be found. Absolutely nothing to tell her who White Eagle was or what he did. The only reward she received for her labors was a verification of what she already knew; White Eagle did receive a good income for something. The labels on his clothing were all well-known, respected names.

"Looking for something?"

His cool voice from the doorway startled her so that she slammed her fingers into a drawer, yelped and spun around to meet his demand with guilt written clearly across her face. "I—uh—I—"

"Yes?"

"Socks!" Whitney blurted, watching the cynical interest in his unfathomable blue gaze. Was he angry? Sometimes it was impossible to tell. "Socks," she repeated, lowering her squeaky tone to a more moderate pitch. "I only have the one pair with me and I was sure that you wouldn't mind."

"No, I don't mind at all." Sedately walking past her, he reached into a drawer and handed her a pair of neatly folded blue socks. The drawer, which Whitney had not had a chance to return to its original state, gave evidence of having been thoroughly searched. "Sorry you had such a rough time finding them," Eagle said politely.

"Yes, well, uh, thank you," Whitney stammered, backing away from him. "I'll, uh, just run out and lock up the car."

"Yes, do that," Eagle agreed pleasantly.

With an artificial smile plastered to her face, Whitney continued to back to the doorway. She backed all way to the steps, then went crashing down them with a small, startled cry of alarm.

White Eagle was leaning over her before she had a chance to gather together either her bruised body or ego. "You really do need to learn to watch where you're going," he told her with mock concern. "Can I give you a hand?"

"No, you may not!" Whitney snapped from her totally undignified sprawl. Damn him! He had watched her! He had known perfectly well that her steps were leading her to the graceless fall.

"As you wish." Shrugging, Eagle turned back into the cabin, a grin playing at the corner of his lips. Whitney winced and pushed the ground with her palms to propel her smarting flesh back to a stand. At least she hadn't really harmed anything except her pride!

"Where are your things?" the voice bellowed irately from the cabin.

"Right there!" Whitney returned exasperated. "My travel bag and the case. They're on the couch—"

White Eagle poked his head from the cabin with an incredulous expression of pure disbelief. "Whitney," he groaned, "we are not going for a week to the Waldorf-

Astoria. We are going into the swamp for you to assimilate a different culture. One change of clothing will be sufficient."

"One change of clothing?" Whitney sputtered. "For a week?"

"In the most contemporary of societies," Eagle said with pointed patience, "people do *wash* clothing."

Glaring at him beligerently, Whitney limped back up the steps and furiously ripped open her suitcase. Grabbing a second pair of jeans and a shirt and a set of matching lacy panties and bra, she stuffed them into her overnight bag and shoved it into his arms. "I am bringing my toothbrush!" she declared haughtily. "I don't feel like rotting my teeth for you to prove some elusive point!"

"By all means, bring your toothbrush," Eagle said with a laugh. He flung the bag back to her and she caught it by reflex. "Sorry, no porters. You carry your own gear." With a mocking bow and quick turnabout, he was out the door.

Throwing the leather shoulder bag over her arm, Whitney followed him outside. The jeep, a new though rugged vehicle, had been pulled around in front, with the large, propellered airboat in tow. Randy was at the wheel with Katie beside him, both patiently waiting.

"I'll just be a second!" Whitney called, racing around the corner of the cabin. Her BMW had been pulled beneath a rear, partially sheltered overhang. Throwing open the driver's door, she pulled her keys from the ignition and hurriedly glanced through the car. Retrieving several packs of cigarettes from the glove compartment, she decided there was nothing else she would need—or be allowed to take!

Eagle was waiting impatiently by the rear of the jeep, his fingers drumming a rhythm on the side of the metal door panel. "Move it, Miss Virginia!" he called. "The bog is awaiting you!"

Raising a brow and tilting her nose, Whitney slowed her

speed to saunter toward the jeep. Eagle's jaw was locked when she reached him, but he said nothing. Pulling her bag from her, he tossed it over the side of the jeep. Then he set the large span of his hands around her waist and hoisted her body over with the same ease before vaulting in himself. His arm stretched behind her as he said, "Better drive on, Randy, before she realizes she's forgotten her Chanel No 5."

Whitney was shivering even as she glared at him indignantly. She could still feel the imprint of his hands upon her ribs, as if his touch had been indelibly etched into her with searing heat. She could sense his arm, so casually lying behind her back, with every nerve of her flesh.

"Eagle!" Katie turned reproachful eyes to her brother, folding an arm over the rear of her seat so that she might converse with them. "Be nice! You like Chanel No 5!" Eagle had no response.

As the jeep pulled along the same road Whitney had stumbled upon the night before, Katie and Randy explained the terrain they would be covering. As well as the seemingly endless marshland of tall sawgrass, the Glades were also composed of high pine lands known as hammocks. The two highways that stretched across the swampland of the southern tip of the state, the Trail and Alligator Alley, had made many areas easily accessible, but there were still countless miles of land that could only be navigated by airboat or canoe. "Many independent Miccosukees live right along the Trail," Katie said, "but the Eagle clan lives deep in the woods."

Whitney leaned forward eagerly in her seat. Katie was a wonderful source of information, and their journey might end at any time. "Tell me something about your family," she begged, mindless of Eagle's stoic expression beside her. "Are your parents living?"

"My father is—" Katie began.

"Katie!" Eagle barked. "I'm sure Miss Latham isn't interested in our dubious bloodlines."

"I'm just going to tell her how they met!" Katie retorted, smiling at Whitney. "My mother and grandmother had marvelously romantic marriages! My mother's father was a businessman who came to the Glades to hunt. He became entranced by the honesty and high moral code of the Miccosukees, and finally the Eagle family grew to respect and trust him in return. Morning Dew fell head over heels in love with him and—at a time when marriage outside the tribe was unheard of—she defied her father and uncles to be with him. But my grandfather loved her very deeply, too. Instead of demanding that she desert her home, he embraced the life of the Miccosukees and gave up his own society."

"That is romantic!" Whitney chuckled. "What about your mother and father?"

Eagle muttered some sort of expletive beside her, but Whitney ignored him. Katie glanced at him with a wounded, I-know-what-I'm-doing expression and continued.

"My father was a charter pilot. He was en route to the Keys from Tampa when his plane went down in the Everglades. He was lost, delirious and barely conscious when my mother found him. She was a beautiful woman, and Dad says he fell in love as soon as he opened his eyes to find her tenderly nursing his wounds. They were married both by tribal law and in my father's church."

Whitney had a dozen more questions to ask, but White Eagle had had enough. Sitting up in the seat, he put his arm around Whitney's shoulders and forced her attention to the road. "We're making a left here to get down to the Trail," he said. "Straight ahead, you would come to North Naples." Obviously intending that she not have a chance to open her mouth again, he rapidly began pointing out the abundance of birds and foliage surrounding the road, naming things so quickly she was sure she wouldn't remember a word. Then the jeep turned again, and within minutes they were pulling off the road. They had arrived at a small Indian village. Bright, neatly printed signs announced that visitors were welcome, and on the outskirts of the slatted pine enclosure were two large, modern gas pumps. Whitney started to smile with inner relief. They weren't going to be so terribly isolated after all!

"This isn't where we are staying." The laughing whisper in her ear sent mixed shivers of apprehension and delight tingling along the length of her spine. Eagle had an uncanny habit of reading her thoughts.

"Airboat from here," Randy said cheerfully, hopping from the jeep. "Katie could take you into the village for a minute, though—"

"She can see the village next week," Eagle said, vaulting out of the vehicle to join Randy. "You two have to get back."

"I'd like to see the village now—" Whitney began, determined to voice her opinion.

"No time," Eagle shouted from the rear, where he was busily disengaging the airboat. "Don't worry, it won't go away."

Whitney suddenly wished that White Eagle would find a quicksand pit and sink into it. He was drawing her into a trap, one she could see clearly, yet she was powerless to stop the bars from closing around her. He wasn't *forcing* her deeper into the Glades; it was if he had somehow magnetized her. He kept making up the rules, and she kept following them. What else could she do? If she demanded that they see the village now, she would be the one to appear petulant and domineering! Sound reasoning had been given her—there wasn't time.

But there was more to it than that. She just didn't know what. Either I have swamp fever or I've gone crazy, Whitney told herself with disgust. No, that wasn't true. She was going into the swamp because she sincerely cared about her job and the people it involved.

Liar! A voice spoke from her heart with an impetus she couldn't control. She was going because she had never been so fascinated by a man before in her life, and if White

Eagle had challenged her to join him for a flight to Pluto, she would have found an excuse to hop right into the rocket. . . .

"Are you with us?"

Startled, Whitney jumped and turned to Eagle with guilty eyes, praying he hadn't read her thoughts again.

"Are you with us? We're all set. You weren't daydreaming about a luxury suite on the beach, were you?" he queried blandly.

"No . . . no. . . ." Whitney rushed away from him, scampering down the embankment to the canal where the airboat now waited, its propeller beginning to rev.

"Ever been on one of these before?" Randy asked loudly as she picked her way through the weeds and climbed to the flat bed of the airboat.

"I've never even seen one before!" Whitney admitted.

"You're going to love it!"

She did love it. The sensation of racing over the sea of grass was exhilarating. A rush of air whipped around her face and through her clothing as they passed through the canal and over miles of marshland, flushing birds into graceful flight with their noisome coming. Randy slowed the airboat, and Whitney felt that strange current of electricity as White Eagle set an arm around her waist to point out the reason for the delay—her first sight of an in-the-wild alligator.

" 'Gator or crocodile?" Eagle quizzed, his voice and breath whistling softly in her ear.

" 'Gator!" she responded smugly. "Crocodiles are coastal!"

"Right." His arm remained around her as they hovered closer to the beast. Whitney shivered involuntarily. The animal was a green color that blended well with the high grass; its jaw, even as it sat motionless, raised several inches so that she could see the open, waiting mouth and its rows of razor-sharp teeth. Black beady eyes observed them in a silent, chilling stare.

59

The arm around Whitney tightened reassuringly. It was odd; the man teased her mercilessly, yet he intuitively knew when she was really frightened and was there to protect her.

"Next hammock!" Randy said, and in another moment they were pulling up to one of the clumps of earth, pines and cypress.

No one could live here, Whitney decided immediately. They were *nowhere!* Although the region of solid ground seemed to encompass a large enough area of space, she could see no sign of human habitation.

"Ah—home!" Eagle proclaimed, offering Whitney a hand as he jumped off the airboat with a splash. The grin was twitching at his lips at the dismay she was finding difficult to hide. "You can still chicken out, you know," he told her as they sloshed to the shore, Randy and Katie following behind.

Whitney inched her nose into the air and smiled acidly. "No, thank you."

"Don't let him harass you," Katie warned softly from behind. "You can come back with Randy and me."

"She can—and she knows it," Eagle said, his gaze upon her as sharp as blue steel. Taking her hand, he led the way through a path in the trees Whitney would have never noticed. The landscape abruptly made an incredible change as they walked, becoming an exotic subtropical paradise. Strings of wild orchids, blooming in pastel purples and pinks, splashed against the green and brown earth shades with a magical splendor. Vines and moss played upon the trees, giving the woods a mystical beauty that lurked somewhere between a woodsy glen and a jungle in deepest Africa.

The trail broke into a clearing dotted with thatched-roof chickees. A happy, musical sound greeted Whitney's ears: the warm sound of children's laughter. The clearing was indeed alive with human habitation. Eagle called something in his native language and a scurry of colorful activity immediately surrounded them, the children with their excited brown eyes, a cluster of women dressed in beautiful long garments that ranged the spectrum of a rainbow.

Whitney hovered in the background while the others were greeted with hugs and affection. Even Randy, she noticed, was welcomed like a long-lost brother. Though faltering in his speech occasionally, he valiantly attempted to keep up with the flying conversation, and his efforts were obviously appreciated.

The growlingly familiar pang of jealousy suddenly assailed Whitney. A number of the Miccosukee women were very pretty, young and as shapely as slender willows. They wore their adoration for White Eagle nakedly in gentle almond eyes.

"Whitney," he announced, and his crystal eyes came to her as if he had just explained her presence. His hand pulled her into the group, and he repeated her name. "Whitney."

She was now the center of attraction. Shy and soft-spoken, the women offered her gentle smiles. Whatever White Eagle had said about her, it had been complimentary. Eagle began to rattle off names to her, some as common as "Katie," some she wondered if she would ever manage to pronounce, much less remember. It did appear, though, that Eagle's clan intended to accept her into the fold.

"We'd better say hello to Morning Dew and get going," Randy said to Katie, "if we're going to make it back in time."

Eagle and Katie both nodded, and Eagle said something to the group before dragging Whitney along behind him across the clearing. "Where are we going now?" Whitney demanded.

"Deeper into the dome of hell!" Eagle laughed wickedly. "My grandmother prefers to live in solitude. She seeks company on her terms only."

Whitney wanted to question him further, but he dragged her along at such a pace that she found speech impossible. A number of chickens and pigs shared the clearing with its human inhabitants, and avoiding the clucking and squealing animals gave her mind thorough occupation. Gritting her teeth as they left the melée behind and entered another trail through the wilderness, Whitney felt with a heavily sinking heart that Eagle had been right in his taunts—she was too soft. She would never be able to stick out the week. In about two minutes she was going to turn, duck tail and run helter-skelter for the airboat, her last link with the known world. . . .

"This, my dear, brave Miss Latham, is it."

Whitney crashed into his back as he halted his rapid stride abruptly. Peering around his shoulder, she saw that they had come to another clearing, one occupied by only three well-spaced chickees. One was floorless, and a large pot issuing steam sat in the middle over a crackling fire. One was far to the left with planking three feet off the ground; the last was to the right and identical, shaded by massive pines. As Whitney blinked, an old Indian woman, wrinkled like a prune from countless years of exposure to the sun and elements but as tall and straight as an iron rod, came to them on a soft and silent tread. Her eyes were as black as coal, and despite her great age it was easy to see that Eagle and Katie had inherited their lustrous hair from her. She was dressed regally in the gaudy calico of her people, and row upon row of beads adorned the entire length of her neck. Her pleasure at the sight of her grandchildren was obvious and yet subdued; she accepted them like a queen receiving homage. Once again Whitney hovered in the background, lost while they conversed in the Miccosukee language. The old woman's eyes were upon her with unabashed speculation, and Whitney's ears pricked like a dog's when she began to hear her own name and that of Jonathan Stewart mentioned.

She was surprised and dismayed when Morning Dew

frowned, angered over whatever was being said. It was she who clutched Whitney and pulled her into the group, her gnarled hands amazingly strong and her words vehement although still soft and controlled. Eagle said something impatiently, then as if remembering whom he addressed, he quieted his own tone and went into a lengthy explanation. Whitney caught Randy Harris's eye and imploringly demanded, "What is going on?"

Suddenly they all went silent.

"Eagle will tell you," Katie said hastily, kissing her grandmother's cheek and grabbing Randy's hand. "We've got to go. Are you sure you'll be okay?"

Eagle was staring at her with his bright blue eyes full of mockery and challenge. "Well?"

"I—I—yes, but what—"

"See you next week, then," Katie interrupted, impulsively kissing her cheek, too. "Don't worry—Gram isn't mad at you. 'Bye!"

"Good luck!" Randy called.

They started back through the path in a sprint, and Whitney was left to helplessly watch them go. Eagle came behind her and his steel-sinewed arms encircled her waist.

"Would you run?" he whispered in a husky taunt. "If so, run now. In another minute you will irrefutably be my woman for the coming week. You have entered the devil's den, and the devil is about to demand his due."

Gut panic gripped Whitney like a wall of ice. It was more than a teasing threat that Eagle had issued. There was an underlying tension in his voice that hinted of a deep fury, as if he was extracting vengeance.

For what, she wondered.

Then, as she snapped around in his arms to make a fear-inspired, acidic retort, she knew.

She was going to pay for her impulsive words when they met—for calling him an Indian with shocked amazement, for haughtily demanding if he could speak English.

Worst of all, she was going to pay because he had read

what she felt in her heart—that she was superior to him. And now there was nothing left to do except bluff her way through it. If his arms were steel, her will would be concrete. She would prove her mettle and take great pleasure in forcing White Eagle to realize he was not dealing with a hothouse Southern belle!

"Devil's den?" She smiled sweetly with mock innocence. "This is a paradise. I'm going to love it!"

"Hmmm . . . I hope so," Eagle replied, tapping her chin lightly with a playful gesture. The threat was still in his eyes as he stared down at her, yet it was tempered now with a mixture of other emotions, all of which were veiled. What were those emotions, Whitney wondered. A dawning of respect along with something else?

A shiver coursed through her. In the heart of her femininity she had finally read the blatant message of coolly controlled desire. White Eagle had been touched by the same inexplicable, electric attraction as she. He knew her fascination; he knew her fear and doubt.

And he played a waiting game, on his own territory, where he was sure that he would win.

Knowing the answer before she voiced the question, Whitney could not hide the waver in her tone as she demanded, "You never did tell me what you expect to get out of this bet."

"That's rather obvious, isn't it?" he drawled, and the current between them was almost visible in the air. "You."

CHAPTER FOUR

Whitney sat hunched upon her rock, her arms wrapped tiredly around her knees, a single eye resting sorrowfully upon the hand that cradled her cheek. She had never known it was possible to achieve so many calluses in one day, and her nails—usually perfectly manicured and sporting the latest in fashion colors—were broken, chipped and split. She shifted slightly and soreness riddled her back. Groaning, she awkwardly tried to massage the pain.

It wasn't Eagle but Morning Dew who had proved to be her taskmaster. In one afternoon Whitney had learned that the life of an Indian woman was still rugged indeed. So far she had been called upon to wash clothes by hand, tend the garden of late summer vegetables, feed an assortment of domesticated animals, sew until her fingers could no longer hold a needle and pound upon a strange root until it became a powdery substance that would be used as flour.

Not that Morning Dew hadn't been kind. She had clucked in perfect English like a mother hen over Whitney and taken her under a competent wing. Immediately after Eagle had stated his terms, he had spun from her as if the interchange had never existed, spoken to his grandmother, then informed Whitney that he would see her later. When she had asked where he was going, he raised and wiggled a teasing brow. "Off to play Indian brave, of course."

Sunset was coming to the Everglades. As Whitney

watched, the sky began to take on a myriad crimson and golden hues. The colors rippled and danced upon the calm, glassy sheet of the lake she sat before, creating a dazzling display. Numerous long-legged birds, trusting in her stillness, stood sentinel along the shore, forming silhouettes against the brilliant pink horizon. She realized her earlier words of bravado had not been a lie—visions of pure paradise lurked within the desolate hammocks of the deep woods.

"Ooohhh. . . ." she moaned again, trying to shift in order to ease the throbbing of newly discovered muscles.

"Rough day, huh?"

Whitney spun with a belligerent stare to see that Eagle was standing two feet behind her. Damn him! she muttered inwardly with irritation. His ability to come upon her totally undetected was most annoying.

"Not at all," she retorted nastily. "The washer didn't clog up once and I didn't have a bit of trouble at the grocery store."

Laughing, Eagle took a step and eradicated the distance between them. Before Whitney could protest, he had pushed her shoulders back and begun massaging her neck with strong fingers that brought a mixture of new torment and sweet, easing relief. Giving in to the overwhelming urge to relish the comfort brought by his powerful hands, Whitney sighed and allowed her head to rest again upon her hands.

"Where have you been all day?" she demanded impertinently, determined that he not know how grateful she was for his soothing ministrations.

"Oh, you know . . . hunting, fishing, warring with the cavalry," he replied airily.

"Very amusing," Whitney snapped. His thumb worked into her collarbone and an unexpected surge of excitement spread through her bloodstream like hot mercury. She jerked with confusion, wondering if he had felt her reaction to his touch. "You don't have to rip me apart!" she muttered hastily. "I'm quite sore enough as it is!"

Ignoring her viperish tongue, Eagle pulled her back into position. "Sit still. If I don't work out the kinks for you, you'll be in agony tomorrow. And I don't want you slacking off around the chickee!"

Whitney clamped her teeth together and stared out over the lake. He was right and she knew it. She would awake as stiff as a poker in the morning if she didn't allow him to work the knots out of her sore muscles.

But she had to maintain her guard with this man. For the first time in her life she was at a loss emotionally and physically. She was attracted to him like a moth to flame, yet unlike a moth, she had the sense to see the fire. He was an enigma to her, and yet his motives seemed as crystal clear as his eyes. He dared her, he mocked her. He had brought her into a world where he didn't need to lift a finger to inflict punishment. And he wanted her.

The why of it all troubled Whitney. Intuition told her that a man like Eagle would have strong passions and be proficient in the realm of sensual delights. She knew beyond a doubt that he would attract any number of the feminine sex—and that countless women would be more than happy to appease his appetites.

So why her? Why go through this elaborate charade to win what he could obviously have for the taking? Especially when he must realize the effect his mere proximity had on her. There were moments of electricity between them that were so intense Whitney would gladly come to him with eager submission, except. . . .

That he was an Indian? An alien to her world? He frightened her as she had never been frightened before.
. . .

And yet that wasn't it, either. If she was really frightened of something, it wasn't White Eagle. She had come to realize that he lived by a code of ethics that might put any city-bred man to shame.

True admission of her real fears hovered in her consciousness, but they were too deep to surface. Too painful. They had nothing to do with morality. In her heart she knew that anything between them would be right because such a feeling could come only once in a lifetime.

. . .

"Isn't it?"

Whitney blinked. She had grown drowsy and content while he worked his magic upon her body, and now she hadn't heard a word he had said.

Yawning, she perked her head back up. "Sorry—isn't what?"

"The lake beautiful—and very inviting."

"Yes, yes it is."

His hands left her shoulders, and she felt a sense of loss. "Join me?" The blue of his eyes was very bright against the bronze of his face in the twilight as he casually began opening the buttons on his shirt.

"Join you?" Whitney echoed blankly.

"For a swim. The water here is always cool and pleasant. A swim makes you feel a hell of a lot better in this climate—much less like a salt lick for cattle."

His shirt was gone, cast over a nearby bush. "Scoot over," he commanded, sliding down beside her on the rock to remove his boots. The heat of his body absorbed her as he nonchalantly pulled at the high zippers to free his feet and roll his socks. Like an unabashed child at a swimming hole, he stood again and Whitney heard the quick slide of his jeans zipper.

"I don't have a suit," Whitney whispered, hastily averting her eyes to look at the water before her.

"Neither do I."

A whoosh sounded through the air and she knew that his jeans and briefs had joined the shirt on the bush. He was a streak of perfect bronze as he whipped past her into the lake with a clear-cut, graceful dive.

"Come on!" There was deviltry to his invitation.

"I—I—"

"I'm not going to attack you!" Eagle called cynically, rising with the cool water dripping from his form. The lake covered him to his waist and he stood facing her regally, his hands planted firmly on his hips. His hair was slicked back by the water, defining the rugged lines of his profile as he grinned.

Whitney fought the blush that was rising to her cheeks. He was laughing at her, mocking her fear.

"What about snakes?" she countered.

"This pool is clear," he assured her. "And I'll be with you."

Whitney hesitated slightly, an eyetooth gnawing at her lip. He definitely wasn't going to attack her—he was almost contemptuous of her—which wasn't particularly flattering! The water did look inviting, and the humid temperature of the Glades *had* left her feeling like a large salt deposit. She rose slowly and dully set to work on the snaps of her tailored blouse.

If she had expected him to turn away, she was in for a surprise. He watched her every movement intently, his hands still upon his hips, his magnetizing eyes still bright with amusement—and appreciation. Whitney managed to doff her shirt, jeans and boots with nonchalance; then she froze, inhibited despite his words of assurance.

Eagle laughed again as she stood on the shore in panties and bra, confused. Yet he wasn't laughing at her, she realized, but rather with a sympathetic understanding.

"Okay!" she yelled at him, assessing the communication for what it was. "You could make this a little easier for me by taking a big jump into the lake—deep!"

He shook his head sternly. "You are beautiful, Whitney. Very fine, very delicate. Don't hide from me."

Unnerved by his bluntness, Whitney felt the blush of her cheeks spread through her body. "Does that mean I have no right to be modest?" she mumbled sarcastically, lowering her head as she fumbled for the hook of her bra.

His answer was soft. "No, Whitney. But we are hardly strangers. You know that as well as I."

Unable to meet his eyes, Whitney dropped the white lacy bra to her feet and slipped from the brief bikini pants with an inborn sensuality that would have stunned her were she aware of it. There was a sharp whistle of air on the wind, but as she wasn't watching White Eagle, she didn't know that the sound had been that of his indrawn breath.

Eagle was thinking that her suggestion that he jump more deeply into the lake might be just what he needed. He had just calmly informed her that he would not touch her, but he had never felt a more potent rush of pure desire in his life. His natural comment that she was beautiful had been a tremendous understatement—she surpassed any terminology in any language. "Gorgeous" would not sufficiently describe her. Although slender and petite, she was built with subtle voluptuousness; her breasts were not heavy but high and firm, rosy-tipped, her hips trim and yet ever so pleasantly rounded. Her legs were long and shapely, graceful like those of a gazelle. She had been married for a year, he knew—he knew a great deal about her, in fact. Yet about her there was an air of innocence. Of trust. She could be feisty, proud, arrogant and haughty. Still . . . that beguiling essence remained with her. . . .

A flash of heat that ripped through him in spasms assailed Eagle with crude violence as she sprinted into the water. Impatiently he cursed at himself, raised his arms high and plunged into the depths of the lake. With powerful strokes he whipped through the water, not surfacing until he had vigorously brought his telling body back into a semblance of control.

The water was delicious, Whitney decided instantly, relishing in its wonderfully cool feeling upon her skin. Not the swimmer that Eagle was, she contented herself with splashing around near the shore. Rising after a moment to shield her eyes against the setting sun and scan the lake for White Eagle, she frowned. "Where the hell is he, anyway?" she muttered.

Beneath her, she discovered an immediate reply as her ankle was deftly wrenched and she tumbled full length into the lake. Sputtering and choking, she kicked her way back up and sought her adversary. He was about a foot away, chuckling. Without bothering to think, she threw herself at him, determined to douse his smug face beneath the surface.

But he had anticipated her impulsive response and he caught her, his hands strong against her midriff. He held her inches away, with the peaks of her nipples brushing the smoothness of his chest, gloating. For a split second he kept her there, and their eyes met in elemental challenge. Then she was once more doused.

Fuming beneath the surface, Whitney swam as far as her lungs would carry her. When she finally broke above the water, he was still watching her, still smiling smugly, still gloating. To him there was no contest.

"Never attack a stronger enemy!" he said with a laugh, verifying her thoughts. "Use strategy!" Then he was swimming away again, the certain victor.

Strategy, Whitney silently repeated. She would use strategy all right, strategy and patience. It would be a dangerous battle, but she couldn't resist. He had the galling capacity to make her forget logic and reason and respond with pure warlike tactics. But she did intend to win—even the little battles, the skirmishes.

When he surfaced again and looked for her, she laughed enchantingly.

"You're right!" she called gaily. "I never will get you under!" Smiling with coquettish invitation, she began an easy sidestroke, emphasizing the languorousness of her movements.

As she had planned, he swam toward her. As she hadn't planned, his nearness threw her completely. The water itself heated between them, like a whirling hot tub. She

71

was painfully aware of his powerful sleekness, swallowing to resist the temptation to run her hands along the glistening limbs that moved beside her.

Strategy! she reminded herself coolly, inching back to a depth where she could stand. A little thrill shot its way exultantly to her mind as she remembered his tone when he had told her she was beautiful. In her little game of retaliation, she didn't intend to make him lose control, she simply wanted to draw on a few of his instincts. Just draw him a few little inches into her lair. . . .

Purposely she slowly brushed against him as they both found their footing. It was a dangerous game. The contact of his bare flesh was exhilarating; her own instincts screamed that she cling to it.

But she faced him instead, her smile a little coy, a little captivating. Surely he wouldn't refuse an overt gesture . . . yet she couldn't let him become in the least suspicious.

Whitney stretched a long finger to touch his raven hair, as if unwittingly fascinated. His response was gentle as he captured her hand and drew her irrevocably to him. Feigning hesitant submission, Whitney inched along his frame, gasping involuntarily with a shock that had nothing to do with the game. It was already going too well. Proof that she could elicit his desire touched along the tender flesh of her lower abdomen as her legs entangled with his.

Now! Whitney told herself as she met his tense stare. Now, while she could still break his unprepared grip, before his lips fell to claim hers.

With all her strength she plunged beneath the surface, and with unimaginable speed she clasped his ankle with both hands and jerked. It was working! His foot rose and his knee bent. . . .

But he didn't fall and crash into the lake. The bent leg tensed and she was disbelievingly being dragged back. Stupidly realizing her mistake, Whitney released his ankle and started a mad dash away.

Too late. His hand sank into her hair, the fingers curled and she was pulled back, his grip not painful but forceful.

Her eyes were clouded with fear when they met his cold ones. "Dirty play, wasn't that?" he inquired tautly.

"All's fair in love and war, isn't it?" Whitney demanded flippantly. His features were tense and his jaw was crookedly locked.

"Those are the rules," Eagle agreed, the glint of his eyes a glacial blue. "As long as they apply to both parties."

A shudder of fear gripped her, but he gave no notice. The hand that laced her hair tilted her head back, and his mouth slowly and surely came over hers. Whitney's lips were parted with amazement, aiding and abetting his assault, which certainly couldn't be called unprovoked. She had gambled and lost. But how far would he carry his retaliation? How far did she want him to carry it? She had stiffened, ready to fight him no matter how feeble her efforts. But her fight lasted less than ten seconds. His kiss, a strange combination of harsh demand and persuasive tenderness, was drugging her, numbing her to acquiescent submission. His foot wedged around hers, holding her his prey, while his tongue deeply plundered the recesses of her mouth, seeking hers, hypnotizing it into a return play.

Immersed in the warm, assured command of his mouth, she thrust deeply herself, tasting and seeking, running the tip of her tongue in light discovery of his pearl white teeth. His mouth left hers to follow a slow, moist suctioning trail across the softness of her cheek to her earlobe, down the length of her neck, to the shadowed hollow of her breasts. His sleek length along hers held no secrets, and she found she was no longer pushing against his broad chest but burrowing into it, striving to be submissively accessible to the wonder of his driving touch.

His hands were on the small of her back, pressing her closer and closer. They lowered to cradle her buttocks and lift her slightly, arch her hips to his so that she could feel the full force of the virile masculinity she had tauntingly elicited against her body. A sigh escaped her, and her lips fell to his shoulder, where her teeth grazed gently as tremors scurried from her head to her toes, flashing convulsively with dizzying heat. She was freezing with fear but burning with anticipation. One of his hands moved in seductive exploration, rounding the contour it held, gently splaying her thigh in search of further secrets.

Torn by irresistible sensation, Whitney realized she was getting so much more than she had bargained for, so much more than she had known existed . . . God! She longed for it to go on, to savor the feel of him, to taste, touch and explore. She wanted the trembling, aching torment to find its way to ultimate culmination. . . .

But she was afraid. So very afraid.

His mouth moved to the high peak of her breast, and his teeth raked it just slightly. The searing sensation was so great that she totally lost her breath; and as her flesh rippled with the jolt, a fear of the crippling delight that rendered her helpless despite her desire suddenly bubbled to the surface.

Her sigh became a plea. . . .

Eagle released her so abruptly that she spattered back into the water, barely keeping her face above the surface. His face was a cold mask; his eyes were glittering orbs. "Go, rabbit," he said icily, "run. I told you I wouldn't force you. If and when you're feeling like a woman, you can come to me." He turned, leaving her wide-eyed and quivering in the water, her mouth bruised, her ego in a peculiar state between relief and humiliation.

Eagle was cursing beneath his breath as he cut through the water for the shore with strong strides. The little bitch! She had known damn well what she was doing. By every right he should have taken her there, by the shore. She had responded to him; her body had melded to his in perfect unison; her sensuality had risen instinctively to meet his. The hidden passion he had tasted hinted of a coming together even he couldn't imagine. . . . But here he was instead, rushing out of the water because he had sensed her fear. A sucker! he told himself disgustedly. A real sap. She probably played her little games a million times, and that feigned innocence saved her. . . .

Pulling his jeans over his legs, he tucked his shirt in and impatiently jerked up his zipper. Glancing out of the corner of his eye, he felt his temper begin to subside. She didn't know that he watched her, and her face and eyes were unguarded. There was none of the usual arrogance apparent. At the moment she looked like a wounded doe, lost, bewildered and delicately stunning. Her arms were clasped protectively around her chest, and her hair, soaking wet, curled long past her waist, covering her modestly like a modern-day Godiva. There was a secret to her, Eagle decided, and he intended to unravel that secret. He wanted her to come to him with complete trust. He had the strange intuition that once would never be enough. If he drank her sweet nectar he would thirst again, and again and again. . . .

He walked to her then and set his hands on her shoulders, groaning inwardly as she flinched at his touch and clutched her clothing tightly to her breast. Tilting her chin to force her eyes to his, he smiled with warmth. "Don't get all cold and withdrawn on me again, huh? You are exquisite, and I don't think you'd be tremendously happy if I didn't think so and tell you!" Not waiting for a reply, he became very businesslike and brusquely began helping her back into her bra, managing the lace-frothed hook with competence.

Whitney stood compliantly still, then ducked quickly into her underwear and jeans. He began speaking again as she snapped her shirt together.

"You are about to taste the fruits of our combined day's labor," he said blandly. "I'm sure my grandmother is waiting for us at the *sofki* pot; we usually eat our evening meals as stews. Some of the vegetables you tended will be in it, and the venison we bagged today. I hope you like it.

75

We also eat tropical fruit at supper—mangoes, papayas, guavas. And bread from the *koonti* root you pounded." His arm came casually around her shoulder as he led her through the pine trail that would bring them back to Morning Dew's three chickees. How could he change so quickly, Whitney wondered with amazement. He had gone from passion to anger to ambivalence in the wink of an eye, while she was still a barely controlled jumble of boiling blood and frazzled nerves . . . no, she told herself solidly, not *barely* controlled. Controlled. She *would* manage to be as nonchalant as he.

"I'm starving," she answered him idly. "I have a feeling I'm going to love that stew—no matter what's in it."

"Even alligator?" he teased.

Whitney eyed him suspiciously. "Do you really eat alligator?"

"Yes, sometimes, but not tonight. We respect the season. They are an endangered species. If you're game, I'll see that you get to try it sometime. If smoked correctly, it's delicious."

"Fine." Whitney shrugged, musing over his words. What did "sometime" mean? In a week's time she would be in Naples, back in the world of business. Her days would be full with meetings, schedules and plans. Eagle would be back in his cabin. . . .

Or would he? She didn't know where he actually lived. He adapted to his habitation easily. Was his real home another chickee in another village?

It didn't matter. At the end of the week she would accept his help with Stewart as her due. Then this tumultuous span of days in her life would fade to the background and things would return to normal.

No. Things would never return to normal again. Whatever this man was, she was never going to be able to forget him.

Little pricks of unbidden excitement started finding their way back into her system. A wave of hot panic washed over her in a black wall that momentarily blanked her vision. *What if she lost?* What if she found she couldn't stand up to the rigors after a few days of grueling labor? Was she really to be his winning stake? She was walking normally beside him, but she felt as if her feet did not quite touch the ground, as if helium held her afloat. Would he really demand payment?

God! The groan reverberated within her own mind. She didn't know what she wanted herself. There had been seconds in the water when she had wanted him to forget his words and promises—moments when she had wished that he would take her and let her discover what it could be like . . . force her into knowing if the ecstasy she had felt hints of could really exist. . . .

She glanced at him to find him surreptitiously watching her with his keen, probing stare. Flushing, she searched her mind for a topic of casual conversation. There were always a million things she wanted to ask him when he was walking away from her!

"What was your grandmother angry about this morning?" she asked hastily.

Eagle chuckled pleasantly in his low baritone. Watching the amusement spread into his features, Whitney was again struck by the appeal his face had for her. It wasn't a "pretty" face, but it was strongly molded and so full of character as to be arrestingly interesting. No one would ever forget his relentless stare or his charming, boyish laugh. He was a creature of fascinating conflict, a rogue, a gallant. Sometimes she was sure she would never grow tired of looking into those crystal blue eyes.

"My grandmother was angry with me because of you," he said.

"Why?"

"Because she thinks I dragged a naive, sweet innocent into the woods to lure into a dishonorable situation."

"Oh." Startled by the honesty of his reply, Whitney

stopped to adjust a boot, lowering her hair over her eyes as she moistened her lips for her next question.

"How did you convince her that that wasn't the case?"

Eagle shrugged. "I didn't. Believe it or not, we live by high moral codes. She saw you—I would never be able to convince her that I wasn't after that shapely little body!"

"So?"

"So what?"

"So why isn't she angry anymore?" Whitney persisted with exasperation.

"Oh, that 'so.'" He stared at her again with a brow twitched high in cynical amusement. "I told her I was going to marry you at the Corn Dance."

"*What?*" The shout erupted incredulously from Whitney.

His eyes hardened and narrowed a fraction. "Don't worry about it—the ceremony won't be legal to you. You won't be obligated in any way."

Whitney realized her jaw was hanging open when she attempted to speak. Closing it, she moistened her lips. "Would you mind telling me what the hell the Corn Dance is and what type of illegal ceremony you think you're going to coerce me into?"

"As I said," he replied coolly, "it won't really affect you. And don't pull that indignant, affronted-maiden bit on me. I've discovered you have more than a bit of the teasing vixen in you, and if you persist in provoking me far enough, I'm sure that I can discover some real savage in myself and knock that royal superiority right off your sweet face."

"Why you—you arrogant brute!" Whitney hissed, clenching her fists tightly by her side as rage engulfed her. A saving grace of prudence kept her from tackling him. She was learning certain lessons.

"Watch that forked tongue," Eagle warned grimly, his stance as tense as hers. "Don't count on my not losing my patience. I have my limits, too, Whitney."

"Damn you!" Whitney swirled around and slammed her fist into a pine. She had to hit something!

"Smart move," Eagle drawled lazily. "There is hope for you."

Crooking her elbow, Whitney lowered her head onto it and leaned against the pine, striving for composure. In a muffled voice she politely demanded, "Would you please explain this Corn Dance ceremony to me? I know you like to be secretive, but I do believe I have a right to know certain things, since you plan on my participation."

"Witty and sarcastic still," Eagle commented assessively, "but the language and phrasing are much improved. The Corn Dance is one of a few remaining rituals to survive the times. It takes place once a year, and major tribal decisions are made and domestic matters handled. The Miccosukees seldom break the white man's laws, and our law is recognized within the tribe and the state. The date of the Corn Dance is kept a secret; very few outsiders are ever privileged to attend. As it happens, the Corn Dance begins tomorrow. If you are really interested in the tribe, you should count yourself lucky. You're being given a golden opportunity."

"Talk about people who think they're superior!" Whitney muttered caustically. "You'll pardon me if I don't kiss your feet for this golden opportunity! I want to understand a little more about this. You actually had the audacity to tell your grandmother you were marrying me at this—this war party? I thought Miccosukees didn't lie."

Eagle rubbed his temple patiently, and she could see clearly that he was in the mental process of counting to ten. "It is not a war party; it is the Green Corn Dance and it dates back to the festival held by our Georgia Creek ancestry. I did not lie to my grandmother. I have every intention of going through with the ceremony, and I can't see any reason it should annoy you to humor an old woman."

"Humor an old woman!" Whitney shrieked. "You want

me to take part in a farcical marriage in front of some totem pole—"

"No totem pole," Eagle interrupted irritably. "We are the Seminole Nation and this is the Florida Everglades, not the Great Plains. Really, Whitney, you have to stop thinking that all Indians are painted savages who ride around on pinto ponies."

Whitney ground her teeth together and glared at him coldly. "I do know where I am." Pushing herself from the tree, she squared her shoulders and started back down the path.

"Get back here!" he growled with menace, spinning her around curtly with a clamped grip on her wrist. "You are not walking back to that encampment and upsetting my grandmother."

Whitney met his darkly challenging eyes for a minute, then shifted her gaze to her wrist. "I have no intention of upsetting Morning Dew," she told him, hoping her voice held no quaver.

"Fine. Then walk back with me nicely." His fingers interlaced with hers firmly and he strolled ahead of her. It was a small gesture, but it left Whitney seething. He thinks he's got it all sewn up, she thought angrily.

"You should like the festivities," Eagle said cheerfully as they neared the chickees. "It will be a chance for you to socialize with many clans and"—he gave her a glance of wriggled-brow mockery—"it will keep us both occupied so that we're not tearing at each other's hair."

"Black clouds do have silver linings," Whitney said through gritted teeth.

Their conversation was cut off, as Morning Dew had seen them and was waving happily. The majority of her affection was oddly lavished on Whitney rather than her grandson. Whitney decided with a great deal of satisfaction that the stern old woman was on her side and still annoyed with White Eagle. Breaking into fast-clipped speech at their approach about how worried she'd been,

Morning Dew came to her, slid an arm around her shoulder and led her to the cooking fire. Whitney sat as beckoned, looking at Eagle innocently.

"It seems you found yourself a fan while I was gone," he said briefly.

Whitney could not prevent a smug smile of satisfaction from curling her lips even as she lowered her head to hide it.

The meal was strangely peaceful and pleasant; the stew Eagle had referred to delicious. After the food had been consumed, Morning Dew served aromatic coffee in large ceramic mugs. The scent of the fresh brew reminded Whitney that she hadn't had a cigarette for hours. Eagle had been right; she had actually been too busy to miss the nicotine, but now she longed for a relaxing cigarette.

"I'll get them for you," Eagle said, reading her thoughts with a grin as he followed her eyes to the left chickee, where she had stowed her things.

"Thanks," she murmured.

Morning Dew began to pick up after the meal while he was gone, and when Whitney attempted to help, she was firmly motioned to sit. This night she was a guest. As soon as Eagle returned, Morning Dew spoke to him quickly, said good night to Whitney and left them.

Eagle lit a cigarette and handed it to Whitney as he sank back down beside her. "We'd better get to sleep soon ourselves," he remarked casually. "Our days are long."

Whitney inhaled deeply, annoyed to find her fingers shaking. The whole thing was so incongruous! Twenty-four hours ago she had met him; they were attracted with the force of magnetic poles, yet they clashed like a thunderstorm and argued with the ferocity of cats and dogs.

And here they were sipping coffee in the outlands of the Glades and casually discussing bedtime.

Crushing her cigarette carefully, Whitney finished her coffee with a quick gulp, yawned and stretched. There would be safety in sleep.

"You're right; these days are long," she said nervously. "Sleep sounds good." She started across the moonlit clearing and then hesitated. "Are you coming?"

"In a minute. My grandmother left you a present—you'll find it with the bedding."

Eagle spoke to her absently, as if his thoughts were far away. Shrugging, Whitney hurried over to their chickee and climbed up to the platform. The sleeping quarters, she knew, were high off the ground for security from snakes and other pests, just as the cooking house was built on a space of flat ground to avoid fire. She had learned during dinner that the Seminoles and other southeastern Indians had originally built log cabins, but due to their flight into the Glades and repeated attacks by a government determined to rout them, they had adapted to the thatched-roof homes.

Whitney prepared their bedding with surprising ease. Rather than the misery she had expected, the abode provided ample comfort. Mosquito netting kept the insects at bay, and thick quilts made the platform mattress undeniably soft. Straightening a cover, Whitney found the present Eagle had spoken of.

It was a sheer white gown, floor length and intricately and lovingly hand-sewn: a bride's gown.

Whitney stared at the beautiful costume for a minute of touched amazement; then her temper began to rise. Morning Dew had offered her nothing but kindness, and the old woman was being horribly deceived. How could her own grandson do such a thing to her!

"What's wrong? Don't you like it?"

Eagle had silently pounced onto the platform and now stood looking at her, his eyes curiously glittering in the gentle glow of fire and moon.

"Like it?" Whitney grated. "I like it just fine! But I have no intention of accepting such a gift. What you are doing to that woman is criminal!"

"I'll worry about my own actions," Eagle told her curtly, checking the nets as he once again began doffing his clothes. Fuming, Whitney discarded her boots and curled onto the floor-bed, her eyes tightly closed. He was calmly stripping with the same thoughtless abandon as before, but she certainly wasn't joining in a second time. The results of the first were still shatteringly fresh in her mind.

A moment later Eagle joined her, his length inches from her own. He was silent for so long she was sure he slept; then he spoke harshly in the darkness. "You're being ridiculous."

"About what?"

"Do you really think one or a hundred garments would stop me if I decided to attack your precious body? Don't flatter yourself that you are such a prize, and don't deceive yourself into thinking you don't want me. You were mine for the taking from the moment we met." The low gravel sound of his voice increased as he spoke. "But don't worry —I taunted you for a reaction this morning. If you leave these woods, you owe me nothing. If you stick to your part of the bargain, you'll still receive whatever assistance I can give you." He rolled away from her. "I'll even try to forget that you think we're all a pack of barbarians."

"But I don't!" Whitney protested.

"No?" He swung back and challenged her with remote curiosity. "Then just what is your problem?"

"I—I—I—"

"Un-unh!" he exclaimed impatiently. "For once, just talk. Try being a little honest with yourself."

Shivering in the moonlight, Whitney stared miserably into his searching eyes. How could she explain what she didn't understand? Suddenly his hand was on her cheek, his thumb caressing her smooth skin. With rough tenderness he traced a pattern down and across her lips, a hard look of longing tautening his features. She read physical desire in his tense demand, but it was coupled with something else—evidence that that desire could only be appeased if it was reciprocated.

Swallowing, Whitney closed her eyes, shivering but unprotesting. His lips found hers and cajoled sweetly until her mouth opened and offered and received. The seeking, stabbing warmth of his commanding tongue was easily drugging her into submissive euphoria again; his whisper-light touch upon her body was a magic she had long anticipated but never expected to experience. The natural masculine scent of him came to her with its intoxicating woodsy aroma, and she lifted her hands to touch the raven hair, the rippled golden muscles of his shoulders. Her shivers became shudders of awed excitement, and a low moan escaped her throat as his lips left hers to travel down the line to her breasts as he began to unsnap the buttons of her shirt slowly, one by one by one, his tongue making little darting forays of moistness upon her flesh.

His fingers slipped into the waistband of her pants, and while they assuredly found the button, he met her heavy-lidded gaze with eyes smoldering gray from the intensity of his desire. Their locked stare sent another heat wave of shivers coursing through her, and even as he watched her, his breath coming in deeper and deeper pants, she heard the slow, steady sound of her zipper sliding open to his gentle, determined insistence.

His eyes continued to hold hers as his lips came back to drink more fully of her mouth, and his fingers splayed over her hip and the skin of her upper abdomen, conquering the area newly exposed to his touch, easing the material firmly lower. Her fingers had clung to his back, then frozen; his free hand rose to catch her right one, guiding it along his length to his hip, to the rigid tautness of his stomach, to the intimate warmth of pulsating strength that was shockingly vibrant and alive. . . .

Whitney gasped, and then the panic set in. She felt innate terror that she couldn't possibly handle or please a man of such demanding virility. Her body went rigid; her moan became a fervent denial. Releasing him as if she had been burned, she pushed at his massive shoulders, pushed fiercely upon his broad chest.

Eagle jerked away from her, and his face was a basilisk of dark anger. With a muttered oath he sprang to his feet and impatiently stepped into his jeans, yanking them over his long legs in a furious motion.

Tears were forming in Whitney's eyes. "Where are you going?" she asked quickly, before he could hear the thickness in her voice.

"I'm taking my undesirable presence out to the alligators," he retorted, his eyes blazing and his mouth a grim white line. A second later he swung off the platform and was gone into the night.

CHAPTER FIVE

Stunned, Whitney stared after him as the seconds ticked by. He was gone, her mind kept repeating numbly. He thought she delighted in tormenting him, then calling a halt. He thought she would only tease and withdraw because he was unworthy of her. . . .

And still he would walk away before he would hurt her. . . .

Suddenly she couldn't bear his believing that her behavior was spawned by such motives. She couldn't define her feelings; she only knew that if he walked away tonight, she would lose something special, something that she craved desperately, needed. The void of his absence was already ripping apart her heart and soul.

Talk, he had told her. She didn't know what to say, but if only she could find him, the words would have to come. She had so terribly much at stake!

Scrambling to her feet, she hesitated. The hand-sewn gown lay strewn at the foot of the bedding. Whitney impulsively pulled off her clothing, ripping at the pearl snaps in her haste, and quickly put on the white gown. A supple swing brought her to the ground, and she peered anxiously down the pine path to the lake. Was that the way he had gone? A wraith in white beneath the moonlight, Whitney started down the path, terrified but determined. The trees, which offered gentle shade in the daytime, were a sinister refuge for macabre creatures in the night.

She started running as she neared the lake, praying that

he would be there, praying that he wouldn't reject her. She stumbled from the trees and a sob escaped her as she fell to her knees before the water. He was there, sitting on the rock, watching the moon play on the water.

"Whitney!" He was beside her in a second, drawing her protectively to his side, his anger erased by concern. "What happened? What's wrong? Are you hurt? My grandmother—"

"No, no," Whitney gasped, burrowing her face in his neck. "Nothing is wrong, nothing happened. Morning Dew is fine. I—I wanted to talk to you, and I frightened myself in the trees."

"Oh." She felt his chest contract as he expelled a breath of relief. Then his hands were over her head, crushing the soft wings of her hair as he tilted her face upward. "What did you want to say that was so important?"

Whitney's mind went blank and she watched him with dismay. She had to talk or he would completely lose patience with her! "I don't know where to begin," she murmured unhappily.

"They usually do suggest that you begin at the beginning," Eagle said with a gentle grin. "Let's sit by the shore. Maybe if you watch the water, it will help."

He led her to the water's edge and they lowered themselves to the grass and sand shore. The effect *was* lulling, Whitney thought, as she cast her eyes over the luminescent star glow of the water. Eagle was beside her, but he didn't touch her. He was quiet, watching the water also, waiting with soothing patience. Whitney glanced at him, then returned her stare to the water.

"You really don't understand—"

"I want to," he interrupted softly.

"My problem isn't you; it's me. I would be a liar to deny I felt an immediate attraction to you. I'd also be a liar to say I've sometimes thought you weren't . . . good enough for me." Sucking in her breath to begin again, Whitney kept her eyes studiously in front of her. If she were to see his crystal gaze now, she would falter; she would not be able to go on. She was going to try to say things she had kept submerged from her own thoughts. "I—I think there is something wrong with me, although I don't know what a technical definition would be. I didn't know it until I was married. I guess I expected to get something out of sex, and then—then Gerry—my husband . . ." Whitney broke off, crunching her lip.

"Damn the man!" Eagle exclaimed, his anger a raw thing, explosive. "What did the bastard do to you? Did he hurt you, Whitney?"

Whitney glanced at him quickly with surprise. "Oh, no!" she explained quickly. "Gerry isn't a bastard. He's a very nice man. He never even raised his voice to me. It wasn't that . . ."

Eagle's dark brow knitted high above his eyes. She was trying; she was really trying. Breathing deeply to hold his impatience and perplexed curiosity in check, he told himself he must speak and move very slowly. She had to be led along on a very tender line. "What then, Whitney?" His voice was nothing more than a soft urging on the breeze.

Her eyes flashed to his apologetically. "I guess I was brought up to be the Miss Virginia you tease me about. My entire life was set up for me. I went to private schools, then the University of Virginia. When I graduated I fell in with what was expected of me. Gerry was—and still is—my father's law partner. He came from a 'good' family, too. He's almost twenty years older than I am, but no one ever thought anything of that. He would be a good husband, father and provider. He belonged to all the right clubs; he sailed, played tennis and golf." Whitney lifted her hands helplessly. "I don't think I was ever in love with him, but I did care a great deal about him, and according to the old Southern aristocracy, love can grow if the elements are right . . ." There was a stick on the shore, and Whitney began to draw lines in the dirt as she settled her chin on

88

her hugged knees. "This is what I'm not sure how to explain. I was always overly protected, so Gerry was, of course, my first real sexual experience. I was young, and I guess I was a romantic. I thought Gerry would adore me and we would create skyrockets together. Then that first night—" Whitney shuddered and stopped.

Eagle was ready to pull his own hair out. Instead he put a tender arm around her shoulders and lightly stroked the wispy wings of her hair. "What happened that first night?"

Whitney opened her mouth, but nothing came.

"Tell me, Whitney," Eagle urged sternly.

Somehow, in spite of sputtering, stopping and beginning again out of sequence, Whitney finally managed to explain. She told him how horrified her husband had been to find her eager to explore her sexuality, how seldom he had touched her, how they had only made love in the dark while remaining partially clothed. If she ever made a sound, he would turn from her, appalled, revolted.

"I—I always displeased him," Whitney finished awkwardly. "And I guess that's what so terrifies me now."

Eagle shook his head incredulously. "It's unbelievable."

"I wouldn't go through this to lie," Whitney strangled out, blinking furiously. Had she unburdened her heart and soul only to be ridiculed?

"No, no, little rabbit," he said with a smile, leaning back onto the earth and pulling her with him. "That's not what I meant at all! I don't believe a man could have you and not worship all that sexy beauty!" He was staring at her kindly, his blue eyes orbs of tender concern, his lips a twitch of sensuous relief. When he spoke, his voice was husky, a tone that sent quivers racing into her blood.

"Do you trust me?" he demanded suddenly, his touch still light.

Her eyes were wide in the moonlight; her answer a silken sigh. "Yes."

He spoke to her for a long, long time in that husky velvet voice before he began to make love to her. He told pleased him just to see her, that she was built ... ythical goddess of love, that her hips and thighs ... slender perfection, her breasts flowers of sensuality th. t begged to be touched. As he talked, his jeans were again cast aside, and he very gently pulled the white gown from her body.

"Look at me," he commanded as he lay his flesh against hers and she fluttered her lashes. "Look at me, Whitney." His features were incredibly tense with desire, but he smiled even as his eyes blazed.

"There is no way, sweet thing, that you could possibly displease me," he said, his voice becoming a harsher and harsher rasp. "And I want to hear you, my darling. I want you to touch me, I want you to forget everything except what you feel and I want you to scream if you feel like it
. . ."

Whitney obediently kept her eyes open, locked with his in a tremulous hypnotism. His hand began a play upon her flesh as he continued to whisper in increasingly ragged breaths just how beautiful she was. His touch was very slow, very tender and yet masterful. His fingers traced lightly over her skin, drawing her with infinite finesse into his web. An instinctive reflex brought her hand to stop his as he caressed the rose-hued peaks of her nipples, but he deftly changed position and anchored her arms. His gentle play continued with stern control; his hands went on to explore fully the contours of her hips, her abdomen and the tender flesh of her inner thighs. Again reflex caused her to tense her slender legs together. "Trust me, Whitney," he murmured.

And she did. Teetering on the fine borderline between abandon and fear, Whitney crashed wildly into total submission as his seduction took an abrupt change and became demanding and urgent. His lips claimed hers with a fervency that left her breathless. His fingers deserted their eloquent teasing to plunge and exquisitely torture the

90

tender, sensitive secrets of her flesh. A gasped moan escaped her, and Eagle replied with unbridled passion.

"Don't stop it, darling, don't stop it. Tell me . . . Touch me . . ."

Tentatively, hesitantly, she began to touch him. The shudders her fingers caused him excited her further and further until she was lost in a wonderful new world of exotic ecstasy. Hot kisses rained over her entire body, following the trails blazed by his knowing fingers. Enveloped in whirling, roller-coaster passion, Whitney writhed uncontrollably, arching into his glorious heat, straining wildly to give the erotic pleasure she received. She died a thousand little deaths.

"Eagle!" Her plea was a tormented whisper.

"Tell me!" he demanded, "Cry it out. Let me know."

"Oh, Eagle," she countered breathlessly. "I want you. I want you so very much . . ."

He filled her, he ignited her, he took her with the devastating passion she craved, his rhythm ever increasing with each new level of consuming exhilaration. And all the while he whispered, groaned, shuddered, driving her ever upward. They were locked together as one; Whitney's fingers dug desperately into his back, then a moan tore from her throat, a cry that was his name, an echo of the unleashed ecstasy that surged through her with a final convulsive, sweetly delicious tremble. The urgent passion subsided slowly, slowly, to be replaced by a feeling equally cherished. In that moment Whitney gave herself to him completely and was filled by him in a way that inexplicably bound her to him forever. Later she would have to think, to reason, to make light of her own fantastic thoughts, but for now she wore his brand, she could still relish in the scent of his body on hers; she was simply, irrevocably, in the most elemental of male-female responses—his.

Eagle shifted himself beside her and raised his head while he bent an elbow so that he could look at her again.

In the aftermath of the intensity of their union, her damp body glistened in the moonlight, and he shook his head slightly to himself as he marveled at the perfect, cream beauty of her form. Her breasts rose and fell with the depth of her breathing, emphasizing the lovely contours and hollows of her collarbone and tightly flat abdomen. Her hair splayed in a wild fan beneath them both, while the fluffed wings framed her face in delicate curls. Heat filled him again as he watched her, and burning tenseness constricted within him. Drawing a finger down the line between the curves of her breasts to her navel, Eagle was consumed by emotions very similar to hers, and even more untamed. It was irrational, he knew, but he felt fiercely and unrestrainedly possessive. Irrational be damned! He would have her over and over again, he and only he.

. . .

Her eyes flew open at his touch, and she smiled shyly.

"Skyrockets?" he inquired.

"And fireworks," she admitted.

He smiled in return, but his voice was grave as he curled a lock of her hair tenderly around his finger. "No more fears, Whitney? That husband of yours was the wrong one, you know. Do you believe me?"

"Yes."

"You are the most exquisitely pleasing creature I have ever known."

She couldn't reply to that. Did he mean it? Or was he bolstering her confidence? She wouldn't worry about it now . . . or wonder just how many "pleasing creatures" he had known. Lazy with satisfaction, she rolled into his chest and curled happily against it. Tonight was special. She didn't want to talk anymore; she had talked enough. For the moment nothing else mattered. She was wallowing in the satiated joy of lying next to the strength and power of this superbly created man. . . .

"No going to sleep on me!" he teased, nudging her. "Not here, anyway. I'm not that trusting of the snakes!"

As he had expected, the word "snakes" sent her flying to her feet. "You told me the lake was clear!" she accused in a wail.

"Well, it is, mostly. But I prefer to sleep off the ground —just in case!" He laughed, reaching for her hand. "Come on, sweetie, give an old man a hand up."

"Old man! How aged are you?"

"Three and a half decades come fall."

"I wouldn't have guessed you were a day over thirty-four."

"That's because Indians age well. Clean living, you know." Grinning, he collected her gown and his pants, then swung her dramatically into his arms. "This has always been one of my fantasies," he told her as she slipped her arms around his neck, "running naked through the woods with a captive woman. Have you ever seen yourself carried off like this?"

"No," Whitney said with a laugh. "And I don't know if it's such a hot idea now. Your grandmother could wake up—"

"My grandmother would love it. She's a true romantic —crazy about 'hot' ideas like this!"

In a few minutes they were back in the chickee. As Whitney curled back into the covers with Eagle stretched beside her, contentment filled her. This bed in the woods was the most wonderful she had ever known. A belief in magic had been returned to her, and she was sailing on top of the world despite the crazy fact that she was falling in love with a man who would probably walk right back out of her life. . . .

Don't be silly, she chastised herself as she snuggled closer to him. She wasn't in love, nor was he. They had simply become "lovers." Odd terminology. . . .

She suddenly realized that Eagle was persistently touching her beneath the covers and that her body was automatically responding to his demands. "I thought we

93

needed to get some sleep!" she teased, rubbing her cheek against his smooth chest.

"We do!" he whispered back. "I want to make sure we're really tired."

Whitney started giggling softly. Moon fever, she told herself.

"Stop that!" Eagle commanded, springing to pin her shoulders to their mat and to straddle her. "I taught you to moan, not laugh! I guess we have to refresh the lesson in your mind."

"Please," Whitney taunted with half-closed eyes. "I'm a slow learner."

"No, little witch," Eagle returned, his stare growing dark and passionately hard, his voice throaty. "You learn with natural ease. If you grow much more proficient, you could become a lethal weapon. You could please me into an early grave. . . ."

Her giggles quickly became panted moans as he lowered his head and fastened his teeth lightly over a nipple to begin the exquisite torment all over again. Whitney's fingers raked into his blue-raven hair as she arched to meet his tantalizing lovemaking. A willing captive. That was her last coherent thought. She had indeed become his captive.

"Up, rabbit!"

She was awakened by a firm tap on the rear end, to find Eagle standing above her, fully clothed, his costume today a braided Seminole shirt. Blinking groggily, Whitney graced him with a reproachful stare. Even he would have to admit that the hour was uncivilized.

Completely stoic, he arched a hand over his eyes and gesticulated to the horizon. "Pink trails of dawn are now consumed by golden eye of rising sun. Time for dedicated squaw to move rear like willow and get with it!"

"You've been watching too many John Wayne movies," Whitney muttered in cynical reply. But the night had changed her, and she couldn't resist an impish smile. "Couldn't you go fight the cavalry late today? Surely Indians must get sick leave, too!"

"No, no sick leave, not today." Smiling in return, he bent to kiss her lips lightly. "We have a lot of preparation to do. The Green Corn Dance begins at sunset—and you become a bride by nightfall. Even in the civilized world women do not laze around on their wedding days."

A frown puckered Whitney's brow and the soft womb of pleasure she had felt at wakening drained from her. How could he still be insisting that they take it all like a tremendous joke? In her one day here she was finding great respect for Morning Dew and the Miccosukee tribe, and she didn't feel like mocking their customs. Eagle was a Miccosukee! And he had told her to trust him. To play games to such an extent seemed nothing short of callous.

"I don't want to go through with the ceremony," she said stubbornly, drawing the covers to her chin.

The light in his eyes immediately disappeared. "I told you," he said harshly, "you won't have to consider any of it legal."

"That's not the point—" Whitney began. "Oh, never mind!" she interrupted herself. What *was* the point? That she was falling in love and didn't want any part of what she had to remember was a farce? "We'll go through with it. I don't ever seem to win an argument with you, anyway."

Eagle's face remained dark and hard even after her agreement. "Get dressed," he said curtly. "There is a lot to be done. I've brought you an Indian skirt and blouse set. I thought you might like to attend the day in customary style."

He was gone before she could think of anything more to say. Scrambling from the covers, Whitney found the outfit. It was as carefully sewn and edged and braided as the white bridal gown. Sighing, Whitney slipped into the comfortable, porous material. She was fascinated by the prospect of attending the Corn Dance, even if it did raise a few moral dilemmas. She would have days ahead of her to talk with White Eagle . . . and tell him what? I realize that I'm supposed to be the sophisticated one and that a night of love in the chickee does not signify eternal devotion, but I think you taught your lessons a little too well and . . . what? God, what did she feel for him? He was like a fever in her blood . . . undefinable.

Eagle was out of sight when she approached the *sofki* pot, but Morning Dew was busily bustling about. She greeted Whitney with a wide smile and a cup of coffee, then, pointing to the pot, told Whitney to eat.

It was some kind of porridge, Whitney realized as she scooped up a bowl, smiled and tasted it. Ugh. Still she kept the smile plastered on her face, not wanting to hurt her hostess's feelings. Must be something you have to acquire a taste for, she thought wryly, grateful that at least she had a decent cup of coffee.

The now-familiar calls of several Glades birds—herons, egrets and beautiful wood ibis—came to her as she sipped her coffee, and Whitney was again struck by the strange sense of peace one could absorb in the woody environment. Listening to the birds, watching the gentle sway of moss upon cypress, she began to feel languorous. One more cup of coffee and a cigarette and I'll get going, she promised herself. A quick dart back to the chickee and a trip to the coffee pot and she was all set, comfortably lodged before the cooking fire, her silver lighter flashing quickly as she inhaled deeply. Ahh . . . nicotine. A sip of invigorating caffeine, and then another inhalation of soothing smoke. . . .

"Oh!" she yelped, startled and dismayed as the cigarette was suddenly wrenched from her fingers. Turning baleful, indignant, then increasingly angry eyes, she saw that Eagle was tossing the remainder of her cigarette into the cooking fire, his face a closed, stoic mask.

"What the hell do you think you're doing?" she demanded, jumping to her feet and facing him with her hands on her hips. "We agreed that my personal habits were my own business—"

"And that they are," he retorted rudely. "But I also mentioned that you wouldn't have time to laze around all day with a cigarette. You've work to do. Now. We need corn ground before we leave."

Whatever happened to the tender lover who had cherished her through the night, Whitney wondered fleetingly. Then her anger replaced any other feelings. "Now?" she queried imperiously. She reached for her pack of cigarettes, coolly eyeing him, and slowly lit another, inhaling and exhaling as calmly as if she were sitting in an elegant bar with a piña colada in her left hand. "I'll be with you in five minutes," she said with icy dismissal, tossing her head as she reclaimed her seat by the fire.

"I said *now!*" Eagle repeated softly, bending over her to wrench the second cigarette away. As Whitney struggled in rebellious protest, he also secured the entire pack and the silver lighter.

Never before accosted by such a situation, Whitney gave vent to frustrated rage, screaming, "Give those back! You have no right! Damn you—"

Ignoring her tantrum, Eagle swung on his heel. "Go take over the corn grinding for my grandmother. If you're a good, productive girl, I'll give you a cigarette break before we leave."

For a fraction of a second Whitney stood stunned, astounded that he would dare dictate her behavior to such an extent. Then she flew after him and pounded on his back ferociously. Her anger began a climb to disastrous heights as she realized he was laughing, and the next thing she knew, he had dragged her from his back to the ground and pinned her beneath him. With one hand he effortlessly secured both of hers over her head, grinned evilly and held the pack in front of him, pretending to muse seriously over the situation. "If I break them one by one," he said slowly, "you won't have any left!"

"No!" Whitney breathed.

"No what?" Eagle demanded.

Whitney broke into a string of abusive language she hadn't been aware that she knew.

"Un-huh, un-huh!" Eagle warned, clicking his teeth reproachfully.

Helpless with him above her, Whitney could not, nevertheless, control her temper. Wild rage decreed that she pit her entire strength against him, and she did so, writhing desperately against his weight and boalike grip on her wrists.

"Hmmm . . ." was his only response, his eyes assuming a brilliant twinkle. "That feels great. I think I like you mad."

"Ohhh," Whitney groaned, gritting her teeth. But he was right; the grinding of their hips together was bringing back memories of last night when they had joined together. . . .

"Let me up!" she demanded quickly, "and I'll go pound your damned corn or whatever it is you want done!"

Smiling, he came to his feet and helped her up. "Now that's the spirit! Whoever said that nicotine addiction couldn't be a good thing? You're going to want that cigarette so bad you'll just plow through the work!"

He chuckled as she stared at him furiously, her eyes snapping emeralds, her beautiful face taut with rebellion, her entire body seething. What perversity goaded him to provoke her, he wondered. Maybe a hint of the arrogance she accused him of. He really didn't give a damn about the corn himself . . . but watching her before the fire had reminded him too clearly that she had no part of this world that he could never really leave behind. She had become a wanton in his arms, instinctively pleasing him as no other woman, however well versed in the arts, ever had. He wanted to grab her and force her back to the chickee, or to a bed, or, hell, on the ground—anywhere. He wanted to take her and take her and take her until she was so indelibly bound to him and filled by him that she would never think of touching another man. . . .

That thought—a vision of her in the arms of another man, touching him, her lips upon him—sobered Eagle. He had only the next few days . . . just a few more days to possess and win her completely.

"Well, go on!" he growled abruptly, unable to control the forces that gripped him like a madman. Elemental power was all that he had.

She spun past him, muttering about what he was beneath her breath. Brute. Domineering. Uncouth. He even rated "chauvinist." Her hips swayed enticingly as she walked away. "Damnit!" was the last thing he heard her murmur.

The corn grinder was simply a section of large log, fashioned with a hollow to hold shelled corn. The corn became pulverized by the dropping of a heavy wooden pestle.

Whitney's arms were aching within a few minutes, but her anger kept her moving. Morning Dew helped her, instructing her in the easiest way to control the heavy pestle. Then she was on her own. Everyone in the village was busy preparing supplies for the festival.

When she had finally finished with the offending corn, Whitney realized it couldn't be more than nine A.M., yet she felt as if the day should be over. Anyway, she certainly deserved her break! Strolling back to the cooking fire, she found hot coffee and her cigarettes. Wary lest Eagle come upon her and decree that she was supposed to have scrubbed the dirt floor, Whitney took her coffee and cigarette through the little alcove in the trees that led to the lake, found a level stump and sat to enjoy her brief spell of relaxation. God, but she hurt all over! And she was one hell of a fool. What was possessing her to stay and endure such treatment? The answer came to her immediately. Eagle. She *was* possessed.

A smile twitched her lips. So she was going to become his bride tonight! He would certainly be sorry he had been so rough on her. The continually joked about excuse of a headache had to be a frequent reality for an Indian wife. Headache, nothing! Everything that was part of her ached!

"I'll have you grind the corn more often if it makes you this happy!"

Whitney glanced from the smoke of her cigarette to Eagle, who had come upon her with his usual irritating silence. A smart retort died in her throat as she stared at him.

He was still clad in the richly colorful Seminole shirt, but he had added to his native costume. His dark head was adorned by a turban of white egret feathers and a warlike band of silver encircled his neck. He had shed his jeans for the brief "skirt" of the kind the Seminoles wore hundreds of years ago, and his high boots were now of buckskin. A knife was strapped to one thigh, and he carried a large, lethal-looking bow, while arrow points peeked over his shoulder. Surely, Whitney decided, Osceola himself had never looked so awe inspiring and fearsome when he arrogantly turned down any terms of peace. Through the decades Eagle had inherited the structure and aura of relentless pride, of independence, of stubborn, ruthless willpower. The bright blue of his eyes and the gauntness of his high-boned face gave conclusive evidence of his white heritage, but that merely seemed to accentuate the ruggedness of his chosen native stance.

"You might want to shut your mouth," he suggested blandly, a spark of humor discernible in the wry twist of his lips. "You could trap a mosquito if you're not careful."

Whitney snapped her mouth shut. "You look . . . uh . . . you look . . ."

"Barbaric?"

100

Whitney shook her head. "No," she said softly. "Regal. Like a chief. Are you a chief?"

"No," he replied, joining her on the stump. "We don't have chiefs these days. We have council members."

Speaking her thoughts aloud, Whitney continued. "Well, you do look just like I picture Osceola to have looked."

Eagle laughed aloud easily, but Whitney felt comfortable with the pleasant sound. Reaching over his shoulder into the leather satchel that held his arrows, he said easily, "Here—I brought you your cigarettes."

"Thanks," Whitney replied sardonically. "I just smoked one." Then, realizing she might be put on another "cold turkey" spell, she accepted the pack from him and lit up. He started to laugh again and she tweaked an inquiring brow at him.

"*You* look like one of those feminist cigarette ads! Old-fashioned dress from head to toe, hiding away in the bushes to smoke!"

"Aren't you glad I'm not a real women's libber? I'd never be in these woods!"

His light banter ceased suddenly and he took her chin gently in his hand. The timbre of his voice was soft and low. "What are you, Whitney? What are you really?"

"I don't know what you mean," she replied, annoyed that her answer warbled nervously. Their relationship was such a strange one. It was business between them, then hostility, then passion and chemistry. But passion was one thing in the throes of ecstasy in his arms; friendship was another. She was terrified to come too close, to put demands on an intimacy that he had probably shared before yet to her was . . . skyrockets.

He didn't release her chin, and his next question was blunt and audacious. "Were you divorced because of the sex problem? Don't start blushing—after last night it's a little late for secrets or hedging with me."

Whitney managed to extract her chin on the pretense of

101

taking a drag of her cigarette. Staring straight ahead of her, she honestly replied, "No. I didn't even realize at the time that I was missing anything. We just made each other miserable. I wanted to work; Gerry wanted a wife who was always home looking pretty. He wouldn't force me to quit, and I couldn't volunteer. One day I just sat down and told him that what we were doing was ridiculous. We were—and are—friends. We wanted different things, that's all."

The tiny alcove seemed very hushed when she finished speaking. Eagle eventually asked, "And what is it that you want?"

"I don't know exactly," Whitney answered truthfully. "To be respected, I suppose. To have my opinions matter. To care deeply . . ." She crushed her cigarette, very carefully grinding it into the dirt. "What do you want out of life?"

"Probably the very same things," he answered her levelly, his blue eyes warmly sincere for the moment. "I think we all do."

He stood abruptly, and the close intimacy was broken. "Come, Whitney. Your dugout awaits."

Whitney rose obediently and placed her hand in his outstretched one. They were both guarded again, and yet something more had been forged between them than the chemistry that had promised that they would be lovers just as surely as the sun would rise.

But, Whitney thought wryly, just as surely as that sun would rise, the moon would follow. They were both willful, stubborn and demanding. They would love, but would they hate with equal depth and ferocity?

As the dugout trailed through the marshy land to take them to the Green Corn Dance, Eagle explained something of the festival. The majority of the Miccosukees in Florida would attend, even those living in more northern parts of the state. Although the Muskogee or Cow Creek

Seminoles held their own dance, many of them would also come. Many ancient customs would be adhered to, and many men, who usually wore jeans these days, would dress in tribal costume. The Indians hunted with shotguns; the bow and arrows he carried were for games, although they were not a competitive people. The idea of a contest was not to win but to excel as far as one could for one's own benefit and satisfaction. The good of the family and tribe was the main consideration for all Seminoles. "Actually," Eagle said with a grin, "we don't call ourselves Seminoles; in Muskogee we are *Istichatee*, in Miccosukee, we are *Yakitisee*. Both terms mean 'red people.'"

"I hope I remember all this!" Whitney said, watching the strong play of muscles in his arms as he unerringly guided the dugout canoe that carried the two of them and Morning Dew with fixed precision through what appeared to be endless miles of identical marshland. "And I do hope that the venerable J. E. Stewart is impressed!"

If she hadn't been preoccupied with her own thoughts, Whitney might have noticed that Eagle grimaced ruefully. As it was, she frowned and continued in the same vein. "Although I'm still at a loss as to what I should be understanding. From what I've learned, the Indians do live hard lives! Think how much easier life could be for your grandmother if she had a washing machine and electricity and—"

"Have you been unhappy, Whitney?"

The question interrupted her with a hushed, sensual quality. Blushing, Whitney trailed a hand over the top of the water and whispered, "No." Then she raised her eyes to his with timid mischief. "But you can be pushy at times! Argumentative and demanding!"

He smiled rakishly in return. "That's right. When one deals with a dedicated reformer, one must be prepared to demand."

Before Whitney could think of a suitable reply, Eagle

pointed over her shoulder with a paddle. "Ceremony grounds."

Ceremony grounds! Whitney groaned, twisting to see the mass activity. There had to be close to a thousand Indians. A faint, tremulous fear edged over her.

Fortunately she didn't have long to dwell on her sense of uneasiness. The gathering was a social occasion, and they were shortly bustling through crowds with greetings being called all around them. Makeshift chickees had been arranged by each family, and along with the other Eagles, they were soon settling into their clan sector. Whitney was turned over to Morning Dew for the afternoon, since Eagle was called upon to join with his male peers for certain functions. Whitney rather sullenly let it be known that she didn't particularly approve of such sexism.

"Don't pout!" Eagle said with a laugh. "Our women run the domestic activities—heredity is matrilineal. It has only been in the last century that we have begun to take our fathers' names—and that because of white influence." Suddenly he grasped her tightly to him and whispered, "And that, darling, is why it shall be to my mother's ancestral home that I bring my bride this evening for her nuptials."

His voice held threat; it held promise. A quivering of anticipation made Whitney loath to move her face from the harbor of his chest. He taunted her, and yet he enthralled her. She should be denying the hypocrisy of the farce, but she couldn't. She was waiting for the night and a Miccosukee blessing of their strange union.

It wasn't long in coming. Morning Dew spent the afternoon entertaining various of her women friends. Some of the conversations were in the Miccosukee tongue, with Morning Dew translating for Whitney, and she was affectionately drawn into the circle of women who blatantly studied her, but did it with such warmth, interest and sincerity that she could feel no resentment. It was touching to see the pride Morning Dew exhibited in her, heartwarming and painful. But Whitney was obsessed by the evening; she couldn't and wouldn't put a stop to the events that were due to occur. She had been swept into a strange dream from which she had no desire to awaken.

Then the sun made its slow descent into the horizon. Whitney, bathed and dressed, her hair carefully braided, was led to the center of the celebration, where a massive bonfire burned. Men and women were joining by the fire, and as Whitney watched, they began a dance. The music of a flute could be heard accompanying a slow chant, which was joined by the rattle of shells and the pulsations of drumbeats upon various devices.

Eagle, clad in a multitude of feathers that turbaned around his head, was among the dancers. For a moment his eyes locked with hers through the mystical orange glow of the firelight. They were brilliant, triumphant, exultant—and a shade devilish and wild. An ember of fear raged through Whitney, interrupting the trancelike quality of the dream she lived. What was she getting into? Three days ago the man staring at her with victorious possession had been unknown to her.

Eagle's view of her was whipped away as the dance increased in tempo, and Whitney was back in her trance. She didn't care. Past and future held no meaning. Whoever or whatever he was didn't matter. She wanted him with pure and unadulterated yearning and love. The trappings of the man meant nothing—he was the essence of all she had ever sought and desired in a male—a lover, a provider, a mate.

The dance ended. Suddenly Whitney became part of the activities—the main part. She was standing before the elders of the tribe and the councilmen and her tongue was unglueing to form alien syllables in repetition. Eagle was beside her; she was his. It was over, yet still the bonfire raged and the ancient hypnotism of the ritual remained. The dream would continue.

Only one incident occurred to remind her that she was

still residing in the twentieth century. She was about to be led away for her "honeymoon" night when the head of the council, a weathered and stately old Indian man, kissed her cheek in a very Anglo fashion.

"Congratulations, my dear," he told her, his English enunciated in a clear, only slightly accented voice. "I hope you'll be very happy."

But Whitney had no chance to muse over his perfect use of her own language. She was taken to a secluded chickee in the shelter of warm, welcoming pines. She was left standing, a beautiful young bride, awaiting her husband, her noble warrior man.

CHAPTER SIX

She stood in ethereal splendor as he approached, a vision of spectral loveliness. The moonlight danced upon the dark waves of her hair, which had been loosened to form a glorious cloak around her shoulders. She was still, perfectly still, as if she didn't even breathe, and the glow upon her skin gave it the cast of silken cream alabaster. In the darkness her eyes were prisms of jade, bright and liquid against the whiteness of her face.

She didn't see him on the path, Eagle knew, and he allowed himself the luxury of simply watching her. He had no desire to rush anything. In his heart he would be claiming his bride, and despite all that he knew, all that had come before, she was defenseless and as tender as a trusting doe as she waited.

Her eyes came to his and he saw that they were tremulous, that a faint shivering held her body in its grip. He stared at her a moment longer, then slowly walked to her, his eyes never leaving hers. He moved like a panther in the night, his sleek muscles fluid, his steps sure. The passion that would be culminated had begun with that first searing eye contact, which had locked them together in a union beyond description but known to man since the beginning of time.

Eagle leaped to the platform with a muffled thump and stood just inches from her, inhaling the soft perfume of her femininity, absorbing the radiating warmth of her nearness. Tonight there was no need to talk. She was fright-

107

ened, but willing and eager. It was all still new. Her eyes told everything.

His fingers trembled slightly as he moved them to unfasten the strings of the gown she wore. It fell to her feet in a soft rustle, and he drank in the beauty of her nakedness slowly with his eyes, worshipping her as he might a statue of the finest marble. But she wasn't marble, she was flesh and blood and her quivering form cried out to be touched as her eyes met his again with mute pleading.

Still, he could not rush. He brought his hands to her shoulders, slowly down the soft length of her arms, along the exquisite contours of her delicately molded back. His lips claimed hers, slowly, seductively, savoring each new depth of the warmth of her moist mouth. Heat grew within him, embering, flaring, yet he kept it within rigid control. His kisses blazed new trails from her mouth, down the swanlike length of her neck, onward across her breasts to tease, torment and demand upon the hard rosy peaks that rose instinctively to his touch against the firm roundness that arched into his hands. A famished man, his head swimming, he went on to thirst and thirst, tasting the taut flesh of her rib cage, the tiny indentation of her navel, the sweet, sweet skin of her abdomen and the soft skin that lurked below hiding all that was his. And all the while that he enticed, teased and cajoled, his own desire intensified like a tornado, spinning, whipping, spiraling as her quivers became sensuous undulations and her silence a series of moans and sighs that pleaded and demanded in return.

Then it was she who became the aggressor. No longer able to stand, she fell to her knees and buried herself against him. Their fingers worked together to cast aside his clothing, and she was drinking of his smooth, tight flesh, relishing the spasm of muscles beneath her lips and hands, drawing the same pleasure as he from the wanton excitement she elicited. She couldn't touch him, feel him, taste the fine salt of his body enough . . . nor could she satiate the appetite that raged like a bonfire, gnawing, creating a hunger as demanding and unquenchable as his.

A hoarse cry rumbled in the depth of his powerful chest, and the mute satisfaction of a woman who has equally seduced a man in loving torment mingled naturally into Whitney's primal level of ecstasy, spurring her still further into the realm of sensuous magic. Then it was he who commanded again, he who navigated her writhing body, he who took her with a rough urgency that propelled them into shock wave after shock wave of ceaseless sweet pleasure until the unbearable exploded into a high of delicious fulfillment so wonderful that they floated in a land where time stood still until the crest washed back in a wave of complete, giving satisfaction.

They were silent again in the aftermath of the incredible maelstrom of their lovemaking. It wasn't a time to talk, Whitney thought dreamily, feeling the breadth of his chest expanding and contracting beneath the light touch of her slender fingers. It was a time to cherish sensations, to mindlessly enjoy all that had transpired and simply hold on to the beauty. With her head upon his shoulder, her arm casually slung over him, her body melded against his, she gave in to her euphoria and total physical and mental exhaustion. A final shudder rippled its way through her limbs; a long sigh of happiness whistled softly through her lips. She slept, in the peace and security that would envelope her wherever this man might be.

Eagle stared briefly at the moonglow through the trees. He was thinking about the future and the woman who was confidently coiled to his length—so fragile, so fine and yet so strong. And, for reasons of her own, she trusted him. He had taught her, but it was he, the teacher, who knew just how special and precious the ties that bound them were. He glanced tenderly at the face nestled in his shoulder. Her dark lashes swept her cheeks in sleep and her lips were prettily curved, even at rest. Tomorrow, he told himself. Tomorrow he would talk to her; he would explain what he had done. In that night he had learned the true meaning of his fanatical desire to possess her completely, and he was once more convinced that he would never let her go. Closing his eyes, he felt the perfect warmth of his discovery and the age-old, masculine, triumphant comfort of having his beautiful woman wedged to his strength. He slept, too, his lips curved into a smile with the satisfaction that she had come to him first in a bed in the woods.

It was the morning song of a chorus of birds that woke Whitney, a symphony that rang sweetly in the dew damp air. She listened lazily for a moment without opening her eyes, luxuriating in the fresh scent and feel of the new day—and in the contentment of languorous satiation that had stayed with her through the night. She was experiencing a rush of womanly wonder at the beauty of the world, awed that Eagle was beside her still, his male strength enveloping her fragility. . . .

He stirred beside her, and his eyes were sensuously heavy lidded as they met hers. In the night they had shifted, and he was leaning over her, his leg thrown casually over hers, his arm gently entrapping her breasts. He kissed her lips lightly, then reverently he kissed the tender peak of each mound beneath his arm's captivity. He smiled, and Whitney gently drew her knuckles over his cheek, smiling in return.

Something rustled in the bushes, and a look of alarm crossed Whitney's face. She automatically reached for the coverings, but his imprisoning arm held her firm.

"Just the birds," he murmured, "just the birds, my sweet." He chuckled and released her reluctantly to stand and rustle through their belongings. Whitney relaxed and narrowed her eyes to watch him through covert slits. He was incredible, she thought with smug, feminine satisfaction. Incredibly powerful, incredibly superb, incredibly masculine. It was marvelous just to watch the blending of sinewed muscles and tendons as he moved near, unconscious of the nakedness that was natural when he was with her.

He found a pair of briefs and jeans and stepped into them, pausing only for a second to glance at her with hesitant longing as she lay curled like a kitten near his feet, enticingly half covered. But the commotion of the birds was a warning that daybreak had come and a scurry of activity would shortly begin. Willpower snapped him from his enchanted reverie, and he pulled up the zipper of his snug jeans. "Let's take a walk," he suggested huskily.

Whitney grinned her agreement and stretched. "What about your costume today?" she asked.

He grimaced wryly. "There will be games and contests today—among them alligator wrestling." He raised a rueful brow and knelt back beside her, unable to resist the temptation to trace a finger down her curved, beautifully sculpted back to the tiny hollows that dimpled at its base. "Even those sworn to custom wear jeans for the alligators —they have fast-snapping, powerful jaws."

"You really wrestle alligators?"

"Ummmm," he smiled at the concern in her eyes and gave in to another temptation—that of drawing her from her cocoon of sheets and taking her into his arms. He allowed himself a drawn-out kiss while caressing her enticing body before pulling away with a shaky breath and handing her her clothing. "It's late."

"Telling time by the sun?" she teased, obediently dressing.

"As a matter of fact, yes," he retorted, grinning. "And I'll be ribbed mercilessly if we don't make an appearance soon, but I want to walk with you in a private fantasy for a while." Hopping lithely to the ground, he added, "Finish dressing, my love, and follow me. I won't lead you astray."

"Hah!" Whitney quipped, but she happily placed her hands upon his shoulders to leap to the ground with the assistance of his warm, muscle-corded arms. Snuggled to his side, she complacently followed his leading footsteps into the pines, content as he for the moment to wallow in the exquisite beauty between them and around them.

It was a short nature hike. Eagle held her close to his beating heart while he shushed her and pointed out the precious foliage and creatures that created the one-of-a-kind paradise of the Everglades: rare flowers carried by ocean currents north from the tropics in ancient times when the land was forming, animals from the north that had adapted to the south, long-legged birds that added their pastel splendor to the darker wood hues.

Eagle held her still against him as they silently watched a great blue heron take flight in smooth majesty. His arms were circled around her waist, and his breath tickled her ear. "We have to get back," he said with a sigh. " 'Gator time."

"You're serious."

"I'm serious." He laughed, taking her hand. "Come on!"

They retraced the pine trail back to the main ceremony grounds, where they approached an area of sturdy fencing where others were beginning to congregate.

"Be careful," she pleaded.

He gave her a thumbs-up sign. "I learned this from the best at seventeen—and I'm always careful!"

Whitney was then left as a spectator while Eagle joined the men for their exhibitions in the pit. She watched with fearful fascination as the men entered and maneuvered the animals skillfully—always careful, as Eagle had said—expertly watching while working to see that no opening jaws were behind them. The angry hissing increased as the prodded animals scampered for their reserves of water, moving with a startling speed.

"They can outrun a racehorse for a short distance, at sixty-five miles an hour," a friendly voice told Whitney.

"Randy!" she exclaimed happily, turning to see him with Katie Eagle.

"How are you enjoying the festivities?" Katie asked.

"Randy and I are late because of some herd problems, but I hear my brother did connive you into the wedding my grandmother demanded."

"Ah . . . yes," Whitney murmured, turning her gaze back to the alligator pit. Eagle was entering, and she drew in a sharp breath.

"Don't worry," Katie said with a chuckle, "he knows what he's doing."

Apparently he did. Barefoot and bare-chested as the other men had been, Eagle held his pole and scampered around the creatures with cautious grace. He singled out his animal and drew it to the center by the tail. Then he had the jaws in a careful grip and performed the stunt of holding them closed against his chest by the strength of his chin alone. Finally he put the animal to sleep by rubbing sand on the pale underbelly.

"They fall asleep," Randy said, "because of the rush of blood from their tails to their heads. He won't leave it long, though—it could be harmful to the animal."

Suddenly Eagle was back with them. His words were for Katie; they were sharp and in the Miccosukee tongue. Katie seemed to deny something indignantly, and Eagle's voice began to soften. An apology? Whitney wondered. For what? He had gone into what seemed to be an explanation. Katie began agreeing with a soft smile that switched mischievously to Whitney. Whitney realized with sinking clarity that it all had something to do with the Miccosukee wedding. Katie and Randy had to know that it was a sham. A dizzying sensation froze Whitney. She didn't want it to be a sham. All morning she had walked beside him and talked with him in a lighthearted flippancy, one that bespoke of tender, reciprocated intimacy. She didn't want shades of reality intruding now.

But neither was she a fool. They were discussing her as if she weren't there, and she just wasn't going to have it. "Excuse me, you two!" she interrupted. "What's going on?"

She received a simultaneous pair of "nothings" that were riddled with guilt. Randy Harris looked at her uneasily. His eyes darted back to Eagle. "I hate like hell to come between 'newlyweds,'" he said hollowly, "but it seems to me we have to split up this party. I believe they're expecting you at the council meeting."

"Yeah . . . uh . . . yeah. . . ." Eagle murmured. He brushed his lips over Whitney's and gave her a warm smile. "Stick with Katie. I'll see you later." Raising his brows with a grimace, he added, "Tribal powwow, you know."

Randy and Eagle disappeared into the crowd that hovered around the pit, and Whitney looked at Katie. She had given Whitney answers before, and now she chatted like a magpie—about anything but her brother or their family. It would be useless to question Katie, Whitney shrewdly realized. She was thoroughly under Eagle's control.

Whitney wasn't sure that she wanted to question her, anyway. She had the intuition that knowledge would hurt her. Better to enjoy what was for her allotted time than to begin already to chastise herself for falling into the arms of a compelling man without having the sense to think about what she was doing.

Katie, relieved to find she wasn't going to be cross-examined, dropped her inane wanderings and suggested they join a game. It resembled lacrosse, and men and women were joining in alike, all in good spirits and camaraderie. Whitney protested that she would bring certain defeat to her team, but she was ignored and soon she was running through the field, laughing like a child. She knew surreptitious glances were often cast her way, and that they all wondered about the woman who had "married" Eagle. Did she read envy in certain eyes? She hoped so. She wanted to fit into this society, which had accepted her with warmth and sincerity.

Whitney didn't get to see much more of Eagle during the day and evening. The council meeting was long; there

114

were many disputes to be settled. She ate with Katie, Morning Dew and other women of the Eagle family; then she was again a spectator of the all-male ritual of the "Black Drink." The Corn Dance, Katie explained, was a time to come back to the tribe, to reevaluate oneself and, in old times of battle, the *Asi* or Black Drink had been a war potion for the braves as well as a purifier. The men drank, cried to the spirits and danced. When the ritual was over, Eagle was again swarmed over by his peers, who seemed to have much to discuss. Whitney found herself returning to the Eagle camp with Katie to await her new husband's return.

The woods were ominous without Eagle. Whitney was a jumble of nerves, half afire for him with burning anticipation, half afraid of the night noises that she recognized yet still didn't trust—rustlings in the pines, the call of birds, . . . the soft note of a John Denver tune coming to her over the breeze.

John Denver! Whitney sat bolt upright, listening. Yes, she could hear a guitar and a singer with a pleasant tenor warbling a charming strain to "Rocky Mountain High." Who? Where? It was impossible! She couldn't be hearing what she was hearing—Denver music in the woods.

But she was.

And it wasn't an acoustical guitar she was hearing. It was definitely electric.

After a while the music ceased. Whitney lay her head back down, pondering the puzzle. But the days had been too much for her. She yawned, dozing into sleep despite her desires and fears. She would ask Eagle who had been the pleasant tenor, she decided. As soon as she saw him.

But electricity in the woods? Maybe she *had* imagined that . . . Eagle would explain.

But she never had a chance to ask him. When he returned she was aroused rather than awakened, and it was late in the night when she contentedly drifted into slumber again, her curiosity blissfully forgotten.

Whitney sat outside the chickee thinking of the night she had spent in Eagle's arms. If only she weren't so tired! The nights of wild exhilaration were wonderful dreams, but lack of actual sleeping hours was taking a toll. She was a woebegone sight as she sat before the chickee, her native costume bunched about her knees, her hair framing bright green eyes that peered above mauve shadows. She yawned with a shake of her head. How did Eagle do it? He had been up and gone before she had managed to blink.

"My goodness! Where did you come from?"

Whitney quickly glanced up from the ground where she had been drawing patterns with her finger to find herself facing a tall, slim man with a pleasant crop of neat, snow-white hair. He was dressed in a sedate three-piece suit of navy that was obviously well tailored. As she frowned at him with confusion, he smiled. The friendly grin that twisted his lips stretched to his eyes—eyes that were a brilliant, vivid blue.

Whitney scrambled to her feet, dusting her hands against her calico skirt. She knew she was staring rudely, but the resemblance was extraordinary. Extending her hand while she searched for her tongue, Whitney smiled. "How do you do?" she managed. "My name is Whitney Latham. Eagle—your son, I know he must be your son!—brought me out here. I am—I mean I was—am!—with T and C Development and he thought I might be interested in learning the real way of life of the Indians involved in our transactions. We met in the woods, you see . . ." How ridiculous she was sounding! Cool, poised Whitney Latham, who could face the presidents of multimillion-dollar corporations without the flicker of an eyelash! Why was she babbling before this dignified, friendly, middle-aged man?

Because he was her father-in-law and knew nothing of the bogus wedding? No; he wasn't really her father-in-law.

But he was Eagle's father, that she knew beyond a doubt. And absurd as it was, she loved Eagle. She wanted so desperately to know his father . . . and her curiosity about his heritage was so strong that she couldn't possibly ask everything at once!

The man laughed, an easy, good-natured sound. "Slow down, Miss Latham. This is a most intriguing situation! You met—uh—Eagle, you say, in the woods. And he brought you out here?"

Whitney blushed slightly and explained how she had stumbled into the cabin off Alligator Alley. Lifting her hands in confused offering, she ended with, "So you see, Eagle thought I could best learn what I don't know by actually living it."

"And what has he been teaching you?"

"How to grind corn, prepare vegetables . . ."

The dignified old man with the beautiful, crinkling eyes interrupted Whitney's recital with laughter.

"Oh, I am sorry, my dear. Forgive me!" he begged, seeing her bewilderment. "That son of mine! What else has he been up to? Never mind, I think I have an idea. He has taken you for a real ride!"

Whitney smiled and attempted to sound nonchalant. "Oh? Please go on!" She forced the trembling that had assailed her to cease, and the look of confusion left her face as she gave him her most beguiling grin. "Perhaps I can take your son for a little ride in return!" Just right, she decided. She sounded like a female intent on a slight teasing revenge, not a woman ready to explode with rage and pain. Ride! she seethed inwardly. Ride! What kind of ride?

"Perhaps I'm being vague," the man said cheerfully, "but I'm not sure why my son brought you to his grandmother. You see, the majority of the Indians today are educated and well aware of the offerings of our society. Several of the families run stores and businesses on the Trail. A number of the men and women hold jobs in the cities, such as in Naples, Miami and Homestead. If they

117

want electricity they have it installed. If they want corn-meal, well, they usually buy it. Especially the younger crowd. Schools have exposed them to the niceties—and the headaches!—of civilization."

Denver, Whitney thought dully, that was why she had heard the John Denver music. That was why the head of the council had expressed his best wishes in English. They probably all spoke English, and she had played the complete fool. . . . "Do you mean," she began aloud, "that none of this is real?"

"No, no! Forgive me again! This is very real! Morning Dew is an old-time Miccosukee," he told her warmly. "This is her way of life. She desires no contact with so-called civilization. I'm shocked that she allowed Eagle to bring you here like this. How did he manage it?"

Whitney couldn't bring herself to mention the tribal wedding. She only hoped she could escape the gentle man before he discovered the extent of her relationship with his son. Escape! How? But she had to get away.

"I—I'm not sure," she whispered vaguely.

"How did Eagle con *you* into this?"

"He . . . uh . . . he promised to smooth things over for me with Jonathan Stewart."

It was the white-haired man's turn to look puzzled. "I don't understand, but I think I'd like to. Smooth what things over? You see, I am Jonathan Stewart."

Oh God! Whitney mutely groaned. Of course! That was the secrecy regarding his paternity! That was why Eagle was so sure he had all the influence he needed. "I don't see what you don't understand, Mr. Stewart," she began politely. "Surely you know you are due to meet with me next week on a solution to the land problem."

His brows raised in a high arch, so like Eagle's that a fierce stab of pain ripped into her heart. "You're to meet with me next week?"

"Yes, sir. With Mr. Jonathan E. Stewart."

"Oh, my dear Miss Latham! You *have* been taken for

a ride, and I can see I'll be having a long discussion with my son! It isn't me that you're supposed to be meeting. I'm Jonathan Lee Stewart. You were destined to meet my son from the beginning—you merely came upon him prematurely. He is Jonathan E. Stewart. Eagle. Jonathan Eagle Stewart. The Miccosukees call him White Eagle because of me, his father."

Whitney had never fainted, but she was sure the blackness enveloping her would soon cause a hasty descent to the ground. Her knees buckled beneath her. "I think I'll sit for a minute," she said, and her voice had a buzzing quality as it came to her ears. How had she been so wretchedly stupid and naive? She had been baited—Miss Virginia, indeed!—and fallen hook, line and sinker for every deception dangled before her.

"Are you all right, Miss Latham?" Jonathan Stewart, his blue eyes pools of concern, knelt beside her, mindless of his impeccable suit in the earth.

"Fine. . . ." Whitney murmured faintly, dredging up a reassuring grin. Stewart seemed to think of it all as a friendly, harmless practical joke. But he didn't know how terribly involved it had been! He didn't know that his son had solicited her love and trust while subtly stabbing her in the back all the while! Oh, God! Whitney thought over everything that had happened in a flash in her mind, like the last visions of a drowning victim. Her demand to know if Eagle spoke English. Her often unintended and naive remarks about the Indians and their way of life. . . .

Yes, it had all been a plot to put her in her place. The tender passion of his lovemaking had been nothing but part of the plan. Lord! How he probably intended to laugh when she walked into his Naples office. . . .

He would never have the chance, Whitney determined, and the blackness that encompassed her became a brilliant white light of fury. Now it was her turn. She wasn't sure of her move yet, but she was getting out of these woods—

without seeing Eagle again. She would face him in his Naples office—prepared!

"Miss Latham?"

"I'm fine—I really am!" Whitney assured the senior Stewart. "And please call me Whitney." There was no reason to hurt this kindly man because she was swearing vengeance on his son! "Tell me, sir, how do you happen to be out here?"

"That's easy," Stewart said as he grinned amicably. "I came because of Morning Dew. I see her whenever I come to the South. I live in Chicago, and the one offering of civilization that Morning Dew appreciates is Fanny Mae candy." He patted his jacket. "I always bring her a box."

"Oh," Whitney murmured. "Then you have no problems finding this elusive Corn Dance?"

Stewart gave her another of his gentle smiles. "No. I am also an Eagle by marriage, and the Miccosukees know that I respect their privacy and culture. I lived with them many years."

"Yes . . . yes . . . of course," Whitney replied. He was here to see his family, except that he had come upon her first, and thankfully he didn't know a thing about what was going on. She hoped he would never know just how badly she had been subjugated.

"Where is my son? Council meeting?"

"Yes, I think so," Whitney replied, glancing quickly at the handsome profile beside her. Stewart's voice held paternal pride. Obviously he was happy to see Eagle fit so precisely into both worlds.

"Well, then," he said with a wink, "you and I will certainly get at him when he returns!"

"No . . . uh . . . please," Whitney protested, straining to wink in return. "I'll get him myself, if you don't mind. In fact, I'd appreciate it very much if you didn't mention that we've met. I have to . . . umm . . . I have to try and find your daughter—" she fabricated quickly. "I promised to tour a bit of the encampment with her and Randy."

"Okay," Stewart agreed mischievously. "I won't say a thing. But when you do find Katie and Randy, see if you can think of a good excuse to send them by here. I'll be in Naples for the next three weeks, but I'd like to surprise them all today."

"I'm sure they'll be surprised," Whitney said sweetly.

Impulsively she kissed Stewart's well-lined but attractive, endearing face. She could have grown very fond of him. So many subtle nuances of his had been inherited by his son! And she was in love with the son. . . . *No!* Whitney screamed to herself. No more. She would forget him, forget the nights when he had taught her the secrets of her own desires, forget the intensity of the intimacy they had shared.

No, she could never forget. But she could use the memory of his betrayal to strengthen her cause. He would be the fool this time.

"Mr. Stewart," she said, rising, "it has been a great pleasure, I assure you. I'm going to run now, if you don't mind. Morning Dew—I think—went visiting. She should be back any minute. I do want to find Katie, if you'll excuse me."

"Surely!" Stewart rose next to her and accepted her offered hand. "And I promise you, my dear, the pleasure has been mine. I don't mind saying that I can see why my son kidnapped you! I look forward to our meeting again."

"Yes . . . yes. . . ." Whitney lied. She rushed away before he could see the trace of tears blurring her eyes. She blinked them away furiously. She had to think and move quickly. To make her getaway she would need to have complete control over her emotions!

Whitney forced herself to walk into the chickee she had shared with Eagle. Refusing to dwell upon any memories, she kept her gaze from the bedding, from the neat bundles of Eagle's clothing. It was good, she decided grimly, that he had made her travel light. Casting aside her Indian clothing, she scrambled into jeans and a blouse, looped the strap of her bag over her shoulder and hopped from the platform of her "honeymoon" suite once more—for the last time. With her eyes straight ahead, she resolutely walked the return trip on the trail. She couldn't look back. Her lips were already trembling.

Nearing the clearing, Whitney froze. The joyful sound of two distinct male voices came her way. Eagle had discovered that his father was there.

Unable to resist, Whitney crept wraithlike into the trees. The two men were embracing naturally—a father and son who not only loved but respected one another, both tall, strong and determined.

Whitney drew a jagged breath. Her eyes now were only for the son. She stared at him, as if by doing so she could etch every line and angle of him into her memory forever —the flashing blue eyes, the arrogant hawklike nose, the height of his proud cheekbones, the bronze of his smooth skin, the large, long-fingered, slightly calloused hands. . . . She closed her eyes, and still she saw him. Soon, though, she told herself, stiffening, he would know that his father had given him away. When she didn't reappear by nightfall, someone would grow worried. Then Stewart would have to admit that he had seen her.

And how would Eagle take the news? She was sure he would harbor no anger against his father. He would probably shrug and accept the fact that his game had been up a little early. He might even vaguely regret the loss of his bed partner. Then his blue eyes would begin to twinkle and he would anticipate their meeting—a meeting when he could look into her eyes with the amused knowledge that he had completely fooled and debased the imperious "Miss Virginia" who had wandered into his web.

Whitney strangled back a moan of anguish. How could she ever walk into his office? All the things he knew about her! Her past . . . her vulnerabilities! How could she ever look him in the eyes again? She couldn't.

She could turn around and leave the southern marshlands altogether. Take her BMW and head right back to marvelously cultured Virginia, where . . .

Her father and Gerry waited, expecting that she would find defeat on her own.

No. She would be dead and buried first. She had a few days left to lick her wounds and plan her strategy. Then she would face Mr. Jonathan Eagle Stewart on territory where she was familiar and practiced. And she would emerge the victor.

Whitney opened her eyes. With a final impression of blue-black hair, she shifted quietly through the foliage. Out of range of the Eagle clan sector, she began to run, desperation moving her quickly from the alligator pits to the council platforms to the nightly bonfire area. Where were they? Finally Whitney saw a patch of sandy hair in the midst of coal black. Randy was playing in a ball game. Katie had to be nearby.

Crunching her lip in preparation for the lie she was about to embellish, Whitney raced around the edges until she found Katie.

"Katie!" Whitney wailed desperately, startling the beautiful woman as she pounced upon her and swung her around. "Oh, Katie, I've been looking for you everywhere! I need help desperately. I—I have to get back to my car and I can't find Eagle."

"Calm down!" Katie soothed kindly, making Whitney wince. "Whatever it is, Randy and I will help you."

"You're going to think this terribly foolish of me," Whitney continued, hating herself but seeing no other way. "I forgot a rather serious problem. I have to be in Naples by evening. My father might be there, and if he doesn't find me he'll have the damned National Guard searching the Everglades. I am so sorry—" She *was* sorry to be inventing such an absurd tale. "It had all simply slipped my mind, but you don't know the man!"

Katie chuckled. "I know all about fathers. Mine kept

123

me on a leash until I married Randy. Between him and Eagle, it's amazing we ever had a date!"

Whitney breathed a sigh of sick relief as Katie gestured to Randy to bring him to the sidelines. Katie explained the situation to her husband quickly, and if Randy thought such sudden panic wearisome, he gave no indication. "We'll get you out of here," he promised quickly.

"I hate to be such a bother," Whitney said sincerely.

"No bother. The trip to the car will only be an hour. An hour back . . ." Randy shrugged. "We won't miss anything. If you'd rather, though, I'm sure that I can find Eagle for you—"

"No! Um . . . I think he's with the council. If you're sure you don't mind, you can explain for me. I'll see him as soon as I can."

"Whatever you say," Randy agreed. He was wearing one of those concealed grins that clearly stated that compliance was much easier than trying to reason with a panicky woman, no matter how feeble her explanations. "If you're ready, we'll go. The airboat is tethered thataway."

Whitney turned her back on the Miccosukees and the Green Corn Dance. She was sorry to use Katie and Randy, but then it was fitting that Eagle's own sister and brother-in-law would be the instruments of her escape.

CHAPTER SEVEN

Alligator Alley was desolate even with a bright sun shining overhead. Whitney looked nervously at her gas-tank gauge, praying that her car would live up to its promised highway mileage and bring her the thirty remaining miles to a service station. She had no intention of ever making a trek into unknown swampland again.

It was amazing, Whitney thought, that she was driving normally. Her eyes were on the road, her hands on the wheel. She looked normal! Inside she felt like the fuming, bubbling lava of a volcano. If only she could erupt!

To ease her frustration she fiddled with the radio, trying to find a station. After a fair amount of static she landed on something clear. Unfortunately what she heard was a John Denver song. Just what she needed. Another reminder that the Miccosukee Indians were well aware of the white world. Another reminder that Eagle had led her down a yellow brick road of fantasy, encouraging her belief that she dealt with backwoods people. . . .

She switched off the radio. Too bad she couldn't turn off her tormented mind with equal ease. None of it would have been so bad if only she hadn't fallen in love with him! *That*, she admitted in her deepest subconscious, was the root of her fury. And she had been dreaming that he loved her too and that at the end of the week some magical miracle would occur to keep them together.

And while she was dreaming, he was playing with her. Whitney reached the service station and had her tank filled with gas and her car checked completely. The attendant gave her directions, and within another half-hour she was pulling into a motel in North Naples. Upon reaching her room she paced energetically back and forth. If nothing else, the vigorous exercise did drain some of the tension from her muscles.

"Civilization!" she proclaimed aloud. "Blessed civilization!" A thorough scrub in a scalding hot shower was at hand, then a quiet dinner and a glass of wine from room service.

No, a carafe of wine. She would drink the entire thing herself and then sleep until she woke. Sleep until her heartache eased. . . .

And it would ease, she promised herself stoically. Time was the healer. Tomorrow she would laze around the pool and check into the offices of T and C. By nightfall she would be ready to check out whatever nightlife Naples offered.

As if determined to erase the very essence of the past days, Whitney pampered herself ridiculously. She plucked her brows, shaved her legs, poured more than ample lotion into the bath water and smeared herself with perfumed skin conditioners she never used. She rolled her hair in electric curlers with a bitter grimace, and manicured her cracked nails.

Still, the trace of calluses remained on her hands. Just as the image of Eagle remained on her mind, within her, constant.

And even a full bottle of Sauvignon failed to put her to sleep with the comfort and ease of just knowing that Eagle was beside her.

After a brisk swim in the morning and an hour of soaking in the sun, Whitney called the offices of T and C, informing the secretary that she would be in after lunch to go over the briefings. The relief evident in the young

126

woman's voice at hearing that Whitney had safely arrived sent little chills into her even before she heard the reason.

Whitney had always hated to lie, not simply because of principle but because of a faint tinge of superstition. Even for a necessary little fib, she would never use the excuse of someone being sick in case she should be foretelling the truth and that person become ill. She would never invent an accident.

And now she knew why. Her lie to Katie and Randy was coming true. Her father had been trying to contact her for the entire five days, and according to the secretary, he was beginning to sound like a madman. By tomorrow he would have helicopters searching the Glades and have an all-points alarm out.

"Damn!" Whitney groaned into the phone.

"I'm sorry, Miss Latham," Susie, the secretary apologized. "We've tried to assure him that you weren't late, that you probably were seeing a bit of the countryside. But he just wouldn't listen."

"Whitney," Whitney interposed automatically. "And please don't apologize. I do know my father! I'm sorry he has been harassing you! I'll get hold of him right away."

Whitney rang off quickly and stared rebelliously at the phone. "Damn!" she repeated inanely. When would he ever believe that she had grown up? It was embarrassing! Men were despicable creatures all the way around, she decided.

She picked up the phone and put her call through to Richmond. As soon as her father heard her voice, he expounded a lecture that sent Whitney hurling back to a pillow, holding the receiver away from her ear so that she wouldn't have to hear his words but would know when she was supposed to mutter a response.

"Dad!" she interjected once. "I'm a full quarter of a century old! I'm legal, remember, and adult! I never promised to call in!"

"You had your mother, Gerry and me worried silly!"

"Gerry and I are divorced."

"Another silly whim of yours."

Whitney exhaled and counted slowly. "Dad, I'm fine. I wanted to see a little of the terrain."

"*Alone!*"

She could almost see the veins bulging in her father's temple.

"No . . . uh . . . I had an Indian guide."

That was good for another five minutes on trusting no-account woodsmen.

"Dad," Whitney interrupted, wishing she could simply record the word. "I was visiting a tribe of Miccosukee Indians. They are moral and upright people. I will be dealing with them—" Whitney broke off suddenly. She was furious with her father, she realized, and not because of the interference she had learned to tolerate from him. He was saying things wildly, in ignorance. *As she once had.* And she was left to defend the Indians.

Choosing her words carefully, Whitney went into her own lecture, telling her father in concise terms that the Indians were far more civil and trustworthy than most men she knew. Relenting at the end, she added softly, "I love you, Dad, and I wouldn't purposely hurt Mom for the world! But I'm a big girl. I can take care of myself."

"Hmmmph!" The phone was silent for a few seconds, then her father found a new vein of rebuke.

"And what is this 'Miss' they call you at the office? You are a 'Mrs.' "

"Actually, I'm a 'Ms.,' " Whitney said and started chuckling. "What on earth difference does it make?"

"You had a husband!"

"I don't now." Or did she? A strong, noble man with blue eyes. . . .

"—will be down late next week . . ."

"What?" Oh, God, what had he said while she was wandering?

"Gerry. I'm sending him down. He needs a little sun

and sand anyway, and you know how concerned he is, even if you did walk out on him."

"No, Dad, no."

"You mean you'd refuse to see him—as an old friend?"

"Of course not. It's just—"

"Good. You'll see him next week. He can accurately assess the situation. Take care of yourself, now, daughter, and we'll expect to hear from you soon."

The phone went dead. Whitney stared at it incredulously for countless seconds before she again turned to her pillow. Thank God none of them could see her now! she thought grimly, pounding her fist into the padded receptacle. They would label her certifiably insane and have her put away for good!

But she had to pound the pillow. When she was through, she would prepare to prove her strength of will calmly and ruthlessly to all of them, mindless of any toes that had to be stepped on.

The land problem proved to be far more complex than Eagle had explained. The Miccosukees and the Cow Creek Seminoles were two entirely different tribes, with separate interests. Both were claiming pieces of the land purchased from the government by T and C. Jonathan E. Stewart was representing both tribes, but separate deals had to be made with each.

Greg Tanner, the friendly, fortyish manager of the Naples office, scratched his forehead distractedly as he tried to explain the confusing situation. "Neither tribe is fiercely against selling land—it's this particular *piece* of land. Maybe a stubborn streak; I don't know. That's where you fit in. When you meet with Stewart, you'll hopefully understand."

Whitney smiled enigmatically. "I'm sure Mr. Stewart and I will understand one another perfectly," she purred.

"We do want that land," Greg said with a sigh.

"We'll get it," Whitney assured him. "The right

amount of pressure might be just what Stewart needs. I think I know the pressure points."

"Oh, Whitney—" Susie stuck her head into the inner office and pushed her stylish gold-rimmed spectacles back up the bridge of her nose. "Mr. Stewart's secretary just called. She wanted to make sure the meeting was still on for today."

"Yes, it's still on," Whitney said and smiled. So Eagle thought he had sent her running!

"Mr. Stewart would like to make it lunch, then. One o'clock at the Golden Dragon. Will that be all right?"

"One thirty," Whitney corrected, "will be fine." She might as well let him have fair warning that he wouldn't be twisting her by the tail anymore!

Besides, she wanted to run back to her motel room before she met him. She wanted to be absolutely perfect— Miss Virginia to a *t*.

And she was. Her few days of lounging in the sun had given her a lovely golden tan, which she emphasized by wearing a cool white knit dress that left her arms and shoulders bare and lightly formed to her figure, flattering it in a subtle way that left the observer wondering how such a chaste dress could mold so accurately around slender curves. She left the feathery waves of her hair fluttering around her face while she swept the waist-length back portion into a sophisticated twirl that would add a few inches to her height. Her compact purse and trim heels were a matching green, coordinates to her eyes.

At precisely one thirty she arrived at the Golden Dragon, sure that she would meet Eagle with cool, unflinching eyes.

Unfortunately she hadn't counted on Eagle's drastic change of appearance. She met him in the lounge, and she didn't flinch because she was too busy—to her extreme annoyance—gaping.

The long black hair was gone. It still reached to his collar, but the cut was stylish. He wore a vested navy pinstripe suit with a casual finesse that would immediately draw any feminine eye. The stark white of his tailored shirt set off a light blue tie to perfection—the silk was an exact match to his eyes. When his eyes finally lit upon her, Whitney momentarily forgot all her resolves. He had never looked sexier; he was refined, yet still rugged. Like a chameleon, he had changed to suit his environment and done it remarkably well. His Indian blood was still apparent; it always would be in the strong lines of his bronze face, but no one on earth would ever take him for an unsophisticated backwoodsman or question his capabilities in speaking the Queen's own English.

"Miss Latham." He stated her name coolly, with his blue gaze flicking lightly over her as he left his stance by the bar to greet her. A crooked smile came to his lips—the almost-sneer she had been expecting. "What's the matter, cat got your tongue? I'm sure you have a lot to say."

"Of course I do!" Whitney snapped irritably. "I—it just took me a minute to recognize you."

"Really?" His brows rose in an arch of doubt, then he snapped his fingers and frowned in self-reproach. "I'm sorry! I forgot to wear my feathers! That would have led you right to me!"

"Droll!" Whitney retorted. "Very droll!" She could feel her temper rising and she was determined to remain cool and aloof.

Eagle placed a firm grip upon her elbow and led her from the lounge to the main dining room. "I guess we'd better take our places in the combat zone," he murmured as he walked, then smiled suavely to the maître d', who rushed to them with a deference that further annoyed Whitney. Her companion, it seemed, had the ability to make people jump wherever he went.

"Ah . . . Mr. Stewart! Right this way, sir. I have you and the lady set in the alcove," the white-jacketed man gushed. "Please don't hesitate to request anything at all. . . ."

131

Eagle himself seated a very stiff Whitney and nodded a friendly concordance. "Thanks, Henry. I'm sure things will be superb as usual."

Whitney immediately began to study the menu, although she wasn't really seeing a word. She needed time—time to adjust to the assault on her senses his mere presence instigated. During sleepless nights she had imagined his woodsy, masculine scent on the air . . . in her dreams his firm hands had caressed her skin . . . and now here he was, in the flesh, alive and vital. She had prepared herself; yet she now had to remind herself that she hated him. He had purposely made a complete idiot out of her. Time to bite back.

Outwardly Whitney exuded the aura she desired. Her appearance was that of a sophisticated, lovely young woman—confident, self-assured. A flick of an eyelash could convey disdain; a tilt of her head could draw instant response to a commanding authority.

Witch! Eagle thought bitterly, scanning her over the top of his own menu. She had her stubborn mind set. She had no intention of listening to anything he had to say. And it was all so stupid! He had the wild urge to drag her out of the restaurant and force her to listen to him, to force her back into his arms. The pain was like a hot coiled thing that gnawed away at him deep within.

He stiffened imperceptibly. Damn her beautiful little face straight to hell! She thought she had him now. Well, she didn't. She wanted a fight—a civil fight—and she was going to get one.

Suddenly she looked at him very sweetly. "I'm surprised you chose this place. I don't see catfish, alligator or *sofki* under the entrées."

"I'll suffer," Eagle returned. He politely took the silver lighter from Whitney's hand and lit the cigarette she had pulled from her bag. "May I suggest a bottle of their Sauvignon '72?"

"You may suggest anything you please."

132

Eagle would have liked to suggest a good swat on the rear end. Instead he returned her steady smile and met the hostile challenge in her eyes.

"The duckling a l'orange is excellent."

"Really?"

"Ah! And they do serve frog legs. I don't believe you've attempted that delicacy yet."

"There are certain things I have no desire to try, Mr. Stewart."

"And others you sample lavishly before suddenly deciding you have no taste for them?"

Whitney snapped her menu closed with precision and folded her hands over the snowy tablecloth. "One can find that certain things which are at first palatable leave an incredibly bitter aftertaste."

Eagle lightly lifted a brow and shrugged, but Whitney knew her barb had struck from the tic that pulsed in the hard line of his jaw. Smiling pleasantly through locked teeth, he reached nonchalantly across the table and casually lifted her right hand. Whitney tensed automatically, but trying to withdraw her hand from his hold, she discovered that his apparently light touch had the force of steel.

Smiling more deeply at her attempted resistance—and the dilemma that was obvious in her eyes with the realization that she must endure his touch or create an embarrassing scene—Eagle turned her palm upward and rubbed the soft flesh in a circular pattern with his thumb. He stared at her hand with mock admiration, then met her eyes again, drawling, "What lovely skin, Miss Latham. It's as silky as satin. Such exquisite perfection, to be marred by such a calloused tongue."

Whitney didn't need to jerk her hand away. He dropped it like a hot rock.

"If my tongue is calloused, Mr. Stewart, it has only become so recently, from what I believe is referred to as association with one afflicted with the forked-tongue syndrome." Whitney curtly delivered her speech without batting an eyelash.

The timely arrival of a stoic waiter saved Whitney from an immediate reprisal on her comment.

"I believe the lady wishes to order for herself," Eagle said coolly, inclining his head.

Whitney decided on the shrimp cocktail and roast lamb. Eagle ordered oysters on the half shell and frog legs. As an afterthought he ordered the wine. "Two glasses, please, although I'm not sure the lady will be joining me."

He stared at Whitney, his blue eyes glacial daggers, until the waiter returned with the wine and hovered uncertainly after Eagle's initial taste and murmur of, "Very good," perplexed over how to handle the situation.

"Miss Latham," Eagle prompted, "you have this poor man in distress. Wine?"

Whitney shrugged. "If you insist."

"Oh, Miss Latham," Eagle protested sardonically, "I never insist. But you know that."

Resisting an urge to kick him beneath the table, Whitney turned a dazzling smile on the waiter. "Thank you. I'll be delighted to try the wine."

The waiter poured the wine and promptly disappeared. Eagle raised his glass to her in a toast. "To 'civil' compromises."

Whitney raised her glass in return, quirking her lips with skepticism. "Certainly."

Eagle watched her as they sipped the wine. "I hope this is palatable, Miss Latham, and that you're not plagued by a bitter aftertaste."

"I doubt that I shall be, Mr. Stewart. This is a reputable establishment. I'm sure the wine lives up to its fine label."

"I see. What you see is what you get?"

"Precisely."

"You are reading books by their covers," Eagle mused with a twist of acid mirth. "Tell me, what difference does a change of jacket make—especially when you are well aware of the contents of the pages?"

His insinuations were brash, but Whitney, though fighting the color that threatened to engulf her, was determined not to let him wedge beneath her skin. She issued an exaggerated sigh and spoke to the rim of her wineglass. "Are we speaking of contents? Or another cliché? It seems you can take the man out of the swamp but not the swamp out of the man." Her gaze lifted pointedly to his. "I suppose I'm lucky you wore a shirt of any kind."

Calculated to demoralize, her comment brought a laugh instead. Mocking hurt shock, Eagle objected politely. "Miss Latham! You wound me to the quick. I always wear a shirt. Except when I'm alligator wrestling. Or"—the timbre of his voice lowered a shade and his fingers lightly covered hers again—"when I'm bathing. Or in bed—sleeping, or engaging in other activities. But then I'm telling you things you already know again."

Whitney didn't need to worry about color. The blood drained from her face. She wrenched her fingers away quickly so that he couldn't sense their trembling and curled them around her wineglass. She couldn't chance meeting his eyes and stared at the golden liquid instead. The gentle caress of his fingertips alone had filled her mind with startling recall, heating a core deep within her—a traitorous physical core. But she had to indifferently deny him. . . .

"My memory can be short, Mr. Stewart, very short. Especially when things are best forgotten. We are here to discuss land, anyway, not clothing."

"You brought up the subject, Miss Latham, not I."

"Fine; then I shall also drop it."

Neither one of them had raised his or her voice a hair, nor had they dropped the glacial smiles that twisted their faces into frozen masks of conviviality. Still, the atmosphere itself was charged. Whitney realized just how thick an aura of animosity surrounded them when the waiter chose to return at that moment. He served their appetizers with trembling fingers and dashed away, practically tripping over the wine stand.

"Let's get to land, Mr. Stewart," Whitney said, glad she could concentrate on spearing her shrimp. "I'll be very blunt. We're prepared to offer the Indians—both tribes—substantial restitution. If you don't care to accept our generous offers, I shall be more than happy to drag you into court."

Eagle calmly swallowed an oyster. "May I say, Miss Latham, that I'm glad you are with the diplomatic corps of T and C Development and not the United Nations?"

Whitney smiled and viciously twisted her lemon wedge. "As I've told you, Mr. Stewart, you may say or suggest anything you please."

"A charming concession," Eagle grated.

"Well?"

"You will not get that land, Whitney."

"But I will—Mr. Jonathan 'White Eagle' Stewart."

Eagle dipped his head and swallowed his last oyster, and the appetizer plates were immediately whisked away. Their entrées were carefully served and more wine poured —by the maitre d', Whitney noticed vaguely, rather than their nerve-racked waiter.

"How is the lamb, Miss Latham?" Eagle inquired politely.

"Quite tender, thank you."

Cutting a morsel of his own food, Eagle chewed thoughtfully. "Tender and delectable," he mused. "However, I—like you—have recently discovered how the most tender and delectable . . . ah . . . tastes . . . can become quite sour. One is enticed to feast and then *voilà!* The banquet disappears!"

Banquet! He had made his statement innocently, innocuously, but still his voice rang with caustic insinuation. She had never been anything more than a diversion, like a meal, pleasingly gourmet as it may have been. Her face was no longer ashen; it flooded scarlet. The man had no scruples whatsoever. Neither would she. Her temper was rising, but she had to keep cool. They were on her territory now, and a verbal battle was one she could win.

"Banquet, sir? Rather a fish hooked and dangled on a line, deceived by the lie of a lure. But even fish that look like easy prey can sense deception and slip hooks."

"I see. Now we're talking about wolves in sheep's clothing."

"You flatter yourself, Stewart," Whitney flared. "We're talking about liars, con men, despicable cheats—" she choked off her own words. What was she saying, she wondered sinkingly. He was goading her into comments that were childishly imperious. Even while wishing she could take back her remark, she knew she couldn't. Her name-calling was below the belt, but she couldn't afford the weakness of an apology. Whatever he thought of her snobbishness, he would just have to think.

Eagle's eyes narrowed to slits of ice blue. "You intend to make two tribes of Indians suffer because you imagine you've been done a wrong by one man?"

Whitney pushed at her lamb toyingly with her fork. She had lost her appetite. "Suffer? I don't intend to make anyone suffer. You took me out to meet the Indians so that I could have a good understanding of what I was doing. Well, I do. I'm convinced that they need all the help I can give them. Grinding corn all day may be your idea of amusement, but it isn't mine. There is no need for anyone to spend every waking moment in grueling labor these days. There is no need for anyone to live in a thatched hut. The community we're offering will provide well-paying jobs for men and women alike. Surely you can't resent that, Mr. Stewart."

"I don't resent your community. Build it, by all means. The economic advantages will most certainly be enjoyed by some; the interaction between the white and Indian societies will no doubt be beneficial. I'm simply afraid that

137

you'll have to build elsewhere. I will be happy to help you find another suitable spot."

"Mr. Stewart, we had men in the field for months trying to find the perfect location," Whitney said stubbornly, positive that she held the edge. That Eagle had pushed aside his own plate and now stared at her calmly, his arms crossed confidently over his chest as he leaned back in his chair, merely served to strengthen her determination.

"The land is not perfect if it belongs to someone else."

Whitney expelled a condescending sigh of exasperation. "We are willing to buy the land for more than it is actually worth! Honestly, *White Eagle,* there are times when I feel they definitely misnamed you! Balking Mule would have been much more apt!"

"How clever!" Eagle arched a black brow high. "Coffee, Miss Latham?" Without her consent, he motioned to the waiter, who set steaming cups before them. When they were again alone, he moved like a coiled snake and leaned across the table. His voice was a smooth, silky hiss that left Whitney struggling with her willpower simply not to jump back from his advance.

"Since we're being clever here, Whitney, I'll let you in on an astute observation. Someone should take you over a knee, plant a few good whacks on your behind and send you back to Virginia to be grounded until you grow up! I'm sure you have brains and a mind, but I'm equally sure that you must be sitting on them! You won't be winning this one. If you persist in this cause—still not understanding a thing that's going on even though it all sits directly beneath your haughty little nose—you're likely to propel yourself right out of a job."

Blood spewed into Whitney's head and her temples began to pound furiously as she gasped in outrage. "How dare you!" she grated, unable to keep a cool tone in her voice any longer. "Of all the audacious, arrogant and egotistical statements! I can guarantee you that I will not be out of a job! It is you, Mr. Stewart, who will find yourself on the defensive! *You* who will lose—a fool through and through to both communities by the time I finish with you! You may have an advantage in the backwoods of the Everglades, Eagle, and you certainly did manage a few tricks! But we are far from there now. Nor can you keep me from discovering real truths!" Gritting her teeth, Whitney spoke her last words between them, very slowly. "I—will—bring—you—down!"

Eagle didn't quirk a muscle. The only sign of his own anger was a pulse that worked furiously in twin veins along the sides of his taut neck. Motioning again to the waiter, he silently signed the check. With silent menace he assisted Whitney from her chair and firmly escorted her from the restaurant. Wincing with protest at the iron grip propelling her, Whitney tried to wrench her arm away. "Stop it!" Eagle hissed in her ear. "This is one of your 'civilized' restaurants, and I refuse to brawl in public!"

A moment later they were standing in the parking lot by the BMW. "Give me your keys!" Eagle growled.

"I hardly think—"

"You're right. You don't think. Give me the damn keys." Eagle curtly grasped them from her fumbling fingers and none too politely ushered her into the car. "Don't worry," he advised acidly as he joined her, "I won't be with you long. I only have one or two things to say, but you are going to listen to them without a pack of snotty remarks in return."

"I don't have to—"

"The hell you don't!" Eagle's grip was now around her wrist, and she could barely twist her fingers, much less escape him. His handsome face, tense and rigid with anger, was inches from her own. A quivering of fear began to dance over her spine and she stared motionlessly into the flaring, hypnotizing blue of his eyes.

"Now, Miss Latham, since I seem to have your attention, I shall try to be very diplomatic. The land you have chosen has special tribal value to the Indians. Sentiment—

not dollars and cents. No matter what you offer, they will not sell. And they can prove in a court of law that the land is theirs. Keep your vendetta against me personal and wise up about the land. You'll hurt a lot of people by trying to spite me."

"I'm not making a business decision out of spite!" Whitney sputtered. "I know they can use what I want to give them!"

"Then handle this with the PR with which you are supposedly so proficient!"

"I—"

"Shut up for a minute!" Eagle commanded harshly. "Take some time and think. What you are doing is because of me, and I'm not even sure quite why. Just exactly what did I do to you? I couldn't tell you who I was that night—you would have put on your little professional act immediately, and I wouldn't have been able to make you understand a thing. I never lied to you. I am White Eagle and I did bring you to my family and they do live that way! Yes, some of our people have electricity and modern conveniences and some even live in your whitewashed houses! It's your anger against me that is keeping you from seeing anything! I gave you a culture, Whitney, and it doesn't seem to mean a damned thing to you! All you see is dollar signs and grocery stores and washing machines."

"You gave me a culture!" Whitney blurted furiously. "You did a hell of a lot more than that. You—you—"

"I what? I made love to you? I let you know that you were very much alive? That you were a warm, sensuous woman? You want to destroy me because of that?"

"Don't be ridiculous!" Whitney seethed. "You keep flattering yourself. You're are not so incredibly special! I—I loathe your touch, I—"

"You," Eagle interrupted scathingly, encircling her other wrist, "have turned into more than a self-righteous, misinformed do-gooder. You've become a liar."

140

"A liar!" Her voice was rising to a shrill shriek. "Get out of my car!"

"I intend to—in just a minute." He had twisted over her now, and his breath was a warm, moist breeze against her cheeks. "I'm giving you fair warning, Whitney. I can take you, and if you force my hand, I will. I can take you in any game you want to play."

"You'll have to prove that!" she hissed.

"I will."

The lips that had been hovering over hers were suddenly upon them, bruising and demanding. The assault was so swift that Whitney was momentarily in shock, unable to protest. By the time she gathered her wits back together, he had taken total advantage of the situation, prying into the cavern of her mouth with an insistent tongue. And in her stupor she was responding. Her senses had taken over, and after the days of deprivation, there was nothing more natural than the sweet, addictive ambrosia of his masculine lips invading hers, or the delicious eroticism of his commanding hands seeking the swells of her breasts, which rose automatically to curve for his pleasure as she arched to him. . . .

"No!" Logic, reason and fury finally tamed the wanton, instinctive physical response. Pushing the slender fingers that had risen to entangle in his black hair against him, Whitney echoed the choked scream. Eagle acquiesced—at his own speed, releasing her slowly. Whitney met the sardonic amusement in his eyes with desperate venom. She was dangerously close to tears she would never allow him to see her shed.

"Get out of my car—now!"

"I'm going." He sounded infuriatingly unperturbed, as well he should. He had controlled the kiss from the beginning. Had he chosen, Whitney thought with horror, he could have easily overridden her feeble objection. "I think," he said concisely, exiting the BMW with his fluid motion, "that I have proved my point."

Whitney watched in stunned immobility as he walked across the parking lot, tall, sinewed and exceedingly masculine in the perfectly tailored jacket that accentuated the breadth of his shoulders and the trimness of his hips and long legs. Then a white-hot flash of heat invaded her with renewed fury. She stormed from the BMW after him, catching up with him just as he entered the driver's seat of his own car, a quiet gray Mercedes.

Clutching the windowsill with white-knuckled hands, Whitney rushed into scathing speech. "You haven't proved a thing, Mr. Stewart," she declared vehemently. "You play tricks and take people unaware. That is all. I happen to know that I am right. That land is right where it should be—accessible! To your people. I intend to show them the benefits, and I intend to bring you into a court of law, where your devious ways will be ripped to shreds. I, Mr. Stewart, am giving you fair warning. Take some time yourself and go out and find yourself a good lawyer!"

A deadly grin stretched Eagle's grim lips.

"My dear Miss Latham, I am a lawyer. You just don't ever seem to have the pertinent facts, do you? I'm even considered to be a good lawyer. That's why I—an outsider —am representing the Indians."

The volcano was about to spew forth. Whitney spun on her heels just as the Mercedes roared into action.

CHAPTER EIGHT

It was a terrible thing to suspect you might be wrong, Whitney thought as she shifted in her lawn chair before the pool and tossed her towel over her burning face. Terrible, when you wanted so desperately to be right!

Almost a week had passed since her luncheon encounter with Eagle. Hate and anger had sustained her through the first few days; then uncertainty had set in. Was she so bent on vengeance that she had become blind? T and C had supported her ultimatum that they take the matter to court, but now she was doubting her own single-minded vision. A woman scorned, she thought bitterly. Well, her tantrums with Eagle could hardly be called mature.

"Aha! I've found you! Believe it or not, old man that I am, I would recognize that body anywhere!"

Whitney ripped the towel from her face and stared incredulously at the crinkling blue eyes of a smiling Jonathan L. Stewart. He was clad today in tan leisure slacks and a beige tennis shirt, and as he stood above her, his hands idly in his pockets, Whitney was again struck by the resemblance between father and son. Unwittingly she smiled. There was little else to do when met with the dazzling, genteel gaze of the senior Stewart.

"I hear you're on the outs with my son," Stewart said cheerfully, drawing another lawn chair next to Whitney's. "I hope you won't hold that against the father."

Whitney grinned sheepishly. "No, sir."

"Call me Jon," he suggested. "All my friends do."

"No, Jon," Whitney said. "I hold nothing against you." She frowned and grimaced suddenly and reached for her dark sunglasses in a pretense of blinking from the heat of the sun. He must know everything now! she thought in a rash of embarrassment. Well, not *everything*, but enough to allow his imagination to do the rest.

"Did your son send you here?" she asked suspiciously.

Jon chuckled. "You must be kidding, Miss Latham. My son is as stubborn—if not more so—as you are. I think he would stand his ground until the next Ice Age overtook it."

"Oh." She didn't voice the question, but it was in the air: *Then why are you here?*

"I'd like to see if you'd be willing to humor a senior citizen and spend an afternoon with me. I'll promise the reward of a excellent dinner in exchange for any boredom you have to endure," Jon said solemnly.

"Is this an appeal to my better nature?"

"Yes, frankly it is. If I know my son, if he became irritated, he never would get around to explaining things fully."

He didn't, Whitney thought silently. I didn't give him much of a chance.

"I shall be delighted to spend the afternoon with you, Jon."

"Good! Oh . . . uh . . . we won't mention this to anyone, if that's agreeable."

Whitney rose and stretched, chuckling. "*I* certainly won't say anything! Where are we going and what should I wear?"

Thirty minutes later they were back along a lonely stretch of Alligator Alley. A natural, comfortable friendship had grown between them, and they had discussed everything from world politics to the atrocious cost of meat in the supermarkets. Jon hadn't brought up his son's name. Neither had Whitney.

Jon's eyes slid from the road to Whitney. "Know where we are yet?"

"If I'm not mistaken," Whitney replied, "from the maps I've seen, we're close to 'the' land."

"Precisely."

Whitney stared into the marsh. There wasn't a thing about the area of swampland that could remotely be termed special. As if reading her mind, Jon curled his lips. "You won't see anything," he told her. "Not until we park."

"Park?" Having been away from the crude environ of the Glades, Whitney shivered involuntarily.

"Trust me!" Jon said with a laugh, and Whitney smiled feebly. Hadn't the son said much the same thing?

They turned onto a path that remained hard and solid for several miles. Eventually it wound around to bring them to a small hammock.

"This is part of the land parcel," Stewart said amiably. With a friendly arm around her shoulder, he led Whitney down a pretty, overgrown trail of flower-strewn pines. A moment later he stopped.

At first Whitney didn't see anything unusual. That was because all the earth tones blended in the scenery. Then she realized that there was a box ahead in a small clearing, resting upon a squat structure of logs. Alongside the six-foot box were strewn tattered and half-buried remnants of pottery, utensils and fabric. Years of exposure to the elements had made the entire picture part of the landscape, but as Whitney swallowed a lump in her throat, she could slowly discern bits and pieces of a human life. From ashes to ashes; dust to dust. She didn't need to ask where she was.

"The land is a burial ground," she whispered weakly.

"Yes," Stewart said softly.

An eerie feeling of pain seemed to transmit itself from the elderly man to Whitney, and she was suddenly sure of something else. They hadn't just stumbled upon any grave.

"This is your wife's—Eagle's mother's—grave."

"Yes," Stewart said again simply. He made no move to go closer to the coffin but stood in silent meditation for a moment. Then he squeezed Whitney's shoulders and led her back along the trail. They were in the car again before either of them spoke.

"Are there others?" Whitney asked softly.

"Many," Jon Stewart replied. "The government has begun to offer interment in special plots, but the grave site you've just seen is the way of the Miccosukees. For countless years they have taken their dead into remote spots in the swamp. Civilization has been closing in, but the swamp is vast. My wife, as I believe Katie told you, was half white, yet she was raised as a Miccosukee. It was her wish to die as one."

"What was she like?"

The wistful question was out before Whitney realized she had voiced it. Stewart didn't seem to mind. A tender smile filtered onto his lips with beautiful poignancy.

"She was everything to me—the sun, the moon, the stars. Lovely, soft, gentle. She had a way with her . . . even wounded animals found their way to her doorstep, whether we were in the woodland or in my town house in the city. Katie is much like her mother."

"What—what happened?" Whitney asked thickly.

Jon shrugged. "A stray bullet from an out-of-season poacher."

"Oh, God!" Whitney's whisper was half gasp and half sob. "I'm really so very sorry."

Jon Stewart lifted a hand from the wheel to pat hers briefly. "Don't be, really; not for me. I was a very lucky man. Not everyone gets to find love like that."

He was quiet during the long drive back, and Whitney was left to her reflections. The man beside her, she decided, was extraordinary. He spoke of life and love with a grave simplicity that was astounding in its depth. Man enough openly to declare his emotions with romantic reverence, he had lived his beliefs regardless of obstacles or opinions. Whitney was sure he would never marry again, yet his lost love did not make him morose. It was something he treasured quietly in the recesses of his heart.

And suddenly, as she sat mutely in the car, Whitney knew exactly what she wanted in life. To love and be loved—like J. L. Stewart and his Indian bride. To find a love that supported her and could sustain itself against the problems and idiosyncrasies of living together, a light in any darkness.

She sighed shakily. There was a man she could love that way. The man on whom she had declared bitter war.

"I promised you dinner," Jon said with a cheerful smile, "and I know a terrific little place on the shore, if you like seafood."

"Love it," Whitney assured him.

The restaurant did offer wonderful fresh seafood served in a rustic atmosphere that was pleasant and relaxing. Through the meal Whitney found herself confiding in Jon Stewart naturally, although she didn't go into much detail. She talked about her childhood, Virginia and even her brief marriage. Stewart, in return, talked about Chicago and his love for museums and theaters, and then how he loved to come back to Naples and spend quiet, peaceful times in the Glades with nature.

"I'm not much of a hunter," he told her, "but I do love to fish and I'm an avid bird-watcher!"

Their meeting at the Corn Dance was never brought up, nor was any mention of Eagle. The tone of their discussion had been so mellow and lulling that Whitney was taken by complete surprise when Stewart returned her to her motel room and bluntly asked, "What are you going to do now?"

"I—I suppose I'll battle T and C and look for other land," Whitney said. "I think I can eventually swing it."

"Will you tell my son?"

"No," Whitney said softly. "If we can come up with something else, he'll know when we meet in the planning conference."

Stewart hesitated for a second, then cleared his throat. "Whitney, I don't tend to interfere in other people's business, and I won't say much now. I know Eagle played quite a trick on you, but I think you might want to take a look at his motives."

Whitney bit her lip. She longed for the release of throwing herself into the gentle arms of the kindly, paternal man who had become her friend and to confess all that she was feeling, but she couldn't. She felt that she knew Eagle's motives all too clearly.

No, they had not been vicious. Devilish would be more like it. He had treated her to rare streaks of kindness and understanding. But to him it had all meant nothing. He had given, but in that giving he had torn her to shreds.

And she did still have her pride. The man had accomplished the feat easily of making an unmitigated fool of her.

"Jon," Whitney said lightly, "you have done your good deed for the day. I will get to work on a rational solution to this thing. But I have no intention of renewing a friendship with your son. And," she said as she grinned with rueful bitterness, "I sincerely doubt if your son cares one way or another. If he feels anything for me, I'm sure an accurate description might be contemptuous indifference." She felt herself beginning to blush. Should she add that Eagle might have found her an amusing bedmate? God forbid! This man she respected was most certainly well aware already of the more embarrassing details!

Damn! she thought, meeting his astute blue gaze. He was reading her mind! "Whitney," he said gently, "I'm going to say one more thing and leave. I promise. I don't expect any response. But listen, and then think about what I say. I know my son. His greatest sin is pride. He would

148

never come to you now. But he married you in a ceremony that he holds sacred. He loves you, and if I haven't gone senile I'm pretty sure you're in love with him too."

"He doesn't love me, Mr. Stewart," Whitney said with quiet dignity. "He married me because he loves his grandmother. He was very careful to tell me it wouldn't be a legal commitment. Besides . . ." she tried a nonchalant chuckle, "he married me when we had only known one another a few days. It's impossible to be in love that fast."

Stewart shrugged with an easy grin. "Oh, I don't know about that. I opened my eyes once and fell in love before I could blink. But I promised I wouldn't say anything more. I'm going to get going. And remember—our whole day is a secret, okay?"

"I'll remember," Whitney vowed.

She had barely closed the door before the phone started to ring.

"Whitney?"

The voice, she knew immediately, belonged to Katie. For an uncontrollable minute she started to laugh. It seemed that every Stewart she knew wanted to talk to her—except the one whose voice she wanted desperately to hear.

"Whitney? Are you there? Are you all right?"

"Yes, Katie," Whitney said, sobering. "I'm fine. What can I do for you?"

"I wanted to know if you were still interested in visiting the reservation and some of the independent villages along the Trail."

"Yes, I'd like very much to do some visiting," Whitney admitted. "When?"

"Tomorrow would be good for us—it's Sunday. How is that for you?"

"Fine."

They agreed on an early start, and just before she hung up, Katie asked the inevitable question.

"Oh—uh—Whitney, you won't mention this to my brother?"

"No, Katie, I won't," Whitney said dryly. "I really don't expect that I'll be talking to your brother."

There was nothing on the wire for several seconds except a slight static. "I'll—ah—see you in the morning, then," Katie said.

By late afternoon of the following day Whitney felt that she had been through a crash course on history and current events. Her curiosity over the Miccosukees had become insatiable, and she knew it had little to do with her job. She had reentered Eagle's world, and all that she learned was as much a part of him as the stunning and immaculately tailored suit he had worn to their elegant luncheon. She couldn't have him, but somehow being with Katie among the Indians was strangely comforting—although it also brought memories that ripped her heart to anguished pieces.

During the day she met men and women who lived extremely varied lives. She visited homes that ranged from the typical chickee to the whitewashed house of her own community. Some of the Indians, like Morning Dew, stayed in the densest woods and lived off the land, while others held important jobs. She even learned how electricity could be installed in a chickee.

As the day drew to a close Whitney stood with Katie near the cattle pens on the reservation, watching the final roundup as she chewed on a blade of grass. As she crunched into the sweet root, a frown furrowed its way deeper and deeper into her brow.

"What is that look for?" Katie demanded with a chuckle.

Whitney glanced at her guiltily. They had skirted the subject of Eagle and the past all day, but now it was she who wanted to ask a question.

"I've been wondering . . . I mean, I don't understand

150

your brother at all." Whitney glanced shamefaced at her hands to avoid Katie's eyes. "When I came down here I guess I really felt that the Indians needed help and that that was why they had a white man handling their affairs. Why didn't he start out by showing me how brilliant some of these men are—how far they have come in so many ways?"

Katie climbed up on the fence and stared out at the horizon, where the golden beauty of the setting sun in the Everglades could be seen. "You just said it yourself, Whitney. 'How far they have come.' Don't you see, you're going by your standards, which are fine. Our people are firm believers in live and let live. If you want a nine-to-five job in the city and a little yellow house with green trim and a flower garden, that's fine. But a lot of these people like to live in the Glades, the way their ancestors did for centuries. My grandmother grinds corn because she wants to. My father and brother are both wealthy men. Morning Dew could have anything in the world she wants. But she does have what she wants: custom and culture. She is happy to tend her garden and greet her family when they come back to her and the old ways, seeking comfort from the modern world. And we do go back to her, all of us. Eagle and I were raised to have pride in all that we are. I love my father and all that he is. And I love my grandmother, and I'm fiercely proud to be a Miccosukee. I can't speak for my brother, but I don't think he ever intended to hurt you. To tease you, yes; that's Eagle's way. He can be fierce, but I've never known my brother to be malicious. Have I made any sense?"

"Yes," Whitney said quickly. "Yes, of course." Ridiculous tears were forming in her eyes. Blinking rapidly, she pretended to feel a pebble in her boot and bent to remove it, shake it and put it back on.

"I think I should tell you, Katie," she said clearly, "that I'm going to try to find new land. I may have problems with the company, so I'm not going to make any promises.

151

We could still wind up bitter opponents in a long drawn-out court battle."

Katie laughed and jumped off the fence. "I'm not worried. We have certain sayings among our people. One of them fits you well, and it's a particular favorite of my family. When someone goes after something with determination and integrity, we say that they fly like an eagle. You, Whitney, fly like an eagle."

"Thanks," Whitney said and grinned. "That's quite a compliment. But, then, I've been flying with a few Eagles, so I've had some practice!"

It was so easy to hug Katie. Why was it, Whitney wondered, that she could earn the love and respect of the entire family except for the son?

Convincing T and C that another spot could be found for the community was a long and tedious job, especially after she had originally sworn to see the thing through in court and fight it out. The hierarchy sympathetically understood the intricacies of invading a burial ground, but Whitney was sure that the chairman of the board would dig up his own mother for a profitable venture. It fell to her to find new land, solve the problems of land fill and access roads and even deal with the new complaints of the builders. All within a suffocating schedule.

But she did it. A plot of land owned neither by the Indians nor by the government as national park space was finally located. Things began to fall into place and finally meshed on the Friday morning just before the conference scheduled for T and C management and members of the Seminole and Miccosukee councils—and Jonathan E. Stewart.

As she sat waiting at the vast conference table in the pleasant but comtemporary and austere meeting room, Whitney shuffled her papers and plans in a supreme effort to appear poised and unruffled.

She wasn't feeling in the least calm or sure of herself.

She yearned for a sight of Eagle, but she desperately feared her reactions. Just knowing that he would walk through the door at any minute was causing her pulse to beat erratically at atrocious speed. Her palms remained moist no matter how many times she tried to dry them on a tissue. She was terrified that the pounding of her heart would muffle her speech.

That was one fear she needn't have worried about. When he walked up and stood in the doorway, nodding to her curtly before his cool blue gaze swept over the room, her heart seemed simply to stop. One glance at his broad shoulders, encased today in tan tweed, his stern, rugged profile and his tall, imposing figure was all she needed to stop her entire respiratory process. She couldn't look his way again. Draining the water glass before her to ease a throat that had turned to cotton, Whitney returned her sightless gaze to her papers. Soon the room was full—and as soon as she looked up, Whitney wished she could crawl under the conference table and disappear.

She had completely forgotten that the council would consist of the same men she had stood before for her Miccosukee wedding.

Whitney felt like a frozen mold. She vaguely heard all the company introductions; then she was being asked for the proposal. She managed to stand, then she managed to make her lips move. She was thankful that all her information was in front of her in black and white; if it hadn't been, she wouldn't have even remembered what they were talking about.

The conference, she saw vaguely, was her victory. The Indians, Seminole and Miccosukee alike, who were as capable as Eagle of remaining completely stoic and giving no hint of any emotion, actually smiled. T and C Development employees were looking equally pleased; it was advantageous to look like the nice guy.

Whitney was the only one in the room who felt ill. As soon as she finished her presentation, she whispered the excuse of a severe headache to her associates and slunk quietly from the room. She couldn't face either Jonathan Eagle Stewart or the Miccosukee council. The refuge of her motel room was all that she sought.

But driving into the motel's parking lot, Whitney became convinced that there was such a thing as karma—and that she had done something truly rotten in a previous life to deserve the day she was having. Something that decreed she receive full and drastic punishment.

For standing at her door, impatiently studying his wristwatch, was her ex-husband, Gerry Latham. Slim, impeccable, graying Gerry. Mr. Right. Her father had carried out his threat.

It was difficult to conceal her irritation as she slammed the door of the BMW, gathered her briefcase and handbag and clicked her heels across the concrete as she walked to meet him.

"Hello, Gerry."

"Thank goodness you got here," he began immediately, taking her things and her room key in complete charge and efficiency. "I've been worried sick! Isn't that job of yours finished at five o'clock? I thought you'd been dragged back into the woods by another Indian!"

"What?"

"Your father told me all about it." Gerry looked distastefully around the adequate room and sighed. "You know, Whitney, I really don't understand you. We had such a beautiful home! A really nice thing. You are so young . . . I can see where you needed a little more time, but all this is so absurd—"

"Gerry, Gerry, wait." Whitney held up a hand and sank wearily into a recliner. "Stop. Whoa. Hold it. Let me correct you. I wasn't dragged into the woods by an Indian." A spark of mischief lit into her. "It was just the opposite. I dragged the Indian into the woods. And I molested him terribly!"

"Whitney!"

She should have had some sympathy for his look of horror, but after her long day she couldn't seem to help herself.

"Oh, Gerry! You just don't know! All those dances and secret meetings! It's so incredible—you couldn't imagine. The wild parties every night. . . ." He was still staring at her with such a dumbstruck expression that Whitney finally relented. "Gerry, I'm kidding. Believe me, dear ex, even you couldn't question the virtue of those Indians!"

Gerry shook his head and seated himself on the bed, musing over his slim hands. "I don't like it, Whitney. Neither does your father."

"Oh, Gerry! What's to like or dislike? This is my life!" Whitney settled her forehead in her palm and sighed. "And anyway, I've been working for T and C for years now! It's a highly reputable company. I'm good at what I do, and I enjoy it." The satisfaction of all that she had achieved warmed her, along with an old affection for a friend. Gerry would never understand her, but he did care about her. "Come on," she told him, rising and patting the top of his head. "Let's go get some dinner and I'll tell you about my job."

Maybe it was a good thing that Gerry had shown up, Whitney decided as they sipped predinner cocktails. If he hadn't, she would probably have given in to the tide of emotions surging through her and spent the evening in a crying jag. Being with Gerry didn't take Eagle out of her mind; he was always in her mind; she was always waging battles against herself. Sometimes she dreamed that the phone would ring and it would be Eagle calling her. But he didn't call. It was becoming increasingly obvious that he cared nothing for her, and that if he ever had, she had doused his feelings with her irate behavior. Sitting alone in her room at night, she would fight herself when her heart demanded that she find him, beg his forgiveness and be anything to him, even a casual playmate. Then she would come to grips with herself. She wouldn't allow him to make an even greater fool of her. But the pain of seeing him today. . . .

"So where is the new land?"

"Pardon?"

"The land. Whitney, have you been paying any attention to me?"

"I'm sorry, Gerry. It's not far. I'll show you the new site tomorrow if you like."

"I might as well see what you're getting into," Gerry replied grimly. "Although why on earth you want to run around playing in some godforsaken swamp—"

"Gerry," Whitney interrupted impatiently, "I do not play. I work, and I've worked particularly hard to make this whole thing come about amicably . . ." Whitney's final words trailed into a convictionless whisper. Beyond Gerry's shoulder, she saw the arrival of a handsome couple at the bar. The woman was a tall, willowy, natural blonde, probably a few years older than herself.

The man was Eagle, strikingly debonair in black velvet.

Whitney was vaguely aware that Gerry had launched into another lecture, luckily one that required little response. Her eyes and mind were on the dark, raven-haired man who towered above his slim companion and solicitously escorted her to a bar stool. His blue gaze was light, radiating a devastating masculine charm and charisma as he leaned to catch a response from the pale, lovely blonde.

Whitney had never known that jealousy could be such a brutal emotion. It washed over her in waves of agony, drying her throat, strangling her breath and seeming to stab a thousand little daggers into her insides. While Gerry droned on, she desperately tried to breathe normally and drag her riveted eyes from the couple before Eagle could see her.

Succeeding painfully in bringing her attention back to her escort, Whitney interrupted him. "Gerry, let's go. I—I'm getting a ghastly headache."

Gerry stopped speaking and peered at her suspiciously

through the muted light of the lounge. "You do look pale—almost green in here! Swamp fever, I'll bet," he said with satisfaction. "You should have never—"

"Oh, for God's sake, Gerry! I do not have swamp fever!"

"Then you must need something to eat. We've already given our name for a table. We'll dine as soon as possible and leave."

Every bone in Whitney's body felt as if it had gone as stiff as steel. "Gerry, I do not want to eat. I am not a child, and I know what I want. You stay if you're hungry. I'm leaving."

But she didn't get a chance to leave. Even as she leaned across the small cocktail table to hiss her words with quiet vehemence, a feeling of acute unease was making her senses tingle. Before she could withdraw from the apparent intimacy of her position, she knew beyond a doubt that Eagle had seen her and had come to their table. The light scent that was enticingly pleasant yet all male was on the air, though his footsteps were as silent in the lounge as they were on the trails of the marsh.

"Good evening, Miss Latham. Sir—" Eagle nodded to Gerry with stiff courtesy. "I hope you'll excuse the interruption, but I'd like to have a word with you, Whitney. Perhaps your friend won't mind if I steal you for a dance. I promise to return you directly."

Eagle had no concern for a reply from either Gerry or Whitney. He corralled her elbow and assisted her up while still speaking, turned a daring smile to Gerry while his eyes caught his in a frosty chill, and led her out to the dance floor, where a few couples were already swaying to the easy tempo of a mellow country band.

Whitney was stunned and spellbound. Still paralyzed by the jolt of his unexpected appearance, she was further bewitched and rattled by the inner tremors elicited by his manipulating touch. She had no thought for the blonde, or for Gerry, for that matter. Thought in its entirety had been swept aside momentarily by pure sensation.

And as they came together on the dance floor, Whitney experienced a rush of bliss. She nestled into his arms as if their forms had been made as a perfect fit for one another. Her head rested automatically on his shoulder; his chin was tickled by the soft silk of her hair. The arms that held her were fierce and possessive—angry, Whitney thought on a whim. Yet she would willingly take angry; she would take anything. . . . .

"I wanted to thank you on behalf of the tribal councils, Miss Latham," Eagle said curtly, dispelling the cloud of dreams upon which Whitney waltzed with the glacial tone of his voice. "I'm glad that you decided to see reason. You saved us all quite a bit of trouble with an early surrender."

Surrender! Was that how he saw her endless hours of work? A cowardly surrender because of fear of a meeting with him in court?

It was impossible to pull out of his arms, but he surely must have felt the steel that meshed into her spine. "My 'surrender,' as you call it, Mr. Stewart, had nothing to do with you whatsoever! I simply came across a few people who considered me bright enough to comprehend the spoken word. They merely explained the situation to me, and with amazing clarity I grasped the problem. They didn't even have to threaten me with exile to the nearest alligator pit!"

"Glib as ever," Eagle retorted, and the arms that held Whitney became stiff and wooden. "What was your previous assignment—a passionate encounter with the Blarney Stone?"

"Mr. Stewart," Whitney said concisely, tossing her head back to meet the icy blue daggers of his eyes with cool emerald, "you are the one who seems to be—ah—full of blarney, shall we say."

"I never lied to you."

Was there a touch of beseechment in his tone? No. That

158

was wishful thinking on her part. His eyes hadn't lost a fraction of their cold hostility; his grip hadn't gentled a shade.

"Omitting the truth is lying," Whitney said miserably. "You made me think you were an Indian—"

The hold that had been stiff was now painful and crushing. "I am an Indian, Miss Latham. For you to think otherwise—that is deception. I am the man that you met in the swamp that first night—unworthy, uneducated, uncultured—whatever that was to you."

Whitney wanted to protest, to explain that that wasn't what she had meant at all. She couldn't seem to summon breath or form words as he stared down at her, the pride and fury of his forebears stamped rigidly onto a countenance that gave no hint of relenting.

Lowering her eyes with a casual shrug seemed the only way to come to a draw. "What difference does it make? It's obvious that your blond friend doesn't care what you are. Perhaps you should bring me back to my table now and return to her. You've performed your duty on behalf of the councils."

"And you'd like to get back to performing yourself?"

"Pardon?"

"Always such lovely, wide-eyed innocence, Whitney!" Eagle marveled disdainfully. "Your executive over there. I gave you lessons; now you're eager to carry on with practice. He looks like a suitable specimen."

Whitney was dumbstruck. The music, the couples around her, even the man who taunted her blurred together in a seething haze that could only be composed of steam from her own burning body.

How could he possibly think that she could share the absolute intimacy that had raged between them with anyone else? His words sounded like a death knell as they hit her mind with the accuracy of a physical blow. Her nails dug automatically into the palms of her hands and she stiffened with flaming, narrowed eyes, subtly counterforcing to free herself from his hold with dignity.

But just as subtly his hold switched to the base of her spine and she was dipped back precariously. "Don't try to fight me, Whitney," Eagle warned with mocking menace. "You may have come out of your civil little meeting like a water lily, but I wouldn't push on a one-to-one basis."

"You are not a gentleman!" Whitney spat.

"No? Not always, I suppose. But then I seem to remember occasions when your behavior couldn't quite be called ladylike. Funny—neither of us was offended. In fact, I really didn't mind in the least seeing you be a female instead of a lady—"

Whitney clenched her teeth tightly together and grated, "If there was a civil bone in your body—"

"But there isn't," Eagle interrupted in a deathly chilling tone. "And not being civil or a gentleman, I tend to say whatever comes into my mind."

Whitney longed to cry that she wanted only to be the female in his arms, but to what end would her words be? His contempt for her was pathetically obvious. He would surely laugh and—worse—return to the lithesome blonde anyway.

Tilting her head back, she smiled at him sweetly through half-closed eyes. "Whatever we are, White Eagle —lady and gentleman or not"—she sniffed disdainfully in opposition to her sultry, feigned grin—"I do suggest we get back to our respective partners. As you say, I'm eager to practice, and it appears that the lady entwined with the bar stool might be hungry to teach the teacher a few new tricks."

There was a combustible moment following her acidic speech when Whitney held her breath in terror, certain that the anger within Eagle would explode and she would be the recipient of unleashed violence. A play of emotions filtered rapidly through his eyes, moving so quickly she couldn't begin to fathom them. His grip, she knew, would leave bruises on her flesh, so tense was it.

Then, miraculously, he released her. "Don't let me hold you up," he said. "Go back to your friend. I don't want to be the cooling factor in anything that might be getting hot. The blonde entwined with the bar stool happens to be my secretary and the tricks she performs are with a typewriter, but you're right, I should get back to her. It would be showing my uncivilized tendencies to leave her any longer."

Eagle nodded briefly and quickly walked away, leaving Whitney on the dance floor, tears brimming in her eyes. Blinking, she made her way through the dancers and out the front door.

Gerry would have to pay the check and follow. She had to get out of the room before she fell apart.

But Eagle wasn't watching her, so he didn't see the unguarded pain that filled her eyes and sent her wretchedly into the night. He was fighting his own lack of control, fiercely battling instincts that demanded he sweep her from the bar and abduct her back to the woods and make love to her over and over until she realized that it could never be the same with anyone else. The idea of her with another man was driving him mad, eating up his insides inch by inch. If he looked at her one more time he would become irrational.

Damnit! He behaved irrationally every time he saw her now! He, the attorney, the Indian, the man born and trained to ultimate concealment of emotions, allowed himself to be ruled by his possessive anger and to lash out heedlessly when he really meant to crush her in his arms.

The lawyer in his mind told him he had no right.

But the man in him decreed that he did.

And in the space of time it took him to return to the bar and order another drink, the man won the battle.

She was his, although she didn't know it. They had declared their vows before the Supreme Being—One who

161

was surely the same to all men. She was his wife. And he meant to keep her. All the desire, possession, protection, irrationality and anger added up to one thing that made the most complete sense in the world.

He loved her.

CHAPTER NINE

For once in her life Whitney didn't have a single difficulty in dealing with Gerry. She refused point-blank, no non-sense, to answer any of his questions. In unsparing terms she informed him that she was his friend and that was it. He was welcome to be an interested party in her work; he was welcome to view his trip as a visit to a friend.

The rest of her life was none of his business, and, as nicely as possible, he was welcome to tell her father the same thing.

Gerry, as disbelieving as he had been when she asked for the divorce, shook his head with little patience but wisely left her alone at her motel. He wound up having a solitary dinner surrounded by boisterous teenagers at a local hamburger joint.

Whitney spent the night in abject misery. Locked in the privacy of her room, she paced the floor relentlessly, exhausted herself, then threw herself on the bed and moaned for sleep, then paced the floor again. Intermittently she would grow angry, sure she had been used; then the tears would start and she would be sure she had only herself to blame for acting impetuously and speaking without thinking.

Not that it really mattered anymore. Whatever had existed between her and Eagle was now irrevocably over. Maybe she should think up an excuse and run back to Virginia. Here she ran the chance of seeing Eagle again frequently. The tear in her heart would constantly be reopened and she would never have the time needed to heal such a wound.

If time really did heal broken hearts. At the moment she was certain the pain she felt could never be assuaged.

It was close to dawn when exhaustion finally brought her relief in sleep. She felt she had barely closed her eyes when the insistent ringing of the phone brought her back to an unhappy stage of consciousness.

A second of wild hope at the sound of a male voice was immediately dashed.

"It's Gerry," the voice said irritably. "Latham. Remember me? You're still using my name."

"Oh. Good morning. What—ah—time is it?"

"Eight. As a friend, I thought you might be willing to join me for breakfast. In a decent restaurant. I had heartburn all night."

She had to get out of bed, and she had to face the world. She had offered to take him to the new land site, and since she was scheduled for a meeting with the land-fill people and the environmentalists, she should really take a trip for her own benefit. Even if she did decide to tuck tail and request another transfer, she had to keep up with her work until a replacement could be hired, and then she would be required to make damn sure that everything was up to date and handled smoothly.

"Sure, Gerry. The motel has a nice coffee shop. We'll have a good breakfast and I'll show you where the development will be."

"Fifteen minutes?"

"Twenty." Whitney made a face to the phone and hung up.

The face that greeted her in the bathroom mirror looked like hell. Groaning, she showered quickly and spent the remainder of her twenty minutes trying to repair the damage done her by the sleepless night.

Funny how she had felt after a different sleepless night.

Then she had been making love, and she had awakened feeling tired but content. The world had been beautiful.

Today she felt as if she should be lowered into the nearest hole in the ground.

"Life goes on," she told her reflection. She had been living without Eagle for weeks now. Why should anything be different?

Because she had thought the land hearings would change everything. Eagle should have raced after her when she left the conference room. He should have told her that he had loved her all along.

She had been living a pipe dream, but real life had intervened. And now she had to face reality. Head on. It wouldn't get any easier. She had lost her heart, but she did still have her pride. And with a good base coat of makeup over the shadows beneath her eyes, no one else would ever need to know that the dream in her life was over.

A light touch of blush took the white hue from her face. What the heck, she told herself, applying a light green shadow and brown mascara. Go all the way. With a coat of moist lipstick, she actually looked good.

Or so she thought.

"You look like hell," Gerry told her.

"So I've been told," she replied, adding silently, by myself! "Could we forget me and my looks for a while?" she begged. "Tell me about home. How is my mom doing with her garden?"

Gerry amicably kept the conversation light while they ate, filling her in on all the little happenings since she had left Richmond. His tone remained easy the entire morning, until Whitney drove to Alligator Alley and down the path that led to the proposed sight in a company jeep.

Reaching the land filled Whitney with a sense of contentment and keen satisfaction. It was largely marsh right now, but she had been assured that filling the area was highly feasible without causing damage to the expanse of the Everglades. She could envision the planned community—affordable, pleasant, widely spaced homes that were encircled by the natural beauty of the area. Children would live in the homes, and they would have old-fashioned swings tied to the sturdy branches of the old cypress trees. The builders would work around the canals and lakes, and the unusual animal life would not be uprooted from its natural habitat.

Gerry was not sharing her future vision, Whitney realized quickly. He began ranting as his shoe slipped in the mud while he followed her on a short footpath that led to a 'gator hole.

"This is it, Whitney! The grand finale! That you haven't already killed yourself is amazing! Why on earth do you want to wander around this horrible hellhole anyway? Damnation!" He swatted viciously at a mosquito. "Dratted things. What the hell else is around here? Snakes, I'm sure. And God only knows what other creatures. You're going to need a fumigation squad before anything else! And it isn't for you. I never saw you swat a fly, Whitney. You look nice in dresses, not mud. We are going to leave this minute, and if you won't listen to me I'll have your father down here—"

"Gerry!" Whitney shouted his name in disgust. "My father cannot send me to my room! Neither can you! I live here now. And I'll be spending many days in this 'hellhole.' Christ, Gerry, look around you with an open mind! There's beauty here, Gerry. If you can't see it, I do! And I'm not budging. You go back to Virginia! Tell my father whatever you want. And if he can't appreciate any of this, he can just go home, too!"

"Whitney!" Gerry gasped. "What has gotten into you? Have you no respect for the man who raised you? I just can't believe this. I refuse to believe this!" He set a slim hand over hers with purpose. "We are leaving now. You don't know what you're doing, and somebody has to take responsibility for you."

"I am not going anywhere! I have things to see here.

166

When I finish I will take you back to the city. And then I'll drive you to the airport!"

Gerry's hand didn't move. He stared at Whitney as if she were a belligerent child.

"Excuse me, but I think you heard the lady. Let her go."

Both Whitney and Gerry spun in the direction of the softly spoken but forceful, determined words. Neither had heard a thing in the wilderness to warn them that a third party had come upon them.

A weakness came into Whitney's system. It was Eagle.

He was all Miccosukee as he stood before them, his legs apart in tight jeans, his arms crossed over a chest that was covered by a braided jacket. His blue-raven hair gleamed in the traces of light that shimmered around him.

The look in his brilliant eyes was all challenge, all warrior.

"Who the hell are you?" Gerry demanded.

Eagle raised a single, imperious brow and advanced toward them with his cat tread. "What difference does that make?"

Whitney had to stifle a smile. Poor Gerry! He was in beyond his league, and he didn't recognize the man from the previous evening. How could her ex be so blind, Whitney wondered. She would recognize Eagle's piercing blue eyes and majestic stance if he were dyed green and covered in snow!

"It makes a tremendous difference!" Gerry said heatedly, confused but refusing to be daunted by an Indian in the woods. "You're interrupting a private matter between a husband and wife—"

"She is no longer your wife," Eagle interrupted quietly.

"What?" Gerry stuttered.

"She is no longer your wife."

"All right, then! Ex-wife! But I'm responsible for her well-being and she doesn't know what she's doing out here and I'm taking her back to the civilized world!"

"Whitney is free and over twenty-one. Where she chooses to be is her own concern."

"Whitney!" Gerry repeated explosively. He stared at her accusingly. "You know this man?"

"Yes. I do," Whitney said quickly. She felt as if she had been watching a tennis match, following the ball back and forth across the net, an observer, not a participant.

"All right, so you know my wife—" Gerry began again to Eagle.

"Ex-wife. I underline 'ex,'" Eagle said calmly.

"Ex. Ex, ex," Gerry sputtered. "What difference does it make to you? This is a private matter and none of your business."

"This is very much my business," Eagle replied with deadly certainty. "I find Whitney to be rather capable. I believe she knows exactly what she is doing out here. It is her right to stay. As to my rights—well"—he allowed his gaze to roam contemplatively over Whitney, the slightest hint of a mischievous twinkle in the depths of his blue eyes—"that, sir, is why I find myself stressing the preface 'ex.' You see, the lady is my wife now. And although I find her completely responsible myself, I assure you that you have no need to worry yourself over her further. I take that upon myself."

Whitney didn't know whether to cry or to burst into laughter. Gerry's amazed statement voiced her sentiments exactly.

"I don't believe this!" he ejaculated.

What was going on, Whitney wondered. Did Eagle mean what he was saying? Did he really consider her his wife? More likely he had stumbled upon them and simply decided to help her—now that he knew who Gerry was—out of simple pity. Perhaps he felt he owed her one because of the land.

"Believe what you like, Mr. Latham," Eagle said with a shrug. "But Whitney and I were married almost a month ago. Just a few days after she came south. It was one of those shotgun affairs"—Whitney could clearly see the teasing light beneath the darkly arched brows—"except it was my grandmother after us instead of the usual bride's father."

"This is preposterous!" Gerry stated rigidly. "Whitney, is this true?"

"Yes—"

"It can't be legal! You're not tied to this—this—"

"Indian?" Whitney supplied innocently.

Gerry glanced at her reproachfully. "This man," he said indignantly. His eyes narrowed as he looked at Eagle, then widened as dawning comprehension came into them. "The restaurant!" he exclaimed. "That was you—"

"Yes," Eagle said pleasantly. "That was me. And while we're on the subject, my name is Stewart. Legally, that is. And you do seem to be concerned with legalities."

"I'm a lawyer—" Gerry began.

"So am I," Eagle interrupted, waving a hand coolly in dismissal, "and as such, sir, I've learned that human nature has little to do with the law. It's my understanding that you and Whitney have no legal ties. And yet you are here, and she is with you. That is a tie, one that goes beyond a piece of paper. I believe that you are legitimately concerned for her, and that she cares for you—as a friend. That's why I'm making such an effort to maintain patience." He walked forward to them on his silent tread until he stood just a foot away from Whitney, and though he continued to speak as if he were addressing Gerry, his eyes were hypnotically locked on hers. "However legal that ceremony was, Whitney is tied to me. I think she knows it." For a moment he continued to stare at her, and the hammock in the woods was held in an eerie silence, as if time had stopped and they all waited in suspended animation. Whitney was suddenly keenly aware of all the little sounds in the cypress glen: the breeze rustling softly through moss and sawgrass, the drone of a fly, the light crackle of dipping branches.

And she was aware of Eagle. He did not touch her, yet he did. It seemed as if the blue steel of his eyes bore through her, searching out her soul, commanding her heart. But she didn't dare move or speak; his eyes were as hard and relentless as his ramrod stance, and fathomless. Was he telling her that they were even, that the score had been settled?

Or was he really staking a claim to her?

He stepped back and turned once more to Gerry. "I hope," he said with a slight edge of contempt, "that I shall never need to depend on a legality or a piece of paper to hold what is mine. Should that ever be the case, I doubt if there would really be anything to keep." He nodded grimly to Gerry, pivoted and started back up the path.

Immobilized, Whitney watched him until his broad shoulders disappeared into the brush. Then her feet took flight, and completely forgetting Gerry, she raced after him, to catch him breathlessly as he was hopping into his own jeep, which was parked behind hers.

"Eagle!" She shouted his name, but as he settled into the driver's seat and acknowledged her, her throat constricted and her words refused to come. There wasn't a hint of softening in the blue chill of his eyes, nor did he encourage her to come to him in any way. Halting a few steps from the jeep, she stared at him blankly, at a loss.

"Yes?"

"Thank you," she said inanely.

Did she imagine it? Or did a trace of disappointment filter through the glacial blue steel?

"Not at all," he said wryly. "Is that it?"

"I—I—" she floundered.

Muttering an impatient oath, Eagle sprang from the jeep. Stalking her roughly, he gripped her shoulders with tense fingers that bit into her flesh. She winced, but he didn't care. He had come to claim her, simply to demand her by right. And if he stayed much longer, he would.

But the scene he had come upon had changed his mind.

170

At first he had wanted to act like any normal jealous male and rip Whitney away from the man who threatened her, shove her protectively behind his back and simply proceed to settle the matter with his fists.

But something had held him back. It might have even been pity. Gerry Latham was not really his rival. It was clear that he no longer had any hold on Whitney. Despite his highhanded tactics, it was pathetically obvious that he still loved his ex-wife.

Without thinking, or rather because he had been thinking, Eagle gave Whitney a rough shake. And where she was tongue-tied, he found words he never meant to say tumbling curtly from his mouth.

"What is he doing here? Why have you brought him out here to begin with?"

Whitney slowly leaned her head back so that her hair fell behind her in a long, dark wave and her emerald eyes met his. They had been strangely blank; now they turned tremulous, and then defiant, and Eagle wished fervently that he had handled the whole matter differently.

He had meant what he said to Gerry—Whitney was his, but only because the tie would be of her own choosing.

And that was the way he wanted it.

"Do I owe you an explanation?" Whitney demanded.

"Yes," Eagle said, and softly added, "if you feel that you do."

Before she could answer him, Eagle pulled her to him and his lips descended over hers. They came down hard, and the punishing grip on her shoulders shifted to the small of her back, pressing her to him.

Her form was pliant. It molded to his, which was what he wanted. He wanted her to feel his strength and heat, the way his hands could take her delicate form, the way his body could press to her with natural need.

Then, as she clung to him with the response he had barely dared hope for, had desired with all his heart, his

171

kiss took on a subtle change, teasing softly, his tongue parrying lightly where it had plundered.

He was gambling.

She was arched to him, straining against him; the fullness of her soft breasts crushed into his chest, begging to be held and caressed.

Eagle allowed his hands to move enticingly along her back. His fingers roamed just beneath the material of her shirt, inch by inch up her ribs. . . .

And then he pulled away.

Whitney was stunned. She blinked, and then a flood of humiliation washed through her at the ease with which he could draw complete capitulation from her and then coolly set her aside. What was it the man really wanted? Shakily she opened her mouth to say something—anything—as long as it was suitably scathing.

"I—" was as far as she got.

"You," Eagle interrupted, and as his crystal gaze held her he was a cross between that man who had boldly declared himself to Gerry in no uncertain terms with assured control and the one who had leaped from the jeep to claim her, "have some thinking to do. And"—he lifted a brow and tilted his head toward the path where they could now hear Gerry stumbling through the brush—"a little unfinished business to attend to." Running a finger lightly from the tip of a high cheekbone to her chin, he added huskily, "You have to decide just where your ties are, Whitney. I want you, but though I don't wish to subjugate you, I promise that being mine, I will be the dominating force in your life. As you will be—and have been—in my own." His lips curled ruefully at the corners. "I'm learning that I can be very dominating, demanding and possessive where you're concerned. But you hold the cards, my love. The final play is yours. I've told you what is, what will be. The choice is yours." He tapped the tip of her nose lightly. "If you want me, Whitney, come to me."

172

The trees near the clearing were beginning to crackle as Gerry, muttering curses to the mosquitoes and the uneven path, neared them. Eagle smiled briefly and both brows raised in sardonic amusement. "Pick a husband, Whitney. Personally, it's my suggestion that you get that one back on a plane for Richmond. He may not be a bad guy—it's obvious that he does care about you—but he's dismally out of place here. And with you—I know that now. I guess I knew it from the beginning; I just needed to *feel* it."

With a last little salute he spun around and vaulted back into the jeep. Whitney, still searching for her tongue, stared after him, amazed. She had listened with virtual speechlessness to all he had had to say, and after his first angry questions, he hadn't expected a single answer. He had told her to come to him, and then he had walked away.

"Whitney!" Gerry stumbled from the trees, dusting his cuffs, as Eagle's jeep graveled away in a cloud of dust.

"You didn't have to leave me alone!" Gerry grumbled gruffly. Whitney finally peeled her eyes from the disappearing vehicle to turn distractedly to her ex-husband.

"What?"

"Oh, never mind." Oddly enough, Gerry seemed amused. He set an arm lightly around her shoulders. "Get me out of here, will you? Then you can get back to your Indian."

"Pardon?"

"Listen, Whitney," Gerry said with a smile, still brushing at his clothing uneasily, "on that score I don't need a road map." He flicked a tendril of her hair softly from her face with a sigh of sadness. "Whitney, I did come here for the wrong reasons. I wanted to bring you back to Richmond—and back to me. But Stewart had some things to say that made sense. And more than that, Whit, I saw the way you looked at him. You never looked at me like that."

"Oh, Gerry," Whitney said miserably.

173

"Don't," Gerry interrupted, "it's okay." He headed for the jeep. "Shall I drive?"

Whitney nodded mutely and climbed in beside him. Her heart, mind and emotions were spinning crazy cartwheels.

Eagle had come to the Glades to find her. In straight terms he had announced that he believed in her, he had defended her in front of Gerry. . . .

And he had claimed her as his—if that was what she wanted.

Even his brief streak of jealousy had come quickly under control. He was a towering pinnacle of strength, one that neither suffocated nor strangled but stood sturdy, offering support.

She had really been a fool, allowing anger and pride to come between them. She had walked out on him once without giving him a chance at explanation.

And since then she had given him little but argument.

Now she had a chance to walk back into his life. Many things still needed to be said on both sides, but they were all so inconsequential.

A small smile curved her lips. He had threatened to dominate, but she was learning that love's domination could be a wonderful thing. It did not hinder or bind but led to growth and wove those webs that were of one's own choosing.

All she needed now was nerve. And belief.

Cartwheels were churning in her stomach again. It would be so hard to go to him! Already niggling doubts were worming their way into her resolution.

Had he really said he wanted her? And, she wondered wistfully, did he love her?

He had yet to say the words.

CHAPTER TEN

True to his word, Gerry was ready to take the first available shuttle out of Naples. In less than two hours since they left the Glades, Whitney was standing with him before the gate that led to his small plane.

With his hands upon her shoulders, he smiled affectionately and kissed both her cheeks. "Good luck, Whitney."

Impulsively Whitney hugged him back. "The right woman is out there for you somewhere, Gerry, and when you find her you'll know it beyond a doubt."

"Oh? How?" he asked skeptically.

"Skyrockets!" she told him impishly. "You'd better get on that plane."

And then she watched as her "unfinished business" rumbled, circled and flew north.

It was showdown time, and her nerves began to jitter even as she left the airport. And as she had once wondered in the waters of the hammock lake, her question was, Where is that damned man?

Come to me. Where? And then she was suddenly sure. He had gone to the place where they had sealed the vows of their love before any commitment had been spoken.

Nervous but determined to follow her course, Whitney stopped at her room and called her office to announce that she would be gone for a few days. Susie cheerfully accepted her message and then had one to give her.

"Mr. Stewart called for you this morning. I told him I

believed you had gone to the land site. Did he ever get hold of you?"

"Yes," Whitney said and smiled. "He certainly did."

Saying good-bye, she slowly replaced the receiver, elation adding to her jitters.

Eagle had not just stumbled upon her. He had come out purposely to find her.

Slow, she told her pounding heart. Before she allowed herself to take flight in dreams, she still had much to do, and she had to be sure. . . .

Picking up the phone again, she dialed his office. She could now picture the soft-spoken blonde who informed her that Eagle Stewart had left the office early that morning and would be out indefinitely on personal business.

This time her hand was shaking so badly she had to fumble with the receiver twice before she reset it correctly. She was holding a very special happiness in the palm of her hand.

Don't let me lose it, God! she prayed silently.

There was one more call she had to make—the hardest. But the day was fading fast, and there was only one way she knew of to reach the Eagle settlement deep in the Glades. . . .

Flipping through her address book, she found the number for the Big Cypress Reservation. As she was passed from person to person and put on hold, desperation began to grow within her, a stifled sob catching in her throat as she waited.

She had to reach Eagle today. She couldn't bear another night of uncertainty . . . and if she waited, the doubts and fears would come back full force and she might lose her chance.

"Randy!" She breathed a sigh of relief as he finally came to the phone. "I really hate to do this to you again," she began after he had happily greeted her. "But I need another favor. This time I have to get back *into* the reservation. I have to find Eagle, and I'm sure he must be out with

Morning Dew. Randy, I know you must be busy, but is there any way you could get me out there today?"

Randy chuckled, and Whitney could well imagine him grinning on the other end of the wire. He would be wearing that lopsided smile that stated he found women irrational yet wonderful little creatures that needed to be humored. Maybe he was feeling like a smug-as-pie matchmaker.

Whitney didn't care. As long as he felt like humoring her at the moment.

"I'm sure I can work something out, Whitney. Go on out to Eagle's cabin in the woods, and I'll round up Katie and meet you as soon as possible. You do know the way to the cabin?"

"By heart," Whitney replied wryly.

"Good. Then see you soon."

Whitney was standing and grabbing her shoulder bag before they could say good-bye. She raced out of her room and to the BMW and out once more to Alligator Alley.

A rueful smile curved her lips as she pulled into the long dirt drive that led to the cabin. Had it only been a month since she had first followed this trail—a different Whitney, so sure of her convictions?

It had all started here, a slow process of learning, taught by a man of quiet strength whom she had given herself to before she had begun to understand. It was almost as if fate had sent her, frightened and blind, down this trail and directly into the arms of the man who would open her eyes to love.

Randy arrived with Katie in just moments, and they set out together in the jeep. Neither of the Harrises had any questions or comments to make about her mad desire to see Eagle as soon as possible; indeed, they acted as if her calling them to rush from work to take the long ride into the heart of the swamp was the most natural thing in the world.

Their conversation was casual yet strangely close and

intimate in the jeep. Once they had begun the trek through the sawgrass in the airboat, they all had little to say.

Whitney scanned the acres of marshland with growing trepidation. Was this what Eagle had meant? Was her coming to him in the deep Glades the sign of trust he needed?

"*Pa hay okee,*" Katie said softly.

"Pardon?" Whitney was jolted from her fearful reflections to turn to her.

"*Pa hay okee,*" Katie repeated, spreading her arms to encompass the land they streaked through. "River of grass. It is our homeland; it succors and supports us, because we love and cherish it for all that it is. I think it is your homeland, too, Whitney."

"*Pa hay okee,*" Whitney whispered, smiling at Katie. She didn't need to say any more; a slender bond existed between the two women, one of the ties Eagle had spoken of, born of friendship, understanding and mutual respect.

When Randy finally pulled off to the high hammock of the Eagle clan, Whitney felt her nervous jitters escalate into full-scale, trembling fear. The closer she came to that which she most desired, the more terrified she became of rejection. Reason warred against her fears. All those things Eagle had said! The way he had held her . . . the way he had kissed her. He had to really want her! Still, she was grateful for the company of Katie and Randy.

Except, she discovered, she was about to lose that company.

Katie kissed her cheek. "See you later, Whitney. I'm going to like having a sister!"

Were these people all mind readers, Whitney wondered as she quickly demanded, "Where are you going? Aren't you going to stop and see your grandmother? Randy? I'm sure Morning Dew will be very upset if you don't—"

"I think," Randy interrupted gently, "that Morning Dew is probably expecting you. My brother-in-law may be sweating it out a bit, but Morning Dew isn't. You go on,

Whitney. This is your family, too. This is your special time. Find Eagle."

Whitney's eyes darted from Harris to Harris. It was a little late for doubt, but she was riddled with it. Was Eagle really here, waiting?

"Katie—"

"Whitney, go on!" Katie laughed as the airboat propeller began to spin. The craft moved off into the marsh and Katie waved and called, "You will find him!"

Alone, Whitney fought the butterflies in her stomach and searched out the little trail in the cypress. A moment later she came upon the village. The women and children acknowledged her with smiles and words of greeting.

They were not surprised to see her.

Following the second trail, Whitney came to Morning Dew. The old woman with the keen, bright eyes and weathered face was sitting before the cooking fire, complacently sewing. She didn't look up until Whitney stood before her; then she smiled as if welcoming a child who had made it home promptly on time for dinner. Whitney knelt beside her and took a gnarled and work-worn hand into her own.

How much did Morning Dew know, Whitney wondered. What did she think of her disappearance from the Corn Dance? Would she understand how long the road had been?

The Indian woman stared at her with gentle eyes that seemed omniscient and all understanding. Whitney realized she needed no explanations; there would be nothing new that she could tell her.

"Eagle," she whispered simply, controlling the tone of desperation that was edging her voice. "Eagle," she practically sobbed. "Oh, Morning Dew! Do you know where he is?"

"Hush, little one," Morning Dew soothed in her perfect, unaccented English. "He is here. Where your heart has led you. He is by the lake. He waits." Her wizened features formed a grimace. "Eagle is not all Indian, you know, and right now he is living with a white man's fears. You must go to him and calm his soul and your own. He has not put his faith in the laws of the spirits."

Whitney bit her lip lightly, afraid to leave the absolute conviction of the older woman.

"Go now," Morning Dew prodded. "We will have time, you and I, later. Years to learn better of one another. But now you must go. My grandson—your husband—awaits you."

Whitney needed no further urging. With a last smile for Morning Dew, she raced down the trail to the lake with her heart plummeting crazily. She sped through the cypress as if chased by the devil, then halted, mesmerized by shivering apprehension.

Here she was, in the swamp, by the lake, where her journey had taken her. But what now? Oh God, what now? What did she say?

And Eagle was there. She saw his back first, rippled with tight muscles and bared to glow bronze beneath the dying sun. She itched to run her fingers over the sleek skin of his broad shoulders and press her lips against his flesh, to reach up and touch the thick raven hair. . . .

But she held back. He hadn't seen her yet. She couldn't see his eyes, couldn't read into his heart.

He turned suddenly, knowing that she was there, framed by the ridge of the cypress. Whitney's breath caught in her throat. He was just staring at her, his hands in the pockets of his form-hugging jeans. A gentle lash of waves from the quiet lake washed over his feet, soaking his pants legs, but he didn't seem to notice. He was frozen like a statue, watching her, his blue gaze startling and compelling but fathomless.

The man who stood as solidly as an oak was trembling inside like a young boy. She had come! Guided by the chemistry of hearts and minds that beat together, she had sought him out. As he watched her, her quivering immobility between the flanking cypress trees, he thought lovingly of all that she was. So delicate beside him! Yet like the beautiful orchids of the Everglades, she was strong and tenacious. From that very first night he had loved her, although he had fought against it. And now he wanted to speak; he wanted to reach out and touch the petal softness of her face. He needed to take her into his arms and promise that they would never be apart again.

Whitney was growing desperate. Damn him! She had come all this way, and he wasn't saying a thing! If his relentless stare of steel persisted much longer, she would run screaming back into the woods.

No, she had come this far. If it was another step that she must take first, then she must take that step.

What could she say? How could she begin?

Maybe it was one of those times when action would say more than words. And time to turn the tables a little.

She was shaking, but a show of bravado could be perpetuated. Leaving the haven of the trees, Whitney stalked slowly toward the lake, keeping her eyes locked with Eagle's. He followed her every movement but still stood silent.

Three feet from the water Whitney began to undo the buttons of her blouse. Removing the garment with a sultry lack of haste, she tossed it to him, smiling mischievously when his reflexes forced him to catch it. With slow deliberation she stooped, unzipped her boots and kicked them nonchalantly aside.

It was the first strip-tease she had ever performed, and it was hard to calculate its effect on her audience, but feminine instinct told her it was going well. Eagle hadn't spoken, but the pulses in his neck were becoming fast and erratic. A feeling of happy power was coming over her. The desire she was hoping to elicit made sultry emeralds of her eyes, and she shimmied from her jeans with a tantalizing rhythm.

Eagle could have moved then. He could have reached

out, crushed her to him and allowed his hard, burning body to demand all that she was offering. But he waited, now with tender, aching amusement. What she was doing was sheer torture, yet it was the sweetest bliss! His body was as taut as a thinly stretched tightrope; his nerves clamored in a cry of thrill and agony for him simply to force her curvaceous, taunting form into his arms and take her with blunt command to appease the rising passion that strained to be released.

But somehow he knew it would be worth it to wait, as he had already waited all these weeks. The smile that was slowly curving his lips was an assured one; he would soon reap his just rewards for superhuman patience.

Whitney saw the smile and her heart skipped a beat. What she had begun, she knew beyond a shadow of a doubt, he would finish. Her fingers suddenly became leaden, and as she slipped the stubborn hooks of her French-cut bra and hastily discarded her panties, her cool was somewhat lost. Not all that practiced at being a seductress, her nerve was ebbing, especially as she realized that the eyes watching her had gone a murky midnight blue that promised of things to come. . . .

Whitney ran her fingers through her dark hair and tossed her head back. Feigning complete innocence, she plunged into the deliciously cool water, swam a bit for distance and rose like a mermaid from the depths. Water streamed from her hair and over her breasts in tiny rivulets of crystal. Watching form the shore, Eagle shuddered as a jolt of flaming, uncontrollable desire burst inside him and ripped its way through his entire length.

"Join me?" she teased breathlessly. "I assure you, I will not attack you." Her voice lowered a shade and the husky tone held a note of beseechment. "It is your move, White Eagle."

It was his move all right, Eagle groaned to himself, but could he make it to the water? He'd never had more trouble unbuckling a belt in his life.

"Hey, there!" Whitney laughed. "What's the problem, Flapping Feather? Get in here!"

Eagle grinned. He finally managed to undo the brass buckle and release the fly on his pants. "What's the hurry?" he drawled. "I mean, after all, honey, if you *don't* attack. . . ."

His voice trailed away as his clothes fell to the dust and he entered the water in all his natural, ultravirile, male splendor.

"Even the best of us can be provoked," Whitney murmured.

His raven head suddenly disappeared beneath the water, and Whitney caught her breath. She plunged below the surface herself and began to swim blindly in an elusive manner. It was a foolish gesture. She would never outmatch his prowess in the water.

A powerful hand clamped around her ankle and she sputtered awkwardly to the top, flailing for balance as he continued to hold her foot high.

"Let go of my foot!" Whitney demanded in between a fit of giggles. "You uncouth rogue!"

"As you say, madame," Eagle replied politely. He jerked her foot and released it, sending her back to the bottom.

Whitney rose to the surface gasping. "Okay, Flapping Feather!" she choked. "This is it. You will get yours!"

Eagle's blue eyes danced with a hellfire. "Oh, I do hope so!" he declared. "I'm counting on it."

Whitney crashed through the water and into his arms. Her breasts crushed into his chest and the nipples hardened at the sizzling contact. Her face nestled into the curve of his neck and she clung to him, radiating in the simple ecstasy of being back where she belonged, of feeling their hearts beat as one.

Eagle caught the hair at the base of her neck and forced her to face him. The bronze skin was stretched tautly over his proud features; the dancing light in his eyes had been replaced by the smoldering cobalt blue. "Are you sure you don't want to talk first, Whitney?" he demanded harshly.

"No!" She shook her head vehemently.

He held her tensely for a second and then sighed his relief. "Good. I don't think I could do much talking."

His lips came down on hers with a fierce possessiveness that left her quaking and gasping for more. Then his head disappeared beneath the water again, but this time his game was in earnest. His teeth moved over a nipple with a gentle tug that sent sparks igniting to her core. Then his erotic water kisses and nibbles moved leisurely all the way down to her toes. When he surfaced again, it was to scoop her into his arms.

Whitney's breath was coming in short pants as she slipped her arms around his neck and looked tenderly into his beloved face. "Much more of that and I could quite cheerfully drown," she purred huskily in spurts of air. "I'm glad we're heading for shore."

"We may not make shore," he muttered hoarsely. His arms tightened around her and his murky-lashed lids fell so that his eyes were sensuous slits. "And I intend that you should drown, my love. Drown in me forever."

They reached the shore—just. Eagle set her down gently so that the water still washed in ripples along her legs.

Then he moved over her, and foreplay was discarded as they both emitted strangled groans and became entwined in a desperate and urgent mutual hunger. Tears of unprecedented joy came to Whitney's eyes as their unleashed passion raged to new pinnacles of erotic, shattering, mystical sensation and Eagle urged her ever onward, telling her of his gnawing need, of the awesome pleasure of all that she did, of the perfection and beauty of her undulating hips.

The culmination of their fierce intensity was explosive. Whitney's cry of sweet, sweet ecstasy rent the twilight air, and before its echo had settled into the sheltering cypress, she was moaning slightly, her contentment so great that the world continued to swirl until her form slowly, slowly began to relax. As always, Eagle held her tightly to him as they regained their footing on solid earth, his touch gentle and soothing now, no longer a rough and demanding magic.

He was glorious when he made love, Whitney decided. Most delightfully glorious. She wouldn't have it any other way.

He shifted after a moment and leaned on an elbow to watch her as he ran enticing patterns over her belly.

"I love you, you know," he said with velvet softness. "More than I'll ever be able to tell you. I'm not sure exactly how or when, but you wound me hopelessly around that delicate little finger of yours."

Whitney inched more closely to his chest, relishing the wonderful masculine scent of him. "I love you."

"I want to marry you in a church as soon as possible."

Whitney chuckled. "That's lovely, darling, and I'd like it very much. But, my dear Jonathan White Eagle Stewart, you had better start considering yourself a married man right now. You have had a wife since the first night of the Corn Dance."

"Oh? Is that so?" Moving with his startling agility, he pounced over her and his eyes blazed with teasing menace into hers. "Then you'd better consider this! Don't you dare—ever!—get it into your mind to pull another disappearing act or I'll skin you alive and tan your hide! Got it?"

"Yes, sir, yes, sir!" Whitney pledged with mock, round-eyed obedience. "But, Counselor, I only plead guilty with an explanation to the first charge! You were leading me down a primrose trail and laughing your rear off all the while."

"No, I wasn't, Whitney," Eagle said, suddenly serious. "I admit I did want to get to you, but it was more than that. I knew there was something special about you from the moment I plucked you from the mud. Even when you

185

were being an impudent snob, I really wanted you to understand. It was important to me that you realize chickees were not hovels, and, of course, that I do speak English. Rather well, in fact."

"Oh, quit!" Whitney pleaded. "Won't you ever let me live that down."

"Never, love. I cherish all my memories too dearly."

Whitney frowned suddenly and ran her fingers tenderly down his cheek. "So do I," she whispered. "Especially my memory of this morning. But I don't understand. After last night—"

"Last night," Eagle said sheepishly, running his fingers through her hair, "I behaved like a thwarted lover. I had no idea whom you were with, and seeing you with another man—when I had become sure we could work things out—drove me half wild. Then I began to cool down, realizing things weren't always what they seemed. You had thought I was 'with' my secretary. I finally put two and two together. I realized the man you were with had to be the infamous Gerry. I had ribbed you cruelly because of simple jealousy. And as far as I was concerned, too, darling, you were already my wife. It frustrated the hell out of me not to be able to do anything about it! I called your office in the morning, determined to have an honest showdown, and they told me you were going out to the land site. I decided to follow you."

"Thank God you did!"

Eagle's brows knit tightly together. "At first I wanted to strangle that ex-husband of yours. I knew a lot about your relationship, but he was with you, and love isn't always rational. He didn't look like a terrible person. Are you sure it's over?"

"I never said Gerry was a terrible person!" Whitney laughed. "He was amazingly decent after your appearance. He was as positive as I that it was all over. He told me to go to you, and I put him on a plane. Everything is over for me that doesn't concern a wonderfully crazy Indian attorney!"

Whitney's eyes shone with bright emerald love, and their track of conversation was temporarily lost as Eagle kissed her with gentle sweetness, savoring the magic moments of revelation. When he finally pulled away, it was to draw a long, shaky breath. "Where were we?" he murmured, bewildered at the way he could lose himself completely in her enchanting warmth.

"Right here, love," Whitney whispered dreamily.

"Now wait a minute, wanton witch," Eagle said with a laugh, catching the slender hand that teased along the length of his back. "I have a few questions. What made you change your mind when it was so stubbornly set? About the land, and me."

"It was simple—your father told me I was trying to build on a burial ground. Then your sister convinced me that you were right—culture and custom mean more to many people than convenience and electric stoves. I'm really a very reasonable person!"

"Hah!"

"I am."

"It may take you a few years to convince me of that," Eagle said with a chuckle, running a finger over her lips with thorough fascination. "So that old coot of a father of mine went after you, huh? No wonder he was so smug about things working out!"

"He's something special," Whitney said softly, "And I'm very grateful to him! Without him, there wouldn't be a you!" She raised a questioning brow. "Is he still in town? He told me he lived in Chicago."

"Yeah, he's still in town. He told me he missed the first wedding so he wanted to hang around for the second!"

Whitney giggled. "I think you're all a pack of Hindu mystics, not Indians! By the way," she demanded, "just what will my name be?"

"Mrs. Jonathan Eagle Stewart, of course."

187

"Of course!" she mimicked with an impish grin. "And where will we really live?"

"We"—Eagle scowled—"will really live at my permanent address—a nice little house in a pretty beach section of Naples called Port Royal. However, I do own the cabin in the woods. And I have permanent reservations for a certain chickee. Do you mind?"

"Not in the least," Whitney assured him innocently. "Although I admit I'm not certain I could spend my life in a chickee, I have become partial to certain of the dwellings. And I love rustic little cabins in the woods. Besides, my love," she told him huskily, "my ties are firmly knotted. I would sleep with you anywhere."

"Sleeping wasn't exactly what I had in mind," Eagle declared with silky insinuation. "Not yet, anyway. Strenuous activity before bedtime is known to improve the quality of your rest. Did you know that?"

"No. Really?" Whitney fluttered her lashes guilelessly and ran a taunting finger lightly over his taut abdomen, delighting in the quiver and sharp intake of breath that were his response. "Then, since we seem to be busy people who need their rest, I suggest we engage in lots of strenuous activity."

Eagle laughed and pulled her tightly to his hardening body. "A most pleasurable suggestion." His lips began a knowing forage against the sensitive flesh of her throat.

"Ummmmm . . ." Whitney murmured, allowing her fingers the wonder of sinking possessively into his sleek raven hair.

He continued to play upon her body with expertise and draw from it the response of a beautiful, perfectly tuned instrument.

The golden globe of a shimmering orange sun sank slowly in its descent into the horizon. The light was dazzling upon the glassy water in reflection and cast graceful shadows upon the birds caught in silhouette like shadows in the dusk. For a second Whitney mused upon the vivid, primitive loveliness of the land she could now call home.

Then it all became part of a splendor that was rightfully hers. Her lover claimed her undivided attention again and she was among those that soared the gold-streaked skies, in flight with an eagle forever.

WHEN NEXT WE LOVE

For E. D. Graham,
who taught us dreams could be real.

PROLOGUE

She had known him for years, yet she didn't know him at all.
They had been the best of friends, the worst of enemies.

But tonight it didn't matter. There was no past, and of course,
as only she knew, there would be no future.

Just the night.

And she hadn't even planned it. Things were simply working
out that way, and she was powerless to call a halt. She didn't
want to call a halt. In the back of her mind she knew she had
wanted him for an eternity. But consciously, even with the surrounding magic and music—and the fair amount of liquor she
had consumed!—she would never admit that it was really him
she wanted, or that want had a deep root in her emotions involv-
ing him.

And it wasn't really *her* who wanted *him*. It was the exotic
belly dancer of her disguise who was falling in love with the
handsome and noble King Arthur of his whimsical attire.

And he didn't know who she really was.

The opportunity was too good to miss. He would never know.
The rinse had successfully colored her hair black; the blue-tinged
contact lenses completely hid her own eye color. Heavily applied
bronze-toned pancake makeup had taken her normally cream
complexion to a much darker hue, while carefully drawn lines
and heavy shadows of dark rich color had given her eyes a
mysterious, Far East cast. The lower portion of her face was
misted by a veil of fine silk gauze. Perpetually leaning to the slim
side, the trauma she had endured over the past few months had
taken its toll upon her weight, and her costume, floating and
flaring over curves now highlighted by gaunt shadows, did the
rest to assure her complete change of person so that not even her
mother would have recognized her.

It had started as a lark. She had intended to announce her

identity later in the evening. Then it had all gone so well . . . of course, it was understandable. She hadn't seen any of them in a very long time.

He had singled her out immediately. Their eyes had met across the room, and his had swept over her with astute appreciation. And before she knew it, she was in his arms.

And it felt so good, so *right* !

Had he been King Arthur in truth, Lancelot would have never stood a chance. He was everything wonderful—tall, strong, arrogantly masculine, and yet unceasingly tender.

When he suggested that they leave, she didn't blink an eye. She didn't bother to think about the deceit she was weaving; it didn't occur to her. She was caught in her own fantasy, unmindful of the repercussions that could follow. To her, they were strangers who had known one another forever, timeless lovers, partners in a dance that had just begun.

She vaguely noted that Pinocchio and a Dresden doll were discussing the London Company as they neared the pair, lamenting the death of the lead guitarist, Richard Tremayne.

"They're still on top, though," Pinocchio said admiringly. "I always did say that Derek Mallory was the talent behind the group."

"Yes, but Tremayne was exceptional," the Dresden doll commented.

"Umm—a genius," interrupted a Fruit of the Loom grape. "I hear his wife helped him, too. Has anyone seen her? They say she clammed up, wouldn't see or talk to anyone."

"I invited Leigh," Pinocchio said. "I guess she couldn't make it."

"Maybe she knew Derek would be here," someone snickered. "And he knows—"

"He knows what?"

The demand came curtly from King Arthur. She was forced to stop and snap into reality for a moment as he challenged the group.

"Nothing, nothing," was the mumbled reply.

194

"Leigh Tremayne is a sweet lady," Pinocchio said sincerely.

"She was my best friend's wife," King Arthur returned in a deadly voice that held definite warning. "I don't like to hear gossip about either of them. Richard is dead. Let him rest in peace."

"We all loved Richard," the Dresden doll said softly, easing the tension that had risen. Then she smiled at Arthur. "You're not leaving, are you?"

"Yes," Arthur said. "But thanks for a super party."

Pinocchio glanced longingly at the belly dancer by King Arthur's side. "You can't leave! We still haven't figured out the true identity of your lovely lady here."

"Neither have I!" Arthur chuckled, grinning at her. "But I intend to."

She almost panicked. They were scrutinizing her too intently. But she held on to her composure and smiled, then affected a superb Irish accent learned from a doting grandparent. "You'll have to think on it then, friends, for we are indeed leaving. But I add my thanks for a terrific night."

They were watched as they left the party. He, because he would always draw attention by the authority of his regal size and unusual eyes, she because she was simply stunning, an enchantress tonight. The eyes that observed their departure mirrored many human emotions—admiration, wistfulness, curiosity, envy, and downright jealousy.

They were barely conscious of the stares that followed them. He was too enamored; she was too busy fighting her nervousness and pushing all the little fears that confronted her to the back of her mind.

He'll never know! she repeated over and over to herself. And finally, she was convinced.

And so began the fantasy, the most wonderful night of her life.

It was slow and easy and wonderful. He took her to a house he was borrowing from a friend for the weekend nestled among the magnolia trees, and they listened to the gentle strains of classical music before the light radiating from the mellow fire.

They talked for hours, as the embers cast their dying glow, and she was relieved as the shadows became deeper, and the darkness became the protector of her identity. Even after he had asked her to remove her veil, he learned nothing of her, nor did he press. He too seemed to know that the night was mystical, a fantasy spun with silken thread.

Their talking tapered into comfortable silence. He rose slowly and offered her his hand. By mute agreement she trustingly accepted him, and when she, too, was standing, he swept her as effortlessly as stardust into his arms and lay her tenderly on the bed, where he began to disrobe her with loving reverence.

She was naked now, more susceptible than ever to discovery. But she was lost in an endless field of longing and desire, totally absorbed by the magnificent male form before her, framed in a silhouette by the pale light of the moon like a true king. His lips touched her flesh and created a wildfire, his hands worshipped her, his limbs, against hers, demanded and possessed. He teased and tormented, feathery light, soft as a breeze. Then his tongue traced the mound of a firm breast and he drew his teeth over a hardening nipple. She moaned low in her throat and her fingers sank into his hair. Gentleness was lost in a swirling, urgent vortex of passion as darkness surrounded them. He whispered husky words to her, words of hunger, of thirst, of sweetness, of awe. He would never have his fill of her.

And she whispered back. Shyly at first, then boldly as she learned she held the same captivating power over him that he did over her. She did, in fact, learn much that night, for he had not lied. He could not drink his full of her soft enchantment. He possessed her as she had never been possessed before, loved her with a beauty she had never imagined. Through the night she marveled at the wonder of giving herself to such a man, of being so completely his. He demanded, he took, and he gave her ecstasy, a ceaseless cloud of sensual adoration and pleasure.

Too soon the dawn broke across the heavens. She awoke with a start to find herself entwined with him, her head resting on his golden-haired chest. Pain raged through her mind with the acuteness of a cruel stabbing. It was over. Carefully, very carefully so as not to waken her sleeping king, she disengaged herself and quickly redonned her costume. The contact lenses were cutting her eyes like a thousand slivers, but she didn't dare remove them until she was far away. She scampered to the door, but stopped. She had to go back. Just for a moment. Just to kiss his sleep-eased brow one more time.

Her lips touched his skin, then she backed away. His eyes were beginning to flicker. She made it to the door before he awoke and called for her to stop. Begged, demanded. But he knew that she was fleeing. "I'll find you!" he assured her, stumbling for his pants.

"No," she said, and her voice was torn with sadness. "You don't know where to look."

Then she was gone, racing away, plummeting back to undeniable reality. She knew he chased her, but the gods of fantasy were with her. Like the magic created, she disappeared into thin air.

Well, actually, she disappeared into a city cab. But it made no difference. She was gone to him forever.

Because she was a real woman, and he despised the real woman who she was.

CHAPTER ONE

Leigh Tremayne shrugged away the chill that assailed her as an unattached voice demanded her name and business after her Audi pulled to a halt in front of the massive iron gate. It wasn't really the voice that bothered her, she realized. She had been to Derek's Star Island estate before and knew what to expect. What was disturbing her, she admitted, was that she was coming closer and closer to the inevitable—her meeting with Derek.

"It's Mrs. Tremayne," she called irritably. "And you'll have to ask your boss what my business is!"

The gate rolled silently open. For a moment she merely stared at it, her fingers frozen on the wheel of her car. She was suddenly panicking, wishing she had never agreed to come. Then she pushed such ridiculous notions aside and turned the key in the ignition. There was no reason for her not to come; there was no reason for her to fear an encounter with Derek Mallory.

She drove slowly up the gravel driveway and past the manicured lawns, unconsciously smoothing back a wispy tendril of light auburn hair. Acutely aware that there was a good possibility that she was being observed by an electronic eye, she made no attempt to check her appearance. Besides, Richard had once assured her—in the days before he had begun to find fault—that her beauty lay in her "classic nobility of presence." And at twenty-seven she had come to an age when she was capable of assessing herself objectively. She might not be a great beauty, but she was an attractive woman. Almost elegant at times, thanks to the sophistication Richard had laboriously drilled into her. And today she had drawn on every natural asset and every grain of hauteur learned from her late husband. Her copper hair was knotted simply on her head beneath the rim of her low-angled beige hat; her large hazel eyes were subtly highlighted by blended

198

green and brown shadows; her "classic" cheekbones were pronounced by a slight touch of blush.

As she crawled lithely from the car, she casually straightened her beige skirt. She had chosen the outfit, and the three-inch heels despite her slender five-nine frame, for a businesslike and aloof effect. Derek certainly hadn't called her to renew an old friendship. He had made his opinion of her quite clear at Richard's funeral, and they hadn't parted on the best of terms.

Derek, although he didn't say it in so many words, blamed her for the wasteful demise of his friend and partner, Richard Tremayne, undoubtedly one of the finest musicians of the twentieth century. The world mourned Richard sincerely while it seemed to Derek that his widow did not.

But what Derek didn't realize, she thought wryly, was that she had mourned the loss of her husband long before his death. And she had loved him. She had given him her heart, soul, and mind and catered to him completely until she began to lose her own existence in the shadow of his growing tantrums and demands. Then she awoke one day with the bitter and sad assimilation of the truth. Richard loved her in his way, but not enough to grant her the individual devotion of a normal marriage partner. Toward the end he cruelly pointed out that she should be grateful just for the privilege of being his wife. He kept her well; she could have anything in the world. He had literally given her fame and fortune. His laughter when she tried to explain that she didn't want the world but a stable home and family had been the final straw. She had filed for divorce, but Richard's untimely death had left her a widow instead of a "Ms."

The shrill cry of a mockingbird startled her into realizing that she had been staring blankly at the whitewashed facade of Derek's deco mansion. Shaking herself sternly, she climbed the five tile steps of the curved outer doorway and briskly clanged the heavy brass knocker. She was happy now, meeting each day with cheerful anticipation. She had mourned, but the past, with all its good and bad, belonged in its proper perspective. And if Derek Mallory intended to tear down her present complacency with accusations and disapproval, she would be back out the door before she ever sat down.

"Come in, please, Mrs. Tremayne."

Leigh was greeted by Derek's staid and proper butler, an English import like his Waterford crystal. Although Derek and the group spent most of their time in the States, they still considered Great Britain their home and often liked elements of "home" around them. Leigh also knew that the popular conception that the group had risen from the slums of Liverpool was absurdly far from the truth. Each of the five original members of the band had been born to affluent families. Derek, in fact, would one day be Lord Mallory.

"Thank you, James," she told the austere butler. A slightly wicked smile curved her lips. It always amazed her that James, so amazingly dignified and correct, could consistently maintain his rigid discipline of manner amidst the frequent cacophony of his employer's world. "How have you been?"

"Fine, madam, thank you," James replied without a twitch of his countenance. "Now if you'll follow me, please, I'll take you to Mr. Mallory. He's been expecting you, you know."

"Yes, I know," Leigh said smoothly, but James was moving down the cathedral-domed hallway before the words were out of her mouth. She hurried after him, listening to the sharp click of her heels on the Venetian tile of the floor. James was leading her to Derek's large office, a room where he carried out his business affairs and also kept a perfectly tuned grand piano so that he could work whenever the impulse came to him.

James swung open a set of varnished oak double doors, and Leigh stopped abruptly behind him, her eyes drawn to the man at the cherry-wood desk.

Derek was casually seated. His long, jean-clad legs were stretched on top of the desk, crossed at the ankle. A pair of Adidas sneakers adorned his feet, a simple navy tank top exposed more of his broad, golden-haired chest than it covered. His sturdy tanned hands and incredibly long fingers were engaged in holding a ledger and scribbling upon it. His handsome features—

high arched brows, deep golden-brown eyes, long aquiline nose, and beard-fringed, sensual mouth—were taut, tense, and engrossed, as if the ledger before him posed infinite problems. At the sound of their approach, he glanced up sharply, his gaze falling quickly from James to Leigh, a dark, fathomless gaze that seemed to strike her with the force of a physical blow, divest her of chic clothing down to the vulnerable flesh, even go beyond the flesh and bare the terrible beating of her heart to open view. How ridiculous! she admonished herself. Cowardly whimsy. Derek couldn't possibly see a thing except a well-dressed young woman.

"Mr. Mallory, Mrs. Tremayne," James announced unnecessarily. He made a clipped goose step and disappeared down the hall.

"Hello, Derek," Leigh said coolly, striding into the room with what she hoped was assurance.

He rose slowly, almost insolently, from his relaxed pose, towering several inches over her despite her own regal height in heels. A shaft of light streamed in from the huge bay windows, highlighting his hair, his beard, and rippled chest to reddish gold as he reached out a hand to take hers, enveloping its fine-boned smoothness in a firm grip. Leigh struggled inwardly to prevent her facial muscles from forming a wince. She was experiencing a far worse reaction than she had expected. It felt as if the long fingers that held her so lightly were charged with electricity, sending shock waves of heat through her entire system. She withdrew her hand as quickly as she could after his slow return of, "Hello, Leigh," dismayed to note the flash of amusement that flickered through his golden-brown eyes at her obvious haste.

"Sit down, will you," he suggested cordially, indicating a comfortable straight-backed but thickly padded chair opposite the desk. She silently acquiesced, taking the opportunity to study him covertly from beneath the shade of her downcast, fluffy lashes.

Derek was undeniably possessed of an innate, animalistic charm. It was something he had a vague acceptance of, like his thick, shaggy hair or deep, compelling eyes. He was superbly built, sinewed but slender, his height belying his true strength and breadth. Powerful, taut shoulders tapered to a steel-flat waist and trim hips and long, well-muscled thighs. Yet his sensuality was not a physical thing, not in that sense. It was part of his languorous movements, his shrewd eyes, his deceptive conviviality. Derek was like a cobra. A woman could find herself hypnotized by those magnetic eyes, lulled by that sleek, fluid grace, then suddenly struck, the victim of a swift and venomous attack. A woman could, if she allowed herself to be vulnerable. And vulnerable, Leigh swore silently, she would never be. In the early days of her marriage she had adored him. Her husband's best friend had become her own. Even then she had been acutely aware of his devastating sexuality. But in those days she had considered herself immune. Her equally charming and talented husband demanded her complete concentration. And then of course Derek would never have dreamed of touching her. Since Leigh was his best friend's wife, Leigh knew that Derek would rather die than touch her.

But they had been close. For a time, very close. When things began going wrong, Leigh reached for him. And that was when she began to despise him. He turned on her coldly, accusing her of being heartless and mercenary, a frigid, uncaring wife.

Sustained by her memories, she stiffened rigidly in the chair and stared up at Derek imperially. He was now standing before the desk, leaning haphazardly against it, scrutinizing her as she had been him, except openly.

"Why did you ask me here?" she snapped bluntly.

"I wanted to see you," he returned immediately, undaunted by her antagonistic tone.

"Obviously!" she drawled with tart sarcasm. "Why?"

He grinned easily. "My, my!" he mocked. "The ever-sweet, conniving little wife did turn into a waspish widow. Defensive and suspicious. Why not take this at face value? Why not believe that I was simply concerned for your welfare?"

She grinned back with equal malice. "Because I know better.

And defensive, Derek, I'm not. Suspicious—yes. Very. Why don't you get to the point? *What do you want?*"

"First," he replied firmly, "I want you to have a drink. It might have a dulling effect on that razor-edged tongue you're brandishing." He didn't wait for her assent, but clanged a bell on his desk, his eyes never leaving hers. "What would you like?"

She stood angrily and protested, "I do not want a drink! I want to finish this meeting and get out of here!"

She gasped with shock when all appearance of polite cordiality dropped from his features and he took one menacing step toward her, planting his hands on her shoulders and pushing her roughly back into the chair. "Sit, Mrs. Tremayne, and have a drink!" he ordered in a low growl. He did not release her, but continued to challenge her, his fingers biting into her flesh in subtle warning. "I insist."

The features above her were rigid and grim; the muscles that held her in their command were tense and strained. For a moment she stared into his angry brown eyes with indecision. She was no match for him on a physical level, but she could scream! Yet, what good would that do? She had the uneasy feeling that James would merely walk in stiffly with his usual calm, set a tray of drinks on the desk, ask Derek if there would be anything else, and totally ignore her whether she was screaming bloody murder or not!

"I'll take a glass of wine," she said glacially, refusing to blink as she met his commanding stare with marked resentment.

Derek moved away instantly. "Good, love. I'm glad to see that you're beginning to see things my way."

Leigh forgot her aloof reserve. "I'll never see things your way!" she cried, shocked by her own vehemence. Why was she allowing herself to become emotional?

Derek raised an arched brow in mock surprise. "What? Is that a crack I'm seeing in Madam Frost? How amazing! I thought that blood had long ago ceased to run in your veins!"

Leigh contained a retort as James chose that moment to enter the room. Derek requested a carafe of wine and as poker-faced as ever James exited to comply. As soon as the double doors were tightly closed, Leigh was once more on her feet, this time ready to do battle. A springing leap put the barrier of the chair between her and Derek

"I'm getting out of here, Derek," she hissed with ringing bravado. "I was crazy to come. I knew all you wanted to do was insult me and—"

"Stop, please," Derek said quietly. He scratched his forehead tiredly and sighed. "I really didn't mean it to be like this. I'm sorry. It's just that you sailed in here like Her Majesty the Queen and I reacted badly. I knew this would be difficult for both of us. But maybe it's better that we started out this way. Maybe we've cleared the air a bit. Please, sit. We won't talk about the past or anything personal except in the context of the present. Agreed?"

Leigh watched Derek guardedly, feeling like a fox being conned by a hound. If only he had continued to be rude and harsh! Then she could have logically called a halt to their meeting and blamed the disaster on him!

She had to admit that she wanted to stay. When she had heard from Derek, after fourteen months of silence, she had been quite surprised. She told herself it was only curiosity that caused her to accept his invitation to Star Island for a "mutually beneficial" meeting. But although she would never admit it on a conscious level, it had not been curiosity that had brought her. Honestly not understanding why they *had* become bitter enemies, she still simply wanted to see him.

"All right, Derek," she said slowly, sidling back into the chair. "I'm willing to listen to what you've got to say."

This time he didn't hedge for a second. "I want to finish the rock opera on Henry the Eighth," he said bluntly.

She stared at him for several seconds without a muscle in her face moving. Then she whispered, "Why?"

"Because it is good."

Leigh looked down at her hands, dismayed to find that they were trembling. The rock opera was hers. Although Richard had

204

often taken her work and ideas and claimed them as his, he had scoffed at the one composition she had put her most loving effort into. He told her it would never sell; he wanted nothing to do with it. To the best of her knowledge, Derek had only seen the rough draft once. He had displayed interest in the project, but that interest was quickly squelched by Richard, who had dismissed it with a wave of his hand, telling Derek with apparent loving humor that it was just an "exercise" for his wife. Leigh hadn't bothered to dispute him.

Now she glanced back to Derek, trying to find a motive for his renewed interest in his penetrating eyes. His expression told her nothing. Careful to keep her voice nonchalant, she reminded him, "You know that Richard didn't write any of the songs. He helped me with the music, but he didn't even like the work he did himself."

"I know."

Leigh crossed her legs and reached into her bag for a cigarette. Moving with surprising grace for a man his size, Derek took a marble lighter from his desk and was on his haunches in front of her to light a flame before she could. She wished she had never dived for the cigarette. It was hard enough to hide her pleasure over his apparent belief in her work with him several feet away; having him so close that she could feel his warm breath on her cheeks had made it an impossible task.

"I haven't looked at it since Richard died," she said noncommittally.

"I doubted that you had," Derek said without moving. His presence at her side, literally at her feet, was totally unnerving. She could smell a pleasant hint of musky cologne, feel the vigorous, coiled tension that made him so very alive and exciting.

Exhaling a long plume of smoke, avoiding his eyes, she asked quietly, "What did you have in mind?"

He raised teasing brows and she blushed. "I mean, do you want me to give you what I have? Are you going to take it from there? Are we going to bill it as Richard's final work? I'm not sure he'd like that."

Derek finally stood and ambled back to his desk, running his fingers through his curly hair. "No, no, no, and you're probably right. I want you to plan on staying here for the next month. You and I will finish it together. We won't bill it as Richard's work, although he will be listed in the credits."

A knock on the double doors prevented Leigh from making a stunned reply. James entered with the wine on a silver tray as she had expected. He deftly poured and delivered two glasses, nodded in response to their mumbled thank yous, and decorously left them, closing the doors with a definitive snap. Leigh took a long sip of wine and finally spoke, breaking the uncomfortable silence that had formed between them. "You are either crazy, a sadist, a masochist, or all three!" she breathed uneasily.

Derek broke into spontaneous laughter and hefted himself to a sitting position on his desk. "I can never say you aren't honest about your feelings!" He chuckled. He twirled his wineglass and absently watched the gold liquid as it rolled about. His voice tightened harshly as he added, "But don't worry. I know what they are. Still, we got along very well at one time. I think we could work together on a strictly professional basis."

"But, Derek!" Leigh protested. "I couldn't possibly stay *here*!"

"And why not?"

"Because . . . because . . ."

"Are you worried about your reputation?" he demanded scornfully.

"No . . ."

"Then what's the problem?"

"Oh, Derek!" she exclaimed with disgust. "You know perfectly well what the problem is! I have no intention of staying with or working with a man who considers me responsible for—" She choked, unable to go on.

"Don't!" he scoffed coldly. "Don't play the bereaved widow with me! I know all about the divorce papers! I know Richard asked you for a reconciliation! I know you turned him down flat. So let's keep everything on an honest level. I think the work you were doing was good. I'm sure you'd like to see it become a reality. I can help you. We both make money, we possibly come out with a memorable piece of music. That's all."

Leigh wanted to scream. She wanted to shout the truth into Derek's callous face. Sure, Richard had never wanted the divorce. But he wanted their marriage to stay on *his terms.* And those terms meant that Richard did what and saw whom he wanted. Leigh stayed home, always there when he decided he needed her, quiet, loving, and unquestioning, even when Richard came in at four A.M. with lipstick stains on his shirts and musky odors of unfamiliar perfumes.

She didn't scream or shout. Rising slowly, she crushed out her cigarette and set her half-consumed glass of wine on the desk, ignoring Derek. She walked back to the chair and picked up her bag before turning to him. "Derek, I can't work with you. We don't seem to be able to carry on a simple conversation. You have your opinions . . . I can't seem to change them and I don't know if I care what you think anyway. Thanks for calling me, though, it was a nice thought."

She should have completed her explanation, spun on her heels, and walked right out the doors with her dignity intact. But she didn't. She hesitated, just a second, but a second too long. Derek was at her side, cajoling her with a pointed challenge.

"Really, Leigh!" he admonished as he gently took her bag from her and tossed it back on the chair. "I never thought of you as the whiny, oversensitive kind. I do apologize—I did promise not to bring up the past. But madam! To run so quickly! If my memory isn't faulty, love, you do know how to put one in one's place. You aren't afraid of me, are you?"

"No!" Leigh exclaimed. She hoped her voice held conviction.

"Marvelous." Derek grinned wickedly and Leigh inwardly acknowledged and saluted his charisma and power of persuasion. It was easy to understand why nations of women, from teenyboppers to graying matrons, fell madly, if distantly, in love with him. He was the strength, the vision, the talent that had kept the group at the top of music charts for almost twenty years.

"Now," he continued, and she realized that he had subtly guided her to the highly polished grand piano. "Refresh my mind. Let me hear the opening song."

"I—I can't!" she faltered.

"Why not? I don't see any broken fingers on your hands!" He pretended to test them for mobility as he manipulated her body onto the bench. "And don't tell me you haven't played since Richard's death!" he chastised her sternly. "I won't believe you!"

Leigh glanced nervously over her shoulder to find that he had taken a stance behind her, his hands in his pockets, his eyes riveted on the piano keys. "But I told you!" she hedged, "I haven't looked at 'Henry the Eighth' since . . . then." Moistening her lips, she tried to bring the blurring black and white keys into focus. She couldn't play! Not with Derek standing over her shoulder! The scene was too familiar. She trembled as it brought the sharp pain of memory. Leigh, sitting at the piano, aglow with excitement and the desire to please, Richard changing that excitement to misery with harsh and amused showers of ridicule . . .

"Leigh . . ." It was amazing how soft and gentle Derek's voice could be at times. "The piece is good. So okay, you'll be rusty. You haven't played it in a while. This isn't a royal performance. I just want to get the taste in my mouth."

Three of Leigh's delicate, manicured fingers touched lightly on ivory, but the freezing chill of fear that assaulted her was too strong. If she stayed at the keyboard any longer, her hands would fly to her face and she would dissolve into a mass of sobbing shudders. And dear Lord! That was something she could never do in front of Derek! He wouldn't understand, and he'd rip her apart.

Holding her head high, she slid with feigned indifference from the stool. "Sorry, Derek," she said coolly. "It's no good. I just don't remember any of it." She stooped nonchalantly for her bag and glided regally for the door. "But like I said, thanks for the thought!"

She was surprised when Derek made no attempt to stop her

departure. Pausing at the door to wave a crisp good-bye, she found that he had taken her position at the piano and was softly playing the chords of one of the group's top hits—a mellow love ballad he had written fifteen years ago but which could still be heard frequently on a multitude of radio stations.

"Bye, Leigh," he said without glancing up. "Sorry I had you take the long drive for nothing. Keep in touch."

A large knot seemed to restrict her throat. Derek had started to sing the words in his husky tenor, a voice that had undoubtedly helped in many a seduction throughout the world. It sent a sharp stab of yearning through her even as she realized that what she listened to was just a well-written song performed by a gifted singer. Hell! she thought miserably. The haunting power of music was unfair.

"Good-bye, Derek," she called, marching out the doors and closing them tightly behind her. She started down the tiled hallway, still hearing the dimmed, but nevertheless compelling, sound of his voice. She clicked her heels loudly, yet even that didn't help. By the time she reached the outer doorway, she had come face to face with a terrible truth.

She, just like a million other heartsick "groupies," was in love with Derek Mallory. She had been, for quite some time. Only self-defense had allowed her the illusion that she had used him.

Oh, Lord! she prayed silently as she continued down the steps to her car. Please, just let me get out of here before I do something stupid in front of this electronic eye!

Although she was walking normally, her mind was racing with tormented confusion. How could she be such a fool as to be in love with Derek? Even if he cared two cents for her, *he was just like Richard.* Another musician, another *star.* One in a lifetime was burden enough for any one human to bear. Besides, she rationalized as she reached the haven of her car, she couldn't really be in love with Derek. She hadn't seen him until today in half a year. And sane people didn't fall in love with people who considered them to be cold, cruel, conniving, and mercenary!

She tilted the brim of her hat and slid her key into the ignition.

It would be all right; in just a matter of minutes she would be across the Island bridge and she would probably never see him again. She would get over her absurd fancy and continue with her life as usual, calm now, uncomplicated and complacent.

At first she thought the car's refusal to start was a figment of her wildly rushing imagination. Perhaps she hadn't really turned the key yet. But as she twisted it a second time to no avail, she was forced to accept the fact that for some reason the Audi had gone stone-cold dead. She sat dazed for a moment, incredulous that such a thing could be happening. She had had her mechanic check beneath the hood and fill the car with gas only that morning, just an hour before she had left her Key West home to travel the few hours north to Miami. Furiously, she turned the key a third, fourth, and fifth time, but the Audi refused to choke out a single sound.

Derek! The man would stoop to anything to get his own way. Her recent self-admittance of her emotions regarding him added fuel to the fire of her wrath. Steaming to a point of explosion, she scrambled from the car, viciously slammed the door, and stormed back into the house, brushing past James imperiously and striding down the hall toward Derek's office with long, angry steps. She burst in on him like a tornado, seething so hotly that she not only forgot her aloofness entirely, but found it difficult not to rush straight for his neck and attempt to throttle him.

"What did you do to my car?" she raged.

Derek glanced at her disdainfully from the piano bench, twisting his wiry frame to observe better her irate, quivering form. "I didn't do a damn thing to your car," he said coldly.

"Then why won't it start?" Leigh challenged.

"How the hell would I know!" he exclaimed impatiently. "I'm not omniscient!" His eyes roamed with indifferent amusement from the brim of her hat to her crisp beige heels, then he turned back to the keyboard with a shrug. "Buzz James. He'll get someone to look at it for you."

Leigh's pent-up emotions erupted. With a shrill curse she sent her bag flying across the room, hurtling it with such venomous

210

force and an uncannily correct aim that it struck Derek smartly in the back of his leonine head. Leigh gasped with shock, horrified by her own behavior, and was immediately filled with remorse. Her anger drained from her as she watched Derek slowly turn again, rising to his full, imposing height, and move swiftly toward her, his eyes narrowed and glittering with glacial fury. She opened her mouth to apologize, but no sound came. The possible repercussions of her hostile act were dawning on her with rapid clarity. Derek, when pushed to anger, showed little mercy. She knew he often restrained his emotions because, once let loose, his temper could be a terrible thing, savage and wild.

It had only been seconds since Leigh had struck him with her flying missile, but time seemed frozen as he approached her. Thoughts whirled through her mind with the speed of light. It was too bad he didn't seem to have a sense of humor at the moment. It was almost funny. She usually couldn't hit the side of a barn with a tennis ball!

Her stunned immobility came to an end when Derek was almost upon her. A flash of logical panic came to her and she decided to make a hasty retreat. She had only seen him really angry once, but she knew she didn't want to see him so again—especially if she were to be the object of that anger. Spinning with the true speed of acute fear, she scurried for the doors and escape.

Her effort came too late. Even as she turned, her hat went flying from her head, and her attempt to flee was painfully curtailed as Derek's forceful fingers gripped into the neat knot of auburn hair, sending the pins cascading to the floor, wrenching her into an abrupt aboutface. She cried out; her liquid eyes and trembling lips begged silently for forgiveness. But Derek was not yet ready to show compassion. His fingers remained tightly clenched in the now tumbled, soft disarray of her hair, pulling her head back so that her neck arched cruelly and she had no choice but to meet his stern, unrelenting features, stare into his smoldering golden-brown eyes. His other hand, she noted vaguely, had fallen to her waist, pressing her dangerously close to his lean hips and powerfully muscled thighs. She could feel his breath on her cheeks, see a row of clenched, straight white teeth, sense the tickle of his soft beard on her flesh. For a brief moment she wondered if he were going to strike her or kiss her. . . .

He did neither. A struggle for control played across his features, then he released her and walked tensely to his desk, leaned against it, and rang the buzzer. Scrutinizing her with quiet contempt, he advised, "You might want to brush your hair. James will be here in a second."

Shaking with humiliation, Leigh scurried across the room for her bag, extracted her brush, and tried to put some order into the long, thick tresses, which hung over her face and down her back in gold-hued, fluffy tangles. She had just completed her task when James entered the room, but if he noticed that their guest had lost her hat and sophisticated upsweep, he gave no sign. Derek explained that Mrs. Tremayne was having auto difficulty and would James please see to it. The butler nodded and started to leave but Derek halted him with, "Oh, and, James, will you ask Emma to prepare a guest room and tell her that Mrs. Tremayne will be staying for dinner? Thank you." The oak doors were closed again.

Leigh shot Derek a hostile glance and stated firmly, "Mrs. Tremayne will not be staying the night!"

"Then Mrs. Tremayne is a bigger fool than I thought," Derek said smoothly. "Don't you ever read weather reports or listen to the radio?"

Leigh's hostility changed to confusion. "I—I don't know what you're talking about!"

"The tropical storm over Cuba has increased to hurricane velocity," Derek said, idly searching the cobalt shag of his office carpeting for her hairpins. "You would have been all right if you could have left now, but, say, five or six hours from now the outer winds will be hitting the Keys. Unless it takes a radical change of course."

212

"Oh." Leigh stood awkwardly. She was a fool! She had heard something about a tropical storm brewing in the Caribbean. Why hadn't she paid more attention to the reports? She should have never left her home to begin with! As a native "Conch," or Key Westerner, she had seen many a storm thunder its ferocity upon the island. Her home, she felt, was safe. Knowing her native habitat as she did, she had insisted that Richard have it built to exacting specifications. Usually when storm warnings threatened, she stocked the house well, filled every receptacle in it with water, and offered it as a harbor to others in less fortunate positions—those who were not able to evacuate or felt their own homes were dangerous during the deluge of water and wrecking winds.

But in the last few days she had been terribly absentminded. All she had thought about was her approaching appointment with Derek. She had not picked up a newspaper, barely glanced at the TV, and, if she had heard a radio, she didn't remember a thing said.

And now here she was, virtually a prisoner of the feckless gods of fate, stuck with Derek due to the haphazard whimsy of the weather. "I'm sure there can't be anything seriously wrong with my car," she said in a small voice tinged with hope as she absently reknotted her hair.

Derek, holding his cache of pins, advanced on her nonchalantly. "Don't," he said curtly, pushing her hands from her hair. "It looks much nicer down. I never did like the way Richard tried to dress you up like a porcelain doll." He handed her the pins and strode with assurance toward the doors. "Excuse me, I need to shower and change for dinner."

"But, Derek . . ." Leigh's protest trailed away.

"Yes?"

"I—I can't stay! I have nothing with me!"

He hesitated slightly, one powerful hand curling around the edge of a door. A small, humorously tender smile showed beneath the trimmed hair of his beard. "I remember you used to wear Richard's tailored shirts to bed." His grin broadened across his face. "I have a zillion shirts. Take your pick. And Emma's always prepared for anything. She keeps a horde of soap, toothpaste, shampoo, and the like that would make a drugstore look understocked. She'll take care of you."

The door began to close but Leigh once more felt compelled to stop her host, deciding the temperance of his behavior after her own childish display warranted an apology. "Derek!" she called again stiffly, not quite able to sound truly humble. "I'm sorry."

"Are you? How nice." The friendly grin had left his face and the eyes that bored into her were unfathomable. He seemed distracted for a moment, then added in a low tone with a rough edge that could only be deciphered as a warning, "But you should learn to guard that temper of yours. Richard might have tolerated it—he had to, you were his wife. But I rarely make allowances more than once."

"Well how good of you to leave me unscathed this once!" Leigh drawled sarcastically. Although she knew better, she couldn't seem to stop herself from goading him. "If—" she stated with pronounced accusation, "if my car hadn't gone mysteriously dead, it never would have happened!"

"My dear Mrs. Tremayne," he said, shaking his head slightly as if he had been delegated the task of explaining something to a very small child. A scornful smile twisted his handsome features. "Dear, dear woman! Do you really imagine I would ever have to stoop to trickery to keep a lady in the house if I so desired?"

A scarlet blush rose unbidden to her cheeks. Tossing her hair behind her shoulders, she attempted a comeback to dispel the miserable feeling of utter ridiculousness he had instilled in her. "My dear Mr. Mallory! Believe it or not, there are women in the world who value the trait of modesty. You never know, one of them might be more than willing to turn you down!"

"True, love, but the sea is full of fish."

"And one black cat is just like another in the dark?"

"You got it."

Leigh gave him a saccharin-sweet smile. "That's what you think now, Derek Mallory. But one day you'll change your tune. You are a mere mortal—or were you aware of that? One day, Mr. Music, you will fall in love. And I hope you're on your knees begging for the feeling to be reciprocated, begging for marriage —"

"Oh doubtful, love! Doubtful!" Derek interrupted casually. "You see, I saw a friend fall in love, and I saw what it did to him. The beautiful, shy little creature that he married turned out to be a heartless bitch. No, I don't foresee the same thing happening to me."

He had barely gotten the words out of his mouth before Leigh was on him, hand raised, nails curved like a feline's in a hissing attack. Once again she hadn't bothered to think about her actions. She had forgotten all about any of her gentler emotions toward Derek; all she knew was that at that moment she hated him with black and thorough rage.

Her blow never found its mark. He must have anticipated that his provoking remark would draw such a response from her. Catching her hand with deft ease, he twisted it cruelly behind her back. "Oh, Leigh!" he said, his voice dripping disgust. "You never do learn, do you? I'm not your doting, besotted husband. Don't ever slap me, I slap back." His jaw tightened savagely. "And believe me, woman, if ever a man lived who thought you deserved a sound thrashing, that man is me. So don't tempt me, huh? I'd love to give you a good taste of your just reward!"

Leigh was in no position to argue. The pain in her steel-trapped arm was barely endurable. But she wouldn't apologize. Not ever again! He was so—so wrong and unfair! Despite the agony she felt, she tilted her head in defiance and stared at him distastefully. "I loathe you, Mr. Mallory," she said, the green overshadowing the amber in her eyes, gleaming emerald with open vehemence. "You are the most arrogant, egotistical, self-righteous, self-centered bas—" she stopped as a cry of agony escaped her lips as Derek twisted her arm even more viciously.

She closed her eyes miserably and fell silent. With a slight push, he released her.

"Sorry, I can't stand here and listen to any more of your opinions," he said as if they had been discussing a song or a book. "I don't want to be late for dinner. I have a guest coming later this evening and I want you tucked in for the night before she arrives. I won't need any of your opinions with her here, either."

He saluted her quickly and headed for the curving staircase that ranged to the right of his office and the hallway. As soon as he moved, Leigh forced her quivering and abused limbs quickly to retrieve her bag for a final time and to rush back down the hallway in a desperate dash for the door. Hurricane or no, she wasn't staying here! She'd happily walk the distance back to the mainland and stand on the causeway until someone picked her up and got her to a phone; she'd do anything to get away from Derek.

"I wouldn't do that if I were you!" his voice suddenly warned as she set her hands on the outer door. "The dogs are out. Nice nasty Dobermans. They chew strangers into little bits!"

Leigh clenched her teeth as she let her hand fall from the door. "Then call me a cab, please."

"Sorry, love." Derek's mock apology echoed frostily against the tile. "Phones are dead. We've been having that problem frequently this past month. Cable trouble."

The echo died slowly as he continued up the stairway. "Damn you!" Leigh cried, shaking with misery and despair. "Damn you, Derek! Why did you make me come here?"

But he was gone. He didn't hear her, nor did he see the abject tears that shimmered on her eyelashes and fell to her cheeks, or the frightened unhappiness that trembled on her lips.

CHAPTER TWO

The view from the arched balcony off the guest bedroom Leigh had been allotted was stunning. Before her lay the shimmering rectangular pool and beyond it the deep blue water of the channel separating Star Island from the causeway. If she cast her eyes to the left, she could see the high rises of Miami Beach, twinkling now in the dusk like a million merry stars. To the right, in a distant glimmer of reflection, was Biscayne Bay, choppy with the fringe of winds caused by the tropical storm southward. Each foam-flecked wave danced and gleamed like a diamond, caught in the nighttime brilliance of the *Miami Herald* building and the magnificent OMNI complex beyond it.

Graceful steps led from the balcony to the palm-fringed pool, and Leigh was sorely tempted to follow them down and touch the silver enchantment of the water. With a regretful shake of her head she decided against such action. She had already been standing on the balcony, hypnotized by the display of the various surrounding waters, for a good half hour. Derek's housekeeper had supplied her with an assortment of toiletries, and she wanted to shower before dinner even if she did have to redon the same clothing.

The huge, inviting deco tub in the bathroom, along with the enticing bottle of bath oil that had been supplied her, was too much of a temptation to allow her to settle for a simple shower. She filled the claw-footed tub with deliciously hot water, added the oil; then, after carefully hanging her clothes, she sank her tense limbs into the luxurious, misting heat.

It was a pity, Leigh thought, closing her eyes in total surrender to the comfort, that she, considered to be such a cool bastion of reserve, didn't seem to be able to maintain an ounce of casual dignity where Derek was concerned. Why on earth had she allowed herself to behave so badly? Wanting Derek's respect so very much, it seemed she was only capable of drawing his contempt.

Well, the hell with it! she decided, suddenly angry. He had judged her without a trial, formed an opinion without half the facts. He was a devastatingly attractive man, but she had met many an attractive man. And Leigh was a strong realist. Life always went on. She would get away as soon as possible.

A knock on the door interrupted her mental wanderings as she was rising from the tub and rubbing her skin to a rough gleam with a large navy towel. She didn't have time to call out; Derek's cheery housekeeper had tucked her head into the bedroom and was calling out, "Just me, Mrs. Tremayne. May I come in?"

Leigh wrapped the towel tightly around herself and peeked out from the bathroom. "Sure, Emma. But you'll have to pardon my dress!"

Emma Larson was a plump little lady, and although she preferred to stay in the background, she ruled Derek's house with a firm hand, from the domestic employees to Derek himself. Even dignified James bowed before her. The toughest elements of the music industry who paid calls upon Derek behaved like lambs in Emma's presence. With her shrewd, crisp blue eyes, she brought them all down to size, seeing clearly through all their facades. Leigh wondered briefly and with a touch of fear whether or not Emma might also see all too clearly through her. Then she smiled as she exited the bath in her towel. If Emma did come uncomfortably close to reading her mind, she would contain her thoughts. Though they had met only once before, two years ago when Leigh and Richard had come for a week to work out a concert schedule, Leigh and Emma had become friends by some unspoken agreement. Though Emma had always been polite and proper toward Richard, Leigh had the uncanny feeling that Emma was unimpressed by his charm or his person and had secretly pitied Leigh even then.

"Wonderful, sweetie!" Emma proclaimed as she bustled into the room and deposited a couple of boxes on the room's elegant four-poster bed. "I'm glad I caught you before you had time to

218

dress. Derek sent one of the boys over to town to pick up a few things for you."

Leigh stared at the boxes dumbly for a few seconds. "You mean . . ." she said hesitantly, half stunned, half angry, "you mean Derek sent someone out to buy clothing for me?"

"Oh, no, darling!" Emma said with horror. "Derek called the shop himself. All the boy did was pick them up!" She gave Leigh a friendly wink. "Derek claims he knows your taste and your size. He ordered from the same place where he's often purchased your birthday and Christmas gifts!" Emma smiled brightly and turned her little figure for the door. "I'll leave you now, unless I can do something else. Dinner will be about thirty minutes."

"I'm fine, Emma, thank you," Leigh said. It would be fruitless to tell the housekeeper she didn't want anything from Derek Mallory—especially clothing!

She dressed quickly in her own suit, ignoring the boxes. She would inform Derek that she couldn't accept such gifts from him. After brushing and rearranging her hair and freshening her makeup, she walked determinedly to the door. But her determination did not quite make it. Curiosity called her back into the room.

The first box contained a pair of designer jeans and a handsome western shirt. An outfit for the following day, she assumed. Pursing her lips, she closed the box. Opening the second, she let out a shocked gasp. A beautiful, simple beige cocktail dress of angel-fine silk met her eyes. Being female, she couldn't help but draw it from the box and against her form to whirl before the mirror.

The dress, of sleek lines, was made to form sensuously around the body. It was, as Derek had boasted, perfect to her taste and size. She itched to step into it, but though her fingers lovingly caressed the material, she forced herself to fold it carefully and to return it to the box. Repacking the gown, she realized that there was more in the box. A blush rose to her cheeks as she discovered stockings, a slip, bikini underwear, and a lacy, low-cut bra—all also perfectly sized.

Good Lord! she thought, quivering. How could he know her measurements so exactly? Her presents from him over the years had often been clothing, but never such intimate apparel! But then, she thought, with a wry and rueful twist of anger, Derek was a connoisseur of women. He could probably take any female figure and size it up easily. With that in mind she quickly closed the box and marched stiffly from the room.

"Mr. Mallory is on the patio, Mrs. Tremayne," James informed her as she reached the landing. "May I bring you a cocktail?"

Leigh was about to refuse, then she decided a drink might be in order. The right amount of liquor might sharpen her tongue rather than dull it, and she would need a bit of a bite to get through the evening. "Thank you, James," she said. "A vodka and tonic would be nice."

The butler nodded and Leigh braced herself mentally and physically as she made her way through the parlor with its simple yet elegant period furnishings and strode with no visible trace of hesitancy to the poolside.

Derek was standing at the far end, facing the channel. He cradled a glass absently in both hands as his tawny eyes fastened on the blue night before him. He was dressed now in a brown velvet three-piece suit, and Leigh was struck afresh by his aura of power and charisma. The suit, which should have covered his tapered physique, enhanced it. He turned to her then, and as a frown furrowed into his features, she was hit with another, startling realization. He had shaved off his beard!

Surprise was about to make her comment on the disturbing fact but Derek spoke before she could. "Why are you wearing that?" he demanded flatly.

"Because," Leigh replied equally blandly, "though I do appreciate the thought, Derek, I do not care to accept such gifts from you. You needn't have gone to the bother. But I haven't touched the things. You can return them tomorrow." Color was spreading through her face despite the unconcerned tone of her voice. She was remembering the intimate "gifts" and the precision of their order. The wind whipped at the escaping tendrils of her hair and she turned toward the channel with carefully planned nonchalance. "Your turn!" she challenged jauntily. "What happened to your beard?"

Derek lightly rubbed the fresh and tender skin of his squared jawline. "Down the drain, love. And all for your benefit. I remember you saying you hated scratchy beards!" He moved to her and ran a finger along her cheek. "So you see"—his touch was like a whisper of air and his voice as soft—"I'm willing to accommodate you to drastic lengths. I think you could humor me in return and wear the dress."

Those tawny eyes were boring into hers and she didn't seem able to turn away. She felt like a deer trapped in the headlights of an approaching car, hypnotized and searching in spite of the coming danger. But she had to move. She was quite sure that Derek was about to take her into his arms, an easy conquest like his other "interchangeable" cats, and she had to avoid such a catastrophe at all costs. He moved even closer, and she found the strength to force her own unwilling limbs. She took a giant step backward, and tumbled straight into the pool.

Derek's laughter reached her ears even through the insulation of the chlorinated water. Furious from the sound, she refused to surface, but swam the depths to the shallow end instead and climbed up the circular steps, high heels in her hands.

"Looks like you'll have to change after all," he commented evenly.

Leigh didn't reply. She marched for the house, just in time to run into James and her vodka and tonic. "Thank you, James," she said airily, sweeping the glass from the small silver tray. "I'll bring this up with me." She sailed on past him, as cool as he despite the rivulets of water that drained from her. Once inside and out of vision, she pelted up the steps quickly, wondering if James would smirk along with Derek behind her back. Besides, she was freezing. The water had been warm, but the stiff wind had chilled her to the bone.

In the privacy of her room she stripped off her soaking clothing and stepped into a quick shower to rinse the chill and the smell of the chemicals from her skin. Then she donned the new clothing bitterly, noting that Derek couldn't have manipulated her into submission any better had he planned it. Or had he planned it?

What was he up to? she asked herself as she pinned her sodden hair. It wasn't a romantic interlude; he had already told her he was expecting a date later and he wanted her out of the way. Besides, he disliked and distrusted her! She knew his displays of courtesy were often masks. No, he was up to something. She didn't believe for one minute that his sole reason for summoning her had been the music. He could write circles around her any day of the week. Then what? Revenge? Punishment for what she had supposedly done to Richard? How absurd. There wasn't really anything he could do to her.

Or was there? She was already stuck where she didn't want to be in the home of a man she had once sworn never to see again.

She tilted her chin proudly and smiled a brave smile to the woman in the mirror. That was much better. The lost and frightened look was gone. Of course she didn't have to go down to dinner. She could hide up here and simply disappear in the morning without seeing Derek. Yes, she could run away.

No. The smile she gave herself was stronger and more sincere. She was not a gawking, naive teen-ager. She had been the wife of Richard Tremayne; she had learned to hold her own and survive in a rugged world. She would tuck tail and run before no one—not even Derek Mallory! And if he wanted to play games, well, she could play them too. She had proved that once. It was a pity that Derek would never know how well she played a game.

It was a greater pity that she had paid so dearly for that game—paid with dreams, longing, yearning, physical pain.

The sick, agonized look was returning to her eyes. She left the room, pushing the memory to the back of her mind as she usually managed to do. Usually, in rational thought, she pretended that the night had been a dream. The man, the chivalrous King

Arthur, had not been Derek, just as she had not been the exotic belly dancer. It had all been a fantasy, not real. As far as she was concerned, she *hadn't* seen Derek since Richard's funeral; she hadn't even attended the party in Atlanta.

And if she was in love, *it was with a fantasy,* not Derek Mallory.

The attractive male who had been dominating her mind greeted her with a long, low wolf whistle. She had to laugh. Derek, minus the beard, seemed younger tonight, more gallant, more touchable. Had he really razored off his magnificent beard on her behalf? Maybe. But, she reminded herself primly, it would be a grave mistake to lower her guard, no matter what his guise might be. She dug her nails into the palm of her hand. They knew exactly who one another was this night. They could never in reality escape the past or the words that had passed between them.

"Thank you," she said demurely, in full control. She spun a graceful pirouette to allow the folds of the dress to swirl smoothly around her. "You do have a nice eye for clothing, Mr. Mallory."

Derek nodded gravely in acceptance of her compliment, but she noticed that his eyes held a satanish twinkle as he answered, "I have an eye for what would become certain spectacular forms."

"Thank you again," Leigh said casually. "I hope I have delayed dinner. I want to be certain ... haven't ... ... to 'disappear' before your date arrives." She astonished herself with the total lack of concern in her statement.

"Umm . . ." Derek was noncommittal. "I'll be sure to have you well out of the way when she arrives." He wore a pleasant grin as he approached her and offered his arm. "Shall we go in to dinner? James said to come in as soon as you were ready."

Dinner was served in the small nook off the kitchen. Prepared for two, the meal was as elegant as any planned for the most romantic honeymoon. James poured champagne into glittering crystal glasses; candles flickered a mellow glow over the slender centerpiece of red and yellow roses. The main course was stone crabs, a Florida delicacy they both favored. For the first portion of the meal they concentrated on the food and kept the conversation light and bantering. But it was inevitable that trouble spring up, despite the pains taken by James and Emma to create a soothing atmosphere.

It started innocently enough. They had been discussing water levels in Key West when Derek suddenly leaned back, a half smile on his unusually bare features. "You know," he said, idly rubbing a long finger along the ridge of his champagne glass, "I'll never forget the day Richard and I met you. You looked like a little waif coming from the ocean, like the mermaid who sold her soul for human legs." He laughed ruefully. "We were both out to impress you—until we discovered you could outswim us in a matter of seconds! I think Richard fell in love with you the moment you dove out of his reach."

Leigh felt a piece of the tender crab catch in her throat. "Richard always did want what he couldn't reach," she said softly when she could.

If she had meant to keep the peace, she should have kept her mouth shut. But her reply had been nothing less than the truth. Still, she knew as she watched Derek's jawline harden and his gold eyes glimmer as if they were about to light like the fire of the candle before them that he had construed her comment as further criticism of her dead husband. His next words verified her apprehension.

"We were both captivated by you, Mrs. Tremayne," he said coldly. "I, like Richard, believed you to be refreshingly guileless and innocent. I even believed you had no idea who we were."

"I didn't know who you were!" Leigh exclaimed indignantly. "I had heard of the London Company, of course; your first album came out when I was in third grade! But how on earth would I have recognized you? I'd never been to a concert! And you always wore some sort of costume on your album covers! And anyway, *Mr. Mallory*, I might remind you that not everyone is impressed by members of the music world!"

"Possibly," Derek acknowledged. "But most people are impressed by money."

Leigh inhaled sharply and tossed her napkin on the table before rising. "I never wanted Richard's money!" she declared hotly. "Nor his 'impressive' name nor 'impressive' companions! If you care to do some research into my finances, you'll find I've not run wild on anything of his! I live in a home which I helped finance and create, I give large sums to the children's care centers and—"

"Richard wanted a child of his own," Derek interrupted rudely.

"Then he should have stayed home to have one!" Leigh retorted. "Excuse me," she added with regal cool. "This conversation has gone far enough. I don't care to discuss my personal life with Richard with anyone, especially you." She was dangerously close to tears. "Thank you for the gown, thank you for dinner and your hospitality. If my car is ready, I'll probably be gone before you rise. Good luck with whatever."

"Leigh!" Derek's commanding voice stopped her as she reached the door. She turned back to him expressionlessly.

"Where were you when Richard died?"

"I was at home, in Key West. Richard, as you know, was on the West Coast. I hadn't seen him in two months. You must have known that too."

"No, I didn't," Derek said softly.

She didn't quite understand the agony that bared for a brief moment in his eyes. "It doesn't really make any difference."

"No, it doesn't."

For a reason she couldn't define, Leigh hesitated. "Derek?"

"Yes?"

"Do you know exactly what happened?"

"He went off a cliff."

"I know . . . but . . ."

"Cut and dried. No drugs involved. He probably had a few drinks, but he wasn't stoned, if that's what you're referring to." Derek dropped his own napkin on the mahogony table and

225

walked to join her at the door. He very lightly cupped her chin in his hands, and she could feel a tingle that seemed to shoot straight through her as his fingers brushed her temples. For a moment, as his eyes searched hers in an unaccustomed tenderness, the months rolled away and she was frighteningly reminded of that one long-ago night. With painful recall she remembered the feel of his strong arms, the taste of his lips, the wonderful harmony of his sinewed body with hers. With precision she knew the touch of his skin, the shape of his magnificent form, the perfection of his lovemaking. . . .

"Derek, please," she murmured weakly. "I have a terrible headache. I need to get to sleep and your date . . ."

He kissed her, silencing her effectively. She stiffened at first and attempted to push away from him. But she was caught between the wall and his steellike strength; her attempt to budge him was futile and then feeble. His lips, like his eyes, were magnetic. They claimed hers with a firm tenderness, neither forcing nor allowing for escape. And as her resistance failed her, his tongue feathered along her teeth until it probed and found access to her warm, sweet moistness, to demand in earnest. That which had been gentle became passionate and demanding, urgent and hungry. The warnings in Leigh's mind went unheeded as her flesh burned from the arousing possession of his subtly exploring hands. They traced the graceful angle of her neck, warmed her back and shoulders to a glow of anticipation, hovered over her breasts until a hot chill of desire blotted out everything except . . .

The shrill cry of the door bell.

Sanity returned. Leigh stared at Derek with horror, watched as triumphant amusement crept into his eyes, then fled from the doorway and up the staircase just as James was opening the door. Reaching the sanctuary of solitude, she dimly heard the musical tinkle of a female voice as she closed her own bedroom door and bolted it firmly. She was shaking from head to toe, consumed by hot and cold, shamed, humiliated, and . . . empty.

She stared at the bolted door for a while, then began mechanically to pull the pins from her still-damp hair. Glancing over at the bed, she began to tremble anew as she saw an assortment of tailored shirts. Some were short-sleeved, some long-sleeved. They were Derek's. He hadn't forgotten his offer.

Her first instinct was to push the lot of them onto the floor. But that action would be foolish. Emma would be the one to suffer. She watched them warily instead, as if they might come alive and attack her. Then she sighed, kicked off her shoes, and disrobed. She chose a long-sleeved pinstripe with tails that reached halfway to her knees and began to pace the room as she buttoned it. She was coming down with a ferocious headache. Perhaps the night air could help clear the tension causing the pain. Barefoot and clad only in the absurdly large shirt, she opened the sliding doors to the balcony and stepped out into the wind. She slid the door closed behind her and leaned against it as the salt breeze tickled her face. It did feel good. The house was air-conditioned and comfortable, but there was nothing like the air of the sea on a night such as this.

She stood for a long time, thinking. She would never forget the day that she had met Richard and Derek either. She had been idly snorkling in the surf off her father's beach house when she had risen from the water to discover the two handsome young men wandering along, apparently lost. She had informed them that they were on private property, but they had quickly cajoled her into entertaining them. Their names—first ones only were given—didn't mean a thing to her. She knew of the London Company—everyone did. They had cut their first gold album when all were still in their teens. Their work in the first years came out sporadically as each spent time in acclaimed music schools. Then, as graduates, they began to put out a constant flow of quality work. Before the oldest member, Richard, reached thirty, all five members were millionaires and celebrities. They had scored movies and plays, appeared on prestigious television specials, and performed before president and queen.

But when Leigh came across Richard and Derek, she accepted them as a pair of poor, confused British tourists. They had talked

227

awhile, flirted in the gently rolling waves, and then Leigh had invited them for dinner. Her dad had been alive then, and the occasion had been tremendous, her father showing a definite interest in Derek. Both men had courted her teasingly, but Derek had been involved with a buxomy stewardess at the time and it was Richard who pursued her, a little awed at the discovery of his fame, to the altar. Richard wanted a wife. A wife, she discovered, to be a centerpiece. But he was, at times, good to her. He had been her buffer from pain at her father's death; he had chosen Key West as his permanent home because she loved it. For certain kindnesses, she loved him.

And yet, she thought guiltily, she had never felt for Richard what she did for Derek. Her blood had never boiled at the near sight of him, she had never reached the plain of heaven in his arms. . . .

No! Although she didn't scream aloud, the word reverberated in her mind. She clenched her teeth and shivered, miserably regretting the folly of her masquerade with Derek. The night air didn't seem to be helping at all. She would be better off getting back into her room, calling downstairs and requesting a good stiff drink and a couple of aspirins.

She turned to do just that, but the glass wouldn't slide. She tried again, then considered the possibility of literally kicking herself. How could she have been so foolish? Only an idiot could lock herself out!

And she was locked out. She looked at the glass angrily and realized it must lock automatically when closed. Damn!

She pounded on the glass and yelled, but quickly ascertained the futility of such action. No one could hear her. She had only one choice, and that was to follow the stairs down to the patio and pool and re-enter the house on the ground floor. If she was lucky, she would avoid Derek and his date and only encounter Emma or James.

She took a deep breath and rushed down the stairs. If she had to run into someone, she might as well get it over with. She would certainly get nowhere fast by standing on the balcony shivering, her arms clasped tightly around herself.

The pool raced in silent ripples from the ever-increasing wind as she reached the empty patio, the palms bent low with each approaching salt-riddled gust. Leigh's hair whipped about her face in furious dishevelment as she hurried to the house, only to stop with abrupt confusion as she heard Derek's voice come clearly to her.

He was entertaining his guest in the rear salon. If she entered here, she would have to walk past them both and surely offer an explanation. "Damnation!" she muttered aloud. If there was anything she didn't want to do, it was to run into one of Derek's girl friends! And what would his girl friend think of a half-clad woman running about his house?

Cursing beneath her breath, Leigh decided to skirt around to the front of the house. Either James or Emma would answer the door—the front door was always kept locked—and meeting one of the household staff was definitely preferable.

She had not rounded the first corner before she heard the sound of vicious barking. Derek had not lied. The dogs were out. And she knew for a fact that they were Dobermans, mean and nasty unless they knew you and knew you belonged.

She did not belong. There was no time to lose. She ran like she had never run before in her life, back to the patio, straight into the salon. She slammed the door behind her, heart beating like a hunted rabbit's, beads of perspiration breaking out on her forehead. She had made it with just a few feet to spare. Two of the magnificent black creatures had been on her heels. They were now jumping on the door and howling their wrath.

The great gasps of her breathing began to subside, and she swept a stream of tangled auburn hair from her face and focused with dread on the room. Derek was standing; apparently he had been about to check on the cause of the frenzied animals. She expected he would be angry. Her presence in such attire could do little to enhance the romanticism of his date.

But he wasn't angry at all. If anything, his eyes were light and amused. She glanced apprehensively at his date. She wasn't a bit like Leigh would have imagined either. She was a woman of at least thirty-five or forty, attractive, but extremely businesslike and staid. Her rounded features bothered Leigh; she was sure she had seen the woman before.

"Really, Leigh!" Derek admonished in a lazy drawl. "If you wanted to join us, you could have simply dressed and come down the staircase."

Leigh shot him a look of pure hostility, but he seemed not to notice. Turning to the woman on the couch, he said, "Miss White, I believe you've met Leigh Tremayne before." He glanced back to Leigh. "Leigh, you must remember Lavinia White. She interviewed Richard several years ago for her magazine."

If there had been a hole in the floor anywhere, Leigh would have found it and crawled into it. This was ten times worse than breaking up the most passionate of romantic interludes. Derek's words reminded her immediately of where she had seen the woman before. Lavinia White. The queen of gossip columnists. Untouchable because she made sure all her articles were based on researched fact.

There was no hole in the floor to crawl into. Leigh winced with every nerve in her body, then forced herself to move away from the door. "Hello, Miss White," she said, sailing toward the woman and offering her hand as if she were dressed in heels and the most becoming of hostess gowns. "How are you?" Not waiting for a reply, she went on gaily to them both, "Please do excuse me. I'm afraid I locked myself out on the balcony. Terribly foolish, I know. Forgive me for the interruption."

"Oh, not at all, dear!" Lavinia White was smiling as smugly as the cat that had just caught the canary. Her twinkling green eyes told Leigh plainly that she was already planning the words of type to describe the state of dress in which she had found Leigh Tremayne in Derek Mallory's household. "In fact, I would have never forgiven Derek if you hadn't made an appearance. Why the rogue! He didn't even tell me you were here."

"Excuse me, ladies, if you will," Derek interrupted. "I want to see to the dogs." He grinned wickedly at Leigh before he exited and she knew exactly what he was thinking: You got yourself into this—now get yourself out of it!

Despite the sinking sensation in her heart, she smiled at Lavinia brightly. "Derek and I had some business to discuss this afternoon," she explained calmly, "then something went in my car. My home is in Key West, you know, and Derek didn't think it safe for me to drive back late with the storm so close and all . . ."

She had run out of her words of excuse and they were ringing false to her own ears anyway. She was in Derek's shirt, she was standing barefoot and bare-legged in his salon.

Of all the miserable luck!

"Business?" Lavinia queried doubtfully. "What kind of business?"

Leigh was spared a reply by Derek's timely re-entry. "Musical business, of course," he assured the reporter with his charm in full swing. "Leigh is a very talented artist in her own right, Lavinia. We're planning to do some work together."

Leigh glanced at him angrily but his expression remained guileless and easy. She checked her own telltale features and slipped back into her mask of a smile.

Lavinia White clapped her hands ecstatically. "Is that true, dear? How wonderful! And I'm the first to know!"

Leigh hesitated only slightly. If she said yes, she was cornered. She would have to complete the project with Derek. But if she said no . . . she knew her presence could only be construed in one way and her face and name would appear shortly in magazines across the country in a not-very-flattering light.

"Yes, Miss White. I started something with Richard several years ago and Derek thinks it's worth picking up again. Actually, we're not sure yet. We met on this today for the first time . . ."

"Leigh is overly modest," Derek said. "Her work is excellent and we're going to plunge right into it."

Leigh could almost feel bars closing in around her. How had she allowed all this to happen? Her headache was becoming acute. She felt as if a thousand drummers were playing a march behind her eyes. "It was nice to see you again, Miss White—"

"Lavinia."

"Lavinia, but I think I'll excuse myself. I've had a long day and—"

"A terrible headache," Derek supplied sympathetically. He had gotten his own way, he could afford to be magnanimous. "Do go on up to bed, Leigh. You certainly look like you need some sleep."

"Oh, must you?" Lavinia wheedled.

"Yes, she must," Derek answered firmly. He grinned amiably. "Leigh has a rotten temper when she's overtired."

She was tempted to slug him despite the reporter's observant eyes. Her face was strained from the effort of maintaining her false smile. "I am frightfully tired. And I'm not exactly dressed for tea or cocktails!" She shook Lavinia White's hand briefly and attempted to walk across the room nonchalantly. "Good night!"

"Good night, Leigh," Derek called. His eyes followed her up the stairway and they were gloating and triumphant. She returned his stare with shimmering venom until she could no longer see him. Damn him straight to hell! she thought balefully. He would find out just how bad her temper could be in the morning!

But her troubles for the night were still not over. She grimaced as she remembered that she had also bolted the hallway door to her room. She tried the knob anyway, but as she had expected, it was locked tight.

She wasn't going back downstairs. Not for anything. Sighing with exhaustion and resignation, she tried the door to the next room. It opened welcomingly at her touch.

She didn't switch on a light. Her body and mind ached and

all she wanted was the solace of sleep. She walked in the dim light until she found the bed, pulled back the covers, and collapsed. She hoped, as she drifted quickly and mercifully into a sound doze, that Emma wouldn't mind terribly that she had made a mess of two rooms. . . .

CHAPTER THREE

She was dreaming, and it was a pleasant dream. She was floating on an azure sea, kissed by the sun and caressed by the breeze. The water lapped by her side in perfect tranquillity, a feeling of relaxation to be matched by none. Overhead white clouds moved across the sky in soft, billowing puffs; they seemed to reach down and cradle her with a tantalizing warmth. . . .

She hurled herself up in the bed with a gasping cry. She was being touched and it wasn't by clouds. There was a body beside her!

She heard a muttered oath and then an impatient movement. Light flared through the room from a bedside lamp and she found herself face to face with Derek.

"You bastard!" she hissed, shaking so with surprise and anger that her voice wavered even in its harshness. "You are incredible! Get out of my bed. I know you're capable of dirty tricks, but this is too much. How dare you? And you have the nerve to condemn me . . ." Her words trailed away, not because she had run out of venom, but because he was staring at her very peculiarly and not saying a thing in his own defense.

"Would you please get out of here?" she begged in exasperation and confusion.

"I'd be happy to, madam," he replied with maddening deliberation. "Except this is my bed that you are in."

If a bomb had fallen in the middle of the room, she couldn't have been more shaken. She stared back at him helplessly, her eyes registering dismay as she remembered how haphazardly she had chosen a place to sleep. "Oh, Derek . . ." she stammered, venturing to glance around the room and note that the dresser was neatly covered with his toiletries and that the half-opened closet door displayed rows of pressed shirts and trousers. If only she'd turned on a light! "Derek, I am sorry. My door was locked,

234

you see, I mean both doors . . . and I didn't want to come back downstairs, and—and, well, I am sorry."

"Don't bother to be sorry," he drawled lazily. His curious look had become speculative and his eyes, golden with sardonic amusement, roamed from her mane of sleep-tossed hair, to the deep vee created by the open buttons of the tailored shirt, and down to the long slender length of bare legs displayed beneath the tails. "Finding you in my bed has been a surprise, but a most pleasant one." He ran a finger along her kneecap.

Leigh pushed his hand aside angrily. "Damn you, Derek, I explained what happened—"

"Yes, I know." He smiled calmly. He was propped on an elbow and rested his head on his other hand. "You picked this room by chance."

"Yes!"

"Oh."

"Oh, yourself, and take the fast route to hell," Leigh snapped irritably. "Yours is the last bed I'd crawl into on purpose."

"Really?"

He posed the word like a perfectly polite question, but Leigh could sense the stifled laughter he was containing. She attempted to rise, only to discover she had one foot still caught in the sheets. With impatient force she ripped them aside, making a far worse discovery. Derek slept in the nude.

As Leigh gasped in an echo of horrified embarrassment, Derek chuckled, not in the least disturbed by the events that were mortifying to her. "Control yourself, love!" he mocked. "I'm not going anywhere."

Fury choked back any reply Leigh might have made. She emitted a low growl, hurriedly tossed the sheet back over his bronze body, and unscrambled her own legs to make a hasty retreat. But in redraping her unexpected bedmate, she had retangled her own limbs. Her efforts did little but land her unceremoniously on the floor.

"Poor Leigh!" Derek taunted, rolling across to gaze down at her pityingly. "Doesn't seem to be your night, huh?" He patted

235

the bed invitingly. "Why don't you give up this ridiculous charade of touch-me-not chastity and get back up here?"

"*This isn't a charade!*" Speechlessness deserted her as she shouted into his smugly leering face. "I don't like you, Derek, is that so difficult to comprehend? I don't want to be near you. I don't want to be in this house and I particularly don't want to be in your room and I especially don't want to be in your bed! I—"

She was rudely interrupted as Derek's hand clamped over her mouth. Then, with one swift movement, he was on top of her, and when he spoke, his eyes blazed into hers and his voice was a wrathful whisper.

"*You*, Mrs. Tremayne, are a perpetual liar! When I kissed you earlier, love, you certainly responded. With amazing eagerness and expertise, I might add. Of course, you have had your share of practice."

The scathing things she had to say in return were effectively muffled by the force of his hand on her mouth. She twisted her head and struggled and writhed in a frenzy of energy born of anger so intense it filled every nerve and limb of her body. All to no avail. Between the confinement of the sheets and his rock-muscled strength, she was helpless. All she accomplished was to bring them closer together, to dislodge more of the thin material that was all that separated them and bring more flesh against flesh.

Finally she lay still, spent, frustrated, and frightened of the growing heat between them. She closed her eyes, refusing to meet his. When she had been quiet for several minutes, he took his hand from her mouth. Yet he didn't move. She opened her eyes imploringly.

"Derek, please, let me get out of here."

Her answer was an unyielding stare.

"Damn it, Derek, you are a crazy man! Why are you doing this when your opinion of me is so poor? I might be contaminating!"

"I find you very desirable."

"But you hate me!"

He shrugged. "Like you said, all black cats look alike in the dark."

"I'm not your average black cat, remember? I was Richard's wife, the cold, cruel mercenary."

"Richard has been dead a long time."

"And you still haven't forgiven me!"

Derek went on as if he hadn't heard her. "You responded to me, Leigh."

"But I didn't want to! Don't you understand?"

"No, love, I don't. There's a chemistry between us. Nice and normal. Two consenting adults—"

"No!" Leigh was close to tears. Moisture gleamed on her eyelashes. "Please?" A sob caught in her throat. If he didn't release her soon, she would be seduced by the nearness of him, by the raw masculinity she knew could become so demanding and possessing, yet tender. "Please, Derek."

He sighed and rose nimbly to his feet, wrapping the sheet decorously around himself as he did so. He extended a hand to help her up. "Get back in bed," he said. "There's nowhere else to go, at the moment. The room keys are in the kitchen somewhere, and it could take me the rest of the night and half of tomorrow to find them without asking Emma or James where they are. None of the other rooms are made up. Emma believes in making up a bed fresh when a guest arrives." He turned and stalked toward his closet.

"Where are you going?" Leigh asked hesitantly.

His back was to her and she saw his shoulders rise and fall in an unconcerned shrug. "It's almost five. I'll make myself some coffee."

"Five? It can't be!" Leigh exclaimed.

"Well, it is. I guess we both slept quite comfortably for some time before discerning one another's presence." He pulled a shirt and a pressed pair of jeans from the closet. Turning to glare at her impatiently, he added in a growl, "Go back to bed. Get some sleep."

237

Leigh pushed a billowing strand of hair behind her shoulder and remained standing awkwardly. "No—no, Derek," she stammered. "I'll go back downstairs. This is your room."

"Get in bed," he said firmly. "Unless you want me to put you there."

She hastened to obey. Their recent, bruising, crossed-swords encounter was too fresh in her mind to chance arguing further. Pulling her pillow to her chest, she watched as he obtained underwear from a drawer and headed for his bathroom, unwittingly admiring the span of his tanned shoulders as she did so. When the door had closed behind him, she glanced nervously about the room, focusing on the green luminescent face of a clock radio as she scanned it. It wasn't almost 5:00 A.M., it was only 4:30. She gnawed on a nail indecisively as she waited for him to reappear. When he did, she plunged quickly into stilted speech.

"Derek, I, uh, I really don't feel right about kicking you out of your own bedroom. This bed is king-size, and we did sleep well for hours before discovering one another. I mean, we could both stay on a side and go back to sleep." She shimmied as close as she could to the edge. "See?"

He laughed. "Are you serious?"

"Yes, I am."

Rubbing his chin absently, he thought over her suggestion. Then he tossed the sheet he had been trailing to her. "Thanks. I'll admit I'm not crazy about early hours." He tossed off the sneakers he had just donned and crawled back into the bed, safely clad in his jeans and shirt. He switched off the light and settled in.

There was silence for a time and Leigh believed he slept. All that she could hear was their suddenly loud breathing and the howling of the wind. She curled into her pillow, but sleep wouldn't come.

"Leigh?"

She would have feigned sleep, but his question in the darkness startled her so badly that she jumped.

238

"What?"

"I'm sorry."

The gentle tone of his voice tore through her defenses as none of his harsh jeers could. The tears that had threatened before fell silently down her cheeks and she fought for control to reply.

"It's all right."

She felt his weight shift and then the touch of his finger on her cheek. She stiffened as his arm then came around her, drawing her to him.

"Don't," he said softly. "I'm not going to hurt you."

He didn't, but held her close instead, smoothing her hair with a lulling tenderness. She began to relax against him and her tears subsided. As the wind continued to howl, she drifted back into a contented sleep, dreaming again of white puffy clouds and a beautiful azure sea.

The sound of the wind, which had helped put her to sleep, also awakened her. She blinked the fuzziness from her eyes, yawned and stretched, and bolted up as she remembered the night. A quick look about assured her that Derek had arisen ~~~~ left her. At the foot of ~~~ ~~~~~~ ~~~~~~ carrier and ~~~ ~~~~ of the bed lay the box with the second set of clothing he had purchased for her. She smiled with appreciation, then bounded to the window to strip away the curtains and view the action of the ferocious howling.

The sky was dead gray and the palms dipped so low from the screaming gusts that their thin, spidery leaves brushed the ground.

If they weren't in for the full strength of the hurricane, they were still in for some rough weather. The pool, she saw, was being drained, and as she watched, a flurry of activity became apparent. She heard a multitude of masculine voices, among them Derek's. The house was being battened down for the approaching storm.

She turned on the radio as she washed and dressed, hoping to catch a current advisory. She breathed a sigh of relief as she learned that Key West had been spared a direct hit; the hurricane had chosen a path across the central Keys and had taken its toll as far north as Marathon and Largo. It was now moving overland in a strange westerly pattern. It was hoped that it would wear itself out in the dense Florida Everglades, but warnings were up from Miami to Daytona and the north of the state was on hurricane watch.

Leigh tied back her hair and hurried downstairs. Even seeing it, she had not realized the brunt of the wind until she stepped out on the patio and was backed into the wall of the house. Aware now, she moved carefully across the pool area and out to the lawn, stripped now of all rattan and wicker furnishings. Looking up at the house, she saw that all the windows were shuttered, including the huge plate-glass doors.

"What the hell are you doing out here?"

It was not the wind this time that forced her cruelly around but an irate Derek. His face reminded her of chiseled granite as she returned his glare rebelliously.

"Listen, Mallory, I know what I'm doing, I was born here. You're the transplant."

"Wonderful logic. Being a native gives you the right to be a fool."

"You're out here!"

"And I'm coming in as soon as we finish. Get back in the house!"

"I'm not on your payroll! You can't tell me what to do!" she retorted. That his words made sense was irrelevant. His attitude was appalling.

Derek stared at her for a moment, noting the stubborn set of her chin. He opened his mouth as if to speak, shut it, then muttered, "Ah, hell!" The next second he tossed her over his shoulder like a limp sack of potatoes and walked her back into the house himself.

"Damn you!" Leigh sputtered when he had dumped her roughly on the parlor floor. "You're nothing but a muscle-bound idiot! You can't run around treating people like this. You will get yours one day!"

"But not from you, Leigh, so don't worry about it," Derek said stiffly, glaring down at her ignominious position with glittering eyes. "If you'll excuse me, I was busy. Cheer up—maybe I'll blow into the sea."

He turned away from her lithely and strode from the room, leaving her on the floor. She scrambled quickly to her feet, knowing that he once again irked her into poor behavior. "I have to get out of here!" she muttered to herself. Nothing ever changed. They had slept together as friends, but the coming of the morning had cemented their enemy status.

Her stomach emitted a grumble and she realized she was hungry. The alluring scent of freshly brewed coffee led her to the dining room. As she poured herself a cup of the steaming brew from a silver pot, she frowned at the settings on the large mahogony table. There were four of them. She wondered curiously what other guests Derek had invited in the middle of a tropical storm.

"Leigh!" Her voice was called with deep and sincere affection and she turned to see Roger Rosello, the "Duke of Rose" as he was known with the band, the erstwhile drummer of the London Company.

"Roger!" she greeted him with equal pleasure. He was a slender man, short compared to the others at an even six feet, and very dark from a distant Spanish heritage. His disposition was eternally easygoing, and Leigh had always cared for him as she might an older brother had she had one. He kissed her unabashedly on the lips and held her at arm's length to survey her, his dark eyes bright.

"You look great, kid, how are you doing?" he said, a grin splitting his strong features from ear to ear.

"Well, thanks." Leigh smiled comfortably in return. "How's life with you?"

"Can't complain." He let loose her shoulders to pour himself a cup of coffee and direct her to a chair. "We've been working like crazy. Keeping the group afloat with Richard gone—" He cut himself off and cast an apologetic grimace at Leigh. "I'm sorry, I—"

"Don't be sorry, Roger. I'm used to talking about Richard." She put a hand over his. "And he's been dead a long time. You must know too that we weren't in a state of marital bliss when it happened. But I think I look at things very objectively now. I learned a fair amount of bitterness from Richard, but I think of him fondly, not painfully. He was a brilliant man, and he also gave me a great deal of happiness. We all miss him sorely, but he is gone."

"You are quite a lady, Leigh, you always were," Roger said admiringly.

"Thanks!" Leigh took a sip of her coffee and changed the subject cheerfully. "So tell me—not that I'm not delighted to see you—but what are you doing here in the middle of a storm?"

"I have a place on Star Island now too. Derek called to tell me that you were here and invited me over. Kind of a hurricane party, I guess."

"Oh?" Leigh raised delicate brows. "Who else is coming?" The other two original band members, Bobby Welles and Shane McHugh, also had homes in or around Miami to be near the recording studios. But she couldn't imagine them coming over in the current weather. They both had wives and Bobby was the father of a two-year-old daughter.

She was surprised to see Roger looking uncomfortable again. "John Haley," he said finally. In response to Leigh's puzzled expression, he added, "You've met him a few times. He was with an American group until it split up last year. He's an accomplished lead guitarist and flutist." He watched his coffee cup instead of Leigh as he continued. "We wanted to stick with the original foursome. Derek wouldn't think of replacing Richard at first. But you know"—he glanced up again with a rueful grin— "Richard and Derek were the talent behind the group. The rest of us are hangers-on. I don't know if you've kept up with us at all, but the first album we cut without Richard was rough. Then we did a concert tour and everything fell on Derek. He was half dead when we finished. Anyway, we added John shortly after that."

Leigh traced a circle around her cup and chuckled slightly. "Roger, quit apologizing. I'm glad you've hired John. If I remember correctly, he is very talented."

"There you go, John." The voice, coming from the doorway, was Derek's. Beside him was the young man they had been discussing, John Haley. Leigh vaguely remembered meeting him on a few occasions, all of which had been pleasant.

"I told you," Derek continued as the two entered the room and he moved to the coffee pot, "Leigh wouldn't resent you for a second." He handed John a cup of coffee and indicated the seat across from him as he climbed beside Leigh and gave her a brittle smile that didn't quite reach his eyes. "She's not the type to carry, uh, grief too far."

Leigh was sure that no one else caught his sardonic implication, but she mentally devised ways to manage dumping his coffee all over his lap as she smiled back. Then she turned to John with sincere welcome, ready to dispel the trepidation that lurked unhappily in his cool gray eyes. "I think it's marvelous that you've joined the group, John. Richard admired you very much, and I'm sure he'd be happy to know that you were chosen."

The naked pleasure that streaked across the newcomer's pleasant angular features was ample reward for her honest words. "Thanks for saying that, Leigh," he told her quietly, and she was struck by the humble sincerity of his manner. "It's rough to try and take the place of a man like Richard Tremayne. Having your approval means a lot."

"Don't take anyone's place, John," Leigh said, touched by the eager and personable young man. "Be yourself."

"Well," Derek said, "now that this is all settled, let's eat. I'm starving."

Leigh watched Derek with more curiosity than ever as he rose and began to serve them all from the various chafing dishes on the table. What was he up to? It was, she realized, possible that her elongated stay was simple happenstance, and that Derek

243

would have invited his friends and associates over anyway. But for some reason she didn't think so. It all had to do with a plan of his, and not knowing his motives made her very nervous.

"Shouldn't we all really be off the Island altogether?" she asked sweetly. "I understand these small islands can be very dangerous."

"This house has been here since 'thirty-eight," Derek replied, equally amiable as he served her a portion of eggs Benedict. "She was built to withstand the weather—rain, wind, even flooding. We're quite safe. You should know, Leigh. You never left Key West because of a storm."

She smiled vaguely and crunched into a strip of bacon. A point that had been bothering her suddenly came into sharp focus in her mind. Roger had said that Derek *called* him. When she had asked Derek to call her a cab, he had told her that the phones were dead. He was definitely up to something, and in all probability he *had* done the damage to her car!

She never had to do anything on purpose to retaliate. He spoke her name, and she had become so engrossed in her thoughts that she started violently, consequently carrying out her earlier plan. She knocked Derek's cup accidentally and the scalding brew indeed emptied into his lap.

He yelped and jumped to his feet as the burning liquid drenched through material and hit flesh. Leigh rose too, horrified. She had never truly meant to hurt him.

"Lord, Derek, I am so sorry!" she cried, chewing a knuckle with uncertainty. Should she try to help him mop up? She couldn't! Not where the coffee had landed!

"Accidents happen," he replied dryly, but the tone of his voice told her two things. He didn't think it was an accident at all, and he certainly didn't intend to let it pass as one when he got hold of her alone. "Excuse me," he said with clenched teeth, and she knew too that he really was in pain.

She watched him helplessly as he strode from the room, miserable at the turn of events.

"Hey, Leigh, sit!" Roger said sympathetically. He tossed his napkin on the table and stood himself. "I don't think it's all that bad. Don't look so petrified!" He squeezed her shoulder as he passed her and left the room.

Leigh sank back into her chair. She had lost all taste for breakfast.

"I hear you're an honest-to-God Conch," John Haley said, tactfully changing the subject and attempting to dispel the gloom that had settled. "I didn't know anyone was really born in Key West."

"Sure." Leigh smiled in spite of herself. "Key West is an old settlement. There have been Conches for several hundred years. Where are you from?"

"Midwest. A little town in the Nebraska corn country. I enjoy trips back home, but I like the South." He grinned engagingly and Leigh decided he was a very attractive man. She would enjoy spending time in his company. Thank goodness he and Roger had arrived.

"I have a home in Atlanta, too, but you know that. I sent you an invitation to a party I had," John continued.

"Umm, I remember," Leigh replied, surprised she could sound so cool and remote. "I really haven't gone too far since . . . in the last year or so," she corrected herself. "It was nice of you to have thought of me."

"It was a good party!" John chuckled. "Some of the costumes were terrific. We had one real beauty, a gorgeous creature, and I never even figured out who she was and it was my party!" His chuckle expanded to an explosive laugh. "You should have seen Derek that night! He left with the lady and *he* never discovered who she was! The poor boy was fit to be tied. He tore Atlanta apart for a month looking for her."

Leigh forced herself to join his laughter. She was feeling a little ill, having forgotten that John Haley had been her host on that night. . . .

"It must have been a good party," she agreed jauntily. "I'm sorry I missed it."

"Missed what?"

A chill crept down Leigh's neck as Derek came back in, clad in a new pair of jeans. She again had the sensation that his golden eyes were seeing through her, that the light in them pierced straight to her heart.

"I was telling her about that party I had in Atlanta," John explained. "And the one who got away from Derek Mallory."

"Oh," Derek said, pouring himself a fresh cup of coffee and sitting, one leg casually draped over the other. He smiled noncommittally. "I still think I'll find the lady one of these days."

John laughed. "The man never gives up."

"No," Derek agreed. "I never do."

Leigh picked up her coffee cup but the liquid was splashing dangerously. She set it back down. "Can I bother one of you for a cigarette? I seem to have left mine upstairs."

Both men solicitously offered her their packs. As Derek was closer, she accepted one from him. He grinned at the slight trembling apparent in her hand as he offered her a light.

"Nervous this morning, aren't you?"

"Am I?" She inhaled and exhaled. "Maybe. I don't like being confined."

"We'll get some work done and take your mind off the confinement then," Derek said. "Finish up your coffee and your cigarette and we'll get into 'Henry the Eighth.'"

"I'm anxious to hear this," John supplied eagerly.

Leigh's reply was for Derek alone. "I told you I didn't want to do the damn thing!" she snapped.

"And you also told our late-night visitor of the silver pen that you were here on business," Derek reminded her. His sensuous lips were set in a smile, but his eyes were narrowed and gleamed devilishly. His words had been part challenge—part warning?

Leigh stubbed out her cigarette and walked swiftly to the door. "I'll play what I remember, Derek—then you take it from there. I'm going home as soon as the weather clears. And I'm not coming back for months of work. Miss Lavinia White is going to have to write up whatever she feels like, which she probably will anyway!"

She briefly saw anger streak across Derek's face, hardening his rugged jaw, narrowing his eyes still further. But she didn't stay to receive an answer. Striding with determined and lengthy steps, she hurried through the salon and parlor, past the curving staircase and into Derek's office, where Roger already waited. Barely acknowledging him, she slid onto the bench and began to play idly with the ivory keys of the piano.

Derek was angry now, she knew, because she had been so rude to him in front of John Haley. But she was too inflamed to care. She knew that he had schemed the entire situation—plotting her arrival in foul weather, trapping her into agreement in the presence of Lavinia White, bringing part of the group to bear further pressure on her and to keep her from arguing with him. Well, on that score, he was wrong. She was past giving a damn who knew about their grievances.

And it was all supposedly over the music. That she still didn't believe. But if he wanted it, then he could have it. All she wanted to do was get away, get away from the man she hated so fiercely and loved so dearly.

She had lied yesterday. There wasn't a note in any of the songs that she had forgotten. She plunged straight in, mindless of the men who listened, heedless of the barrage of criticism that might follow. Her delicate fingers slid over the keys naturally, her voice rose high and low, clear and sweet. She played straight, locked in a little world of her own, and when she finished, the only audible sound was the call of the wind that raged outside the house around them.

It was Roger who spoke first. "Damn, Leigh! That's not just good, it's brilliant!"

"Bloody brilliant," Derek echoed quietly, and Leigh chanced a glance at him. His eyes had lost their golden glint and were dark with sincerity.

She shrugged, unable to cope with the unusual compliments. "It's all yours," she said. "Use it as you like."

"Tell me," Roger said, moving from the door where he had been standing when John and Derek had followed her into the room after her explosive departure. "Why didn't you ever sing with us before?"

Leigh laughed, honestly surprised by the question. "Because Richard always said I sounded like a dying frog!"

The three men in the room exchanged a glance that Leigh could not interpret. Derek cleared his throat and bent his lengthy frame to join her on the bench. "Let's try it again, shall we? I think I've got the chords."

Leigh was sure that he did. Derek could hear the opening bars of a piece and pick it up from that. "John," he continued, assuming consent by all, "my guitar is behind the desk."

They played the music again and Leigh was amazed at how good it all sounded, the two of them at the piano, John on the guitar, Roger tapping out the beat on his knees. Derek's voice, blending with hers, added the final touches. When they finished this time, she sat quietly staring at her hands, tense with an excitement she was afraid to feel.

"As soon as the weather clears," Derek said, "we'll fly down to Key West and pick up the original music. Then we'll get Shane and Bobby and start work in earnest."

Leigh swallowed and lowered her eyes. He was too close to be nice to her! She could feel his breath as he spoke, smell his warm masculinity and the light aftershave he was wearing.

She moved from the bench. "I'm thrilled that you all like it," she said. "And you're welcome to it. But no one needs to fly to Key West. I'll mail it as soon as I get back."

"What do you mean, you'll mail it?" Roger demanded jovially. "You're in this too, my girl. We wouldn't do it without you!"

"Roger!" Leigh exclaimed. "That's sweet of you. But you don't need me. I can't play anything half as well as any of you do and Derek could write books on what I don't know about music—"

"You'll be singing with me," Derek interrupted.

Leigh gasped with amazement as she stared at him, stunned. He had to be joking! As long as she lived, she would never forget the things that Richard had said about her voice, never accept that they were anything but true.

"Come on, Derek!" she retorted. "Enough is enough."

"What did you do before you met Richard?" he demanded suddenly.

She stared at him with exasperation. "You know what I did! A group of us used to play and sing calypso music for tourists—"

"Exactly."

"I don't understand what you're getting at."

"Did anyone tell you you sounded like a frog then?"

"Don't you get it?" John Haley moaned. "You were Richard's *wife*. He loved you; he didn't want you becoming involved with the band. He probably wanted to keep his private life private."

Had that been it? Leigh wondered. Had Richard's blustering, scornful criticism been part of a deep-seated insecurity? But why? She had never given him cause to doubt her. When she had filed for divorce, he had known exactly what her reasons were.

She looked to Derek and found him studying her inscrutably. He rose when he caught her return glance, stretched, and yawned as if he didn't want her to know what he was thinking. "Anyone for a game of pool? It must be getting close to lunchtime. Let's go play a grand championship and then hit Emma up for some sandwiches."

John and Roger likewise stretched and yawned and agreed with Derek. Leigh began mechanically to follow the two out the door, but Derek's grip on her elbow stopped her. "Go on," he said to John and Roger. "I'll play the winner. I need to speak with Leigh for a minute."

"You can let go now," Leigh said, looking pointedly at his hand on her arm as the door closed.

"Can I?"

She wasn't sure if he were amused or still angry.

"You want to talk—talk." She extricated her arm with a small jerk.

"I want to know if this is settled."

"If what is settled?" She knew what he was talking about but

249

she wanted to stall for time. Her feelings were confused. She knew she should simply get away. But learning that her work had merit and that she could be wanted for her own talents was exhilarating. As accustomed as she had become to Richard's fame and artistry, she had never imagined hearing her own voice on the radio, or seeing her own name in print.

"Dammit, Leigh!" Derek snorted impatiently. "Don't play games with me! Are you going to stay and see this through?"

"I—I don't know," she faltered.

"Why?"

"Why what?"

"Why don't you know?"

"Oh, Derek, what a stupid—"

"Not stupid at all!" he ejaculated, gripping both her arms and flinging her around to face him. "And I'll tell you why. You're afraid of me and that's stupid."

"I keep telling you you're as crazy as a June bug!" Leigh countered defiantly, her hazel eyes blazing. She didn't attempt to break his grip. "You tell me not to be afraid of you, but you're constantly throwing accusations at me or—or attacking me."

"Oh. And you're Madam Tact when you talk to me?"

"You started it all!" Leigh flared.

"And attacking?" He laughed dryly. "You threw your purse at me, you tried to slap me, and then you appear in my bed! Who's attacking whom here?"

"I—"

"And on top of all that, you make a sound effort to destroy my sex life forever by scalding me! Think of my poor parents! They would be heartbroken to think all chance of future Lord Mallorys was wiped out by a viciously thrown coffee cup!"

"Derek! Stop! I beg you!" He had to be teasing her, but she couldn't be sure from his unrelenting features. "I swear to you, it was an accident! I wouldn't have really harmed you on purpose!"

"Perhaps." The faintest ghost of a smile played upon the corners of his mouth. "But I owe you for that one!"

She was absurdly happy as he placed his arm around her shoulder and led her out the door. The idea tingled in the back of her head that Derek's attitude had improved because he slowly was coming to realize that Richard had been capable of telling less than the truth.

"You do want to work on the album," he said thoughtfully, as they followed the U shape of the house to the game room on the opposite side flanking the pool. "I can feel it, no matter what you say. So come on, commit yourself."

She hesitated no longer. "All right, I'm committed."

"Good. As soon as the roads clear, I'll drive to Key West with you and we can pick up the music and the things you'll need."

"I can drive back myself."

"But I don't trust you to return here. Anyway, I could use a few days' vacation. I'd like to do a little fishing and diving."

Derek, when he chose to be, was capable of selling air conditioning to Eskimos. Although she could hardly say they had come to any real understanding, Leigh was lulled into believing they could become, if not friends, at least amiable partners.

Until they neared the game room. Then he stopped her once more. "Oh, Leigh." He spoke as if in afterthought. "Stay away from John. He's just started with the group, you know, and I'd hate to have any trouble."

"John?" Leigh echoed dumbly.

"Always the sweet innocent!" Derek scorned her confusion. "You were coming on to him at breakfast. All those smiles and the shy encouragement. You keep forgetting—I know you!"

Leigh stood stock-still, her muscles wired within as fury boiled to her head with a dizzying pain. Her low, controlled voice was an amazement to her when she spoke.

"Derek, you do not know me at all, because you do not care to. But I'll tell you this, I won't stay away from anyone on your say-so! And if there is any trouble, I can guarantee you'll be the cause of it."

They stood for what seemed like forever, glaring at one another, both aware of the cocoon of hostility generated between them. Derek finally broke the heated silence.

"Well, love," he drawled. "Then I'll guarantee there won't be any trouble at all. I'll see from the beginning that I never give it a chance to exist!"

CHAPTER FOUR

The hurricane whipped and roared and wreaked havoc throughout the day, but by nightfall she had passed on, weakened as the eye itself had hovered inland, and only the outer circumference had played up on the coast. Star Island lost electricity, but few of the inhabitants suffered discomfort. Most had their own emergency generators, as did Derek.

Telephone lines, however, were down. The bridge was impassable. Property damage had been great in many places, but even in the smaller Keys, which had first been struck in the United States, no lives had been lost. A gentle toll for a hurricane of such force.

Leigh wandered from the house just as dusk was descending. The wild lashing of the sea had subsided to slow ripples; the merciless wind had died to a softly blowing breeze. Shades of crimson and gold streaked across the heavens, casting a glow of peace upon the battered land. The air was crisp and incredibly fresh, as it could only be after the cleansing effect of a storm.

She ambled idly down to the dock and sat despite the dampness of the wooden planks. She was glad to see that Derek's yacht, ironically called *Storm Haven*, had weathered the wind and thrashing sea remarkably well. She stood now like a regal lady, proudly silhouetted against the setting sun, rolling lightly in the lapping waves. Behind her the pale streams of a rainbow jetted in a magically disappearing arc.

Hugging her knees to her chest, Leigh watched until the sun sank into the sea. The day, after Derek's cryptic remark, had been a tense one for her. She had been careful to stay away from him, choosing to interrupt Emma and James in the middle of their gin rummy game and assist with lunch rather than enter the game room with Derek. She had played a game of eight ball with Roger when Derek had gone to radio the guardhouse and check on Tim and Nick, the generally invisible employees who nevertheless held considerable import as they manned the electronic eye and assured the safety of Derek's property and privacy and cared for the kennels. When he returned, she yawned and excused herself for a nap.

She had slept for a spell, and when she awoke, it was to hear the rasp of the shutters being lifted. She knew then that the storm had moved on and crept downstairs to sneak outside alone.

"Not too bad, huh?"

She started and went rigid at the sound of Derek's voice. He had the terribly annoying habit of addressing her as if nothing ever went wrong between them.

"The damage here," he continued, taking a seat beside her and wincing as the dampness crept through his clothing. "I've lost a few palms, and the pool looks like a deserted shambles, but that's about it."

"Good for you," Leigh muttered. Maybe he could act like all was peaches and cream, but she surely couldn't!

"Nasty little witch, aren't you?" he queried lightly, hesitating over the "witch" with deliberation.

"Leave me alone," Leigh suggested, "and you won't have to hear any nasty comments."

"Can't leave you alone at the moment, love." He gave her one of his wide smiles, which sent sent a rush of unease trickling down her spine. It was not a smile one could trust.

"Well . . ." She dusted her palms on her jeans. "If you're going to sit here, I'm going to go back in the house."

"Oh, no, darling, let's stay out here a few moments longer."

Leigh was not alarmed at the sudden rise in Derek's voice, but rather quizzical at the out-of-character endearment. She arched a brow at him, ready to ask if he were feeling all right, when he swiftly reached out and drew her into an intimate embrace. She opened her mouth to shout her outrage, but he, sensing her intention and his own advantage, claimed her lips with his own, forcing her teeth farther apart with his steely jaw even as she attempted to bite him in a bid for freedom. Her hands were

254

useless to her, for he caught them both expertly as he pushed her back upon the pier and and held her secure with the weight of his torso.

As she struggled against him vaguely, she sensed that he was not kissing her for the pleasure of the experience. He made no effort to entice or to seduce her, but held her rigidly, tense himself, giving only a fraction of his attention to her. His eyes, like hers, were not closed; they stared intently toward the house, a direction from which she could hear the remote sound of voices.

It was an act, a carefully planned and staged act. She was supposed to be seen in Derek's arms, seen in a position where it would appear that she was perfectly happy, perfectly content, perfectly willing!

The remote voices became more so. In the distance she could hear a sharp click . . . a door closing. Derek removed his muzzle-like hold from her lips, but maintained his clasp on her hands.

She would definitely have struck him if she could have.

Her breathing was ragged and uneven from her struggles, her chest heaving with indignation, making her speech barely coherent, which might have been a blessing. The things she had to say were certainly not nice. She raved in gasps, trying to shout but unable to, casting upon him every name of abuse that would come to her mind. And he sat and stared and listened, never releasing his hold upon her a hair, never interjecting a comment of his own. She cursed him on and on, until her fury sputtered itself out in a final, enervating exhaustion. When she had spewed forth her last words of contempt and scorn, she felt as if she had just run the Boston Marathon.

And that, of course, was exactly what Derek had intended.

"Why?" she breathed, when she had drawn air again.

He shrugged, clearly amused despite the venom that had been rained upon him. "Nothing personal. I told you I'd make sure there was no trouble."

"I see," Leigh said icily. "This was a little act staged for John.

But don't you think you're jumping the gun a bit? What makes you think John is interested in me anyway?"

Derek smiled nicely. "He's a man, a young man at that."

Leigh laughed, the sound dry and bitter. "What flattery! Every man is going to fall head over heels for me?"

"Like I said, John is young."

"No one here is young!" Leigh snapped. "I'm twenty-seven, John has to be at least thirty, and you, you—"

"Bastard?"

"Thanks, it will do—will shortly be thirty-seven! All adults! We're all capable of looking after ourselves!"

"It doesn't matter," Derek said indifferently, but there was a smug look, like that of a contented cat, in his eyes. "I won't have anything to worry about anymore."

"I see. John will think there's something between us."

"Isn't there?"

"Certainly. Dislike and bitterness." Leigh tried to shift but his weight and restraining hands still held her firmly. "Could you move now, please? Your little charade went off quite well. John and Roger are long gone."

"I'll move as soon as I'm sure you're calm," he replied flatly.

"Then you may be here a long, long time!"

"It's a nice night." Derek might not have had a care in the world.

Leigh emitted a low moan of exasperation. "What if I assured you that I have no designs at all upon John Haley? That I promise not to make a problem in any way for any member of the band?"

He moved one hand, securing both of hers in the other with a twist of a long finger, and scratched his chin, mocking her in slow deliberation.

"Well?" she demanded.

"I'm thinking." His free hand moved from his chin to her cheek and and he traced the fine bone structure of her face and brushed aside a lock of loose auburn hair. "You're quivering."

"I am not quivering!" she retorted, dismayed at the way her flesh so easily gave her away. "I'm shuddering!"

"That's not a shudder," Derek murmured in correction, his head lowering over hers. "It's a decided quiver. . . ."

It was indecent, Leigh thought vaguely before giving herself over to the delicious sensation, that anyone should kiss so well, that the mere blending of lips, the meeting of tongues, could destroy all rational thought, could create a boundless heaven of damp wooden planking. . . .

It was a very long time before she realized she was no longer restrained. His hands were too busy—exploring the form beneath the material of her skirt, enticingly creeping, touching each shivering rib, and molding over firm breasts that willfully arched to him—to be involved with keeping her in place.

And there was certainly no need. Her own arms had risen to embrace his back, to feel the warm, taut muscles there, to hold him closer to her as she mindlessly slipped into obedience to the demand of aroused sensations. Her fingers crept into his hair, tantalized by the clean crispness, delicately tracing the breadth of his chest to his flat waist, feeling keenly his heat through the thin material of his shirt. . . .

The pearl snaps on her shirt were coming undone, but she didn't notice, except, maybe, to appreciate the loss of their restriction. It had been so long since her flesh had felt his tender, sensual touch, so long since she had felt such delicious heat burn within her, the ecstatic fulfillment of longing, love, and desire. So right. So very, very right.

But it wasn't right. She loved him; he scorned her. The passion he showed her was just that. Desire, and the arrogant belief that he could use her and manipulate her as fitted his will.

His expert lovemaking—which had just allowed him to undo the snap of her lacy bra and to handle and tease the creamy mounds of her breasts and their rosy, hardening nipples—was skill, learned from years of practice. She, Leigh Tremayne, panting beneath his knowledgeable touch, meant nothing to him. Certainly not love . . . if anything at all, only revenge.

And what better revenge than to make her love him, need him, long for him with every fiber of her being? Then he could repudiate her—as she supposedly had Richard!

He was off guard now. She pushed him with all her strength and he went rolling over, grabbing for her instinctively. Together they plunged off the side of the dock—and into the frigid water below.

The storm had left the normally tepid channel as cold as ice. The chill stabbed Leigh through and through like the savage edge of a knife as she sputtered to the surface. They were not in deep water. Derek was standing as he shot her a furious oath and a glance more chilling than the water. He hooked his arms onto the dock and chinned himself up to shimmy back on the planking. Leigh couldn't stand, nor could she pull herself back up. She swam to where he now stood, hoping his wrath wouldn't be so great that he would leave her foundering in the cold water.

He didn't. His hand shot down and he cruelly pulled her up, his grip merciless, his expression shocked and livid. "What's the matter with you, woman?" he demanded, shaking with his rage, his eyes as gold and hard as newly minted pennies. "You're as hot as a coal one minute and the next . . . You're a vicious tease, just like Richard said!"

Leigh's mouth flew open with a stunned denial. Surely Richard couldn't have said that! "Derek, I—"

"You what? There is no excuse for you!"

"Don't force people and you won't get any surprises!"

"Now you're flattering yourself! That sure as hell wasn't force!"

"But it was!" she cried. "It is force because—"

"Because you don't want me touching you?" He laughed, deep, disdainfully. "You are a perpetual liar, Mrs. Tremayne. You fit to me like a hand in a glove. You lie through your teeth, but your flesh and blood tell the truth." He pulled her inexorably to him and her breasts were pressed to his chest, forming to his heat and strength. He possessed her again with burning kisses that stripped her of will as they moved along her face and down the length of her neck to push aside negligently the wet clothing that covered her collarbone and shoulders. His hot kisses were not an act this time, but nor were they gentle. They had their revenge as they fastened upon her with humiliating ease, audaciously claiming her nipples and breasts. Yet Leigh was a spellbound captive, seething with horror at the realization that he could not help but see the physical response he elicited despite the roughness with which he used her. Her tremulous lips, her rigid nipples, her erratic, gasping breaths—were all dead giveaways.

Then he pushed her away. "So you don't want me, Mrs. Tremayne. I know it is not love for your husband that makes it so. It must be that your lover still waits in the Keys. The same lover for whom you cast aside Richard Tremayne."

Leigh was so stunned that she couldn't speak. And as she stood staring at him, her hair plastered against her face, her lashes dripping the saltwater, and her clothing in dishevelment, she began to understand. It had all been Richard. He had created fictions to suit his convenience. He didn't want her singing; he told her she sounded like a frog. He didn't want a divorce, but he wouldn't change his ways. So he blamed it on her. He told Derek the divorce was her fault—that she wanted it unconditionally; that she had a lover, rather than himself having several.

And she *had* filed the papers. Derek knew it. It was only natural that he believe Richard on everything else. Richard had been his partner, his associate, his lifelong friend.

Derek mistook the wide-eyed shock on her face as an admission of guilt. She knew as his jawline hardened that he thought her surprised only at his knowledge of her affairs. His next words verified this.

"So you thought no one knew, huh? Sorry, I was the closest thing to a brother Richard ever had. He was a broken man, Leigh, he had to talk to someone. But don't become overly alarmed. I am the only one he ever talked to. And out of respect to Richard, I've never mentioned any of this before. When he died, I let the pretty lies go. I let the world go on thinking that

259

Richard had been a happily married man, that his widow had closeted herself away in her grief, that she had stayed sweet and loving to the end. You're safe, Mrs. Tremayne. I am the only one who knows that Richard might have purposely gone off that cliff because the woman who he had adored and married cared only for his money and status and was using them to support a bum of a lover—"

Leigh slapped him with the strength of a madwoman. Had he not been so vicious, had hate not glittered so clearly in the gold of his eyes, she would have tried to explain, she would have told him they had all been duped. But what good would that have done? He would never have believed her. The only man who could have cleared her in Derek's eyes was Richard, and Richard was dead. And now she understood with pathetic clarity what had happened, what had changed the kind and gentle man who had been her friend into a towering volcano of seething animosity bent on justice. She knew that the tender and caring lover she had had so briefly as another woman could never exist for her in truth.

A red mark was rapidly spreading across his cheek where she had struck him, but she didn't care. They couldn't be friends; they might as well be out-and-out enemies. "That's right, Mr. Mallory," she hissed furiously. "Wanton little me. I can't resist the touch of anyone male, including you, even though I do hate you with all my heart! But my friend in the Keys . . . well, he's terribly jealous and demanding and I do love him so I try to control myself. . . ."

Flippant anger was the wrong path to have taken. She stopped speaking because the wrath in his eyes and rigid stance was so murderous that she became frightened. "I told you, Leigh, never to slap me." His voice was as low and ominous as thunder. His fingers abruptly curled into the back of her hair so tightly that tears sprang unbidden to her eyes and she was sure that her scalp would shortly depart from her head. He swung her around in his punishing grip and shoved her toward the house. "This is your last warning—don't do it again."

There was no course for her but to head back inside with her chin lifted. Any further words between them could be deadly as well as futile.

He followed her back to the house, both dripping seawater. They met Roger on the patio, who said, "Bad time to be swimming," merriment playing in his eyes. "I came to warn you dinner was about ready, but . . ."

"We'll be right back down," Derek chuckled, throwing an arm around Leigh's shoulder. "We got a little carried away."

Leigh winced at his touch, ready again to do battle and set all records straight now that Roger was present to buffer her from Derek. But he was, again, prepared for the response he knew she would make. Her words were nothing but a gasp as he easily hoisted her into his arms and carried her to the staircase, his throaty, amorous-sounding laughter drowning out her gulping attempts to protest.

He took her to his own room instead of hers and dumped her on the bed, and when she indignantly tried to stand, he roughly threw her back.

"Just what do you think you're doing, Derek Mallory? You can't keep me away from the others forever! And when I do talk, you will be in trouble!"

"And you will look ridiculous!"

"Oh, and how is that?"

Derek took her chin lightly but with great menace. "Because, my dear, Roger and John are now thoroughly convinced we are having an affair. Flighty and pen-happy Miss Lavinia White will be thrilled to fill her magazine with the news of it; after all, she did see you in a state of undress! And—"

"Affairs end!" Leigh whispered defiantly. "And this one is ending right now."

"No, it's not!"

"Derek, you can't make me do anything! I don't care what anyone thinks or what anyone writes! All I want is to get away—"

"And that's the only thing I'll deny you!"

261

"Why?" Her single word was a cry of despair.

"Why do you think?" he demanded bitterly.

Tears sprang to her eyes and she choked them back. "You're trying to punish me for Richard, but Lord, Derek! I've paid for Richard. You never gave me a chance! You don't know the half of it!"

"I know enough!"

"Richard has been dead a long time! Why now? Why?"

"Because you wouldn't have come before."

Derek uttered his statement dispassionately and finally left her on the bed to walk to his closet, choose a dry outfit, and begin to strip, apparently comfortable doing so in her presence. She glanced longingly at the door to estimate her chances of making a quick escape when he grated, "Don't try it. You'll be sorry."

She replied with a derisive, brittle laugh. "And what will you do?"

"Try it."

"I will, Derek, and if you touch me again, I'll scream bloody murder!" Leigh warned, tossing her head in her most contemptuous manner. She stood with disdainful grace, slowly, as if she thought no more of him than of a harmless fly.

She made it as far as the door. Then he was upon her in two easy strides, naked to the waist. The crisp mat of hair on his chest tingled through the soaked blouse that clung to her skin as he caught her and threw her back even more viciously than before. Caught in his viselike grip, she could only stare with disbelief as he quietly told her, "Why, Leigh? Why all this? Because of Richard, because of me, because of you. There was no judge and jury to take care of you on Richard's behalf. So it falls to me. Stupid, idiotic me. The one who praised you to no end, the one who envied Richard his beautiful and charming wife, the one who would hear no wrong until forced to see it all. You mocked Richard, Leigh, and you made an absolute fool out of me. None of which I ever wanted to believe!"

Leigh hung limp against him. The puzzle pieces were all fitting in, everything was in the open. Any mask of chivalry Derek had worn had been to connive her to stay where he wanted her.

"So what now?" she asked bleakly. "Why don't you just beat me up, macho man, and leave it at that?"

"Too easy!" he muttered.

"Then what?" she demanded flatly, no longer rebellious but tired. "You can't keep me forever to torture . . ."

"No, your sentence isn't life."

He left her again to finish dressing, sure she would not take off again. Leigh lay with her eyes closed, incredulous that he could think he could hold her against her will.

He came back to the bed and jerked her up by the wrist. "Let's go. You have to change before you get pneumonia."

"Wouldn't you like that?" she queried sweetly.

He ignored her and ushered her into the room next door, carefully locking the door after they had come through it. "Your suit is in the closet. Emma cleaned and pressed it." He leaned against the door with crossed arms.

Leigh took her clothing into the bathroom and changed quickly. She brushed out her hair and repaired her makeup. When she emerged, Derek was still against the door, exactly as she had left him.

"Now, Mrs. Tremayne," he said coolly, "the choice is yours. If you walk down those stairs like the nice little lady you always purported to be, the night may go well."

"And if I don't?" It was all too absurd!

"Then you take your chances!" Something in his expression caused her to pale perceptibly. "Let's go."

She wondered as she preceded him downstairs how she could have managed to become part of the nightmare she was living. There had been moments at first, she was sure, when Derek had truly gentled toward her. He knew Richard had lied about a few things! The scene in the office had assured her of that. But now, now it seemed he hated her more than ever. The violent rumblings of hostility he had barely concealed at Richard's funeral were erupting like the lava of a volcano.

263

Dinner, which she dreaded, went amazingly well. Derek slipped back into his mask of conviviality, and became the perfect host. It was an easy meal, comfortable, made so by the bantering between the three men who worked together and who, in that capacity, had shared in one another's lives to a deeper extent than family. Roger was the main entertainment for the meal, telling funny tales of early experiences. Leigh began to wonder how the conversation would have gone had Richard been present instead of she, if the four men would not have fallen into ribald jokes and laughed the night away, eternal friends and conspirators of the night.

They wandered into the game room after dinner, where Roger came upon Derek's picture albums. He ensconced himself into a well-padded couch with Leigh and went through them as Derek and John shot pool. The albums were dated, and Roger started from the first year that the group, then shy and awkward boys, had first started playing together. They appeared in black velvet suits with ruffled white shirts, their hair—daringly long for those days!—curling over their collars.

"James put these all together for Derek, you know," Roger mused, as he and Leigh chuckled over the old pictures. "Staid old James! Pretends he can't stand the music but he bristles with pride over Derek anyway. I wish I had had a James!"

They moved on through the years, looking at remembrances of both the professional and private lives of the London Company. The boys in London, Glasgow, New York, Paris, and so on. Roger with an Orange Bowl Queen, Shane with the Italian girl who would become his wife, and then, Richard and Derek and herself, playing in the surf behind her father's house. Richard . . . tall, slender, handsome, his eyes as blue and light as the surf, his face as endearing and sincere.

Pictures followed of their wedding, Richard, the groom, Derek, the best man, Roger, Shane, and Bobby as ushers. Leigh, a very different Leigh, a bright, beautiful, and radiant bride. Derek, a Derek tender, admiring, respectful, kissing the bride. . . .

Pictures could be painful. Leigh stretched and snapped shut an album. "Those were fun to go through, Roger," she said, standing to uncramp her legs. "They made me feel drowsy, though. I think I'll go on up to bed."

"Don't go yet," Derek called. He paused and surveyed his shot, chalked his stick, and deposited the eight ball in the corner pocket. "Emma was making us some Irish coffees and scones."

He smiled at her caressingly and she smiled back with twisted lips. She wasn't up to arguing with him tonight, or putting any of his threats to a test. "Irish coffee sounds nice."

And it was very nice. They sipped it out on the patio, the breeze having lulled pleasantly. Except for the visible damage to the palms and other plant life, the storm might never have existed.

Derek sat beside Leigh, his arm around her shoulder or his hand resting on hers. She didn't fight him; she was too tired. Tonight the game was his. She could almost ignore the light touch of his long, strong fingers.

"Irish whiskey," Roger mused, thoughtfully scooping his whipped cream with a swizzle stick. His gaze suddenly focused on Leigh. "Weren't your folks Irish?"

"My father was," Leigh replied, idly chewing on the plastic of her swizzle stick. "My mother was Welsh." She started as she felt a spasm surge through the hand Derek was holding.

"McTigh!" He sounded as if he were choking.

Leigh was puzzled. "Yes, my name was McTigh. But my dad was very Americanized. You two know yourselves how easy it is to gain and lose mannerisms and customs! Don't you agree, John?" She laughed. "Why there were times I would have sworn Richard came from southern Georgia rather than London!" She couldn't begin to understand Derek's reaction to the conversation. He had met her father!

"Yes, I'm sure we could all pass as Americans by now," Derek said absently.

"I didn't say that!" Leigh chuckled. "You've picked up a lot of American expressions, but it's obvious you're British every time you open your mouth."

"Just like everyone knows I'm an American!" John supplied. "Even though I'm with the London Company now."

"You know," Roger reflected, leaning his chin in his hands, "we need a name for John. Remember, Derek, when we started the band how we all had the little names printed on our cards? You know what I'm talking about, Leigh. I'm the Duke of Rose, Richard was the Wizard of Oz, Bobby, Sir Robert, Shane, the King of Hearts, and Derek, of course, Lord Mallory. What could we have John be?"

"Something high-sounding too!" John chuckled.

"But American!" Leigh interjected. The liquor was numbing the pain she had been feeling and she was beginning to enjoy herself.

"American . . ." Roger said thoughtfully. "Chief John?"

"Too plain!" John protested.

"The Governor? The President?" Leigh was thinking American.

"How about the Pied Piper?" Derek suggested, apparently involved with the conversation although his eyes still seemed slightly distant and oddly speculative as he watched Leigh. "Pied Piper. For his flute."

"That's it! I love it!" John Haley decided jubilantly.

"And now . . ." Derek sipped at his warm glass and brushed at the mustache that no longer existed. "We need one for Leigh."

"But I'm not with the group!" she cried.

"You will be," he corrected. "For the next album."

"True! True!" Roger delightedly tapped on the aluminum table. "Maybe the Wizardess of Oz?"

"No!" John protested quickly, and Leigh saw by the glance he exchanged with Roger that he was reminding him Leigh now belonged with Derek. "No, Leigh should have her own special name."

"Wonder Woman?" Roger tried.

"Ugh!" from Leigh.

"There's always the Black Widow," Derek proposed innocently. "But actually, I have a better one, The Lady of the Lake. Medieval and quite fitting too, considering Leigh is only truly happy in or around water."

Leigh shrugged and downed the tail end of her drink. The peculiar look Derek continued to give her was making her terribly uneasy. If she were an animal, she would be sniffing the air for danger.

"Sounds good," she said, suppressing a faked yawn. "I think I will go up now, if you all don't mind." Without meaning to, she glanced at Derek for his approval, wincing inwardly at the amusement and spark of triumph that sped briefly through his eyes.

"I'll walk you up," he offered.

"You don't really need to," Leigh demurred. If she could only move quickly enough . . . She planted a light kiss on top of his head and waved jauntily to Roger and John. "You all stay and talk!" She scampered into the house, confident that Derek would not follow now.

But he did. He was knocking at her door even as she closed it.

"What, Derek," she moaned, throwing it back open to admit him.

"I just wanted to tell you good night and"—he leaned against the door with sardonic amusement—"good show."

"Isn't that what you want?" she jeered.

"Umm . . ."

"Well good night and thank you." Her sarcasm ruffled him not at all. He continued to watch her, curiously, as if he had seen something new. Then he chuckled. "Good night . . . me lass!"

He left, closing the door with a snap behind him.

"What ails that man?" Leigh wondered aloud irritably as she bolted the door uneasily. She shook her head with disgust and changed into a shirt with little thought. She was so tired! She had been at Derek's for less than forty-eight hours and he had totally exhausted her.

Yet sleep, when she had tucked herself into the four-poster, was hard to come by. Her eyes kept flying open as her mind raced on.

Derek was blatantly out for revenge. And in a way she understood his feelings. She could well remember the way Richard could tell a story, the way he could make you almost believe it was night when it was day. And she, like a fool, had fostered Derek's belief in her coldhearted infidelity by her impulsive angry words.

At moments, she thought wistfully, Derek honestly wanted her. She instinctively knew when his touch was sincere. But, and she hardened her heart, Derek honestly wanted a number of attractive females. He was a womanizer, like Richard.

Games. All they did was play games together. Hers had been one of unrequited love and desire; his was based entirely on bittersweet revenge. He was making all the plays; as yet, she had hardly had a turn.

But the chance for her move would come. And when it did she asked herself wryly, which way would she turn?

CHAPTER FIVE

"You're a lucky girl, Leigh. Like those model types in the soap operas who manage to waken in perfect form."

Leigh rapidly blinked the sleep from her eyes to stare wrathfully at the figure casually seated, hands around knees, at the foot of her bed.

"How did you get in here?"

"Key, of course. I own the house, remember," Derek replied.

"Good," she told him curtly. "Go find somewhere else in your house to sit!" She turned her back on him and added, "I thought it would take you a day and a half to find the key."

"So it would, except Emma found it for me."

Traitor! Leigh thought silently. "Could you go away, please? I'd like to go back to sleep." She pointedly closed her eyes.

"What? More sleep? You've already slept half the day away!" Derek proclaimed, ripping her covers rudely from her. "Come on downstairs, my love, we're having a party and you're the hostess for the day."

The drapes went flying open and Leigh blinked again, painfully, as she forced her lids up and acknowledged from the angle of the sun streaming through the window that it was late in the day. She groaned and buried her face in her pillow. "Go have your party without me."

"No way, love. It's a work party." His voice had taken on a crisp and authoritative edge. "Get your sweet body up and moving. My office."

Leigh jumped up seething as her door slammed after his exit. She had had just about enough of Derek Mallory. She glanced out the window with narrowed eyes. The sun was brilliantly shining; only a slight breeze whispered through the foliage.

She was getting off Star Island, this morning, alone.

Determined, she showered and flung open the closet door to

find the beige suit that she had worn the night before. It was gone. In its place hung a new assortment of clothing—blouses, pants, and three dresses. It infuriated her further to realize that someone had been very busy in her room while she had thought she was sleeping in privacy.

But if she wanted to leave the room, she had to dress. She chose jeans and a short-sleeved gold-threaded blouse, a comfortable outfit for a drive. Then she moved purposefully down the stairs. She didn't expect to find her own car waiting outside, but if Derek had arranged a "party," then the phones had to be in order and the bridge passable. She would call a cab, and fly back home. The Audi could be picked up later, when Derek had tired of his game.

The receiver was wrenched from her hand before she had dialed the first number.

"What do you think you're doing?" Derek demanded hotly. He must have moved like an Indian into the parlor, she hadn't heard a sound.

"Leaving."

"The hell you are!" Derek propelled her toward his office. "Shane and Bobby are here. We're going to work."

They did work, for hours. Derek barely allowed her a cup of coffee before they began, which startled no one. He was a strict taskmaster, which they all knew, yet he demanded nothing of anyone he wouldn't give himself. Leigh knew that he was most rigid on concert tours, when he jogged five miles a day and refused even a glass of wine with dinner.

They broke late in the afternoon, and when they did, Leigh was trapped thoroughly in a way Derek must have known she would be. Blue-eyed Shane McHugh and eloquent Bobby Welles were, if possible, more enthusiastic about the project than Roger and John had been. They, too, insisted that Leigh must be a part of her own work. Bobby filled her head with images of videodiscs and Shane suggested that they could film a complete program to be sold to various subscription television networks.

"Of course, Leigh," Derek said with sickening sincerity, a look of understanding sympathy on his face that should have won an Emmy, "we will not force you to join us. We can always hire Samantha Downing to do the female harmonies and sections."

Leigh tensed in her chair, but smiled brightly. She would never let Derek know how deeply his barb had struck. Samantha Downing was a singer with a voice like a crystal angel. She had also been one of Richard's first outside "affairs." Did Derek know that?

"That won't be necessary," Leigh said. Derek had sprung another trap, but in this instance her pride forced her to walk into it open-eyed. She batted shy, conniving lashes. "Since you all are willing to bear with my inexperience, I'll thank you for your patience and enjoy the ride!"

It was the perfect response. The cluster of males, minus Derek, hastened to scurry to her and assure her they were more than willing to be as patient and helpful as she would need.

The real party, which followed their rehearsal, was an enjoyable occasion, even though Leigh knew that all present were secretly mulling over the new relationship between her and Derek with glee. What could be more fitting? Derek, caring for his best friend's widow. Leigh, who knew them all, who loved and understood music, with Derek. . . .

Angela McHugh and Tina Welles had come over with Shane and Bobby and Bobby's little girl, Lara. Emma and James were off for the evening since Miami and the Beach had recovered quickly from the effects of the storm. They had, Derek informed Leigh as he escorted her into the kitchen to assist Angie and Tina, made a cute couple as they left for a dinner at Joe's Stone Crab, the proper Englishman and the plump American matron.

"The boys are barbecuing," Angie said as she gave Leigh an alarmingly happy hug. "So we're throwing together some salad and wrapping up some ears of corn."

It was easy, Leigh thought, as she chatted with Angie and Tina, to remember how nice it had been when they had all gotten together. She and the other two wives had become fast friends as had their husbands; they had enjoyed the times when they had

271

been able to meet as a group, any set of normal couples leisurely whiling time away with amiable company.

The conversation between the women was general at first. Little Lara tottered among them, lisping but sweet as she broke in occasionally with her childish voice. She was a beautiful little girl, Leigh thought with a pang, but then she had beautiful parents. Beautiful, happy parents. Bobby Welles, she knew, could be set in the middle of a bevy of naked beauties and he wouldn't notice a one of them. He adored Tina. They had the kind of marriage Leigh had believed that she and Richard would have.

And it was beautiful raven-haired Tina who dropped their bantering chatter to demand, "Why didn't you keep in touch with us, Leigh? Angie and I both wrote . . ."

Leigh raised her hands helplessly. A painful spasm ripped suddenly through her muscles. For a moment she saw their last meeting clearly in her mind, like the slow-motion, brightly colored replay on a television set. Richard lay in an oak box while the birds sang and the sun shone; Derek stood beside her, though distant, a pillar of strength. Tina, Angie, Roger, and the others and a host of strangers to mourn the passing of a brilliant star moved by them, tears in their eyes, unspoken sympathy showing in their drawn faces.

Then they were all gone. All except her and Derek, and Richard between them in the dirt. Then Derek had broken. The towering, proud giant broke and tears came streaming down his face. Leigh tried to comfort him despite the gulf that lay between them. But he wanted nothing from her, he told her in no uncertain terms. She was, he railed, anger and hate returning his strength, a witch, a lying, hypocritical witch. He had had a few more choice words for her before turning on his heel abruptly and leaving.

"I—I needed some time," Leigh said lamely. Roger, as did Derek, had known trouble had stirred between Leigh and Richard. But even he hadn't known about the impending divorce.

"Sure," Tina said, her voice husky. "But time does heal all wounds."

"Hey!" Angie declared, sweeping little Lara into her arms. "If we don't get this corn out we'll never eat! And I'm starving!"

"Starvin'!" repeated little Lara with round eyes.

Leigh chuckled and reached for the little girl, softly touched by the feel of her chubby hands. Would she ever hold such a wonderful bundle of love of her own? It was doubtful. She would be twenty-eight on her next birthday, not old—certainly!—but time was passing by.

"I'm starvin' too, Lara! Let's go hurry your daddy," Leigh said.

As the night wore on, Derek continued in his subtle ways to give the impression that he and Leigh were now a twosome. Tina and Angie would sometimes glue their heads together in soft conversation, and Leigh supposed they were happily considering the chances of a second marriage. She wanted to laugh bitterly. What would they think, she wondered, if she were to stand and calmly announce that Derek didn't give a damn for her, that the whole charade was some type of malicious revenge?

They would think she was crazy. Derek was displaying his complete, suave animalistic charm. He was devastating in the starlight, his jeans tight over his trim hips, his shirt casually unbuttoned and showing the breadth of his deep bronze chest. When he spoke and smiled, his teeth would flash white and perfect against his rugged jawline, his eyes would sparkle like gold against the copper of his strong features. His fingers often touched upon Leigh, awakening her every nerve, sending her into chills of trembling each time.

What if . . . she began to ask herself, what if she went along with his little game. How would he react if she pounced upon him in return, became in public the loving mistress he pretended her to be? She would certainly throw him off, and perhaps find out just what part this mock tenderness played in his ultimate plan.

She didn't have the nerve! She could act all she wanted, but

Derek had the strength. He had the power, because he cared nothing for her while she . . . was going to do it!

She would beat Derek Mallory at his own game!

She might wind up shattered later, but he would never know it. He wanted to think of her as a conniving little cheat, well, by golly, that was exactly what he was going to get. He had said he desired her. When she finished with him, he was going to go crazy with his desire. He wanted everyone to think they were together, she would verify that reasoning. And then she would turn on him, as he had turned on her.

She began with the subtlety he employed himself, fingering his hair as she jauntily checked on the barbecue, pretending to massage his back when he chanced to sit near her, even going so far as to pat his firm rear end when he passed her on his way to the cooler for another beer.

His stunned response left her hard put not to burst into gales of laughter. Unfortunately, her triumph didn't last long. Derek learned to stifle his surprise and in return dropped all pretense of subtlety. She learned abruptly that the tide had changed when she teasingly caressed his neck, only to be drawn into a long and barely controlled kiss, enjoyed with relish by the entire company.

As the fabled moon moved high over Miami, they moved the party inside. Leigh accompanied Tina upstairs to put Lara to sleep in her portable crib, then returned to the game room with the others. Derek caught her as she entered, and maneuvered her into a position where she half reclined against his chest. It was a loving scene, she thought ruefully. His hand moved along her rib cage familiarly and settled beneath her breast as he casually chatted.

"Oh, Leigh!" Tina impulsively interrupted the discussion on the light area damage of the hurricane. "It is so wonderful to have you here with us again!"

"It sure is!" Bobby echoed, hugging his wife closer to him.

"Wonderful," Derek repeated, and only Leigh caught the sardonic inflection in his tone.

Angela muttered something quickly to Bobby in the Italian he had begun to understand and then smiled at the group mischievously. "And so wonderful that it seems you will be with us for a long time, yes?"

An idea ripped madly through Leigh's head. It was the perfect time to call Derek's bluff. Did she dare? She giggled, thinking, the devil made me do it. True in a way. Derek was the closest thing to a real devil she had ever met.

"Oh, darling!" she crooned. "We should tell them!"

Derek jerked and stared down at her adoringly angled head, his eyes narrowing and his pulse suddenly increasing. "Tell them what, *darling?*"

"Really, Derek!" she admonished, pushing playfully from him. "He's so shy!" she exclaimed to the group, a very convincing, loving smile glued to her tolerant lips. She chanced a quick glance his way to find his jaw stiff and eyes glittering suspiciously. She plunged on quickly, "Well, darling, I think they should know." Her smile increased and she faked tremulous tears. "Derek and I are going to be married, as soon as we finish the new album."

Derek's muscles tensed as if he had been hit by a red-hot poker. She could feel the terrible steel coils of his thighs beside hers as the group went pin-dropping silent. Then Angela and Tina jumped to their feet simultaneously, followed by their husbands, to rush to her and Derek and voice their sincere happiness and congratulations.

Leigh felt the first horrible pangs of guilt over her ridiculous announcement. These people were her friends as well as Derek's. There was no need to have involved them in their private problems, no need to have created such excitement, which could only be dashed cruelly upon the shore of lies. At least, she assumed, it would all be over quickly. Derek would now have to denounce her and she would explain it had all been a joke. . . .

But Derek did no such thing. After his initial astonishment, he grinned, accepted the congratulations of his friends, and eyed Leigh levelly.

"Really, Leigh!" he mocked her with silky tones. "Now that

you've let the cat out of the bag, as they say, why should we wait till we finish the album? I never did believe in long engagements. I'm sure we can arrange something nice and suitable in the next few weeks."

It was Leigh's turn to be totally astounded. She couldn't think of a thing to say. Once more her move had viciously backfired. She could only sit and listen to the plans that ricocheted around her, suggestions from Tina and Angela, winks and chuckles from Bobby and Shane, heartfelt good wishes from John and Roger.

It was late when the company finally pulled from the drive. Leigh tried to escape Derek while he said his last good-byes and to race up the stairway before he could catch her, but she never had the chance. He maintained an iron clasp around her until the final car, Roger's gray Mercedes, disappeared down the moonlit path.

"What's the hurry, love?" he demanded dryly as he felt her preparing to spring from him. "Shouldn't we be discussing our wedding plans? Or perhaps be wallowing in the ecstasy of our love beneath this silver moon?"

"If I'm with you, darling," Leigh retorted, "I'm already wallowing."

"Tsk! Tsk! That mouth of yours will get you into trouble one day," Derek warned, ushering her back into the house. "Go to bed. I want you up and ready by seven tomorrow morning!"

"For what?"

"The Overseas Highway has been cleared for traffic. I want to leave early."

"For Key West?"

"Yes."

"Why do you want to go with me now?" Leigh asked, her voice caught between bitterness and pleading. "You know I'll come back. You know that I want to do the album now!"

"You don't like Samantha Downing, huh?" Derek shrugged indifferently. "It doesn't matter. You don't think I'd let my beloved fiancée take that long drive by herself, do you?"

Leigh breathed a sigh of disgust and gripped the banister of the stairway tightly. "I'm sorry I came out with that, Derek, I really am. I was sure you'd come out with the truth. But we have to stop this ridiculousness now."

"Maybe I'm really intending to marry you."

"Hell!" Leigh sniffed. "And I wouldn't marry you—"

"Or," Derek mused, ignoring her statement of derision, "maybe I just want to bed a hot—" He captured her hand in midair as it sailed toward him. "Or maybe I want to make sure your friend in the Keys hears about this. Maybe I want to meet him and be sure to let him know, after I blacken both his eyes, what it feels like when the woman you love jumps into bed with another man."

Anger surged through her like a rushing tide as she stood a prisoner of his encircling fingers. "You can say we're living together, Derek, or you can say we're engaged. Believe it or not, you won't be ruining anything—"

"Oh? You mean he doesn't care if he shares you?"

Leigh ignored that. "And you won't find anyone's eyes to blacken." He had begun to lead her up the stairs. "But my strongest promise is this, Derek Mallory, I will never jump into your bed!"

"Why not?" He was amused suddenly, chuckling. "You've jumped into it before."

"By accident!" Leigh exclaimed. "You know I was locked out! You know that I didn't know that was your bed!"

"Ah, but, love," Derek said gravely, "that's not the occasion I'm talking about!"

In a split second Leigh's hands became clammy; the hairs on the back of her neck seemed to stand straight with cold, creeping fear.

"What . . ." She was choking, her throat constricted. "What are you talking about?" That was better. Her demand came off with irritation.

"You don't know?"

"Of course not!" Good, she was indignant.

Derek smiled lazily, his eyes like some feline predator in the dim light. "Maybe you'll think of it. Good night." He moved on down the hall to his own bedroom doorway. "Oh, Leigh, don't forget, seven A.M. And be ready, or I'll drag you out of bed and dress you myself."

"That should be a new one for you," Leigh muttered crossly beneath her breath. "I would imagine you're much more experienced with undressing women!"

He turned and she cringed, startled that he had heard her.

"I'm quite good at that, too, my love," he said gravely, a mocking smile stealing into the corners of his sensuous lips. "You'll have to try me sometime . . . again."

Leigh had nothing else to say. She slammed into her room, fighting the shakes as she tried to assure herself that she had imagined Derek's last word. He couldn't be referring to Atlanta, he couldn't be! If he had had any suspicions regarding her, he would have confronted her long ago. Besides, he was still determined to find his mysterious and missing date.

Uneasily convinced, Leigh drifted into sleep. Derek, she decided, before succumbing to the comfort of a restful blankness, had merely discovered a new way to taunt her. Her lips curved into a soft, groggy smile. Sticks and stones may break my bones but words will never hurt . . . Darkness claimed her, shutting out any reminders of just how painful words could be.

As they passed through Homestead the following morning, the disc jockey's blaring voice from the Audi's AM/FM radio announced an uninterrupted hour of music by the London Company. Derek, driving, impatiently moved to change the station, telling Leigh sourly that he was not in the mood to hear his own voice.

"Leave it, please," Leigh requested. It was the newest album that would be played, one that she had purchased, but had not been able to bring herself to listen to yet.

Derek, softened perhaps by her politeness, shrugged. He wore dark sunglasses as he drove, preventing her from seeing any of his thoughts.

The album was a pleasant mix of lighthearted fast tunes and

soul-reaching ballads. One was about a child, and as Leigh glanced at Derek he said yes, he had written it especially for Bobby about Lara. The next was a hard, fast piece, the type that toes automatically tap to, about a "vixen beauty" who lied and cheated her way from man to man. Leigh wondered if that particular song had been written with her in mind, but she didn't glance to Derek for confirmation and he kept silent.

The final song of the set, though, was the one that caused her heart to throb in fast-paced agony. She knew beyond a doubt that Derek had written it for and about his mystery woman. His voice filled the small Audi with agonizing clarity, husky with emotion.

> I remember you like a golden sunset;
> I remember you like a fireside.
> Crystal dreams and emerald seas
> Lord, love, how you please.
> Silver lady of the night
> Disappears with dawn's first light . . .

There was more, but Leigh blocked out the words. She lit a cigarette and stared out the window. They were losing the station anyway.

"It's good," she said dispassionately. "Very good. More 'solid gold' in there somewhere, I'm sure."

"Thanks."

They were passing the long strip of A1A that would deliver them into the Keys. Snowy egrets dotted the slender landscape, and out in the deep azure water a pair of cormorants hovered over the horizon, hunting their breakfast. Leigh turned slightly in her seat to watch a great white heron standing proudly on one pencil-thin leg as he majestically surveyed his surroundings. She spun back around; the Audi was slowing as they entered Key Largo. Derek turned off the road shortly.

"What are you doing?" Leigh asked, puzzled. "This is Pennekamp."

"I know where we are," Derek stated flatly.

"All right then," Leigh replied, growing irritated. "What are *we* doing *here?*" John Pennekamp was an underwater state park. It was a beautiful place, boasting miles of protected coral reefs. Leigh had come many times in her life and enjoyed them all. But what was she doing here now, with *Derek.*

"What do people usually do here?" Derek cross-queried sarcastically. "We're going to go snorkeling."

Leigh smashed out her cigarette and exhaled with exasperation. "You are a crazy man, Derek," she said, repeating an earlier observation. "I thought you were in a big hurry to get to Key West."

"No," he corrected, "I was only in a big hurry to get started."

"And we're going to have a terrific time, I suppose?"

"I would think so." Derek grinned boyishly. "We'll be underwater most of the time. You'll have to keep your mouth shut."

"Funny, funny," Leigh muttered. "I don't have a bathing suit. We don't have our snorkel gear—"

"They've a nice little shop here where you can buy a bathing suit and we can rent snorkel equipment." Derek set aside her objections.

Leigh went silent with a resigned twist of her shoulders. If he wanted to stop and take a snorkling trip, he would do it whether she agreed or not. Then a thought came to her as she glanced at Derek's dark glasses. He had probably worn them more to conceal his identity than as shade against the sun. She almost laughed aloud. A devious little plan began to hatch in her mind.

"Perhaps this is a good idea," she mused, keeping a small note of reluctance in her voice. He might become suspicious if she sounded too eager. They parked and she hurried out of the car. "Why don't you check on the excursions and I'll see if I can find a shop."

"Okay." Derek seemed pleased with her affable agreement, and he smiled almost tenderly as he watched her, his eyes swiftly raking over her auburn hair, glinting like spun gold in the sun, and her warm, thick-lashed hazel eyes. "Hurry up. I'll meet you by the rental window."

Leigh remained nonchalant and sedate until he disappeared from view. Then she rushed into the shop and purchased the first suit she could find in her own size, donned it hurriedly in the dressing room, and asked the kindly clerk for a public phone.

With feverishly trembling fingers, she called the local radio station and announced that *the* Derek Mallory of the London Company was at John Pennekamp Coral Reef State Park. To assure the validity of her statement, she even gave her own name, while pleading that it not be divulged.

Then she smiled and hung up the phone, and slowly sauntered over to the rental window to meet Derek.

He came up shortly after she did, dressed in a pair of faded blue cutoffs. Leigh winced for a moment of regret. Clad so scantily, every rippling muscle, every tautly honed limb of his superb physique was visible. He would attract the attention of anything female whether his identity was known or not.

"We leave in forty-five minutes," he told her. "A four-hour trip, all right?" His handsome smile was sincere as he slipped an arm around her shoulder. "Then we can shower, dress, and stop by Marker 88 for a meal before driving on to Key West. How's that sound?"

"It sounds fine," Leigh murmured, feigning attention to the rows of flippers that hung in the window. She didn't want to meet his eyes. Guilt was taking a toll on her. Little pinpricks of uncertainty were telling her that Derek had really been trying to plan a nice day.

They had both just found masks and fins that fit reasonably well when the first shout came, followed by a cacophony of noise and shrill screams

"It is him!"

"There he is!"

"Oh, my God!"

"Derek Mallory in the flesh!"

Within seconds Derek was besieged in a sea of humanity, trapped between countless bodies and the rental window.

His scathing glance caught Leigh once before she was able to

281

scramble away, and she began to regret her impish prank in earnest. The message in his glimmering eyes couldn't have been clearer had he shouted, *You'll pay for this!*

Leigh decided not to wait around to see how Derek would extricate himself from the quickly formed crowd of fans. She scurried down to the dock and searched out the excursion boat they were to take. Luckily, the boat was in her berth. Leigh hopped aboard and found a seat in the stern, hugging her knees and rocking nervously.

It seemed like an eternity before the boat began to fill. She was pulling away from the dock when Derek finally came on board, breathing heavily. He was forced to stop several times as he strode forward, caught by new adulation from those who were scheduled on the same trip. Finally, after speaking to everyone, he pleaded to be thought of as nothing more than a fellow passenger. Leigh watched him with grudging respect and admiration. He managed the situation very well, and she had to admit there was reason for him to be thought of so highly within the business and out.

"Cute!" was his short, terse word for her when he sank down beside her. "I'll thank you not to pull that again!"

She hesitated, then decided upon a play for innocence. "Pull what again? I can't help it if you're a recording star and people recognize . . ."

His tense features and blazing eyes caused her speech to trail away. "Don't do it again, Leigh, I mean it."

She was relieved when it appeared he was going to say nothing more. But at the time he really couldn't have said much more. People were inching over to them, no longer determined to tear Derek apart as a celebrity, but fascinated that he was with them, an ordinary person out to view the beauties of the crystal waters. A number of young couples were on board and the conversation turned to water, sailing, snorkeling, and diving.

They dropped anchor and sent up their dive flag at the reef with the bronze statue of Christ set into the water. Derek and

Leigh wet their equipment and donned it and plunged into the water, peacefully.

He was right; it would be difficult to argue with one's mouth in the water.

The bathing suit Leigh had so quickly purchased was a kelly green bikini. Occasionally Derek's fingers were pulled from hers to ripple down her back so that she might look in a special direction and view whatever it was he pointed out: a tremendous, friendly grouper, a colorful jellyfish to be seen but avoided, a school of brilliant yellow tangs. There was something very sensual about his touch in the water, something extra delicious about the feel of his extraordinary fingers.

Time passed quickly in the eerie little spot of oceanic heaven. Derek motioned her to bring her head out of the water and then suggested they move over to the statue before it was time to go back. Leigh nodded happily and followed him with a stiff kick of her large black flippers.

The others were leaving the statue as they approached it. Leigh inhaled for a deep dive and plunged through the fifteen feet or so of water that would bring her to the base of the bronze Christ. Then she slowly swam up its length, curious as ever about the beautiful piece of art sitting in the coral reef. Suddenly she felt Derek behind her, his hands moving along her waist to her rib cage and on to her back. She didn't fight him; the silky sensation was wonderful and besides, how far could he push in the middle of the reef with scores of people within forty feet of them? At the moment, she thought, he was welcome to be a bit amorous. . . .

But he wasn't being amorous at all. He and the seductive sea had lulled her into a false sense of security. The hand on her back was not loving but devious. It abruptly pulled the strings of the kelly green bikini top and pulled the entire thing from Leigh's body.

Leigh spun in the water but Derek was already a good ten feet away. She was running out of air, forced to surface. She kicked herself up and cleared her snorkle, glancing around desperately for Derek. He broke the surface too, shooting water from his snorkle, then laughing gaily as he caught sight of her furious, perplexed features.

"Damn you, Derek," she shouted, "give that back!"

"In time," was his cool, chuckled response.

Leigh struck out for him in the water and he didn't move. She lunged for his hands to find that neither held her bikini top. "Where is it?" she demanded breathlessly.

"All in good time," Derek replied, a wicked grin planted firmly on his lips. Then his hands began to seek her. Then ran over her velvety flesh, fixed upon the soft mounds of her creamy breasts, began to tease the rosy nipples that were clearly visible in the amazingly translucent water. . . .

Leigh desperately tried to pull away. "Derek, please!" she begged. "There are people . . ." Her struggles were stealing her breath as were his tantalizing maneuvers. "Please!"

He laughed again, a low, throaty sound, and allowed her to escape.

Then he calmly turned and began to swim slowly back to the boat.

"Derek!" Leigh screamed. He couldn't really be doing this to her, leaving her half naked to return to a crowded boat!

He slowly turned to her again, treading water, his brows quirked beneath his mask. "Yes?"

"Please?" she implored again. "I promise, I'll never play another trick on you again!" She waited, her legs flailing the water with strong strokes as he watched her, apparently mulling over a decision. "Derek!" she cried again, mournfully. The boat captain was calling his passengers back on board.

"All right," Derek called.

Leigh waited again, with exasperation. Seconds were becoming minutes and he wasn't moving.

"Throw it to me!" she exploded.

"Un-unh!" he returned with a shake of his curly head that sent a spray of saltwater flying. "You come get it."

Leigh swallowed with resignation and swam to him warily. "Well?" She hovered two feet away from him.

"Get it yourself," he taunted indifferently.

"Where is it?"

With half-closed eyes and a lazy drawl he replied, "Tucked in my pants."

Ten hours of straight sun could not have turned Leigh's body a darker shade of red. But his face was implacable.

If she wanted her green bikini top, she would have to get it herself. Cursing him all the while, she reached gingerly for his trim hips and delved into the faded blue cutoffs, praying she would touch nothing with her delicate fingers except her bikini top.

CHAPTER SIX

"Calm down!" Derek ordered as she continued to curse him while trying to adjust the bathing suit. He was still annoyingly amused. "You'd better let me help you before the boat leaves without us."

Leigh stiffly turned her back on him and allowed him to retie the strings of her bikini. As soon as he finished, she kicked away, but a powerful kick brought him to her side and he jerked her back to face him. "Calm down!" he repeated harshly. "This evens the score. No more little pranks on either side. Agreed?"

"Ohhhh . . . agreed!" Leigh snapped. She really had no other choice. Besides, there could be more trouble back at the docks. Derek's throng of fans might be waiting for his boat to return. . . .

They managed to settle that problem back on board the boat. A sympathetic young man suggested Derek take his loud, tourist-type shirt and battered fishing cap and blend into their group. Derek gratefully accepted his offer, and suggested the convivial conspirators join them later at Marker 88. Needless to say, the man, his wife, and the couple with them were thrilled.

Derek did elude the crowds that had formed with the help of the captain and fellow passengers, promising them all autographed albums if they wished to call his agent. It was well known that he was a man who kept his promises.

An hour later they entered Marker 88 and were ushered to a rear table. The two young couples who had been so helpful on the boat joined them within a few minutes and Derek returned the borrowed shirt and cap. Leigh, who had hardly spoken to Derek since their encounter in the water, was surprised at how pleasant the meal turned out to be. They were bright young people, knowledgeable about many things, and conversation flowed easily. The waitress neatly rattled off the long list of special appetizers and entrees Marker 88 boasted daily, and between them they ordered one of everything. The snorkling trip and the sun and sea had left everyone famished, and Leigh, as well as everyone else, dived ravenously into clams casino, oysters Rockefeller, escargots in mushroom caps, and several other delicacies. She ordered a scrumptiously prepared Florida lobster for her main course, and ignored Derek's look of amusement when she accepted a taste of his king crab.

Sometime during the meal Derek mentioned nonchalantly that Leigh was Richard Tremayne's widow. Leigh shot him a look of pure antagonism as she then was plied with questions, polite at that, about Richard. She was treated to more sympathy, until Darlene, the wife of the man who had lent Derek the loud shirt, squealed, "Oh, my goodness!" She turned to her companions with wide, bright eyes. "Then we're part of an engagement party!" She looked at Leigh enviously. "I just read about it in a fan magazine. I should have remembered."

Leigh felt as if she were short of breath. "Read about what?"

"Oh, it was all in there!" Darlene explained giddily. "That you and Derek were disappearing for a private romantic liaison before working on something new and getting married."

"What—" Leigh moistened dry lips. "What magazine was this?"

It was, of course, Lavinia White's magazine. But where had she gotten the rest of her information? Leigh allowed her suspicious and accusing gaze to fasten on Derek. He met her stare noncommittally, but she knew then that he had been the one to fill in all the blanks.

Derek ordered another round of drinks, and Leigh sipped hers slowly as the talk swirled around her. Damn him! she thought, for at least the hundredth time. And she had felt guilty over the trouble she caused him! Well, Mr. Mallory, she said silently, watching him covertly from the shade of her lashes, the hell with being "even"! You haven't begun to see trouble yet! She downed her vodka and tonic in a single swallow.

It was growing late when they finished their leisurely meal and split company with their still awestruck new friends. Leigh was dismayed as she tripped over the gravel in the drive on their way to the Audi to discover that she had been angrily drinking too fast. Derek gripped her elbow and ushered her into the car.

"I'm going to drive!" she muttered, further annoyed to find her speech slurring. "I have to drive! I have to drop you at a motel and—"

"You're drunk," Derek said flatly, "and you're not driving. And I'll be damned if I'm staying at a motel!"

Leigh carefully enunciated her words when she spoke again. "I'm only a little drunk." She winced. She hated people who drove when they drank. "Okay, you drive. But you can't stay at my house. My housekeeper doesn't live in. The Casa Marina is a beautiful place, people come from all over the world—"

"I'm not staying at any motel," Derek repeated firmly. He flashed her an evil grin. "I'm staying with my beloved fiancée."

Leigh opened her mouth to argue but yawned instead. The food and drink and sunny exercise were combining to drain her of energy. Night had fallen and the lights of the Overseas Highway were mesmerizing her. Before she knew it, her eyes closed, her head fell to rest on Derek's shoulder.

She awoke with a start to feel motion and Derek's strong arms around her. He was carrying her up the path to her house.

"I need the key," he said as he noted her open eyes.

Leigh fumbled in her bag, which Derek had deposited in the curve of her stomach. "You can put me down now," she said. "I'm awake."

"But not terribly with it!" Derek chuckled. With one hand he took the key from her fingers while still holding her and inserted it dexterously into the lock. He kicked the door open and switched on the lights, then proceeded through the living room to the bedroom she had shared with Richard.

"I don't sleep in there anymore," Leigh protested thickly.

Derek's arms stiffened around her. "Where do you sleep?"

"The next room," she murmured. She was so sleepy!

He moved on down the hall and pushed the door open with

his foot. Dim light surged in from the hall so he didn't bother with another switch. He walked straight to the bed and deposited her in it. Leigh immediately began to curl into the comfort of her cool sheets. But she wasn't left alone. Derek was unbuttoning her blouse and pulling at her jeans.

"Don't!" she objected weakly, fighting for consciousness. "Please!"

"Please, what? You little fool," he muttered harshly. "I'm not doing anything, but you can't sleep like that."

"But—"

"I'm not going to see anything I haven't seen before," he interrupted.

She fell silent, a limp rag doll as he hoisted her about to remove her clothing down to her brief panties. Then he tucked her into the covers and walked briskly to the door. Leigh struggled to sit up.

"Derek?"

"What?"

He was silhouetted in the doorway, his handsome form like a classical sculpture.

"Thank you," Leigh whispered, a catch in her throat.

"For what?" There was a rapidly beating pulse apparent in his neck.

Leigh licked her lips to speak. "For helping me. I did overdo it." She couldn't tell him what she was really thinking. *For not pushing or taking advantage when I'm so terribly vulnerable!*

"Yeah." The door was closing. "Good night."

Leigh rose bright and early, strangely cheerful. She threw back her drapes and tilted her chin to drink in the morning sun, then quickly dressed. She ambled into the kitchen to start coffee, but found that her housekeeper, a Cuban woman named Maria Lopez, had already done so. She heard jaunty Spanish singing coming from the living room and hurried out to say hello.

"Ah, senora! It is nice to have you home!" Maria exclaimed joyfully. She gave Leigh an unabashed, motherly hug. Her voice

289

took on a tone of reproach. "You did not say you'd be gone so long." She shook a stubby finger and sniffed. "And who is that man sleeping in the guest room?"

Leigh stifled the urge to chuckle. She was twenty-seven years old, but Maria often treated her like a young girl in need of a duenna.

"That's Derek, Maria, didn't you recognize him?"

"Senor Mallory?" Leigh resented the obvious pleasure in her housekeeper's redundant question. "Oh! How very nice!"

Leigh had tossed her length into a comfortable Victorian love seat but she rose again restlessly. "Yes, how very nice, Senor Mallory." She fingered various knickknacks as she glanced around the room. She had furnished it, like the rest of the house, with Victorian and other turn-of-the-century pieces to match its gingerbread facade. The home, although new, had been copied after those in the old town, down to the widow's walk that stretched around the second-story circumference. The only difference with her "conch"-patterned house was that all the living area was on the first floor; the second floor was filled with musical instruments and recording devices. She didn't use the floor much anymore, but she had always been loathe to change it.

She set down the sand dollar she had idly picked up. "I'll go start breakfast."

"No, no, senora!" Maria dropped her dust cloth and started to bustle for the kitchen. "I will start your breakfast! You have just come home!"

Leigh's protests that she needed something to do went unheeded. Maria, promising exquisite Spanish omelets, shushed her out of the kitchen. Leigh sighed, accepted a cup of scalding black coffee, and wandered out the back door.

Leigh's "backyard" had always been a source of joy to her. Her home was as secluded as possible for the small but bustling island of Key West, set on the gulf side on a spit of beach called Blue Lagoon. And it was indeed blue. Shockingly so, against the bleached white sand, shells, and coral pebbles of the shore.

She walked aimlessly down to the water, beckoned by its still tranquillity. Reaching the edge, she kicked off her shoes and sat, and allowed the quiet tide to ripple over her toes. What am I doing? she asked herself with a hint of desperation. Why am I allowing Derek to walk all over me?

A large gull swooped down beside her, warily out of reach, and eyed her speculatively. Leigh laughed as she watched him comically twist his head and beak. "You think I'm a fool, too, huh?" He cocked his neck again at her voice. "Sorry, buddy," she told the bird. "I haven't a thing on me to offer you."

A piece of fish went flying over her head and the gull greedily and expertly caught it with his extended mouth.

"I take it this guy is a pet," Derek said, sliding next to her in the sand. He waved a plastic bag of fish heads and tails in front of him. "Maria greeted me with a spat of Spanish, stuffed this in my hand, and pushed me out the door."

Leigh chuckled. It was amusing to think of tiny Maria pushing a giant like Derek anywhere.

"No, he's not a special pet. None of them are. They come and go, but they all seem to know this is a good place for a handout."

She glanced at him quickly, then turned her concentration to the gull. The musky odor of his aftershave that she was coming to know so well could rattle the pace of her blood by itself. Looking at him, dressed like a tourist in shorts and a knit shirt, was something she wasn't up to yet. His eyes were becoming too intuitive, his masculine face and form too dear. If she weren't careful, she would forget that his motives were to make her pay . . .

"So." She briskly stood and dusted the sand from her cutoffs. "What are we doing? When do you want to start back for Miami?"

Derek tossed another fish head to the nosy gull. "In a few days. I want to spend some time here."

"Doing what?" Leigh demanded crossly.

"The usual things one does in Key West," Derek replied complacently, "Fishing, boating, sunning . . ."

"You live in Miami," Leigh reminded him. "You can do all that there."

"Star Island is actually Miami Beach."

"Pardon my mistake."

"I want to go sit in Sloppy Joe's bar like Hemingway and sip cold beer. I want to take the Conch Train and listen to the tales about the pirates. I want to hit all the super seafood restaurants and visit Audubon's house. None of that, my love, can be done in Miami or Miami Beach."

"But, Derek"—Leigh was both confused and exasperated—"you've done all that before!"

"I want to do it again," he said firmly.

"Well, go on," Leigh said, "have a good time."

One arched brown brow raised high. "You, dear sweet, are going to do it all with me."

"Oh, no I'm not!" Leigh retorted. "I'm not in a touristy mood."

"Then get into one."

"Aren't you afraid I'll call another radio station?" she taunted.

Derek pretended to consider her question. "No, I'm not afraid." He flashed her a pearly smile. "Because, Mrs. Tremayne, should such a thing happen again, it will be more than a bikini top you find yourself bereft of, and whatever I might have you will not get back."

He was dead serious in spite of the deceitful smile and Leigh knew it. "I told you I wouldn't pull any more pranks anyway," she muttered, summoning a shade of dignity to saunter toward the house. "I'm sure Maria must have breakfast ready by now," she flung over her shoulder.

Typical of Derek, he forced Maria to join them in the omelets. He then plied her with teasing questions about her life, asking about her fisherman husband, her three daughters and two sons. Maria in return blushed like a young girl and giggled giddily as she gave her replies, responding with pride when it came to her children.

"José is in medical school now at the University of Miami," the middle-aged matron told him proudly. Her loving gaze slipped to Leigh. "Thanks to la senora here." Her big brown eyes grew wide. "It is so high, so very, very dear to pay! But Leigh . . . she tells me it is nothing."

Leigh, sipping her coffee, wished that she could fit a muzzle over her housekeeper's mouth. But what could she say? Maria had no notion that Leigh wanted Derek to know nothing about her finances.

"More coffee anyone?" she hopped to her feet to interrupt the flow of conversation. "More toast?"

"No, thanks," Derek barely glanced at her. "I'm enjoying my chat with Maria."

Leigh didn't want to hear anymore. "I'll clear the table, then. When you're ready to go, I'll be out back."

Leigh cleared the few dishes, which looked as if they'd already been washed since Maria really did make an exquisite Spanish omelet, and picked up a horror novel to take to the sand. She settled by the shore, lit a cigarette, and tried to absorb herself in the chilling pages.

The effort was no good. Black ink blurred upon the white pages. She should be adamant about not going, she told herself, still staring at the book but not seeing a word. The truth was, she wanted to go!

"Hey, Leigh!" he was calling her from the screen door. "Ready?"

She scrambled to her feet. Derek was telling Maria not to worry about dinner as she re-entered the house. Maria demurely thanked him and waved them both out to the Audi.

Derek had been to the four-mile island many times and knew exactly where he was going. "Conch Train, first, okay?" Leigh nodded.

They spent an hour on the "train," listening to the bold and adventurous story of Key West's history. Their guide was excellent; she made the pirates and scavengers come alive in color, sometimes dashing, sometimes downright despicable. She talked about Henry Flager's railroad and the hurricane that had destroyed it. They passed Old Town and the western tip of the island and Leigh's father's house.

"Do you still own the place?" Derek asked her.

"Yes," Leigh replied simply. She would never sell her father's house although she would probably never live in it again. It held too many special memories for her.

"Let's stop by when we get off the train," Derek suggested. Leigh glanced at him suspiciously, but he was wearing his dark glasses and she couldn't read a thing from his tone.

"Why?" she asked bluntly.

Derek shrugged and lifted a hand in a casual gesture. "I'm feeling nostalgic, I guess. I remember the good times I had here talking with your father."

"I remember . . . You got along better with my father than Richard did." Leigh attempted to sound nonchalant, but her heart was racing. Why, she wondered, would a trip back to the old house mean anything to Derek? What was he up to?

Fifteen minutes later they were standing on the trellised porch and Leigh was nervously fitting the key into the lock. Derek's hands were in his pockets as he surveyed the exterior.

"It hasn't changed a bit," he observed.

"Not in two hundred years," Leigh commented dryly. She pushed open the door and entered the den, feeling the same surge of emotion that never failed to pulse through her when she came "home." The house was the embodiment of her childhood; a happy time, when she was as free as the gulls that soared the blue skies and as blissfully ignorant. Her world had centered around the sea and her doting father and growing up on the island had been everything a child could ask.

"Not a bit," Derek repeated idly. He brushed past Leigh and ambled slowly around the room, allowing his long fingers to glide lightly over various of her father's "treasures": carved ships in blown glass, porcelain figures of the sea, delicately sculptured meerschaum pipes. He glanced at Leigh suddenly. "It doesn't make you sad to come here, does it?"

"Sad?" Leigh echoed. A tender smile curved its way gently into her features. "No. My memories are very precious. I think I'm lucky to be able to afford to keep the place." Leigh turned abruptly from Derek and walked over to the grand piano and ran her fingers nervously over the keys. Why had she been so stupid as to make a reference to money? Derek would surely come back with something about Richard's legacy. The afternoon, which was going so pleasantly, was sure to be ruined.

But Derek made no sardonic reply. Instead he motioned her past the stairway to the door that led to the beach. "Let's sit out on the sand for a while. I want to talk more about your dad."

"Why?" Leigh mouthed, as surprise prompted her immediately to accept his outstretched hand and mechanically allow him to lead the way.

He answered with his usual haphazard shrug. "Because I want to understand more about you. And him."

Leigh stared at him with doubt, but his golden eyes were sincere and the hand that held hers was warm and supportive. There was no hint of demand about him now, just that openness that bordered on a true reach for friendship.

"I'll tell you about my life." She grinned shyly. "If you'll tell me about yours."

"Deal," Derek agreed. He unhooked the back latch and ushered her through to the weathered planks of the back porch and down to the surf. There he teasingly pushed her to a sitting position and lowered his large frame beside her with the easy grace of a great cat. "You first!" He laughed, his eyes calmly set upon the Atlantic and the massive freighters on the horizon as he drew patterns in the sand in a random motion.

Tentatively at first, then with more ease, Leigh began to talk. She told him that she had no memory of her mother, but that her father had given her a beautiful picture of the woman he had loved, that he had spoken of her cheerfully and often. And he had been both parents to his only child, always there when needed, always willing to listen before commenting, always open to her thoughts and desires. "He seemed like a magician to me when I was little!" Leigh laughed. "So wise! He never raised a hand against me, but I was always eager to please him."

"Now that," Derek said, "is the secret I want to fathom."

"What?" Leigh asked, puzzled.

Derek shifted and lay back in the sand, his head resting in the palm of his hand, supported by a crooked elbow. "What it is that earns respect and love from a child." His eyes traveled from the water to Leigh's. "I didn't learn to love my own father until I met yours."

"You're joking!" Leigh gasped, shocked by his admission. She couldn't imagine not loving a parent.

"No, I'm not joking," Derek returned absently, cupping his free hand around a scoop of sand. "Both Richard and I had very proper parents. We were switched diligently for disobedience. And we became tough little hellions because of it. Oh, my mother was soft, but even she was under my father's thumb. I resented him for years. Now"—he grinned at Leigh—"I actually like the man."

His grin was contagious and Leigh laughed. "What did my father have to do with that?"

"I don't know exactly," Derek mused. "Showed me that people were different and often part of their heritage, I guess. Somehow, just being around him gave me a better understanding of other people." The tawny shade of his eyes darkened a shade but Leigh didn't notice. The conversation between them had lulled her into a sense of security. "Did he come to the States as a young man?" Derek asked, still playing idly with the white grains of sand.

"I think he was about twenty," Leigh answered innocently.

"He really had lost most of his brogue. Where did you learn yours?"

Leigh was now watching the freighters in their apparently slow drift across the ocean and she replied without a thought. "When he was mad you could cut his accent with a butter knife!" She chuckled. "But I suppose I learned to affect the brogue from his mother. She lived with us for several years. They all emigrated together in a bad year for potatoes!"

Derek bowed his head, and Leigh was blissfully unaware of the secret smile of knowing satisfaction that flitted across his face. When he glanced at her again, his expression was bland and guileless.

"When I am a parent," he said, "I hope I can be like your dad." Dusting sand from his body, he reached a hand to Leigh as he rose. "He sure as hell did something right. He left you nothing but good memories, and yet they are more enviable than any of the Mallory fortunes."

"Wait a minute!" Leigh protested. "I still haven't heard—"

"Another day," Derek protested.

"But—"

"I still want to get a beer at Sloppy Joe's and I have some souvenir shopping to do," Derek interrupted impatiently. "Besides, you will meet Lord and Lady Mallory one of these days and that will answer all of your questions."

Leigh's further protests were to no avail. Derek was dragging her back through the house and out to the car like a man who had accomplished a task and was now eager to move on to something else. Uneasy at his sudden change, Leigh searched her mind for a reason, but could think of nothing. Her trepidation over coming to the house with Derek had been groundless. He had been cordial and friendly the entire time. Glancing at his rugged profile as they drove back into town, she began to relax.

"With a childhood like yours," Derek said suddenly, his tone light, "I'm surprised you didn't want children."

Leigh bristled immediately and felt her spine stiffen like a rod down her back. It was coming. Another reference to how she had failed Richard.

"I did want children!" she snapped, turning on him. "But I'm not going to sit here and try to convince you that it was always Richard who was too busy! It's really none of your business and you're going to believe what you want anyway."

"Hold it! Hold it!" Derek laughed. "I'm not accusing you of anything. I was merely curious."

Leigh stared at him, her mouth still open. Finally, she managed to shut it and lean back into the seat, bewildered. Not only was he instigating pleasantries, he was actually refusing to argue with her when she sprang at him!

He remained completely pleasant as they reached Duval Street and ordered beer at Sloppy Joe's, the corner bar made famous by Ernest Hemingway.

"One would think this was your first trip here," Leigh told him as she caught a stray strand of hair blown aside by the huge ceiling fans.

"I know," Derek replied, sipping his beer and licking the foam from his lips. He was wearing the dark glasses again and Leigh found his thoughts impossible to guess. A smile tickled his lips. "Just wait till we hit the souvenir shops! I'll look like I'm fresh off a boat!"

Leigh smiled tentatively in return. As the fan-cooled air stirred around them and the blazing sun shone from the street, they chatted on idly, combatants mellowed to a state of truce by the easy, laid-back atmosphere of the "live and let live" Key colony. After a multitude of discussions that ranged from the best eating fish to the world economy, and after her third beer, Leigh suggested that they should get going.

"If I sit here any longer," she said and chuckled, "I'll fall asleep on you again."

"You're cute when you sleep," Derek replied, and Leigh could not tell if he mocked her or not.

They spent another hour on Duval Street so Derek could comb through the shops. He bought jewelry to bring back for Angela and Tina, fine pieces made of coral and turquoise, toys for Lara, T-shirts and other trivia for the boys in the band, a watch for James, and perfumes for Emma and Maria.

"When you buy souvenirs," Leigh commented, "you don't mess around!"

Derek shrugged casually. "What good is money if you can't spend it for pleasure?"

"Some people pay bills," Leigh replied tartly.

"True." He adjusted his purchases in his arms, pushed the large stuffed dolphin he had bought for Lara toward Leigh, and started down the street to the parking lot where they had left the Audi. He wasn't going to argue with her at the moment. "Come on! It's getting late."

Leigh gripped the fuzzy dolphin and hurried after him. He was strangely quiet as he drove, his jaw squared and tight. As they took a wrong corner, Leigh assumed his self-absorption had caused him to lose direction.

"This isn't right, Derek," she said. "You should have gone straight."

"I'm not going to the house," he replied. "I want to stop by the cemetery."

Leigh fell silent along with him, her skin prickling uneasily. At the wrought-iron gates, Derek bought a spray of flowers, then continued down the winding path until he parked and they walked the remaining distance to Richard's grave site. Leigh followed slightly behind Derek.

Derek placed the flowers in the two bronze vases that flanked Richard's final resting place.

"I'm surprised you didn't send Richard home for burial," Derek said matter-of-factly.

"Home?"

"Yes, to England."

Leigh frowned, puzzled. "Richard had no one left in England," she said. "No one close. . . ." For a few seconds she forgot that Derek was there and thought about the man who had been her husband and now lay beneath the neatly trimmed sod. "I think that's why he needed the adulation so much. He needed to be loved. He needed to be loved by many people." She realized suddenly what she was saying. She bit her lip and glanced at Derek nervously, expecting him to bristle and come up with a comment about her being such a poor companion that Richard had been forced to look for love elsewhere.

But Derek said nothing. He crouched down and dusted a cluster of dirt from the marble headstone. Then he rose and slowly began to walk away, back toward the car. He stopped suddenly and turned back to Leigh. "I'm sorry. Are you ready?"

"Yes." Leigh picked her way through the stones after him and hesitantly accepted the hand he offered her. Neither spoke again until they reached the house, then Derek, casting aside the gloom that had invaded them both, cheerfully commanded her to take a leisurely shower and dress up for the evening.

"Where are we going?" Leigh asked.

"Oh, lots of places!" Derek replied vaguely.

It was difficult for Leigh to control the excitement and happiness that were growing steadily within her. She tried to remind herself that Derek's kindness and friendliness could be a trick far worse than any of his cruelty. But all her stern warnings did little to dissipate the exhilaration that claimed her like a heady drug. The day had gone too well for her to maintain the guard she needed to resist him.

She bathed like a bride preparing for her nuptials, washing her hair with scented shampoo, filling the tub with an oil that lived up to its promise of leaving skin as soft as a baby's. The dress she chose was alluring, bold, and daring—a black silk that plunged to the cleavage of her breasts and completely bared her back. Side slits wavered teasingly as she walked, giving occasional glimpses of her slender legs. To complement the sophistication of the gown, she carefully pinned up her hair, not severely as usual, but in delicate, looping ringlets. She finished off with makeup applied heavier than was her custom, but right for an evening out.

At last she slipped into black, heeled sandals and spun before the full-length mirror in her bedroom, tense with anticipation. She bit a lip with happy excitement. Her eyes, bright with the cheer that could only come from natural elation, were enticing and adventurous. Her hair, high but soft, gleamed rich and red in its coils. The whole effect was perfect. Had she ever been beautiful in her life, it was this night.

Derek, handsome and elite and overwhelmingly masculine in black velvet, was waiting for her in the living room. His eyes roamed over her as she joined him, and for once they held nothing but sincere admiration. He sauntered over to her and offered her a sherry wordlessly. Leigh accepted the drink from him, then spoke quickly, afraid to let the drawing silence continue.

"You look dynamite! You should be in an advertisement for some ungodly expensive men's cologne!"

"Thank you. I'll keep that in mind if all else fails." He caught her arm and spun her in a circle. "May I return the compliment? If you were in the same advertisement, I guarantee you any male seeing it would run to the store in the middle of the night to purchase a cologne which could attract such a divinely stunning female!"

"Thank you," Leigh replied in turn. She sipped her sherry and withdrew her hand to wander idly across the room. "Have you decided where we're going yet?"

"Umm. I thought we'd have dinner at Pier House and move on over to the Casa Marina for after-dinner drinks and dancing."

"Nice," Leigh murmured. She sipped the rest of her sherry and inched toward the door. "I'm really starving tonight. We missed lunch, you know."

"Umm . . ." Derek repeated. The concealed amusement in his tone was evident by the golden twinkle of his eyes. "Nervous again?"

"Just hungry," Leigh lied. She was terribly nervous, not of Derek, but herself. She would soon forget that she didn't trust him. She opened the door herself and moved into the night.

Once they reached Pier House, a casually elegant dining place that overlooked the shimmering sea, Leigh began to relax. She was fine in Derek's company as long as they weren't alone. They chuckled companionably as they argued over appetizers, both having the inclination to order everything on the menu page.

Then Leigh had difficulty deciding between the steak Diane and the lobster thermidor, and Derek laughingly said they would order one of each and create their own surf and turf. They split a bowl of conch chowder, smiling afresh as their spoons continually clashed.

A bottle of Dom Perignon disappeared along with their meal, which Leigh chose assiduously to ignore. She felt marvelous, and when they strolled along the moonlit beach before driving over to the Casa Marina, her steps were steady and her mind, although dreamily clouded, seemed to be functioning fine.

Derek was behaving like a perfect gentleman. He supported her as would any escort, but made no passes of any kind. The only time she fell into his arms was when they danced below the muted lights of the Casa Marina and drank sweet cordials into the small hours of the morning.

Leigh would later berate herself cruelly for her mistaken belief that the amount of alcohol she consumed was all right because she had been eating. She knew she had a low tolerance level, and she later realized Derek knew it too and knew exactly what he was doing as he kept her drinking and dancing, smiling all the while. By the time they left the Casa Marina and drove for her home, she was as relaxed and content as a well-fed kitten purring before a fire.

She was so relaxed that she accepted Derek's kiss with eagerness when they entered the house, accepted his arms around her and automatically brought her own to his back, her hands to caress and to luxuriate in the feel of his heat and strength. She was swept away by dizzying sensation as he lifted her easily and strode smoothly for her bedroom, lost in desire as he stripped aside the coverings and lay her pliant form down.

She didn't think as he pulled off her shoes, didn't resist as her nylons slid sensuously off her legs. It even seemed perfectly normal and right when Derek cast away his black velvet jacket and trousers, crisp silk shirt, and tight-fitting briefs. She knew every line of his magnificent bronze body, remembered with sweet anticipation the ecstasy of joining with his splendor.

He moved beside her and kissed her again, arousing her further with his probing tongue, bringing her body to burn as his own. His lips moved along the satin texture of her throat and she weakly protested, "We can't fall asleep. Maria will find us in the morning."

Derek was gently working on the clasp that held the black dress around her neck. "Maria won't be in tomorrow morning. I told her to take the day off."

Something snapped in Leigh's mind, a blaring suspicion that turned her heated blood cold. "You—you gave Maria the day off?" she repeated, stiffening within his arms despite his tender ministrations.

"Ummmm . . ." He was nuzzling her neck, but she wrenched away. It was all perfectly clear now. From the time they left the house that morning, his every movement, action, and gesture had been planned for just this moment. He had refused to argue with her, even over Richard, to lull her into a sense of comfortable trust. It had all been done just to get her into bed, to possess her, degrade her, use her, and hurt her—as she had supposedly hurt Richard.

"No!" she screamed. As much as she loved and desired Derek, as much as her body cried out for her to stay, it couldn't be this way. "No, let me go!"

His expression, she could see, even in the dim light, was stunned. Then anger slowly filled in as he observed her, propped up on an elbow, narrowing his eyes to cat gold and tightening his lips to a thin line. Freed from his weight and caressing hands, Leigh made a mad scramble to rise. He caught a handful of the black dress and it came apart in his hands as he jerked her back beside him.

"No, Mrs. Tremayne? I think not." His voice was a silky hiss. "But I am willing to hear about this sudden reluctance. You weren't in the least, uh, hesitant last time."

Hysteria was slowly claiming Leigh, creeping upon her as she read the determined intent in his eyes, felt the impregnable steel band of his arm around her.

"You're crazy, Derek, I keep telling you that. There was no last time—"

He growled an impatient oath and his arm tightened. "What do you take me for, a fool? I know damned well that was you in Atlanta! You think I don't know your skin, your voice—Irish accent or not—your shape, your thighs, your every curve and every secret—"

"No!" Leigh cried again, horrified. "You're wrong! All black cats are alike in the dark! You told me so!" Her voice was rising shrilly.

"Not this cat, love, she has a streak of silver."

"No, Derek," she tried desperately for control. "Please . . ."

"If I remember correctly," he went on harshly, ignoring her protests totally, "you might even have been called the 'seducer' that evening. Granted, I was a willing 'victim,' but then, I don't really believe you're unwilling now."

"I am unwilling!" she shouted, grabbing for a last-chance stance of dignified hauteur. "Damn you, Derek, let me go this instant!"

His hold loosened slightly. "What is it, Leigh?" he asked coldly as she scrambled to her feet. "Do you make a habit of nights like that? Did you think it amusing to hoodwink me?" He was rising despite his nudity to face her. "Did you play that little disguise game and run around when Richard was alive? Is that how you met your lover?"

The situation didn't matter anymore. That Derek was standing menacingly before her naked, his every muscle taut and wired with tension, meant nothing. That she would be a fool to cross him never crossed her mind. All she felt was terrible, sick fury. And like a blind animal, all she wanted to do was strike out.

And she did. She flew at him like a wild thing, nails drawn, hands and arms flailing furiously. She was determined to pummel him to pieces, draw blood with her fists as he did with his words.

With agility and speed and raving fury, she delivered one

blow. Then it was all over. "I've warned you a dozen times, love," he whispered coldly as he captured both her arms and held her tightly against him. "*I slap back!*"

And with a gesture that was actually more of a cuff, he did. Leigh went sprawling back on the bed, astounded that he would carry out such a threat.

He was beside her again before she could gather herself into more than a sitting position, gathering her to him in all his bronze glory.

"That's one lesson, love," he said, still in the deadly cold voice. "You're about to get another. Don't play your little teasing games with men, real men, unless you plan to carry them out. You came willingly into this bedroom with me tonight, and now, willing or not, you're going to stay here."

The remaining pieces of the black dress shredded from her body as he ripped it with one swift but powerful movement. Beams of moonlight peeped in from the half-open curtains, displaying her own naked beauty. She huddled, shrinking away from him.

"Derek!" Her cry was a broken plea as he collected her into his arms. "Oh, God, Derek, please, not like this!"

He went rigid for a moment, relaxed, stiffened, groaned. His face sank into the sunset of her hair. A shudder rippled through his length.

"No, my love, not like this. I would have you willingly."

But he did not release her. He began to make love to her again, gently and tenderly, caressing her with hands that softly explored the contours of her face, and more urgently discovered the intimate secrets of her breasts, her hips, and her thighs. And despite the emotions that boiled through Leigh, despite everything that had happened, she began to respond. She was the woman again who wanted nothing more than to touch him, to feel his embering flesh against hers, to wrap herself around him however briefly. . . .

He was creating a whirling vortex of pleasure she couldn't deny, a wonderful pleasure that only he could bring, because she

305

could never, no never, no matter what he said, thought, or did, change the simple fact that she loved him as she had never loved in her life.

And in his arms, with his kisses and demanding, roaming hands consuming her, she soon forgot all else. Her fingers dug into his hair, she matched kiss for kiss. Woven surely into his web of passion, she lost herself in a returning, bold aggression, needing as he did to explore, to caress his broad chest with her lips, to taste the masculine roughness of his cheeks, to feel the muscular contours of his long back and sinewed thighs . . . steel that trembled with warmth and vibrancy at her touch.

When he finally took her, the sweet ecstasy was so great that Leigh sobbed with the shock and a shudder rippled forcefully through her. Their eyes met, and his were infinitely tender.

They were on a plain that surpassed all else, the special lovers inexplicably bound together, both aware of the magnetizing uniqueness that drew them together irrevocably . . . soaringly. . . .

That which had been sparked by anger became beautiful and rapturous. The night passed in a storm of tender passion, and as Derek had promised, Leigh came to him willingly. Again and again.

Whatever happened in the future, she could not regret this night, marked with turmoil as it was, when the cool breeze of the bay caressed the splendor of their love and a silvery moon looked down upon their union with a blessing.

CHAPTER SEVEN

The discordant jangling of her bedside phone woke her. The raucous sound, interrupting her from a deep dreamland, took awhile to penetrate.

"Maria will get it," she mumbled to her pillow.

The sound continued, bringing with it the reality and humiliating memory of her abandoned and painfully quick surrender. She groped a hand quickly to retrieve the receiver before Derek awoke, praying she could dress and escape the room without having to face him in the bright light of day. Maria, of course, would not be getting the phone.

Her hand touched flesh. Derek was already awake, answering her phone.

"Hello? No, don't hang up, you have the right number."

Leigh peeked as she heard a faint and garbled noise from the other end of the line.

"No, no trouble at all." Derek glanced at her with twinkling eyes. "She's not busy, she's, uh, sitting right here."

Leigh pulled the covers to her chin and ripped the phone from his hand, gracing him with a malignant glare. "Hello?"

"Leigh? Who is that? What a marvelous voice! Is it . . . no! It can't be! I won't believe it! Or is it? Is it, Leigh? Is it Derek Mallory?"

The barrage of questions and exclamations came in a rush from her best friend, Sherry Eastman. Leigh had often grit her teeth over the last two years when Sherry raved about Derek, begging her to come to terms with him so that he would return to Key West and, presumably, Sherry's charms.

She lifted her eyes resentfully to Derek. He was fully dressed, and looked as if he'd been up for some time and already out on the beach. Covering the mouthpiece with her hand, she snapped, "Do you mind?"

307

He shrugged and sauntered out of the room, his eyes still twinkling mischievously, his grin still annoyingly smug.

"Yes, Sherry," she sighed to the phone. "That was Derek."

"Oh! Then things went well. Marvelous! When do I get to see him?"

"I—I don't know," Leigh hedged. The last thing in the world she wanted to see at the moment was her best friend falling all over Derek. "I'll have to call you back on that."

"Leigh!" Sherry wailed. "Why don't I just hop over?"

"Not—"

"See you in a few minutes." The line went dead.

Leigh flew from her bed and into the shower. When she emerged, wrapped in a snowy towel, Derek was back in the bedroom, his long form draped casually over the foot of the bed.

Leigh scowled and studiously avoided his eyes. "Would you please get out of here?"

"Don't you think we should talk?"

"Talk! Good Lord! No!" Talk? In the full light of day? Look into his eyes as he mocked and made light of her?

"All right, we won't talk." He patted the bed. "Come here."

"No!"

"Then I'll come there."

Leigh gripped her towel tighter. "Derek, what happened last night—"

"Would have happened sooner or later. Sooner, if you weren't such a little hypocrite." He had reached her and his hands were running slowly along her arms. "You know me, and you know I get my way. You were also truly an ostrich with your head in the sand to believe I didn't know it was you at the costume party."

"It wasn't!" Leigh would never bring herself to admit it.

"I found the contact lenses this morning."

Leigh unwittingly focused her eyes on her dresser. The case was sitting next to her jewelry box. Why hadn't she gotten rid of the damn things?

"How dare you prowl through my room?" she demanded.

308

"Oh, I dare a lot!" He moved his mouth toward hers and his hand slid around to find the tie in her towel. "When I know I'm right."

His head jerked back up suddenly as the door bell began to ring.

"Who the hell is that?" he muttered fiercely.

"Sherry."

"Who?"

"Sherry Eastman," Leigh said faintly. She had been saved by the bell, but she wasn't sure if she was grateful for the interruption or not. "A friend of mine. You talked to her this morning, and you met her a few times—several years ago."

"Oh." He was scowling now as the bell insistently rang again.

"Will you go answer the door please."

"Maybe she'll go away."

"She won't go away," Leigh said firmly. "She knows you're here."

"All right," he grumbled, eyeing her sternly. "I'll entertain your friend while you dress, but you come out and get rid of her. Fast. We are going to talk, whether you like it or not."

"We've nothing to say," Leigh said.

"I have plenty to say, and I expect plenty of answers."

Leigh sighed as she watched his broad-shouldered form leave the room. If there were any chance—even the slightest chance—that he would believe anything that she had to say, she would be happy to talk to him. But Richard had done his undermining well, and her own foolishness in dealing with the night in Atlanta seemed sound proof of all that he'd had to say.

If circumstances were not in her favor that morning, they were definitely against her as the afternoon rolled by. She found Sherry and Derek in the kitchen when she had dressed, discussing the aftereffects of the recent storm. Sherry, she could see, was having a rough time keeping her hands off Derek.

"Leigh!" Pretty blond Sherry greeted her friend with a little hug. "I missed you!"

"I wasn't gone that long," Leigh replied wryly.

309

"But it seemed like forever!" Sherry exclaimed, flipping a piece of bacon, which caused Leigh to survey the cute little domestic scene going on around her. Derek was eyeing the toast and spooning butter over eggs. He was next to Sherry, brushing against her often with apparent comfort.

Just like Richard! Leigh thought painfully. Happy and at ease with anyone attractive and female while demanding everything from her. Her heart constricted and hardened. Well, Derek could play his games, he could extract his revenge, but he would never have a kind word from her, never draw an admittance of any feeling except total disdain!

Leigh sauntered farther into the kitchen and hoisted herself onto the counter. "Forever?" she queried with amusement. "You must have had very dull days!"

"Not at all!" Sherry chuckled. "We had a super beach party. Everyone was there! Except you, of course. Poor Lyle was so upset! He was astounded that you took off for a trip without telling him!"

Leigh winced as Derek's head jerked upward and he turned to her with questioning eyes and an "ah-hah!" expression. Yet when he spoke, his tone was amused and nonchalant.

"Who is poor Lyle?"

"One of our resident artists," Sherry responded quickly, draining the bacon on a paper towel. "Hopelessly enamored of Leigh. He has been for years."

Leigh's fingers curled over the counter. She felt like a drowning woman with no sign of help in sight. Yes, Lyle had a crush on her, and yes, he had had one for years. But the gaunt young artist had also had a crush on Richard! He was respectful though, amusing and a friendly companion, a young man who liked to keep his love life a fantasy that appeared in his beautiful watercolors.

It would be impossible to explain Lyle to Derek, especially when she could see by Derek's grim features that he assumed Lyle to be the "island lover" of Richard's grievance.

The sunny kitchen had drawn strangely tense and silent, and

Sherry, having no conception of what her innocent words had implied, looked between Leigh and Derek with confusion. Then she gave a startled whoop.

"The eggs, Derek! They're burning!"

Somehow, breakfast made it safely to the table. Sherry took over the conversation, amusing Derek with tales of the flighty types that made up their immediate circle of friends. There was Sandra, a prolific but unpublished poet, who wrote most of her ballads for the sea gulls; Herbert, an artist like Lyle who took great pleasure in painting pictures of sand; Shirley, who wrote terrible tragedies for the confession magazines; and Norma and Harold Grant, who chartered their fishing boat for an income but who mysteriously disappeared for months on end to travel the globe when the whim caught their fancy.

"In fact," Sherry said giddily, almost passing out with pleasure as Derek courteously lit her cigarette, "we're having another barbecue tonight down by the beach to hear the calypso singers. Why don't you two come?"

"And meet Sandra and Herbert and Lyle and the rest?" Derek inquired politely.

"Yes!" Sherry exclaimed. "I've been teasing about them really. They are very nice, normal people. I'm sure you'd enjoy them very much."

Derek contemplated her suggestion for a moment, then gave her his charming smile. "I'm afraid we won't be able to make it. We're going to go back to my place on Star Island tonight."

Leigh was so amazed by his sudden decision that she choked over her coffee. What had happened to his vacation plans? "I thought—" she began.

Derek interrupted her quickly and suavely. "We have an album to work on. I want it wrapped up by Christmas, and to do that we'll need every day from here out."

"Oh, Leigh!" Sherry said excitedly. "*You* are working on it too?"

"It's Leigh's album," Derek answered for her. "And we have to fit a wedding in somewhere."

311

Sherry's cup crashed into its saucer. "A wedding!" she shrieked. She looked from one to the other of them quickly, her eyes reproachful and almost hostile when they alighted on Leigh. "You two?" She was decidedly incredulous.

"Yes, us two."

Derek stared at Leigh, his lips twisted into a hard smile, his eyes daring her to dispute his announcement. He stood and came behind her chair to massage her shoulders with fingers that bit into her flesh. "We deserve one another, don't you think?"

It took Sherry several seconds to shut her mouth so that she could reply. "But I thought—I—"

"Yes?" The prompting was pleasant.

"No—nothing," Sherry stammered. She inhaled deeply on her cigarette. "I didn't think you got along particularly well."

Derek laughed and ran a finger along Leigh's cheek. "We get along very well." He chuckled insinuatingly. "When it counts."

Leigh despised the rush of blood that filled her face. She was hot and cold and furious. "Derek—"

"I'm so sorry, love." He feigned an apology. "I suppose you wanted to tell your friend yourself! Well, sweetheart, you got to tell Roger and the others, it seems only fair that I should be the first to tell someone." His hands tightened on her neck. "I guess Sherry will have to tell 'poor Lyle' and the rest of your island friends."

Sherry didn't stay much longer. Her hopes dashed where Derek was concerned, she began to look a little sick. Leigh was almost sorry for her. She determined to tell her the whole truth when Derek's masquerade ended—whenever that would be!

"Marvelous!" Leigh challenged hotly when she had shut the door on Sherry. "Just marvelous! How far do you plan to carry this—this absurd fiasco! Haven't you already gotten what you wanted? Aren't you satisfied yet?"

Derek appeared surprised by her burst of anger at first; then his features took on similar grim lines.

"I'll carry it all the way to the altar, love," he replied with quiet venom. "And I'll be sure the altar I carry it to is a good hundred miles away from 'poor Lyle.'"

Leigh didn't know whether to laugh or cry. When she opened her mouth, it was the first that came out—a hollow laugh, dry and bitter, verging on hysteria. "You're an idiot, Derek, an honest to God idiot! You told me a few days ago you'd never marry because of me, and now you're contemplating marrying me! Because I was such a rotten wife to Richard! What a deal you're making for yourself, Mallory. Are you seeking revenge on me, or on yourself?"

He walked to her slowly and cupped her chin in his hand. "Maybe both of us, love, maybe both of us." Then he walked past her and she heard him move into her bedroom.

She followed him to find him pulling clothing from her closet.

"What the hell are you doing?" she demanded.

"Getting your things," Derek said curtly. "You heard me earlier, we're going back to Star Island."

"You may be, I'm not."

"Oh, you're coming, Leigh," he replied, finishing with the closet and moving on to her dresser. "You're coming with me if I have to truss you up like a spitted deer and throw you in the car myself."

Leigh's mouth worked furiously as she searched for the right words to say. "You can't do this! You can't take me against my will! It's against the law!"

"Really? We'll see." He dragged two suitcases across the room and tossed them onto the bed. "Shall you pack or shall I?" As Leigh continued to stare at him speechlessly, he shrugged and began to stuff her clothing into the suitcases.

"This is all very interesting," she finally said coolly. "But tell me, Mr. Mallory, how do you plan to make me marry you? You can hardly spit a bride like a deer and walk down the aisle with her. And I will never marry you willingly. I will never go through another marriage like—"

"Your marriage with Richard?" Derek jeered.

"Yes, my marriage with Richard."

"That's right, love, you won't. I'm not Richard. But cheer up. If you manage to divorce me, you'll be twice as rich."

Leigh choked back laughter and sat on the bed to watch him. He was dead serious! She blinked back tears. There was nothing in the world she could desire more than a lifetime commitment to him. In her secret dreams she had prayed that Derek would one day discover that he loved her with all his heart, needed her like air to breathe, cherished her as she did him.

And now he was planning to make her his wife. But he didn't love, need, or cherish her. He simply wanted to make sure she had no other life. He would bring her to heel, dominate and overpower her. Then he would go about with his own life, traveling, staying out, seeing whomever else he so desired. *Just like Richard.*

But she had fallen out of love with Richard and his behavior had become bearable. Richard, after their whirlwind courtship when she had given her heart, had quickly proved himself to be an unprincipled liar, weak despite the front he showed the world.

There was no weakness in Derek Mallory. In twenty years he had never thrown a professional temper tantrum, never been accused of anything but a judicious and fair mind, never been attributed characteristics other than generosity, toleration, and dignity.

She would never fall out of love with Derek. And the pain would be forever unbearable. No, she couldn't marry him. Even as her pulses quickened at the thought and her heart pleaded that it was better to have a fraction of his time than nothing, her mind rebelled. He could force her to Star Island, but he could never make her say the words that would bind her to a life of never-ending misery and despair.

"Are you ready?"

Leigh snapped into the present. "Now?"

"Yes, now," he barked impatiently. His eyes roamed over her half-prone position on the bed. "Unless that's an invitation?"

She scrambled up. "I—I have to write Maria a note. That is," she drawled tartly, "unless you've already told her we're leaving again?"

"Write your note. I'll be packing the car."

Leigh stalked into the kitchen and began to write her note to Maria, explaining that she would probably be gone for several weeks. She was in such a turmoil that the pen ripped through the paper and she had to start over. After she had done so, adding Derek's phone number in case the housekeeper should have difficulty finding it if necessary, she wrote out an advance check for the next month. Glancing at her wristwatch, she noticed that the procedure had taken her much longer than she had expected. She was surprised that Derek had not come after her to bully her into hurrying!

She moved into the living room but he wasn't there. A quick glance out the front door showed her that the Audi was packed, but there was no sign of Derek. Puzzled, she walked tentatively down the hall to her bedroom. The door to the room she had shared with Richard stood ajar. She paused and looked in.

Derek was standing very still by Richard's heavy oak desk. His eyes were clouded, seeing nothing, his face white beneath his tan. His strange appearance astounded Leigh so that she, too, stood still for several seconds, watching him. Then she called his name softly, but he didn't hear her.

"Derek!" she called again, more loudly. He started, like a man coming out of a trance, and turned slowly to her. "I'm ready," she said, softly again, unable to fathom the haunted air about him.

A tremor shot through him. He shook himself, as if to remove an unwanted and annoying insect. A faint smile curved his lips but did not reach his eyes. "Good. Did you get the music?"

"The music?" Leigh queried faintly.

"The music. Your rough drafts."

"No, I'll run up and get them now." But she didn't run. She watched him, completely puzzled and not at all sure he was all right. "What are you doing in here?" she finally asked.

315

"The phone . . ." he said vaguely. "I wanted to let James and Emma know that we were coming back."

Leigh didn't dispute him, yet his answer made no sense. There were phones all over the house. "I'll go on up and get the music then . . ." she said, backing out of the room.

"You don't come in here much, do you?" Derek asked suddenly.

"No, no I don't." Leigh's eyes moved over the room, taking in the queen-size water bed that Richard had adored, the Florida pine paneling, the heavy Victorian dressers and desk. "No," she said again. "I moved my things out the day I heard about Richard's . . . accident. I haven't been in here since. Maria comes in to clean."

"Richard's things are still all here?"

Leigh wasn't sure if he were asking her a question or making a rhetorical statement. "I haven't touched anything of Richard's," she said. "I always tell myself I have to get to it but I never do."

Derek nodded as if her words had been the answer to a deep and mystifying puzzle. "Go on," he said gently, "get the music. I'll check the doors and be in the car."

Amazed and incredulous at his abrupt change of behavior, Leigh backed the rest of the way out of the room. She sprinted up the stairway to the studio where she kept her work, organized the composition and her scribbled pages of notes, bound them, and hurried on out to the car. Derek waited at the steering wheel, his eyes dark and pensive, strangely distant. They focused on her sadly as she hopped into the passenger seat.

"Leigh, you're right. I can't make you come to Star Island if you don't want to. I think your work should be published, but I have no right to force you to work on it. We can hire Samantha."

He wasn't taunting her in any way, Leigh saw. In the few minutes that she had spent wording her note, something had happened to change him drastically. But what? She wasn't sure that she liked his new solicitude and uncanny remoteness.

"I—I don't mind working with the group," she said stiffly.

Some emotion raced swiftly through his golden eyes, an emotion Leigh couldn't begin to understand. He turned the key in the ignition and stared straight ahead, his attention on the road.

They rode in silence for miles, neither thinking even to switch on the car radio to alleviate the stilted tension between them. Leigh finally remarked on the beauty of the endless water as they passed over the remarkable seven-mile bridge that spanned the lower islands. Derek responded with an absent yes, and Leigh gave up all attempts at conversation. She didn't speak again until they cleared the Keys and were coming upon the mainland and it wasn't by choice then. The rumblings in her stomach were becoming embarrassingly loud.

"Do you think we could stop to eat?" she asked hesitantly.

Once again Derek looked as if he had been snapped out of a trance.

"I'm sorry. We have gone hours without a meal. Will Durty Nelly's be all right?" he replied.

"Lovely."

Despite its disreputable name, Durty Nelly's was a particularly fine crab house. Derek and Leigh both ordered the specialty, crabs, and draft beers. When the waitress had bustled on her way, Derek watched Leigh's face, his soul-searching eyes oddly intent. Their beers arrived and he sipped his, lit two cigarettes and handed her one.

"I want you to know," he said in a cloud of smoke, "that I'm very sorry. About everything."

Leigh lowered her eyes nervously, unsure of how to relate to this now person. She inhaled, exhaled, and sipped her beer.

"I'm glad you've decided to work on the album," he continued. "You are a talented lady, and your light shouldn't be hidden under a bushel. But you won't be harassed anymore by me. It's reasonable that you stay at my house, but you're free to come and go as you choose. I'll introduce you to the dogs so that you won't have any trouble with them." He paused, sipped his beer again, and absently swiped at the long-gone mustache. He

317

opened his mouth, closed it, and took another long swallow. "About last night . . ."

Leigh uttered a muffled protest and waved her hand. Her eyes were glued on her table mat; she couldn't raise them to meet his. His hand caught hers in the air and covered it on the table.

"No, Leigh," he said. "Listen to what I've got to say. I'm sorry about that too. Very sorry. I promise nothing like that will happen again either. I'd like to go into this as friends. Do you think we can?"

Leigh was speechless, her heart torn in two. That Derek was being unerringly kind, apologetic, and gentle was something that she should love. But what did it mean? Did he no longer want her? Had their evening together, the one that had brought her to a heavenly cloud despite everything, been nothing to him at all? Had he decided she was not worth pursuing? Not until this moment, not until his promise that he would leave her alone, did she realize that, whatever the bitterness, whatever the antagonism that raged between them, she wanted him desperately—on any terms. His vile temper was preferable to his total rejection.

"Leigh?" he prompted.

"Yes, yes we can be friends." She did not trust herself to look up yet and spoke to the table. She moistened her lips. She didn't dare ask him about his sudden change of heart yet; she would hope the opportunity came later when she was in better control. But maybe now he would answer a few of the questions that had plagued her since she first came to his house. "Will you tell me, though, why you invited me to Star Island? And did you have something to do with my car not starting?"

"I did nothing to your car," he said, "and I invited you to Star Island for two reasons. The first is the music. I'll only tell you the second reason if you'll give me an honest answer to one of my questions."

Pinpricks of fear were gathering at her neck. She knew he was going to ask her about Atlanta. She had to find a way to hedge him. Taking a sip of beer, she finally raised her eyes to his. "If you didn't damage my car, how did it happen that I was there with Lavinia White?"

"Lavinia had scheduled an interview with me before I was even sure that you were coming. If you remember, I wasn't responsible for your entering into the interview. I didn't lock you out of your room."

Leigh flushed slightly. "But you did call her with all the information about our supposed romance. You must have. The people we met at Pennekamp had already read all about it!"

Derek frowned, puzzled himself. "No, I didn't call her. But then, again, if you remember, I wasn't the one to make the first announcement about a marriage. You told John and Roger and the group—"

"But you know why I did that!" Leigh exclaimed.

"Do I?"

"Of course!" Leigh retorted, "I was calling your bluff!"

"Well"—he shrugged indifferently—"it doesn't matter. But I would assume one of the group spoke with Lavinia. Roger, probably. He usually handles most of our public relations. Now," his voice lowered and he stared into her eyes intently, "my turn. I want to know—"

"Here we are!" The waitress cheerfully swooped into the conversation by producing Leigh's steaming plate with a flourish and then Derek's. "Can I get you anything else for the moment?"

"No, no thank you," Derek replied, controlling his impatience. "Oh, yes, two more beers please."

"Certainly," the rosy-cheeked waitress replied. She was a heavyset lady of about forty. As she responded to Derek, she began to study him more thoroughly. "English, sir, are you?" she asked politely.

"Yes," Derek said shortly. It wasn't like him to be rude and Leigh could see he was wincing at his own behavior. He glanced to the woman and smiled. "I'm originally from Northumbria."

The waitress suddenly sucked in her breath and exclaimed, "La-di-da! I know who you are now. You looked so familiar! You're the singing star! Oh, if my daughter could see me here!

319

But, oh, honey!" She chuckled. "What the young don't know! Her father and I spent many a night by a warm fireside with your music ourselves."

Her voice was growing louder and Derek was beginning to regret his decision to be polite. "Please!" he shushed her. "I am Derek Mallory, but it's not me you listen to, it's the group, the London Company. And, if you don't mind, I really don't want to be recognized."

"Oh, I'm so sorry. Of course." The waitress lowered her voice. "But would you do me a favor? Could I have an autograph—for my daughter?"

Derek grinned more easily. "Get me a paper quietly," he promised. "And I'll sign all the autographs you want!"

"Thank you!" Flustered and happy, she hurried away.

Leigh plunged in quickly to keep him from getting to his question. "Now see," she whispered teasingly. "You were recognized and it wasn't my fault at all!"

He groaned. "No, it wasn't your fault. But you did cause the fiasco at Pennekamp."

"Yes."

"And you did pour coffee all over me."

"Not on purpose! Really!" They were laughing together, naturally. It was a wonderful feeling, one that relaxed Leigh. She continued thoughtlessly, "Besides, I didn't hurt you badly. You were just fine . . ." Her words trailed into a choked whisper and halted. Last night. You were just fine last night. That was what she had been about to say. But she didn't want to find out about last night. She didn't want to hear that she had been just another black cat in the dark, silver-streaked or not.

This time she could have kissed the waitress. The lady, who told them her name was June, descended upon the table with a pen and sheets of paper in the nick of time to save Leigh from struggling out of her awkward predicament. "One for Cindy, Marilyn, and Louisa, please," she whispered conspiratorially with a wink. "And a special one for June and Dirk, please."

"Surely." Derek set his cocktail fork down and agreeably

made out the autographs. Leigh noticed that diners at nearby tables were beginning to watch them curiously.

"Perhaps we should get the check," she suggested, motioning with her eyes to explain her statement.

"Umm." He finished his last scrawl. "June, would you get our check, please?"

"Right away, Mr. Mallory."

It was easy to stall Derek then. They were both involved with finishing their food quickly. But they had a forty-five-minute drive still ahead of them.

"Ready?" Derek gulped the tail end of his beer.

"Yes," Leigh picked up her own beer and gulped down the remaining half a glass. She was plotting as she rose from the table.

"It's amazing how sleepy a good meal can make you," she yawned as they climbed back into the car.

"And liquor." Derek reminded her.

"Yeah, the beer," Leigh agreed, with another strenuous yawn. She curled into the seat. "I never have had a tolerance . . ."

"Leigh?"

Praying she was a good enough actress to carry off her charade, Leigh failed to respond. She kept her eyes closed as he repeated her name. Was it possible to fall asleep so quickly?

At any rate Derek didn't push her, and as the car rolled along the road, drowsiness began to overtake her in reality. She awoke with a true start to find that they were parked in front of the Star Island estate.

"We're here," Derek said, nudging her gently. "Can you make it, or shall I carry you?"

"No!" Leigh sprang up and opened her door. "No, I'm awake. I'm fine."

She tripped over the first step. Her faked nap turned real had left her groggy and disoriented. As she wavered for balance, Derek came behind her and scooped her into his arms as James appeared at the front door with a respectful, "Welcome home, sir."

321

"Thank you, James," Derek responded cheerfully. "Mrs. Tremayne fell asleep on me. I'll bring her up to her room. Will you bring in the bags, please? And tell Emma I'd like a cup of coffee in my office."

Leigh nuzzled into his warm chest as he carried her up the stairway, absorbing the scent of him, straining to remember every wonder of him, the feel of his breath, the touch of his skin. Tears were pricking at her eyes again. She had the uncanny feeling that this would be the last time he ever held her in the gentle, imprisoning security of his arms.

He lay her softly on the bed in the room that was once more hers. "Go back to sleep," he whispered. "I'm going to get hold of the group so that we can start tomorrow and look over the sheets you've written."

For a moment he paused, looking down at her. Leigh felt that he was going to kiss her, and she longed for him to do so. But he didn't. He moved a stray lock of hair off her forehead, his fingers lingering tantalizingly. Then he spun quickly away.

Her door closed, then reopened. He stood in the doorway, glancing upon her prone body reflectively. "Leigh," he said quietly, "I want you to tell me one thing. I'll never bring it up again, I promise. But answer me now, and tell me the truth. *Was that you in Atlanta?*"

Thank God the room was dark. Leigh winced and bit her lip. To subdue the tears in her voice she spoke harshly. "Yes. Yes, it was me. Now, can we drop it, please?"

CHAPTER EIGHT

"Stop!"

Derek's voice sounded stridently as the instruments that now crowded his studio discordantly quieted. "You're flat, Leigh, start concentrating!"

Leigh bit her lip and nodded. The others, she knew, were looking at her sympathetically, but no one was going to rush to her defense. This was their last rehearsal before moving into the recording studio, and if Derek was being harsh and nitpicky, well, it could only be expected with the grueling schedule he had set. Leigh also had to admit that her voice had gone flat and that she wasn't concentrating. They had been rehearsing ten hours a day for a month straight. Granted, Derek worked long into the night, hours after the rest of them had called it quits, revising, improving, tearing the original work apart until it was musically perfect.

"Roger, take it back to the beginning. One, two, three, four." He ran his fingers through his hair as Roger began the bars of slow drum beats that introduced the final song. Derek came in on lead guitar, Bobby on bass, and Shane on the keyboard, then the crystal tones of John's flute, a sign from Derek, and their harmonized voices, Leigh taking great care to keep hers high and clear.

The song ended with a repeat of the slow drum beats. On the last Roger threw his sticks in the air and shouted, "Whew! I'm for a drink! Anyone care to join me?"

"I surely will!" Shane replied, rising from his bench and stretching. He tensed his fingers and curled them. "John? Bobby? Leigh?"

Agreement followed all around. They began to troop out the door, Leigh escorted forward by Roger.

"Why isn't Derek coming?" she asked him. "We're done, right? What else can he be doing?"

Roger gave her a quick hug. "Don't worry about Derek, love, he's always like this when he's really into a project. He'll come out when he's ready. Tomorrow things will get better."

Leigh didn't think so. Since the night they had returned from the Keys, Derek had barely spoken to her except during rehearsal and that was usually to yell. In public he had been polite, solicitous, but even then, distant. Leigh lived in his house, slept not forty feet from him, but might as well have been living on another planet. The only meals he took with her were when the entire group ate together. Otherwise, he avoided her like the plague.

"What'll it be, Leigh?" Bobby, self-elected bartender for the night, demanded as he shuffled through Derek's game room liquor cabinet.

"A Coke!" Leigh smiled wanly. "Anything else and I'd crash over on my feet. How do you all stand this pace?"

"You get used to it." Shane chuckled, patting her shoulder in encouragement as she sank into a plump chair. He walked over to the corner phone, saying, " 'Scuse me. I have to call the home front."

"Damn!" Bobby muttered, producing Leigh's Coke. "I'd better do the same. I promised Tina to take her to dinner."

Leigh chatted idly with Roger and John while Bobby and Shane made their phone calls. She was comfortable with the group now, close. Every night they had spent an hour together talking like this, an hour that Roger described as the "wind-down."

"Oh, brother!" Bobby exclaimed with disgust as he rejoined them and sank disheartened into the sofa. "As if Tina isn't annoyed already with this rehearsal schedule! Her mother has come down with the flu and can't sit with Lara for us." He grimaced. "No dinner out."

"Angie and I can take Lara," Shane offered.

"No, you can't, but thank you," Bobby replied, draining his Scotch swiftly. "Angie has her dance class tonight."

"I'm sure she won't mind skipping," Shane said.

"You're not going to ask her." Bobby smiled wanly. "She missed a class for us a few weeks ago."

"Don't you have a live-in housekeeper?" Leigh asked him.

"Mrs. Smikle is on vacation," Bobby responded tiredly. "And Tina is funny about Lara. There are only a few people she'll leave her with."

"Well, how about me?" Leigh queried. "I'm sure Tina would trust me! She knows I'm crazy about Lara."

"Leigh, the offer is great, but no. You're exhausted."

"I'm tired of rehearsing," Leigh agreed amiably. "But I'd love to take care of Lara! And she goes to bed in a few hours."

"Are you sure . . ." Bobby was trying to dissuade her with his words but his eyes leaped with pleasure.

"I'm positive!" Leigh stated firmly. "Call Tina back and tell her you're still going to dinner. I'll change and follow you now. I'm not sure I can find the house by myself."

"There's no need to do that."

Leigh's eyes shot to the doorway where Derek was entering. He rubbed the back of his neck tiredly as he approached the liquor cabinet and poured himself a liberal portion of gin and added a splash of tonic. "Bobby," he continued, "bring Lara over here with her portable crib. She can spend the night. Tina can come to the studio with you in the morning and pick her up." He eased himself into a recliner. "You and Tina can have a whole night alone."

"Gee . . ." Bobby muttered. "That sounds great. But are you two sure you want to do this? You haven't had much time alone yourselves."

Leigh winced and felt pink staining her cheeks. Bobby, as well as the rest of the group, assumed things were still good between Derek and Leigh. Nothing else had ever been said about their impending "marriage," by either of them. The group, knowing their leader as they did, took Derek's often abrupt behavior toward Leigh as normal. He was, they believed, frenzied and harassed by the work load that fell his way.

"I promise you," Leigh said, controlling the note of bitterness and sarcasm that threatened her voice, "Derek and I would both love to have Lara."

"It's settled," Derek told Bobby. "Call Tina."

"Thank you, both. I really appreciate this. And one of these days"—he winked—"I might be able to reciprocate the favor."

Leigh felt her stomach lurch.

An hour later Lara arrived for the night and Bobby and Tina blissfully repeated their thanks and headed off for a romantic evening. Leigh took Lara into the game room, where she read the little girl stories and played pat-a-cake. She was heartily surprised when Derek chose to join them, followed by dignified James with a tray of steaming cocoa.

"Snack, ladies?" he inquired, folding his long legs Indian fashion and sinking to the floor beside them. He patted the loop rug. "Right here will be fine, James."

James knelt to the floor, his brittle old bones creaking. "Sorry, old boy!" Derek chuckled, "I should have taken the tray myself."

Offended, James sniffed. Then his basilisk features actually crinkled into a smile. "I don't mind at all, sir." His smile became reproachful as he continued, "I could do this with considerably more grace, Mr. Mallory, if I were to have more opportunity in the field of catering to little people."

"James!" Derek groaned. "I have my mother to nag me about my lack of procreation, thank you."

"And Lord Mallory," James supplied.

"Yes, and Lord Mallory." Derek agreed. "Well, James," he snapped suddenly, "would you like to join us for cocoa? Or are you going to kneel there and stare at me like a mother hen all night."

"Certainly not, sir!" He rose to his feet with a huff. "I shall be in the kitchen, sir, playing gin rummy with Emma should you require my services."

Lara had scrambled her chubby little limbs to reach her plastic cup of cocoa. Now she called after him, "Thank you, James."

James bowed stiffly, the silly smile back on his face. "A pleasure, Mistress Welles, a great pleasure." He shot Derek a final, reproachful glare, sniffed again, and left them.

"So, Lara," Derek questioned the little girl, "are you enjoying your stay?" A twinkle lit his eyes as they gazed upon the child, but Leigh could see the signs of strain in his face. The thin lines that edged his mouth and eyes were deep, the fine angular cast of his face gaunt. Why did he drive himself so hard? Leigh wondered. She longed to stretch a hand to him and ease his tension with gentle fingers. But she didn't dare. What was going on was more than work, she was sure. Derek was purposely burying himself, and purposely keeping a distance from her.

Lara scrambled to her stubby legs with childish grace, throwing herself into Derek's arms, cocoa and all. "Wuv it, Uncle Derek, wuv it!" she proclaimed.

Derek grimaced as cocoa lapped onto his shirt. "Good, sweetheart. Finish your cocoa now, and have a cookie. We have to get you to bed or your mother will have our necks." He grinned at Leigh with a wink.

Crazy, Leigh thought, how her heart began to pound. He had proved he wanted nothing more to do with her. . . .

"Yes," she said lightly. "Finish up now, Lara, so we can get you into your pajamas."

Lara happily crunched an oatmeal cookie and drank her cocoa to the last drop. She giggled with hysterical delight when Derek swooped her into the air and tickled her tummy. Then Derek looked to Leigh questioningly. "Where is she going to sleep?"

"The crib is in my room," Leigh replied. "I wanted to be sure I'd hear her if she woke." She lifted her hands helplessly. "I was afraid in a different place she might be frightened."

"Okay, munchkin!" he told Lara, tossing her to a position on his shoulders. "Auntie Leigh's room it shall be."

Leigh followed the giggling pair up the stairway. In her room she delved into the bag Tina had packed for her daughter and found her pajamas and teddy bear. Derek waited while Leigh washed Lara, helped her brush her tiny teeth, and changed her into the rag-doll patterned footed sleeper. Then he took over, popping Lara high into the air, kissing her soundly, and tucking her in.

"Lull-by, Uncle Derek," Lara demanded sleepily as she hugged her teddy bear. "Lull-by, please?"

"Kiss Leigh good night, munchkin," Derek said, "then I'll do the number of your choice. Maybe we'll do some harmony."

Leigh leaned over the crib to receive Lara's obedient kiss. Soft hands curled around her neck and she hugged the little girl warmly in return.

"Now, munchkin, your request?" Derek queried.

"One Daddy does," Lara mumbled.

Derek frowned for a moment, thinking. He chuckled. "You mean the one Uncle Shane taught your daddy?"

"Yeth!"

Derek gave Leigh a crooked grin. " 'An Irish Lullaby'," he explained. Although a native Londoner himself, Shane had Irish parentage like Leigh. "Join me. You must know it!"

Leigh did, and she was now used to harmonizing with Derek. They sang the song together, softly, for the child. Their voices rose beautifully, magically, in the night, and Leigh was suddenly overwhelmed by a sense of loss and sadness. This was all she had ever really wanted. A family. A child to love and care for, a man beside her to share that joy. But the child was not hers, nor the man. The man she longed so dearly to touch, the man who had proved himself sensitive and tender as well as proud and arrogant.

"Better than Daddy," Lara muttered to her teddy bear with closing eyes.

"But let's not tell him!" Derek chuckled. His voice dropped to a whisper. "G'night, princess." He inched away from the crib quietly. "Are you coming back downstairs?" he asked Leigh softly.

She shook her head. Her emotions were frazzled. She didn't trust herself in Derek's company tonight. "I think I'll go to sleep myself," she whispered back. "I want to be wide awake at the studio. I'll be the only one with no idea of what I'm doing."

"Good night, then." Derek turned for the door. He hesitated for a second, his back to her. Then he went out.

Leigh shook misty tears from her eyes. Absurd, she thought, how easily tears formed in her eyes these days. It was the hectic pace she lived at, she told herself. She was always tired.

Moving stealthily about the room, she prepared for bed herself, changing into one of Derek's tailored shirts that she had claimed as her own. He had never asked for any of them back, and Leigh continued to wear them, drawing strange comfort when she donned them, like a teen-aged girl with a pathetic puppy-love crush.

It was a long time before she slept, and when she did, it seemed as if she were awakened immediately. Sniffling cries broke into her awareness and she lay confused at first. Another cry came and she bounded from the bed, instantly alert as she remembered that Lara was with her in the crib.

Leigh knew something was very wrong as soon as she gathered the little girl into her arms and carried her from the crib. Her skin was dry, and her body felt as warm as a furnace.

Panic gripped Leigh in a dark vise. She loved children, but knew so little about them! How ill was the child who clung to her so trustingly in her moaning misery?

Leigh couldn't wait, she couldn't take any chances. Tearing out of her room in bare feet, her warm human bundle still in her arms, she burst in on Derek, crawling onto his bed and shaking him as she called his name.

Thankfully, he woke quickly. After one arched-brow look of confusion, he sized up the situation easily by the terror in Leigh's eyes and the warmth of the flesh of her childish package.

"One moment," he told Leigh swiftly. "Let me get some pants

329

on." Not in the least a hypocrite, he made no suggestion to Leigh that she leave or turn her head as he sprang from his bed to clothe himself. "Calm down," was all he told her, with an encouraging smile. "I'm sure Tina put some children's aspirin in her bag."

In seconds Derek was dressed. He led the way back to Leigh's room where he tore through the child's bag. "Here we are!" he said cheerfully. "Let's get a little of this into her."

Leigh looked on tensely as Derek prodded Lara fully awake and she downed a measure of the liquid medicine. "We're going to get a nice, long drink of water now, okay?"

Lara nodded drowsily but dutifully drank the glass of water Derek gave her. Derek grinned at Leigh from his haunched position by the child.

"Just a little teething fever, I think. Molars." He picked up the child and lay her gently back into her crib. Leigh perched nervously at the foot of her bed, feeling helpless and inadequate as Derek competently handled the child.

"Are you sure she's okay?" Leigh asked anxiously in a whisper.

Derek joined her at the foot of the bed. "Pretty sure," he replied cheerfully. "We'll keep a watch on her. But I'll bet"— and his eyes twinkled kindly—"that her fever is down already. Go and see for yourself."

Leigh glanced at him with disbelief, then tiptoed toward the crib. She placed a hand upon Lara's forehead. Amazed to find it cool to her touch, she lightly clutched the little girl's hands. They too were cool and soft, no longer dry and burning. After readjusting the crib quilt, she returned to Derek, baffled.

"I don't understand!" she murmured in bewilderment. "Lara was so hot, just moments ago!" Sitting again, she met his eyes. "How did you know? I mean, how did you know it was nothing serious?"

Derek chuckled softly and set a friendly arm around her shoulder. "No great talent, I assure you. It's just that I've been around since Lara was born and I've been through a number of minor catastrophes with Bobby and Tina. When she was an infant, we all panicked over everything!" He smiled ruefully. "Then we all began to learn a little about parenting. A teaspoon of aspirin and water can save you from a lot of unnecessary, middle-of-the-night hospital trips."

"Should we call Tina and Bobby?"

"No, I don't think so, not yet anyway. Let's let them have their night."

"Yes," Leigh echoed hollowly. "Let's let them have their night."

Something in the sad inflection of her voice reached Derek. "You'd better get back to sleep yourself, young lady, or else the Lady of the Lake *will* sound like a sick bullfrog tomorrow morning."

"I can't—" Leigh began to object, but Derek quickly silenced her.

"Lie down and close your eyes. I'll watch Lara. Here . . ." He pulled a pillow from the top of the bed and laid it across his lap. "Put your head so"—he demonstrated by gently maneuvering her onto his lap—"and you can watch her yourself until you drift off."

"But you need sleep more than I do!" Leigh exclaimed.

"I will go to sleep soon," he murmured.

Leigh wasn't about to argue further; she was afraid to move or even breathe and disturb the strange bond of tranquillity that had formed between them. Lara, she could see, was sleeping peacefully. She allowed her own eyes to flutter and close, aware that Derek was stroking her hair. Then she too fell asleep in a cocoon of borrowed happiness. Sleep led to dreaming, and in her dream she heard Derek's voice and he was saying marvelous things. *I love you, Leigh, God, how I love you!*

Lara, demanding exit from her crib, woke them both. "Up!" she shrilled imperiously. "Up! Uncle Derek."

"I'm up! I'm up!" he groaned. Uncoiling his length in a luxurious stretch, he ambled over and lifted Lara out. "How do you feel?"

"Starvin'!" Lara replied with wide eyes. "Starvin'!"

"Oh, you're always starvin'," Derek chuckled. "Let Leigh get you washed and dressed and then Emma will take you down to the kitchen." He scratched his chin while he gave a groggy Leigh a rueful, "Good morning." Sauntering for the door, he mumbled, "This shaving every day is for the birds. Better get moving, ladies. I'm off to shower and dress myself. We have to be out of here in ninety minutes." He raised his brows at Leigh to make sure she was awake and comprehending.

She had never felt more warmly drawn to him, more aware of the complex personality that made up the man, more attracted to his sensual virility. He stood in the doorway, reddish-gold hair tousled, eyes still lazy with sleep, deep bronze chest bared and hinting of the trim hips and powerful legs beneath the faded jeans below. A catch stuck in her throat, preventing her from speech, so she nodded. What was wrong with them? she wondered sadly. As enemies, they created hate but a marvelous passion. As friends, they could only come so close.

"See you downstairs." He closed the door behind him.

Leigh despondently dressed Lara and called Emma to take the child downstairs so that she might shower and dress herself. She lingered in the shower as long as she dared, donned a light knit dress for the still-warm fall weather, and rushed down the stairway for the dining room, determined not to be late.

Derek did not join her for breakfast. Emma told her that he had grabbed a cup of coffee and piece of toast earlier, then hurried out to see that their instruments were properly loaded in the company van to be moved to the studio. Lara, too, had already eaten and was with Derek.

Leigh absently ate an egg, a few strips of bacon, and toast, forcing herself to do so. She didn't want to become hungry later on company time.

"More coffee, dear?" Emma asked as she bustled about the room, her voice ringing cheerfully.

"No, thank you." Leigh smiled in return. She frowned and looked at the dark liquid in her cup. For some reason Emma's usually delicious fresh-perked coffee was tasting acid and bitter. "I wonder if I might bother you for a cup of tea instead?"

"No bother at all, dear." Emma whisked away her cup and returned quickly with a steaming pot of tea. "Are you feeling all right?"

Leigh grimaced ruefully. "Opening-night jitters, I guess. This will be my first day in a studio as a worker instead of an observer. Butterflies seem to be playing havoc with my insides."

"Oh, you'll get over it!" Emma assured her sweetly. "Just ignore Derek's growl. It's always worse than the bite, you know."

"I suppose . . ." Leigh said vaguely. She drank her tea beneath Emma's benign eye, grateful that the mellow liquid, laced with milk and sugar, seemed to sit much better than the coffee. Then she thanked Emma and braced herself to meet Derek for their trip to the studio.

Recording, Leigh learned quickly, was a perfectionist's dream. Mistakes could be rectified, and if she had found Derek "nit-picky" before, she now found him to be impossible. They did the same things over and over, and over again until Derek was satisfied. At least, she thought, they were working with tracks, which allowed for each instrument to be recorded separately. Her mistakes did not cause endless difficulty for the others in the group. Tracks also allowed more complex instrumentation. John played the guitar for one track, flute for another. Derek played guitar and harpsichord. Shane, drawing upon a much loved but seldom used talent, contributed the haunting cry of his bagpipes in several, specially planned and defined places.

"It's really amazing," Roger told her one day when they were both behind the glass booth, watching John record a flute segment. "When we have the completed project, we'll sound more like a symphony than a group of six. Of course, if we take the album on a concert tour now, we'll have to hire extra musicians."

Leigh smiled faintly. She didn't think there would ever be a concert tour. They had been recording now for a month. The strange night she had shared with Lara and Derek might never have existed. He was distant again, barely aware of her being in his house. At the studio he was harsh, and even when he yelled at her these days he called her "Tremayne." The album, she knew, would be wrapped up within the next week. And then she would go home, alone this time.

"Tacos!" Bobby suddenly sauntered toward them with his happy announcement of lunch. He set the large white cardboard box on an empty chair. "Dig in. We all have thirty minutes."

Leigh reached a slender hand for a taco and then withdrew it.

"What's the matter?" Bobby asked, crestfallen. "I thought you loved tacos!"

"I do!" Leigh promised him quickly. "I'm—I'm going to let them cool for a minute." She grinned brightly, but felt terribly uneasy. She did love tacos, but the spicy aroma of them had churned her stomach. She dismissed the unformed idea that floated on the outskirts of her mind and helped herself to a soda. "I heard we're breaking early today for a meeting," she said. "A meeting about what?"

"The album cover," Bobby told her, grimacing as his taco shell broke. "And title. Right now this thing is just 'Henry the Eighth.' We have to decide if we want to stick with it or not. You get final judgment on that, Leigh. But as a group, we always toss ideas around."

"Believe me," Leigh chuckled, "I'm not averse to ideas! Besides," she added softly, "I hardly recognize my own work anymore. Derek has done so much with it!"

"That is Derek," Roger agreed. "He can change a weed to a rose, and should he get a rose, he can change it into an exquisite garden!"

"Thanks!" Leigh knew he was telling her that her work had been the rose. It was matter-of-fact with them that Derek had unlimited talent.

* * *

334

On Star Island that night they mused for over an hour before anyone came up with any concrete ideas suitable for the cover. Shane ghoulishly thought that a chopping block and ax against a pitch-black background would be perfect.

"The man was a monster," he said, in defense of his scoffed-at idea.

"True," Bobby agreed. "But we always appear on our covers. Why not a medieval scene. Period costumes and the like."

"Leigh?"

She was surprised to find that Derek had spoken her name, drawing her into the discussion.

"Well, I—" she stammered, afraid to voice her suggestion lest it sound ridiculous. "I think we could combine the two ideas. As Shane says, the ax and block center. And then as Bobby says, we can be the background. The king and his retainers and a random wife."

They were all staring at her and a slow flush spread through her cheeks. "It was just an idea . . ." she said weakly.

"And all in favor yell 'aye'!" Bobby called. A hearty chorus echoed him and Leigh looked around at their smiling faces, amazed. Derek, she noticed, was smiling too.

"I'd like to stick with 'Henry the Eighth' for the title," Derek said, "and underneath, 'Loved to Death.' It will fit perfectly with the cover, and also advertise what will probably be the most popular song. Any other suggestions?"

There were none. Everything had been congenially resolved. As the guests trooped out, Leigh moved awkwardly toward the stairway. Being alone with Derek now left her tongue-tied.

"Have a drink with me, will you, Leigh?" he called as she reached the banister. "It's a beautiful night. I'd like to walk down to the dock and watch the stars for a while."

His invitation caught her mid-step and she almost tripped with the shock of it. Turning slowly, she composed her features to nonchalance. "If you like. It does seem to be a pleasant night."

Leigh was stiff and Derek relaxed as he casually put an arm around her waist and led her first to the game room, where he gallantly poured two glasses of wine, and then outside, past the pool and patio and out to the dock. They sat on the planks and sipped their wine while they watched the brilliant stars in the night sky play upon the water. Derek began to rub gentle fingers beneath the hair on Leigh's neck.

"I have to talk to you," he said softly.

She looked at him with tremulous eyes. His face was gentle, the line of his mouth curved. She felt herself lost in the golden-brown hue of his eyes, lost and frightened should she be misreading the tender concern she found in their depths.

He pulled her more closely to him. "What I have to say to you isn't going to be simple. There's a lot that you don't know, a lot that I have to rectify with myself. And it will take time. I don't want any interruptions, I don't want to be worried about schedules or broken strings on guitars. But in a few days we'll be all wrapped up. Will you bide with my temper till then? And then, will you listen to me with an open mind? Part of what I have to tell you is going to be painful, and you may have to adapt to it as I did."

Leigh stared at him and nodded, the commitment of her agreement evident in the shimmering tears that specked her lashes. He hadn't said that he loved her; he'd promised no future for them. She had simply to trust in her love, but that was enough. He had asked her to wait, and she would gladly wait forever.

They didn't speak anymore, but sat by the water contentedly together, feeling the soft ocean breeze, listening to the gentle lap of the tide. Surely, Leigh thought, had she died and gone to heaven she could not have been more blissful and secure.

The chill in the breeze slowly increased as the moon rose full above them. Leigh shuddered involuntarily and Derek immediately suggested they go back to the house. He kissed her lightly as they reached her door, but she couldn't let him go. Her arms curled tightly around his neck and she clung to him.

"Don't go," she whispered desperately. She couldn't bear him to take away his wonderful warmth; leave when she had just found him.

"Leigh . . ." he began in a groan, holding her hands still. "I told you, there's so much you have to know. I have no right—"

"I don't care," she murmured in a choked cry to his chest. "I don't care. And I do know that it's right when we're together."

Whatever demons he fought, he was only human. In the blink of an eye the door crashed open and she was in his arms. He whispered her name over and over with a soft and yearning desire that echoed lovingly of emotion deeper than the spoken word.

Both meant to play love's old game, to tease and to torment. Yet neither could. Sprawled upon the bed, they fumbled with one another's clothing, ripping rather than removing. The month apart had been long, too long. When their clothes were shed, their arms immediately entwined, their lips met with insatiable, feverish hunger.

For a second Derek pulled back, and in that time his eyes devoured her. They were a flame within themselves, and as they quickly roamed over her, Leigh felt her flesh begin to heat. Then his eyes met hers. They asked a mute question, which she answered with a strangled sigh, hurling herself back into his arms. Her thirst for him had to be quenched. She arched herself to him, relishing the feel of her soft breasts crushing into his chest, the grinding of their hips in instant and mutual need.

"Derek, my love," she pleaded.

He needed no further urging. "Oh, honey," he groaned, "you don't know what you do to me."

But she did. As he shifted to take her, she opened to him like a bursting sunrise, and they melded together like molten lead. They were an inferno, feasting as if starved, and the ultimate consummation of their love burned with a fire more fierce than the sun's and left them with a satisfaction and togetherness more thorough than the meeting of the sky and earth.

And as Leigh slept in the serenity of her lover's arms, she knew she would ask no more of life than the heaven he gave her.

337

CHAPTER NINE

Leigh slept fitfully through the night, waking often to assure herself that Derek was still there beside her. He was, of course, his limbs entangled with hers, his arms possessively around her. She awakened fully to the bright light of early morning to find herself still curled comfortably along his length, his easy breathing in her ear, his head resting gently upon the auburn pillow of her hair.

Derek awoke as she gently tried to free her hair. A slow, contented smile curved his lips and highlighted his lazy golden eyes. He stretched long fingers to caress her cheek. "Morning, love," he whispered softly.

"Morning," she replied, subduing a sob that suddenly choked in her throat. He couldn't really be hers. Not this golden giant who had sworn revenge with savage arrogance and then made her a prisoner of his heart while arousing undreamed of passions with his magnificent body. She clutched his hand and kissed it feverishly and rolled atop his deep bronze chest. "Oh, Derek . . ." she murmured into his neck. She almost said, "I love you," but the words caught on her tongue. Their relationship was so very fragile! Ghosts still lay between them, ghosts that could easily destroy them. Not just the tangible spirit of Richard, but the other clouds he had created . . . doubt, mistrust, and fear.

"What is it, Leigh?" Derek asked gently in return, stroking her hair in a comforting gesture. "Talk to me."

She shook her head. "Not yet. Just hold me."

He did, and then he made love to her, slowly, sweetly. And when she shuddered and lay happily content in his arms, he continued to caress lightly the silkiness of her skin with a tenderness that she knew belonged uniquely to her alone. She gave him a dazzling smile.

"Derek, I have to know what's going on," she said, secure in his arms. "Something happened the day we left my house—something that changed everything. I need to talk to you, Derek, but I need you to be honest with me too."

His cat eyes were drawing a film, a shield, closing off from her as she spoke. "Leigh—" he began.

"Don't!" she protested. "Don't shut me out! Can't you see! We've been doing just that to one another all this time. Trust me, at least this once. Whatever it is, I can handle it. I really can, when you're beside me."

Derek was no longer touching her. His hands were clasped behind his head and he stared up at the ceiling. "We have to be at the studio in less than two hours."

"A lot can be said in two hours." Leigh knew she was pushing him, but fear drove her on. She had thought she could wait, take whatever golden moments were theirs and cherish them for just that—beautiful spaces of time that could linger forever in memory.

But she couldn't. She was terrified of whatever it was that lurked in Derek's mind. Life had taught her the bitter lesson that love could turn sour, and if she stayed with Derek any longer, basking in the depth of emotion she felt for him, only to have it all snatched away, she would never survive the blow. Within her soul she would be a cripple. They had to straighten things out. She had to know that he loved her, and that his love was a commitment.

"We have a tendency to argue when we talk," Derek finally said, still watching the ceiling.

"Damn!" Leigh muttered irritably. She was a nervous wreck and he was being completely evasive. "We can't go on not talking."

"You're already arguing."

"I'm not!" Leigh exploded.

Derek whipped around with a strange savagery and planted his weight over Leigh's with his fingers gripped into her shoulders and his golden gaze burning into hers. Tension worked tersely in his facial features and the veins corded and pulsed in

339

the length of his neck. Leigh shivered; she had forgotten the power that he was composed of, the strength, determination, and will that lay coiled at all times within the sinewed frame she so loved.

"All right, Leigh," he enunciated crisply, "I'll talk. But you won't walk out if you don't like what I've got to say. We've made a commitment. It isn't on paper yet, and it isn't legally binding. But we've made it, and you know it as well as I do."

Leigh stared into flaming golden eyes and nodded blankly. He was saying things she wanted to hear; why was his voice so intense and frightening? Didn't he understand that all she needed to know was that he loved her and believed in her and wanted to spend the rest of his life with only her?

As abruptly as he had pounced upon her, he moved away. His movements were erratic as he paced about the room, totally unself-conscious of his nudity, and as splendid and regal as a golden god of ancient times.

"Richard didn't have an accident," he told her matter-of-factly. "He drove off that cliff on purpose. I talked to him the night before and I knew he was very upset about something. He kept mentioning 'her' and I naturally assumed he meant you. Then he started talking about the past. When we were kids growing up together. And he talked about meeting you and how the days we had spent with your dad by the sea had been the best in his life. He kept repeating over and over again that he had 'missed the boat somewhere.' "

Derek stopped his pacing and looked at Leigh. Her eyes were as round as saucers, her face frozen in shock. She had thought herself beyond pain from Richard, but she wasn't. He had killed himself. She hadn't seen what turmoil raged behind his cool aloofness; she hadn't been there when he really needed her. No matter what had gone on between them, she should have been able to help him.

"I told you this wouldn't be easy." Derek's harsh voice broke through her remorse and the terrible guilt that washed over her in waves of agony. "But hear me out." He drew a deep, ragged breath and turned to the window, unable to comfort her until he had finished. "I blamed you. I blamed myself for not realizing how depressed he was when we talked. His last request was that I watch out for you. I laughed it off. I told him that you were a survivor and that he would fall in love again. We had all been in and out of love a dozen times.

"He told me good-bye and thanks. The next thing I heard was that he was dead. I wanted to strangle you. He was more than my partner, more than my friend. He was my brother. All those years when we were kids, when parental love meant boarding schools and an unspared rod, Richard and I had each other."

Derek's tone went very soft. "We were both mesmerized when we met you coming from the ocean like an innocent Venus. Everything about you was fresh and wonderful. The love and respect in your home were totally alien to anything we had ever known. Richard was quick. I remember how awed you were when you realized who you were marrying. But it was he who had found something special, and he knew it. He just didn't know how to handle it."

Leigh allowed her dazed eyes to focus on Derek. He was watching her now, and his eyes held only compassion. None of it made sense. He said he wanted to kill her, then he said that she was special. She didn't understand, but she was too numb to care.

With an impatient oath Derek strode back across the room and gripped both her hands. "Dammit, Leigh! I told you this wasn't the time to go into all this and I'm making a terrible mess of it all. Listen to me! Pay attention to me! Now I've made you feel responsible and that's not the case. I'm trying to make you understand the things I felt and why I behaved the way I did."

"I'm listening," Leigh managed in a whisper.

"I loved you even when you were my best friend's wife. I knew I couldn't have you, so I set you up on a little pedestal. I could be your friend, and I could be near you. I never allowed myself to think about you and Richard in bed . . . in one another's arms. I told myself that one day I would find a woman like you, a woman I wanted to have my children, to live and grow with together, to shelter, to come to. You were perfection to me, your marriage heaven.

"When Richard began to tell me you were running around and wanted out, I couldn't accept it. I had to mask my feelings with hate and anger. After he died, I barely made the funeral. I swore I'd never see you again.

"Then came Atlanta. I wanted it to be you; I was afraid that it had been you. It was gnawing me apart and I had to find out." He ran a finger over her cheek, reverently tracing the fine lines as the timbre of his voice went deeper in a husky whisper. "And I had to have you again. I convinced myself that anything I did would be fair because you deserved whatever I could do for all that had happened to Richard. I knew that I could find a way to trap you if I could just get you here, and perversely, I really was interested in 'Henry the Eighth.' Then, when you came, I was a mess! I loved you, I hated you, I wanted you. It was almost a sickness. I needed to be close to you, to understand you, but I couldn't stop myself from striking out, and I couldn't let you go until I had come to terms with myself."

Leigh watched the strong tan fingers that were curled around her own. Derek was telling her that he loved her. She should be ecstatic. She knew now beyond a doubt now that he wasn't another Richard, that his desire was also for the love and security of a total commitment that she craved.

But she wasn't ecstatic. She was chilled to the bone. Richard still lay between them, now more than ever. She had indirectly failed him and led to his suicide, and no matter what Derek said, in his heart he would never forgive her. She'd have to learn to forgive herself.

"Why are you telling me this now?" she asked thickly. "We haven't got a chance in the world—"

"I'm telling you now because you insisted!" Derek grated, dropping her hands to grip her chin and bring her lifeless eyes to his. "And you could help a bit! I'm botching this entire thing because you're not giving me a single response."

"What do I say? Yes, I didn't understand Richard's frame of mind and so I did nothing? What will that do? Nothing. We both have to learn to live with it—"

"That's the point I haven't gotten to yet. You were not in the least responsible for Richard's actions. I know that for a fact, but even if I didn't, I would have realized by now that none of us can prevent a thing like that."

Leigh frowned, confused. "What?"

"Richard left a letter for me in his desk. You never found it because you never went through his things. I was in the room that day to look through his phone book—I had forgotten my own number because I never dial it—and I found the note. He knew before he left for the West Coast that he wouldn't return. He had a disease of the nervous system that would have slowly killed him, crippling him first, and he couldn't bear to die that way. He didn't want you to know. He said he had caused you enough pain and that you would be able to cope with an accident —an act of God—better than the truth."

The paralyzing dullness of shock suddenly receded from Leigh, and the floodgates of pain opened with a shudder and an agonized cry. "Oh, God! Derek! I didn't know. I didn't know! Why didn't he come to me? He knew that I still loved him . . . that I would have done anything . . . he could have come to me . . ."

"Leigh!" Derek's arms were around her; they held her with infinite tenderness as she sobbed, her tears streaming into the mat of his chest. "Leigh, Richard did know those things. And he did love you— very much. It was that love that wanted to spare you any more grief. It's all in the letter. He said that you had already suffered enough because of him. When enough time had passed, he wanted you to know."

He held her for a good hour while she cried, soft tears for the brilliant young man she had loved and hated, for the waste of his life, for the depth of his love for her that he had shown in his way at the end.

Derek mourned with her. Old scars had been cut afresh, they

343

were bleeding again. Yet now they could heal. In a strange way they had given Richard Tremayne back to one another.

Leigh's tears subsided and Derek gently wiped the dampness from her cheeks. "We go on from here," he said softly.

She nodded against his strength. "I know."

"I love you."

She nodded again.

"I'm still a bastard."

It was a strangled sound, but close to a chuckle. "I know."

"We're both going to make it—together."

The bedside phone rang shrilly and Derek automatically answered it, his eyes never leaving Leigh. He listened for a moment, then muttered, "Thanks, yes, we're coming." Replacing the receiver, he tilted Leigh's chin again. "Hey! You promised me you could handle this. I'm beside you, and I love you. Are you okay?"

"Yes." Leigh attempted to smile but her effort fell flat. "Yes, I'm fine."

"I can cancel the session," Derek offered, his eyes denoting his obvious concern over her lethargy.

"No . . . no," she said faintly.

"Then we have to go. That was James to tell us we're running very late."

Leigh rose, feeling like a zombie. "I'll just hop in the shower."

Derek retrieved his jeans from where they had landed on the floor the night before and slid them over his long muscled legs. "I'll hop into my room then." He grimaced ruefully. "Tonight we'll pick a room and transfer all of our clothing into one spot."

Leigh tried for another smile. "Yes."

Derek walked over to her and enveloped her naked shoulders in his arms, relishing the silky touch of her feminine skin against his. His lips brushed her forehead. "You could say something now, after all I've poured out to you. Something like, 'I love you too.'"

Leigh stared at him, her eyes still saucer-size and glassy. "I do love you, Derek. I have for a long, long time."

"Did you love me in Atlanta?"

"Yes." Leigh buried her head into his chest and rubbed her cheek against the coarse red-gold hairs that tickled her nose, "but I didn't know it then."

Derek groaned and his frame tautened against hers; his flesh became warmer. "I have to get out of here. We're going to finish the tracks today, the pictures tomorrow, and then get out of here. I want you all to myself." He clutched her tightly to him, pulled away and made a hasty retreat.

Leigh walked into the shower, still dazed. What was wrong with her? she wondered. She was shocked by the circumstances surrounding Richard's death. That was natural. But Derek was right; she couldn't have changed anything. Still, it was as if a wound had been ripped back open. She had loved Richard; she had been his wife for three years. He should have come to her. Yet in the end he had chosen a strange type of nobility. He had shielded her from pain; he had even made a vague attempt to clear her of the accusations he had made.

She had told Derek that she could handle whatever troubled him. And she could. It was something else that was bothering her, something she couldn't quite define. There would be time, she told herself philosophically. The man she loved returned her feelings and they would have all the time in the world.

With Derek's determination behind them, they completed the final tracks by five o'clock. Derek had last-minute details to work out with the photographer so he sent Leigh home with Roger. "If I'm late, don't wait up. Tomorrow may be hectic."

Derek was late, very late, but Leigh couldn't sleep anyway. She prowled the house nervously, chiding herself for not settling down. In the last two days her world had made a marvelous turnabout. She should be as happy and as content as a bird.

"There's just so much we have left to discuss!" she told herself aloud. "Plans . . . more admissions and confessions . . ."

Gravel finally crunched in the driveway and Leigh knew that Derek had returned. She raced across the marble to the door, eager to greet him now that she had gotten over her initial shock.

She had been so cold that morning! And in between all the sadness he had had to relate he had also told her many wonderful things. He had loved her as long as she had loved him. . . .

The door swung open and Derek's cat-gold gaze brightened at the sight of her. She had showered and changed into a lingerie set of misty blue gauze, and his frank appraisal and sensuous smile told her that her efforts were approved of and appreciated.

"I told you not to wait up," he murmured after a deep kiss that stole the breath from both of them, "but I'm glad that you did."

"We have a lot of lost time to make up for!" Leigh answered, grinning as the now-familiar heat he could produce raced through her limbs. His trim hips instinctively wedged closer to hers, and color suffused her face at the sure proof against her abdomen that she could arouse him as easily as he could her.

"I'm all for making up for lost time!" he breathed to her earlobe, nibbling as he did so. His lips, growing more urgent and demanding as they traveled, moved erotically along her throat and on to the cleavage enticingly displayed by the negligee. Leigh let escape a sigh that might have been a purr as her body responded to his demands with loving skill. "We're standing in the hallway," she told him dreamily. "I think we should move. This little scene could seriously endanger James's sense of dignity should he awaken and stumble upon it."

Derek lifted his head and laughed, the deep sound that could captivate her a room away. Then she was in his arms and they were moving effortlessly up the stairway. "It's all real!" Leigh said softly, meeting his smoldering eyes.

"Forever," Derek replied. He walked on into his own room and they fell to the bed together. No longer the least bit shy or hesitant, Leigh began working at the buttons of his shirt, teasing him with flicking motions of her tongue each inch of the way.

"You are a vixen!" Derek accused, turning the tables as he ripped away the last button and pinned her to the bed. "Now I shall play the tormentor!" He laughed.

His assault on her senses was slow and complete, his own desire held carefully in check as he teased and tantalized every inch of her sleek skin, savoring the fragrant scent, tasting its sweetness, exploring its perfection. His teeth nipped and grazed over her earlobe, finding each little erogenous zone along her nape. The warmth of his breath alone sent thrilling chills flooding through her spine; his touch, purposely designed to torment with arousal and withdrawal, turned those chills to a current of charged electricity.

"I love you," he murmured, his mouth moving sensuously over her breast. "I'm in heaven when I'm with you. I shall never have my fill of you."

"I love you," Leigh panted in return, moaning deeply as his teeth locked over a highly sensitive nipple and rotated gently.

"Like that?" Derek demanded hoarsely.

"Ummmmmm," Leigh returned breathlessly. "I like everything that you do . . ." Her voice trailed away with a gasp and her fingers dug into his shoulders as his teeth raked gently down her rib cage to begin a new assault on the hollows of her hips.

"And how about that, my love?"

His query was little more than a choked stream of air, as was her answer, yet they both knew that their murmured words of love could elicit deeper and deeper passion.

Derek's voice suddenly took on a peculiar note, which faintly surprised Leigh, but she was cocooned within his realm of expert seduction and it was several seconds before his words registered in her mind.

"And you're all mine, my darling, all mine now. You will never have to look for love from another man again because I will always be there. I shall keep you so happily busy and satisfied you will never have the need . . ."

Leigh felt as if she had been doused in a tub of ice water.

"*What?*"

"Nothing, my love."

Leigh furiously sprang into a sitting position, knocking him aside as she did so.

"What the hell?" Derek demanded, staring at her stunned, his eyes narrowed dangerously.

Leigh didn't care. The green of her own hazel eyes was blazing like dark jade. "I want you to repeat what you just said."

"I don't even know what I just said!"

"Yes, you do!" Tears stung her lids; she knew what had bothered her from earlier in the morning. Derek still didn't believe *her*. He no longer blamed her for Richard, but he had Richard's own words to rely on. It was evident that he still thought her capable of shoddy affairs behind someone's back.

"Dammit, Leigh!" he muttered angrily. "You have to be the only woman in the world who can pick an argument in the middle of making love."

"I want to hear what you said—slowly and clearly."

"What difference does it make?"

"How can you say that?" Leigh sputtered. "You talk about commitments but you think the worst of me! Love is trust and . . . and credibility!"

"What are you talking about?" Derek demanded, growing steadily angrier. "I didn't say I didn't trust you!" He scowled darkly. Lifting his arms to her, he commanded, "Come back here!"

"Not when you think—"

"I don't think anything. What went on between you and Richard and whoever else doesn't matter. The past is over. You might have had every right to—"

"To what?" Leigh prompted icily.

"To seek whatever comfort you did elsewhere." Derek impatiently pushed her shoulders back to the bed and straddled her. "I love you. I don't care. We're beginning anew," he continued, his words a husky, mumbled whisper as he resumed his lovemaking, his tongue sliding over her lips and his hands caressing her torso.

"Derek, stop it!" Leigh insisted. She held herself rigid despite the pulsations of sensuous pleasure her body refused to deny. "Stop it!" But he wouldn't take her protestations seriously. She knew he thought she was playing a feminine game, saying no but meaning yes, wanting to be cajoled into submission.

"Stop—" His lips fell over hers, muffling out the words. Then he was slowly caressing her soft flesh, and she doubted that he would even notice she had pitted all her strength against him. . . .

Then, it didn't matter. He claimed her with sure, knowing expertise, seducing with each demanding thrust of satin, hurtling her along with him into the escalating whirlpool of magic that she no longer desired to deny.

But she could not glow in the aftermath of their mutual satiation, nor seek the comfort and security and contentment of the arms that attempted to hold her with their usual ease. Despite the yearning she felt to settle back and bask in the simple pleasure of her love, she pulled away from the man who would undoubtedly hold her heart for life.

He groaned. "What now?"

Trying with great difficulty to stay completely calm and voice her words softly, Leigh smoothed back her damp auburn hair and said, "You aren't paying any attention to me. You think going to bed solves any problem that pops up. I wanted to talk and you—"

"And I forced you to make love?" Derek raised a skeptical brow.

"No," Leigh said evenly, but she knew her temper was slipping. "I'm not a hypocrite—believe it or not. I love being with you, I love what you do to me, your touch, your scent, everything. You. But that's not enough. I know. You keep saying nothing matters, that the past is gone. But it matters to me, Derek. It matters very much that you trust me and believe what I say. How can we form any kind of a life together without those basics? I want to tell you—"

"I don't want to hear about the past!" Derek grated, interrupting her in a sharp command. "Damn! Can't we just let it rest?"

"No!" She had tried, Lord, she had really tried. Springing from the bed with a furious oath, she stalked for the door, so enraged she completely forgot her state of total undress. Pausing with her fingers clutched around the knob in a white-knuckled grip, she turned back to Derek. "If you think you can listen to me, Mr. Mallory, do it by tomorrow. If not, I'll be heading back to the Keys and 'poor Lyle' by nightfall."

Derek was silent for a moment and their eyes clashed in a battle of willpower. Leigh would not allow hers to fall.

"I don't like ultimatums," Derek finally said coldly. He turned his back on her and sank his head into his pillow.

Shaking with a mixture of rage, pain, and frustration, Leigh threw open the door and flounced into the hall. Suddenly realizing she was as naked as a nymph, she sped toward the door that led to her own room. It was highly improbable that anyone would be roaming the halls at such an hour, but she still felt ridiculous on top of everything else.

But shades of the past were indeed engulfing her. The door was locked.

"Impossible!" Leigh muttered. She rattled the knob again fruitlessly. The door refused to budge. Sinking to the floor, she berated herself for having inherited an Irish temperament that didn't allow room for common sense. When walking out on someone, it was wisest to do it clothed.

Trying not to think, she rose slowly, tilted her chin, and headed back for Derek's room. If she was lucky, she could slip in quietly and grab her negligee. . . .

But she wasn't lucky. Derek was no longer in the bed. He was standing by the window in his dressing gown, gazing down upon the moonlit lawn. His eyes turned to her as soon as she entered the room.

"Back already?" he drawled.

"Just for my clothes!" Leigh hissed, snatching the gown from the floor. "My door is locked," she snapped.

The sardonic brow raised. "Again?"

"Yes!"

"My, you do have problems with doors!"

"Only in this house," Leigh replied sweetly, "so I imagine I won't be worrying about it anymore." Hastily slipping back into the gown and trailing the robe over her shoulder, she smiled a sarcastic "good night" and spun for the door to make a regal exit.

"Where are you going?" Derek inquired politely.

"To find a couch."

"Don't be absurd," Derek sighed. "Sleep here."

"You don't listen—"

"And I thought you weren't a hypocrite. You've slept in my bed before—one more night isn't going to kill you."

"I—"

"No," Derek said softly, leaving the window to walk toward her with the quiet tread of a cat. He touched her cheek just briefly with a single finger. "I won't get into anything else tonight. We're both tired. Let's get some sleep."

Leigh was tired. It had been an incredibly long day, long and traumatic. Her lashes fluttered over her eyes and she fought the urge to cry. "All right, let's go to sleep."

"I thought you might see it my way." Derek chuckled.

Leigh was already crawling into bed, pulling tensely to the far side.

"That's the problem," she retorted bitterly. "You refuse to see *anything* my way!"

Derek doffed his robe and climbed beside her, encircling her protesting form and drawing her against his warmth. "You know, one of the first rules of marriage is never to sleep apart. I heard that from a wise old friend."

"We're not married, Derek, and I don't think it's a likely prospect for the future," Leigh said stiffly, but she was no longer fighting the comfort he offered. It might truly be their last-night together. She had been a partner once in a marriage that lacked communication and understanding. Not even for Derek would she contemplate such a thing again.

He didn't answer and within minutes she found herself yawning. "By the way," she murmured drowsily, "who was the wise old friend who gave you advice on marriage?"

His arm tightened securely around her. "Your father," he whispered smugly.

351

CHAPTER TEN

A park in Coral Gables had been chosen for the picture-taking session. Acres of rolling green grass and high-arched, vine-covered pathways gave credence to a scene from the medieval days of jolly old England.

Derek was a terrific Henry VIII—with his costume, a fake beard, and generous padding, and his own imposing height, he could easily pass for a reincarnation of the arrogant king.

Roger was dressed as the Archbishop of Canterbury, Shane, John, and Bobby as various noblemen of the court.

Leigh was to portray Anne Boleyn, and as the day went on, she was sure Derek had chosen her role with malicious intent. She spent an hour of posing on her knees by his feet, beneath his royal foot on the chopping block, then tearfully clutching his robe abjectly begging for mercy.

Despite the fact that it was fall, the temperature readings were closing in on ninety. Dripping with the heat, Leigh found it harder and harder to keep her temper in check. Derek, she knew, although he seemed entirely nonchalant and easygoing to all other eyes, was still angry. She had warned him again that morning that she was leaving, and his attitude had infuriated her further. He seemed as if he just didn't care. Now he was taunting her, all prefaced with smiles, as if all were well between them and he was any teasingly tender lover.

"Just one more by the block, Leigh," Bernie, the potbellied photographer called out cheerfully. "Then we'll wrap it up."

Gritting her teeth, Leigh once more folded her hands in prayer over the block, her knees sore now from grinding into the dirt. She forced a smile as a young makeup man powdered perspiration from her nose. Derek strode into position behind her; the others took their places in the background.

"I know it's hot," Bernie apologized, pushing his glasses back up his sweat-slick nose. "So we'll hurry the best we can."

"Take your time," Derek responded pleasantly, leaning on a knee and wedging his foot farther into Leigh's back. "We want to get it right," he added, "and besides, I think Mrs. Tremayne looks rather nice on a chopping block."

"Someone should have assassinated the king!" Leigh retorted.

To the left of her Roger started chuckling. Damn men altogether! Leigh thought. Always sticking with one another. Roger knew something was up between them, but he didn't take her seriously either!

"Too bad the Tower of London isn't handy," Derek commented dryly. "We could have gotten a few nice shots of Leigh behind bars."

Leigh opened her mouth for a nasty retort, but this time it was the frazzled photographer who interrupted her. "You have to stop talking or I'll never get *this* shot!" he moaned.

Then the work was finally over. Derek asked the band to join them on Star Island for a "task completion" drink. "Love it!" Roger agreed, his eyes dancing merrily. Leigh smiled grimly. Company was not going to prevent her from driving off the island.

She had packed her bag that morning, so once she returned to the house—in Roger's car—all she had to do was change. But she didn't get a chance to change right away. Roger affectionately pulled her into the game room. "I know you're leaving," he told her. "Derek mentioned it this morning. But you have to have one drink with us." He swept his priestly hat from his head and playfully bowed. "After all, my dear Lady of the Lake, this is your venture we have just completed. You and Derek *are* the London Company now."

Leigh chuckled at his antics, still objecting. "No, Roger, I am now retiring from the London Company. And you all are the London Company. Every one of you is important. I've been the hanger-on."

"Today I shall not argue, Lady," Roger said gallantly. "We

shall resume this ethical question on another occasion. Today is a victory. What can I get you to drink."

"Oh . . . white wine, I guess," Leigh acquiesced. Sadness was slowly creeping through her. She would miss them all so much! In the last months she had learned to love the band and the work that they did. She was a part of their camaraderie, of their family.

And even more a part of Derek. She blinked as tears welled behind her eyelids. It would be so easy to give way and just stay—agree with Derek and be his wife on any terms.

But such a relationship couldn't last. By his attitude he was calling her an out-and-out liar. And he refused to listen to a word from her!

"Hail, hail, the gang's all here!" Bobby called, filing into the game room with John, Shane, and Derek behind him. "Break out the booze!"

"Too quick for you!" Roger laughed, throwing beers on the counter. "Leigh and I are already indulging!"

It was a happy party. Tina, Lara, and Angela appeared to join in the celebration and gleeful, gay conversation filled the room. Feeling as if she were amputating a part of her body, Leigh joined in with the fun for a while. Then she singled out Roger and kissed his cheek. "I have to go now, Roger," she said quietly. "Thanks for everything."

"For what?" Roger scoffed, giving her a brotherly kiss back. His eyes were still dancing away. "You're special to all of us, Lady, and very talented at that. And I have a strange feeling you won't be gone long."

Leigh smiled doubtfully and moved away. Unable to resist, she looked for Derek. He had removed the beard and padding, and looked much as Henry must have as a young king—tall, strong, impeccably noble. But he wasn't watching her. His warm eyes, sparkling with their golden glow of interest, were on Tina, who was telling him something with a great deal of animation. Leigh closed her eyes and forced herself to spin around toward the door and the road out of his life.

She was reaching for the knob when she was abruptly and literally swept off her feet. Stunned, she stared in Derek's eyes.

"You should have told me you were ready sooner, darling," he said complacently, twirling in another circle to stride easily with his burden for the patio doors. "Tell everyone good-bye. A nice wave will do."

"Derek, I don't know what kind of a stunt this is," Leigh hissed as she was jostled in his arms. "But you can put me down this instant."

"I will put you down in a moment," he promised. Raising his voice, he called, "Hey, Roger! Are the bags on the boat?"

"James just put them in," Roger called back jauntily.

They were passing through the crowd, and everyone was innocently smiling at them. Tina, Angela, Bobby, Shane, and John. All smiling and waving as she protested.

"Do something, someone!" Leigh wailed, astounded. "This man is abducting me! He's taking me against my will. He's—"

They were out on the patio and Derek was moving calmly but swiftly down to the dock and the boat. Roger—Roger of all people!—trailed a few feet behind them.

"Don't be mad, Leigh," he pleaded, chuckling as he watched her angry features. "We really think we're looking after your best interests."

"Ooooooooooh!" Leigh spat, before exploding into a stream of oaths. She squirmed and pounded at Derek uselessly. He merely shifted so that she hung ineffectually behind his back, her costume helping to keep her prisoner.

And on the dock, releasing the ties on the *Storm Haven*, was James. Staid James, proper James, grinning away. "Have a nice trip, Mr. Mallory, Mrs. Tremayne."

"I don't believe this!" Leigh moaned as Derek skillfully hopped onto the boat with her in his arms.

"Bon voyage!" Roger yelled. He and James stood waving like a mismatched Laurel and Hardy as the *Storm Haven* drifted from her berth.

"What now, Errol Flynn?" Leigh snapped from her ignominious position. "You can't hold me and drive the boat or maneuver the sails!"

"I'll leave the sails for a while and we'll motor," Derek replied evenly. "And yes—I can hold you and turn on an ignition and steer!"

He went on to prove that he could do so while Leigh sputtered away vigorously until she realized she was wasting her breath. Then she hung limply, gathering strength for the moment when he would have to set her down.

They were out of the channel by the time he finally did, miles from shore. Leigh clamped her lips on a threat that she could swim. Dusk was falling and the shimmering lights on the horizon, blending together in the distance, informed her clearly that she would be a fool to attempt such dramatic bravado as a dive overboard.

Derek was watching her, a smile twitching on the grim set of his lips as he read her thoughts like a large lettered book. Drawing a deep breath for a rush of abuse, Leigh exhaled instead. "Why?" she demanded simply. Lifting helpless hands, she repeated, "Why? Why the dramatics?"

"Because," Derek informed her, his hand on the helm and his eyes scanning the ocean, "I have my faults, and I've been wrong —we'll go into that later—but you have a very major problem. *You* think running away solves everything. I want you in a spot where you can't get mad and take off."

"I didn't just run away! I warned you—"

"What about last night? You get mad so you hop out of bed and go running out stark naked!"

"I came back."

"You had to," Derek acknowledged bitterly. Cutting the engine with a flick of his wrist, he nimbly brushed past her to the aft of the *Storm Haven* and cast the anchor overboard with a whistling swing. If the situation were not so tense, Leigh would have laughed. Henry VIII balancing perfectly by the jinny mast of a twentieth-century yacht.

He turned to stare at her, his form tall and proud against the violet-streaked sky of the dying day. "Get into the cabin and sit," he ordered her curtly. "You wanted to talk—we'll talk. But you're going to get to hear why I didn't want to listen to your version of anything that happened."

"My version!" Leigh exclaimed.

"Go on down!" Derek demanded. "I'll be right there. Oh— and make yourself useful. There's wine in the refrigerator; you should find it easily. It's a small galley."

Squaring her jaw and clutching her long skirts around her, Leigh carefully climbed the wooden ladder down to the cabin. It was dark, but by groping along the wall she found a switch that gently illuminated the galley and adjoining dining room-den. The sailboat, Leigh decided, fitted her captain well. The galley was compact but complete down to a dishwasher; the den area simple but tastefully elegant, pleasingly paneled in a dark wood and decorated with silver gray drapes and matching seat covers. Stooping to reach into the waist-high refrigerator, Leigh found that it had been stocked with more than wine. Carefully shelved were rows of meats, cheeses, fruits, and various other staples. Derek, it seemed, was prepared for a long voyage.

The sound of his feet upon the ladder informed her that he had joined her just as she finished pouring the wine into the chilled glasses she had found beside it. Ignoring her, he drew the drapes to allow a cooling sea breeze to waft into the cabin while he impatiently began to jerk pieces of the Henry VIII costume from his body until he was down to the tight form-fitting pants and the knee-high boots. As he strode back to Leigh, she could read the tension in his face and sense the extent of his anger from the tautness of the muscles that bunched across his back.

"What the hell are *you* mad about?" she demanded crossly. "I'm the one who has been abducted!"

Derek picked up both wineglasses and set them at the mahogony table that flanked the starboard side. Reaching into a cabinet, he extracted an ashtray and a pack of cigarettes. Sliding into the seat, he motioned her next to him. "Sit down. Start talking. I'm listening."

357

Nervously, Leigh took the seat he indicated. She took a swallow of her wine and accepted a light for a cigarette, growing increasingly uneasy beneath the relentless intensity of his dark glower. "Go on," he prompted.

"Tell me why you are angry, first," Leigh suggested hesitantly. She felt totally tongue-tied, at a loss. How could she carry on an intimate conversation when he was acting like a hangman?

"You'll understand in a few minutes," he sighed, seeming unwillingly touched by her confusion. "Start talking—I'll try to help."

Lamely, with broken words, Leigh tried to explain her relationship with Richard: how entranced she had been at first, then how shattered she had become when she realized that Richard had a woman waiting in every city and that she was simply supposed to accept the situation because he was Richard Tremayne. She told him about the constant temper tantrums toward the end, the mental cruelty he would purposely inflict. "I tried to talk to you about Richard then," Leigh said, watching the smoke curl into the air from the glowing tip of her cigarette. "I told Richard a month before I filed the papers that I intended to do so. But Richard had your ear, and he didn't believe I would divorce him. Not until he was served the papers." Forcing herself to meet Derek's eyes squarely, Leigh turned to him and said, "But not once, Derek, not once, no matter what was happening, did I ever see anyone else. I was too hurt and bewildered to chance an involvement. Richard had shattered all my beliefs in what marriage and love meant."

It was Derek who shuttered his gaze and turned away. A lock of reddish-gold hair fell over his forehead, hiding his lowered head completely. Leigh sat tensely watching him, surprised by his silent reaction. Suddenly the hand that held his wineglass rose and slammed back to the table, splintering the fine crystal into minuscule pieces and splaying wine in every direction. His focus turned to Leigh and there was rage and pain in the depths of his eyes, which had turned as dark as the mahogany table.

"Why?" he exploded. "Why do you insist upon lying to me? I told you I didn't care—that I just didn't want to hear!"

"I'm not lying!" Leigh cried, frightened by his vehemence but more bewildered than ever and determined to cross the gulf between them. "Damn, Derek!" she pleaded, resisting the temptation to touch him by clenching her nails into her palms. "You tell me that you love me, but you won't even give me the benefit of doubt! You tell me why! Why are you so convinced that Richard's lies about me were the truth?"

"Because I have it in black and white," Derek said, his voice low and strained.

"What?" Leigh's whisper was a breath of utter disbelief.

"The letter, Leigh. The rest of Richard's letter. It's a damn deathbed confession! He wouldn't have lied to me in that; he wanted me to watch out for you." Shreds of glass covered Derek's hands but he didn't notice. A pool of wine lay over the table, but neither suggested they mop it up.

"I don't believe that either, Derek," Leigh choked sickly. "He wouldn't purposely have lied . . . then."

"God, Leigh," Derek groaned, "don't you see that I do believe in you? I understand how rotten things were for you—Richard did like to play the 'star.' I don't condemn you for anything. But I don't want to start our life with lies, either. We just drop it—whatever was was."

Feeling like a broken record Leigh dropped her forehead into the palm of her hand and repeated, "But I'm not lying!" Lifting her head with sudden inspiration, she asked, "Do you have the letter?"

"Yes, why?"

"Because I may find something in it you didn't!"

Derek shrugged as if the effort was useless, but he rose and disappeared into the forward cabin. Leigh picked up the broken glass while he was gone and searched the cabinets for another. When Derek returned, she had cleaned the table and set the new glass at his place. The little task had kept her from climbing the sailboat's walls.

The letter had been in his wallet, and as Derek pulled it out and handed it to Leigh, she could see the crease marks. He must have read it and replaced and reread it a hundred times.

Leigh glanced at his heavy countenance once, then turned her full attention to the words before her in Richard's sprawling script. The sight of his handwriting alone caused a constriction of sadness to form in her throat, but she had to read the letter. Knowing the fullness of his concern for her at the end, she couldn't believe that he would purposely malign her.

The letter was short, just two paragraphs and a line. The first dealt with his knowledge of his disease and his decision to end it all his own way, which Derek had already told her. Everything Derek had said was true; without going into detail, Richard admitted sadly that he had hurt her. His written word begged that she be spared as much further grief as possible.

It was the second paragraph that unwittingly condemned her:

I don't think Leigh realizes the depth of her own feelings, but she has been in love with a great guy for a long time. I've seen it; I knew it from the very start I suppose, but, well, being me, I just couldn't let her go. A real noble man. Ha-ha. Sorry—you know my bloody sense of humor. Maybe I am a little bitter. Seems like I'm the one that has to go. It was life, and I lived it. My only regret is Leigh. She deserved him in the first place. I hope that she gets more than stolen moments now. See to it, long-time friend and brother, will you?

Good luck, health, and long life to you both.

Leigh read the paragraph and parting line three times; she choked, sobbed, then began to laugh. It was a sad laugh, one that verged on hysteria. Looking from the paper with tear-bright eyes, she met Derek's pained and incredulous stare. It was obvious that he thought she had plummeted over the brink and become totally demented.

"Oh, don't you see? You mammoth idiot! To the music world, Derek, you may be a genius, but you can be as dense as a forest full of trees!" Leigh exclaimed, smiling ruefully through her tears. "Richard is talking about *you*. He understood our feelings before either of us did—before either of us could ever admit such a thing!"

Derek was still staring at her stunned. " 'A noble man,' " Leigh quoted. "Nobleman—dear future Lord Mallory. Richard was far more perceptive than I ever would have imagined. 'Good luck, health, and long life to you both.' This letter does more than ask you to look out for me, it's Richard's blessing. He wanted us to be happy together!"

Derek grabbed the sheet from her hand and his eyes scanned the paper. After a moment he dropped the worn sheet and unraveled his length to walk tiredly to the ladder and lean against it, his face pressed to the cold wood. Oh, God! Leigh thought desperately, he still doesn't believe!

She sat staring at him, in a trance of fear. The world and time stood still; she didn't dare think or even breathe. Lord, why didn't he say something? Didn't he know that she couldn't bear his terrible withdrawal one second longer?

"Derek!" she cried, her calling of his name ripped from her throat in a pathetic screech of agony. It was a beseechment from the soul that would have shattered a heart of stone.

He came back to her then and knelt at her feet, his hands and the tremendously long and powerful fingers that were music themselves locked more tenderly over hers than ever they had graced a keyboard. Tentatively, Leigh withdrew one hand and gently set her own delicate fingers upon the crisp reddish-gold hair of the head bowed over her lap.

"Oh, Lord, Leigh! I couldn't see what was right before my own bloody eyes! I was so afraid . . ." His voice was broken and cracking; his explanation trailed into a groan. "Can you ever forgive me, my dearest love?"

"Forgive you?" Leigh gasped, still trying to assimilate the fact that he was on his knees before her and that their ghosts had finally been laid to rest. For a brief moment she thought of Richard, and she thanked his fading spirit with a silent tear. Then she freed her other hand to clutch it too into the golden curls before her and lift Derek's head so that she could meet his golden eyes. All shadow of doubt was gone. In his gaze she found a wealth of unspoken eloquence, and she knew he offered her everything she had ever desired—not only undying love and devotion, but the complete belief and trust that would allow that love to grow to endless bounds for all the days of their lives. A smile of sheer relief and happiness stretched its way into her eyes, adding the beauty of radiance to the loveliness of her finely chiseled features.

"Forgive you?" she repeated incredulously. "My dear, dear Lord Mallory. I forgive you with all my heart! And I will love you with all my soul and being well into eternity!"

She planted a kiss of infinite tenderness upon his brow, then a spark of mischief lit her eyes and she began to chuckle softly. "Now get off your knees, Lord Mallory!" she commanded. "Your female fan club wouldn't like this one bit!"

"My female fan club can go hang!" Derek declared, slowly grinning. "I seek the approval of only one female in the entire world." He started to rise, but lowered himself back down, a definitely roguish expression settling into his rugged profile. Her chuckle became a knowing laugh; she had never expected her arrogant lover to remain humble for long.

"Hush, woman!" he ordered. "I decided to say one more thing while I'm down here. It's highly unlikely you'll ever get me into this position again!"

Leigh raised impudent brows. "Speak, my lord!"

"This is a proper proposal. Will you marry me?"

"You'll never get out of it!" Leigh vowed. "When?"

"As soon as we can get a license. I'd like to fly to Georgia and spend my wedding night and honeymoon in a certain house on a hill near Atlanta. I was seduced there once by a fantasy witch, a woman from a dream." Derek pounced gracefully to his feet and pulled Leigh up beside him as he whispered on in her ear.

"She was a real vixen, but I fell in love with her then and there and I would have spent my life searching for her." Running his tongue over her earlobe and tracing a pattern of erotic little kisses along her throat, he murmured, "I wonder if she likes to make love on boats. It's a delightful experience beneath the stars . . ."

"I'm sure she'd adore it," Leigh panted, gasping for the breath he was robbing from her lungs. "She is, you know . . ."

"My lady," Derek murmured. "Always."

Somehow, Derek managed to keep his mouth tantalizing her skin while he slid the draping "Boleyn" sleeves from her arms. Then he found himself stumped. "Where's the zipper on this damn thing?" he quizzed, annoyed and impatient.

Leigh smiled seductively and very slowly started to work apart the tiny hooks that held the costume together. "They didn't have zippers in the sixteenth century," she told him innocently. "You rented from an authentic costume shop." Shimmying from the dress seductively, Leigh gave him a wicked smile and bolted up the ladder. Beneath the moon she cast aside the remainder of her flimsy undergarments, knowing that he watched her, knowing his eyes were glittering gold with desire. . . .

Derek reached for her and she turned impishly to throw herself into his arms, only to slide down his length and help him out of the high boots. She watched him with frank feminine approval as he slid out of the tight pants, then waited as he came for her. Their bed was a spot beneath the proud mainmast; their ceiling the star-blanketed sky. The harmony of their voices was that of their bodies and souls as they came together, satisfied for a timeless moment to touch, arms wrapped tenderly around one another, her breasts crushed against the crisp hair of his chest, her hips pressed to his, her long, slender legs interwoven with his longer, more powerful ones.

And yet that moment, beautiful in itself and meant to be cherished, could not, of its own making, last. Still, it was a portent of things to come. Simultaneously, they sank to their knees together, and Derek reverently kissed the palm of her hand and each finger before claiming the sweetness of her mouth.

Tonight was new again, tonight the bonds of their love would be irrevocably sealed beneath the heavens.

Leigh shivered as the intensity of his kiss brought them down together and the easy roll of the *Storm Haven* abetted the rising desire between them. Their tongues did not duel, but sought deeper in demand, until Derek's muffled cry brought them apart, only so that his lips could taste more of her. Tenderly, feverishly, then tenderly again, his lips traveled her flesh, savoring her throat, her breasts turned hard with longing, her stomach, which constricted at his touch, her quivering thighs, her knees, her toes . . . everything; he was compelled to know every inch of her. . . .

And Leigh trembled with the burning sensations of his loving desire, certain that they had become one with the stars as she was consumed bit by bit, as if little flames licked at her, until she could no longer endure the exquisite torture. Crying out for him, she threw her arms out in beseechment, then drew him back to her. Even as he began the culmination of her deliciously agonized longing, she was tasting the salt sea mist of his lips again, grazing her teeth over the satin-smooth tightness of his shoulders, allowing her hands the possessive appeasement of following the sturdy line of his powerful back, her fingers the return enticement of curling into the mat of his chest, of teasing along his ribs. . . .

The mounting cloud of desire that only they could elicit in one another raged until it became a passionate storm that swept away all else. The world itself was eradicated; there were only the two of them, one body, one soul. A beautiful, synchronized harmony that was a love song soaring ever higher with each rhythmic, combustible beat. . . .

And a crescendo of sweet, sweet, exquisite ecstasy. One that left them both satiated to the brim with awe and quaking contentment, loathe to break their entwinement in any way.

Leigh sighed happily and half opened sensuously lazy eyes to the sky. It was with wonder that she realized her fantasy had finally become real, unquestionable and complete. She moved finally to touch the damp tendrils of hair that lay upon her chest. She would always need to touch him.

And he her.

He shifted as she moved, but only to look at her with a knowing smile, and rearrange their positions to place protectively his heavier form against the deck and pull her into the comfort of his shoulder. Neither was really ready to stir yet; they were basking in the blissful, semiconscious state of euphoria that followed such a bout of fully committed and hungrily passionate lovemaking.

Leigh's lids began to droop and her lashes brushed softly against her cheeks. The timeless sensation was still with her, an enveloping feeling of happiness and security with Derek beside her, holding her. She slept, knowing they had forever.

Later, Leigh stirred in her lover's arm and wedged closer for warmth. The moon was high above them in the heavens and the sea breeze chilled the dampness of her contented form.

"Cold?" Derek murmured.

"A little."

"No romance!" Derek grumbled, encircling her closer. "You're supposed to say something like, 'Not with you to warm me!' I am a hot thing to handle, you know."

"Oh, I'd be the last to deny it, believe me." Leigh laughed. "But maybe you could be 'hot' down in your cabin."

"Anywhere you like." Derek started to rise but Leigh stopped him with a wistful smile.

"In just a minute. I want to watch the stars a bit longer."

Sliding his arms around the back of her shoulders, Derek sat, his thumb lovingly brushing her cheek while she cradled her head against his shoulders. "I have another confession to make anyway," Derek said. "So I might as well tell you here. If you decide to jump out of bed on me, you'll wind up in the Atlantic."

"*Another* confession?"

"Umm . . . I played a trick on you last night, but my intentions were the best. I didn't want you getting away. When you pulled your streaking act out of the room, I slipped through the adjoining door and locked yours."

"You didn't!"

"I did. I couldn't bear the thought of going to sleep without you after I had you in my arms again."

"I didn't even know there was an adjoining door! Why you son of a—"

"Hey!" Derek growled teasingly. "Don't you dare say it! My mother is a nice woman and she bears absolutely no resemblance to the canine family."

"I was going to say son of a gun," Leigh protested.

"Nothing metallic in the family line either. But while we're on it"—his voice abruptly grew low and gently serious—"how do you feel about a son?"

"I'd like one very much, but they don't come by order. We could have a daughter," Leigh advised him.

"We can keep trying until we have one of each," Derek mused.

"That sounds terrific," Leigh sighed.

Derek's touch on her chin intensified and he twisted his head to face her. "Really, Leigh, would you mind if we started a family quickly? We have everything to give children, a secure future, a good home, and most important—love."

Leigh crossed a leg and rose gracefully to her feet. The *Storm Haven* swayed beneath her as she placed a slender hand in Derek's and drew him to her. God, how she loved him!

Her hair fell over her shoulders in deep rippling red, curling around her breasts; her eyes gleamed with the devilry of the full moon.

"Quickly?" she queried impishly, giving him her best vixen smile. Yes, quickly. This man of hers did have everything, strength, dignity, love, and compassion. He would make a wonderful parent.

In one fluid motion she came to her feet and stretched out her hand wordlessly, telling him all he wished to know.

EPILOGUE

She had known him for years, yet each day was a voyage of new love and discovery. She was his best friend, his partner, his lover, his mistress, his wife.

And it was a special night. A secret anniversary.

She had wanted him forever, loved him for an eternity.

He was a pirate tonight, a swashbuckling pirate with a rakish air and devilish smile. She was a gypsy, flamboyant and colorful, promising heavenly delight with boldly flirtatious, glittering hazel eyes.

But it didn't matter what their guises. She loved him as a king, as a pirate, as her lordly mate, Derek Mallory.

And he knew exactly who she was. He loved her for exactly who she was, and for all the complexities that were what she was.

His eyes met hers across the room, then swept slowly over her figure with astute appreciation. Before she knew it she was in his arms. It felt so good, so right. He was everything wonderful: tall, strong, arrogantly masculine, and yet unceasingly tender. They belonged to one another as only very special lovers ever could.

He suggested that they leave and she didn't blink an eye. Her slow, suggestive smile was all the answer he needed.

She vaguely noted that a leprechaun and a well-feathered Indian were discussing the London Company as they neared the pair, extolling the virtues of the group's latest album.

"Leigh, Derek!" the Indian joyfully exclaimed. "I was just telling John about the calls I've had. The movie companies are hounding me! Do you believe that? Lord!" he said with a chuckle, "if I do say so myself, with the team of Mallory and Mallory in the lead of the London Company, we surpass genius!"

John, the leprechaun, smiled wryly. "Nothing like patting ourselves on the back!"

"Seriously," Roger groaned, adjusting a loose feather, "what answers do I give these people?"

"Whatever you want," Derek told him, his eyes on his wife. "Just don't commit us to anything until next month. Lord and Lady Mallory have descended upon South Florida to care for their grandson and Leigh and I are leaving for the next four weeks."

"Where—" Roger began.

"Oh, no!" Leigh exclaimed with a smile. "No one knows where we're going! We don't want to be found."

"I'm sure you'll handle whatever comes up, Roger," Derek said patiently. "John, thanks for a super party. Have a good vacation too."

"You two are going now? It's early!"

"We are, indeed, leaving," Leigh chuckled, tucking her hand into her husband's crooked arm. "Why don't you two run over and flirt with Sherry? This is her first big party and she is crazy about musicians!"

They were watched as they left. They were a fantasy couple: both tall, graceful, handsome, enviably in love. Happiness radiated from them and encompassed all who came near.

So began their special night. It was slow and easy and wonderful. They listened to the gentle strains of classical music as they sipped on mulled wine before the light and warmth of a mellow fire. They talked for hours, about their music, their friends, their son, the silken fantasy of their lives.

Their talking tapered into comfortable silence. He rose slowly and offered her his hand. By mute agreement she trustingly accepted him, and when she, too, was standing, he swept her as effortlessly as stardust into his arms and lay her tenderly on the bed, where he disrobed her with loving reverence. She was naked now, susceptible and vulnerable. But his love was her strength, his powerful arms her harbor. And as always, she was lost in an endless field of longing and desire, totally absorbed in the magnificent male form before her, framed in a silhouette by the fire like a true golden king.

"With my body I thee worship," he whispered, his husky voice against her throat sparking the fire that would soon rage through her veins and consume them.

Her fingers locked into his hair as their forms melded together. Lips played upon flesh, hands teased and caressed provocatively. Even as Leigh responded to her lover's whispers of hunger and desire, she knew that they were blessed with the one ingredient for everlasting passion. Love. Then the fire raged out of control, and she no longer thought but surrendered to the ecstasy that enveloped and overwhelmed her. He demanded, he took, he gave, and all through the long night he proved once more that he would never have his fill of her.

Too soon the dawn broke across the heavens. She awoke with a start to find herself entwined with him, her head resting on his golden chest. She smiled with sweet fulfillment and joy, then carefully, so as not to awaken her sleeping king, she disengaged herself and dressed. She scampered to the door, but stopped. She had to go back, just for a second, just to kiss his sleep-eased brow.

Her lips touched his skin, then she backed away. His eyes were beginning to flicker. She made it to the door before he awoke and called for her to stop, demanded to know where she was going.

"For coffee!" She chuckled ruefully. "I thought I could make it back before you awoke and surprise you."

"That's okay." He leaned on an elbow to watch her with contented, lazy eyes that still sparkled golden with insinuation. "You can go."

"Oh?" She raised teasing brows. "And what if I disappear?"

He rose from the bed and sauntered toward her. "You will never disappear, love." He kissed her until she went limp against him, weak and breathless. "You are truly part of me now." He drew her closer to him, his embrace promising that they would be together forever.